T0009730

By ELLE E. IRE

Reel to Real Love
Vicious Circle

NEARLY DEPARTED
Dead Woman's Pond
Dead Woman's Revenge

STORM FRONTS
Threadbare
Patchwork
Woven

Published by DSP PUBLICATIONS
www.dsppublications.com

DEAD WOMAN'S REVENGE

ELLE E. IRE

DSP PUBLICATIONS

Published by
DREAMSPINNER PRESS

5032 Capital Circle SW, Suite 2, PMB# 279,
Tallahassee, FL 32305-7886 USA
www.dreamspinnerpress.com

Dead Woman's Revenge
© 2022 Elle E. Ire

Cover Art
© 2022 Tiferet Design
http://www.tiferetdesign.com/
Cover content is for illustrative purposes only and any person depicted
on the cover is a model.

Mass Market Paperback ISBN: 978-1-64108-309-6
Trade Paperback ISBN: 978-1-64108-308-9
Digital ISBN: 978-1-64108-307-2
Mass Market Paperback published September 2022
v. 1.0

Printed in the United States of America
∞
This paper meets the requirements of
ANSI/NISO Z39.48-1992 (Permanence of Paper).

To those who lost their lives in the real Dead Man's Pond and their families. No curses here, just a road that dead-ends and a speed limit that seems too slow for the highway it serves. I hope they have found peace.

Acknowledgments

SEQUELS CAN be difficult when it comes to beta readers and critique partners. If one hasn't read the first book, then it's hard to offer constructive feedback. I've been fortunate to have a steady group of writing companions to see me through this series. First and foremost is my beloved spouse who is my first reader for everything. Thank you for being both supportive and honest always. Thank you to my former writing group: Ann, Amy, Evergreen, Gary, and Joe who read the first book in this series and all that followed. Their assistance with continuity is priceless. Thank you to my agent, Naomi Davis, who knows when to push me to be better and when to cheerlead me through the harder moments. Thank you to Dreamspinner in its entirety for their belief in my work, but especially to Gus, Yv, Brian, Gin, Naomi, the entire art department, and the administrative team. Special thanks to my cover artist, Anna Sikorska, who took my vague thoughts and turned them into a gorgeous but creepy as all heck cover that gave me chills the first time I saw it. Finally, thank you to my readers, especially MB, Arielle, Don, Dolores, Bob, Mimi, Stephanie, and Kathy who not only buy the books but spread the word about enjoying them. If I've missed anyone, I apologize. There were a lot of people involved in making this happen. Niki, I hope you liked the character I named after you. Thank you for entering my contest!

Chapter 1
Heroes

EVERY TOWN has its heroes. Festivity, Florida, has three.

Their names are engraved on a concrete wall encircling a large tree at the center of town. The first is Simon, a teenager who dedicated the last years of his short, cancer-ridden life to funding and building a veterans' memorial in one of Festivity's many parks. I never met him, but I'm glad he has a memorial of his own.

The second name on the wall belongs to Charlie, the eighty-three-year-old crossing guard who threw himself at a kindergartner, knocking the child from the path of a speeding van and taking the fatal hit himself. Didn't know him either.

And the newest addition is me, Flynn Dalton, immortalized with a bronze plaque for diving into Dead Woman's Pond at the edge of town and pulling a woman from her wrecked, sinking car. I did a lot more than that, actually, including a later scuba dive to the lake's bottom to retrieve a cursed charm that was drawing in all the vehicles in the first place. Town Hall doesn't know about that part. Regular folks, or nulls, as my girlfriend, Genesis, calls them, don't know about a lot of things, and we need to keep it that way.

I'm the only one of the three to be honored while still alive—a dubious distinction, I've come to believe.

Six weeks ago, when all this first happened, I would have declined the honor. Saving a life is what anyone would have done. Who would watch a woman drown and do nothing? Now, as I stand in the heat of a late-August evening, looking down at the names, I accept hero status with a numbness that's become almost second nature to me.

Shit. I don't need a plaque or free meals at the Festivity restaurants or a 10 percent discount at the kitschy little gift shops.

Not that I wouldn't have appreciated the complimentary food a couple of months ago, when I could barely make my pay-by-the-week hotel room rent. But now….

I rub the spot on my left shoulder where a water moccasin bit me during my scuba excursion—one of three bites, actually, all engineered by the evil asshole who made the charm and spelled the snakes, good old Leopold VanDean. Dead now, officially and incorrectly ruled natural causes—heart attack trying to save me from the same water moccasin bites. Good riddance.

My right leg twinges in sympathy with the shoulder. The one bite that healed completely is on my neck. Genesis took care of that, but she had to use dark magic to do it, and she killed Leo in the process. In her own way, she's as scarred as I am.

So yeah, I paid the price for my heroics, and I'm still paying. Gen doesn't know it, and I don't intend to tell her. I can hide pain pretty well. But my limp is getting worse, and my left arm's range of motion is deteriorating.

And every few nights, Gen awakens me with her sobbing.

I don't want a plaque or meals or discounts. I want our fucking lives back.

GENESIS TOSSED and turned, her afternoon nap disrupted by the nightmares. She helplessly gave in to their grasp, once again startled by the clarity, the detail, which made her wonder if these weren't mere dreams, but something else… punishment.

"How old is his sister?"

Genesis frowned, standing beside her brother's hospital bed, watching the artificially induced rise and fall of his chest. The equipment noises and the thin partition curtain didn't drown out the voices beyond the plastic divider.

"Seventeen."

"Damn."

A social worker, and the hospital representative who'd called her.

"She's a senior in high school. They run a business together. Their parents left it to them, along with a lot of money."

"She can't run it by herself."

"No."

A choked sob escaped Gen's throat.

No, she couldn't run the Village Pub alone. (Would a minor even be allowed to try?) But she wasn't going to have to do that. Chris would recover. He had to.

"Not sure what we're going to do with her, or what she'll want to do with herself."

The two women stopped talking as more footsteps echoed on the tile floor. Visitors for the room's other occupant, an elderly woman who'd fallen down a staircase. She spent much of the previous night moaning and begging for God to take her. Gen listened from the room's easy chair, to that stranger on the other side of the curtain, wishing someone could ease the woman's pain, take away the sorrow of her family.

Someone other than Genesis. Because she had nothing to spare.

The hospital rep and social worker murmured a few comforting words to the other woman's relatives and left without pushing aside the partition to see Gen. Just as well. She would have told them to get out.

No, she would have told them to go to hell.

If she were stronger, trained, Gen could have done something. As it was, she'd poured all her magical energies into keeping Chris alive. Sudden Florida downpour, slippery asphalt, car accident. No one's fault.

Brain damage.

He could survive the broken leg, the cracked pelvis, the fractured collarbone. But he'd slipped into a coma, and despite all the doctors' efforts, he hadn't come out of it. Too risky to operate with him in this state, and he needed that operation. They gave him one day, maybe two, before the rest of his body shut down.

They'd just lost their parents. She couldn't lose him too.

Genesis sank into this side of the room's only chair. It crunched around her, brown faux leather with a foot panel that swung out if she pulled a lever. She could sleep in the chair. She had slept in it.

On the other side of the curtain, someone started crying—a child or a young woman. Grief was universal.

"I love you, Grandma."

Gen swallowed hard.

The grandmother didn't answer. She'd been in and out of consciousness since her arrival.

Afternoon wore into evening and evening into night. Gen sat beside the bed, holding Chris's hand, feeding him her energy to the brink of her own collapse. If she fainted, the staff would take her from his side, break the connection, end him.

She stood between her brother and death, and death was winning.

No more sleep. She even feared running to the restroom, certain the machines would scream their alarms if she went to relieve herself.

Like they were screaming now.

Gen jolted from her doze, sitting straight up, then standing while the heart monitor blared a steady, ominous note. Weak, dizzy, what good could she do? The respirators kept pumping, but his heart had stopped.

Chris's hand had slipped from her grasp while she slept, and she scrambled for it, pulling the cold flesh between her equally chilled palms in frantic desperation.

The door slammed open, doctors and nurses bursting through the narrow space, pushing a crash cart ahead of them. An orderly dragged her from Chris's side.

"No!" It came out as a squeak, a feeble protest unheard by the trauma staff. "You don't understand." Sobs she'd kept in since the accident broke free, crippling and contorting her. Before the medical personnel could spare a moment to remove her from the room, she ducked into the attached bath and curled into a ball on the floor behind the cracked-open door.

The doctors worked with fierce determination, stabbing her brother with needles, administering shocks to his chest that made his frail body bounce on the mattress, then settle to complete stillness. After a long while, they shut off the alarms, the monitors, the breather that forced one last lungful of air into Chris with a dying hiss.

They packed their equipment, the wheels of the cart squeaking as they rolled it out the door.

"What happened to the girl?" a nurse asked.

"Ran off, I think," an orderly responded. "She was very upset. I'll radio the other orderlies to keep an eye out for her."

Gen barely heard the words as they all left the room and the door shut. Above Chris's body, a glow formed, taking on a vaguely human shape, Chris's shape, separating itself from its corporeal shell.

"Get. Back. In. There," Genesis snarled, pushing herself up and stalking from the restroom to the bedside.

Other than the old woman beyond the curtain in the bed nearest the door, they were alone.

Chris's spirit hovered, still in contact with his physical form but pulling away. Not solid enough for a conversation, but it had flickered when Gen issued her command, so on some level it heard her. It understood.

It just couldn't obey.

If he couldn't go back into his body, she'd pull him back. Not knowing what she was doing, acting on instinct, Gen plunged her hands into the swirling glow. They vanished to her sight, hidden by the ephemeral form, her arms seeming to end at the wrists.

Genesis sucked in a sharp breath as emotions suffused her: anguish, regret, and a love so deep, so great, tears streamed down her face from the sheer force of it. Love for her. And the brother-sister bond they shared pulled taut, tethering the three of them: Genesis, the ghost, and the corpse.

"No!" she screamed, this time throwing all her self, all her remaining strength into reuniting Chris's body with his spirit.

Not enough.

Her heart pounded, racing, straining. Her breath hissed between her teeth as pain wracked her.

She sought other sources: the gardens outside, the approaching thunderstorms, all the good, the light, the energy Mother Nature kept in its reserve, but these were too far from her reach, and the ones she could tap, still not enough.

Her magic touched the electrical energy buzzing in the equipment all around her, filling the rooms of the ICU, the very walls themselves, but it felt wrong, did nothing, not natural. Perhaps if she'd been trained, she'd know how to make use of it, convert it, but the Registry had invited her for training and she'd declined—too soon after her parents' deaths, too desperate to be with Chris, to be near family, to help him reorganize and keep the bar and restaurant going, to finish high school with her classmates and maintain some degree of normalcy.

At the edges of her awareness, power nudged, teased, tingled. Strong power.

Green.

To her other-sight, the green glow taunted, and she resisted. Green, she knew, meant bad, sickly, tainted. She didn't know how she knew; she just did. When she touched it, just a taste, it felt... corrosive.

Chris's spirit pulled farther from her, floating toward the ceiling, almost beyond the limits of her fingertips.

With a final moan of despair, Genesis thrust one hand behind her, out of Chris, toward the power source, and forced a conduit between them.

The energy passed through her, no longer sickly but invigorating, orgasmic in its pleasurable intensity. Her knees went weak.

The alarms blared once more, beeping and screeching, and she searched the room for the source. Not Chris. The doctors had unplugged his equipment before they left.

The old woman.

Gen grabbed at the curtain with her already outstretched hand and threw it aside with a zing of metal rungs across the metal bar. In the bed beyond, the grandmother thrashed weathered, wrinkled hands, her chest rising and falling irregularly while a pebbly wheeze issued from her gaping mouth.

Beside her, Chris gasped. His eyelids fluttered. His spirit sank back into his body.

And in that moment, Genesis realized what she'd done.

Like a recurring nightmare, the door burst open once more, the same trauma team swarming the room, moving her quickly and firmly to the far side of Chris's divider curtain and closing it to perform their life-saving—no, life-extending—methods on the elderly woman. But Genesis knew in her aching heart they'd be too late.

She peered around the curtain's edge at the woman's sunken facial muscles, devoid of animation, the filmy blue eyes staring at the ceiling, focused on nothing.

Her ghost detached itself from her body much more rapidly than Chris's had, solidifying into a recognizable and stunningly beautiful younger woman. She floated past the doctors and nurses still pumping, shocking, injecting, passed through the curtain, and settled into a regal pose before Genesis, one hand on a curvaceous hip.

The ghost flipped long brown hair over a bare shoulder, her strapless evening gown in a style from a much earlier era flowing around her long, shapely legs. Jewelry sparkled on her wrists and about her neck, catching the overhead lights with an otherworldly brilliance.

"Two in one night. Cursed room," a large male orderly muttered from the curtain's far side. He wasn't much off the mark.

When Gen had wished someone would ease the grandmother's pain, she hadn't intended this.

"This isn't what I wanted," Gen whispered. Behind her, cases clicked shut as the trauma team repacked their gear.

"It's what I wanted," the woman said in a melodious voice incongruous with the cigarette-damaged rasp she'd used with her visitors. "I'm ready. Don't punish yourself." With a grateful smile, she disappeared.

Chris groaned, catching a doctor's attention—a resurgence of life, transferred from the old woman into Chris.

"My God," a nurse cried.

Orderlies shooed Genesis into the hallway while they reconnected the equipment. Shortly after they permitted her to return, Chris opened his eyes and focused on Gen, a slight grin curving his lips, which faded at her stricken expression.

She took his hand in hers, reassuring him while she swallowed bile.

Not a miracle. Not by a long shot.

The scene shifted, as scenes in dreams often did, to… the bedroom Genesis now shared with her girlfriend, Flynn, formerly Leo VanDean's bedroom. And how twisted was that?

He'd left the house and all his assets to those with him at the time of his death, perhaps not considering that the beneficiaries might be the people who *caused* his death.

They'd cleared out the old furnishings: four-poster bed in dark cherrywood, elaborately carved armoire, dressing table (what straight guy owned a dressing table?), and antique full-length standing mirror. In their stead stood light maple furniture, flowered comforters, an easy chair in pastels, lace curtains. Gen had done the decorating; Flynn let her run with it.

The new looks helped disperse the lingering sense of Leo's presence.

Genesis rolled from the bed where she'd lain down for a quick nap—she hadn't been sleeping well since their struggles at Dead Man's Pond, though Flynn insisted on calling it Dead Woman's Pond, a more accurate name. A glance at the bedside clock got her moving faster. Flynn would be home from work soon, should have been home already.

She needed to make herself presentable before Flynn saw her. Matted hair, tear stains, and red-rimmed eyes weren't what she wanted Flynn to see.

Gen went to the mirror, picked up the hairbrush from the side table, and froze.

"Hello, Gen," Leo said, staring out at her from the glass, designer shirt and slacks perfectly pressed, smile wicked. "You pretended to be so good, clinging to your righteous indignation whenever I spoke of the dark powers. I always knew we were two of a kind."

GEN'S OWN sobs woke her. She sat up in the bed, staring across the room at a mirror that only reflected herself. Her heart raced, her breath coming in quick gasps. Third nightmare this week and becoming more intense.

She needed a break before it broke her.

Her limbs trembled as she stood and moved to the window. No sign of Flynn's car—Leo's formerly orange McLaren that Flynn had immediately taken to be painted a more sedate metallic blue.

With the setting of the sun came concern. Flynn had come home later and later since she started back to work at the construction site a couple of weeks prior. Was Flynn avoiding her? Was she afraid of her? Flynn swore she wasn't, but….

She pulled her cell phone from the charger by the bed and dialed her brother.

"Yo, Gen!"

"Chris." Clinking dishware and loud conversation interspersed with cheering carried from the background. "Let me guess, game night?"

"Yankees versus Red Sox. You're messing with fate, here."

Like many other rabid fans, Chris believed if he didn't watch every second of every inning on the huge flatscreens at the Village Pub, the Yankees would lose.

"Don't worry," Gen said, putting on her fake, cliche psychic voice, low and breathy, "they'll make a comeback in the ninth. You got Flynn down there?"

Flynn loved her seat at the corner of the patio bar, sipping her favorite Breckenridge Vanilla Porter and annoying Chris by rooting for whomever the Yankees played against.

"Hang on, Sis." Footsteps followed, then the creaking of a swinging door and a slam. The ambient noise faded with its closing. "Nope, not here. I'm out back. No sign of her car, either." A bit of a snicker on the last statement. Flynn loved the idea of a sports car, but the reality, and the attention that came with it, intimidated her. She'd be more comfortable behind the wheel of her old, now junked, pickup truck. Chris's tone sobered. "You okay? You sound a little off."

Leave it to her brother to sense whatever she wanted hidden. Genesis sighed. "I'm fine, but she's not home yet. I'm not her keeper, but I am a little worried."

Chris laughed. "Of course you're her keeper. You're engaged. Flynn just hasn't figured out her role in it yet. I'll keep an eye out. Don't stress. I'm sure she'll be home soon, probably with a pizza and an apology."

Genesis hoped so. But she'd learned not to ignore her impulses.

Her impulses were screaming. Something bad was coming. Maybe not now, but soon.

Chapter 2
Make Good

I COME home late from work. I don't call to let Gen know I'm okay. I forget to pick up dinner, walk in the door, and basically crash on the couch until I drag my sorry-ass self to bed where I crash again.

You're a bad girlfriend, Flynn. Bad.

I don't deserve her.

I need to make it up to her.

So, now I'm standing in line with Gen to get into Atlantic Dance, a nightclub at the Disney Boardwalk Resort, about fifteen miles from Festivity. Not a gay club, but kind of a safe haven for us. I've been here before, but it was years back, before the housing crash, when I still made a decent living with the construction crew.

At the door, Ed, according to his name tag, gives my ID a cursory glance. Gen's bears more scrutiny. Though twenty-three, she appears younger. But with her smile and charm, she could've talked her way in without an ID.

God, she's hot tonight. Silver ballet flats, ankle-length black peasant skirt, silver off-the-shoulder top that fits skintight like a bodysuit and shows off all her curves. Silver moon earrings dangle from her lobes, catching the spotlight accents on the club's exterior. To complement her, I'm wearing all black from my boots to my vest and shirt, though the vest has some narrow silver striping.

The bass music drifting through the open doorway changes pitch and rhythm, and Gen gives a little squeal of delight. She grabs my sleeve and pulls, and the music engulfs us as we step into the club proper.

Pools of light scatter around the comfortable seating areas, and the occasional multicolored strobe punctuates the dark interior. Central rectangular dance floor with a huge video screen hanging from the ceiling and blocking what was once a stage for big band players.

Atlantic Dance has an impressive and unusual history, a swing club that featured live acts, elegantly costumed waitstaff, and table service. When swing went back out of fashion, the club evolved. They closed the upper-floor martini bar, curtained off the stage, and transformed into a much more traditional Top 40 dance venue.

The speakers blast Lady Gaga's comeback hit, the accompanying video on the screen, and, oh God, what is that woman wearing now? I think it's swiss cheese. I'm pulled across the carpeted walkway, through the seating area, and on the floor before I can blink twice.

Gen catches the rhythm, spinning and twisting and gyrating her lithe form around me, sending heat flowing through my body in a pleasant rush. I become the focus of her movement, the pillar, the foil, the palette. She paints me with her soft curves, her teasing touches, her grinding motion.

Can I dance? Not really. I can keep the beat, move a little without looking stiff and uncomfortable. I can support her when she arches backward, long hair brushing the dance floor. I can twirl her around so her skirt flares, showing off her shapely legs. I can lift her in my arms.

I surprised the guys on my crew when I danced at our engagement party. Anyone who knows me knows I avoid public displays like the plague. But this is different. It's everyone on the floor. And here in particular, that comprises a wide range of ages (from twenty-one to sixty-somethings), styles, and gender pairings. People watch us, yes. Especially a long-haired blond leaning over the wall separating the floor from the bar. I don't mind. We're an unusual enough couple for the older set to stare, so attention is inevitable. But surrounded by others, it doesn't bother me.

I would put up with a lot to keep seeing the current expression on Gen's face: exhilaration, freedom, pure joy. Her red hair flies around her, her skin shining under the hot lights. And her smile—I've seen it far too rarely since the incident at Dead Woman's Pond.

By the fourth straight song, I'm glad I have the next day off to recover. I took some preemptive

Advil, but it's insufficient compared to the heavy-duty prescription stuff I can't take when drinking. I've been careful to catch Genesis with my right arm, brace on my left leg, but when she gives a little leap, forcing me to lift and twirl her or let her hit the floor, both old injuries scream in protest. I grunt with the pain, hoping the music covers the sound and knowing it fails when she lets go of me and steps back.

"Your arm?" Gen practically has to yell to be heard over the music. She frowns and reaches out to brush my upper back beneath the shoulder blade where the snakebite scar lies raw and half-healed. Little tingles follow her fingers, not magical ones, just the positive reaction my body always experiences in response to her touch.

I grimace. Might as well come clean, at least to some extent. "And my leg," I admit. I lean down to speak into her ear. "Twinges, but I could use a short break."

"And a beer, right?" Her smile returns. She leads me off the floor, ahead of me so she doesn't notice how pronounced my limp is, and damn, it hurts a lot more than I let on. I should tell her everything, about the doctor's prognosis that I'm getting worse and will continue to. I recovered from the venom, but not too long after I got out of the hospital, some sort of muscle degradation set in—dark magic damage I'm guessing, invisible on the surface, confusing on the x-rays and ultrasounds, nothing the medical professionals can name of course. This meant more tests and a lot of downplaying on my part. I got the painkiller prescriptions I wanted and stopped going. Not sure what I'm going to do when they run out.

Gen doesn't need to know. Not right now. She doesn't need my stress.

A couple vacates a nice isolated corner table with two rolling cushioned chairs left over from the club's big band days, so Gen snags it. I drop into my seat with a sigh of relief.

"What'll it be, loves?"

I jump at the server's sudden arrival and bristle at the endearment from a stranger, then note the British accent and figure it for a cultural thing. A handsome guy in a bartender's black-and-white uniform hovers beside us. Gen's beaming. She has a thing for accents, especially British ones. Bond films drive her wild.

"She'll have a white zinfandel," I say, double-checking for Gen's nod of confirmation, "and I'll take whatever light beer you've got on tap. Didn't think you still did table service here."

He smiles. Nice smile, late twenties or early thirty-something, that clean-cut look Disney hires for. He gestures out to the dance floor. "Impressive performance. Most of the men and half the women couldn't keep their eyes off you. But it looked like you overdid it a little at the end, so I thought I'd cut you a break."

Gen shoots me a guilty look. I'm sure she's thinking if the bartender noticed my pain and limp, she should have. Sooner or later, she'll have to know it all.

I glance past Peter—name tags are wonderful things—to the beleaguered bar swarming with customers. The two remaining bartenders scramble to fill orders, pour drinks, and run credit cards. Steady chaos, no downtime. I think I might enjoy the job if I ever get out of construction work. Could be just the thing to work on overcoming my shyness. Casual chitchat. Just enough interaction with each person without getting too personal, and not a chance of boredom. Plenty of movement too. "Much appreciated," I say.

He tips an invisible cap and strolls behind the bar, taking Gen's credit card to start a tab.

"Hey, guys!"

We turn toward the familiar voices, spotting my friends Steve and Allie a few feet from the table. Steve is another bartender, at Kissimmee Lanes, my favorite bowling alley. Allie is his waitress and long-term girlfriend. She's been encouraging me to drop some marriage proposal hints Steve's way. After all, if I can pop the question to another *woman*, in public at Festivity's Village Pub of all places, he should damn well be able to work up the nerve.

I've taken him aside and chatted about it. So far, no success, but I suspect it won't be much longer. He mentioned saving up for a ring.

They negotiate with a few nearby tables for a couple of unused chairs, drag them over, and join us, bottled beers already in hand. Peter drops off our drinks, and the four of us chat for a while, but the music volume makes meaningful conversation impossible.

Gen's antsy, bouncing in her seat, feet tapping, fingers keeping the rhythm against the side of her glass. Allie's the same, so I lean over and tell Gen, "Go. Dance."

"No, it's okay," she protests, but her heart isn't in it.

"Seriously, go. Take Steve and Allie with you. She's about to burst. I'll enjoy the show." I waggle my eyebrows, earning a laugh.

"I'll make it a good one." She grabs our friends' hands and hauls them off, positioning the three of them on the floor in a spot where I have a clear view. The two women proceed to seduce Steve through dance, and I get a mental jolt, remembering Genesis is bi.

Chill out, Flynn.

I know it's an issue for me. I tend toward inse-cure in my relationships. A bad breakup will do that to a gal, and my first serious girlfriend dumped me on my ass for her old boyfriend. But Gen wears my engagement ring. Gen is mine, I'm hers, and I won't worry anymore. I can grin at their sexual antics, Gen casting me heated looks beneath lowered eyelids and blowing me kisses, and the jealousy no longer flares. It's a performance, and desire curls hot and low.

I have my leg propped on one of the other chairs, leaning back and sipping the last of my beer, when Peter reappears with a fresh drink. Quite the personal service I'm getting. He must expect a big tip. Either that or he has a thing for lesbians, which is less un-usual than one might think.

He sets the glass before me. Not beer. Something harder. Rum and Coke, maybe, judging from the color. "Um, thanks, but I didn't order this," I say.

He crouches beside me. "Compliments of the lady." Pointing, he indicates the blond woman I'd spotted watching me and Gen dance earlier. She raises an identical drink in a quick toast to me, tosses some long blond curls over her shoulder, then turns back to the bar, where she's perched on one of the red-velvet-covered stools. "Cassie's a regular. She doesn't show interest often, and I've never seen her go after another woman before." Peter leans in farther. "You'd best watch out, love. She doesn't tend to take rejection well."

"Thanks for the tip."

He nods and heads off.

I twirl the short glass on the table's surface, letting the amber liquid catch the light. This doesn't happen to me a lot, and it's been a while since it has. When we go out, it's usually Genesis who gets hit on, mostly by guys who don't realize we're a couple.

I cast a more subtle look in the woman's direction. Flattering, to have someone like her pay me attention. She's well-dressed, a tailored business suit and high heels. Very sophisticated, obviously well-to-do, perfectly put together, but not my type.

Free-spirited women fan my flames. Women like Genesis. And red hair. I have a real thing for redheads.

All that aside, though, even if I were uninvolved, I'd nix things with this one. Peter's comment about her not usually going after women raises all my caution flags. I've been someone's experiment once before and ended up with my heart in pieces. No way would I go through that again.

Best to deal with this head-on. I'm a much rarer target, but this isn't my first rodeo.

Picking up the untouched drink, I walk, well, limp, my way over to the bar.

Chapter 3
Roped and Tied

As if she senses my approach, Cassie swivels her barstool toward me. Up close her young age— maybe twenty-four, twenty-five?—surprises me. Definitely younger than I am. Closer to Gen's age. Mature clothing, makeup applied to make her look older. I can't imagine why any woman would want to age her looks, but then again, if I were in the corporate world and I were that young, a sense of age and experience might help me advance. Her angular face breaks into a predatory grin, shifting her from somewhat attractive to downright scary.

Oh yeah, I need to nip this one quick.

I set the full glass next to hers and lean on the bar. "Hey there. Thanks for the drink, but I'm involved with someone."

She glances over at my abandoned table with its four empty chairs. "Not too involved," she says.

"Dance floor." Gen's group has moved off, more toward the center, so she's hard to spot. I can just make out the silver of her bodice between some of the other bodies.

Cassie shrugs, giving the glass a nudge in my direction. "Well, then. What she doesn't know won't hurt her. Don't waste free alcohol."

The budget cruncher in me wants to accept. Even though I inherited half of Leo VanDean's fortune and I'm filthy freaking rich now, I used to be dirt-poor. The idea of a wasted drink makes my insides cringe. However….

"Can't. Sorry."

"Oh, come on." She attempts a girlish pout, not even coming close to the disappointed innocence she wants to convey. Her hand falls to cover mine, the skin cold despite the heat of the crowded club with its overworked air conditioners. "Think of it as compensation for your earlier performance. I love watching a strong woman dance, imagining what those muscles might do to me."

Her words send a shudder through me. I appreciate blunt and forthright, but this is too much. As smoothly as I can, I slide my hand from beneath hers.

"One drink, no strings," she finishes, making a final play. "I'll be offended if you don't accept."

And Peter seemed to suggest offending her might be a bad idea. "No strings," I repeat.

She holds up one hand, palm turned outward. "On my honor."

Fine. I lift the glass and take a sip. The rum burns down my throat, my eyes watering a bit. Good stuff, but strong, a double at least. If it weren't for the hint of carbonation, I'd wonder if it contained any soda at all. Behind her, Peter shakes his head at me, smiling sadly, before he addresses an older tourist couple in matching flowered shirts and shorts. Didn't he want me to not piss off this woman?

The second sip goes down more easily than the first, and the third runs silken smooth. The alcohol settles in my stomach with a pleasant warmth that flows outward to my limbs and eases the pain in my leg and shoulder. I hate to think what rum of this quality cost her.

Guess I should at least introduce myself. I nod toward the British bartender. "Peter says your name is Cassie. I'm Flynn."

"Flynn." She rolls my name off her tongue like she's savoring a fine wine, and I suppress another shiver. "Like Errol Flynn?"

I smile. "First name, not last."

Cassie waves a dismissive hand. "Doesn't matter. Still suits you. You've got that swashbuckling hero sense about you."

Hero, huh? Back to that again. Part of me wonders if she knew who I was before I told her. I made all the local papers and news broadcasts with my lake dive and rescue. That might explain her intense interest.

I'd planned to withdraw as quickly as possible, but Cassie's good at maintaining the conversation at a quick pace, leaving me no openings to excuse myself without being rude. I keep a watchful eye out for Genesis, fully intending to bring her into the conversation if she decides to leave the dance floor. But she's disappeared into the masses, everyone in rows for a series of line dances I wouldn't have participated in even if my leg didn't hurt.

Which, now that I stop and think about it, isn't actually hurting at all. Not a twinge, not the persistent dull ache that wakes me up in the middle of the night. Nothing. And no pain from the shoulder, either.

Maybe I need to invest in some expensive rum.

She finishes telling me about her job, owning and managing Orlando Match, a localized web-based dating service. The kind that introduces couples online, then arranges group gatherings for them in the area. I checked into it before I met Genesis, but the "finder's fees" went beyond my construction worker paychecks. They have a great reputation, though. Lots of success stories with both straight and gay clients. And she founded the company. Cassie makes some serious money.

I keep my personal details to a minimum, but I hear about her two cats, her last romantic partner (a guy), and her preferred sexual positions, which is way too much info coming from someone I just met. She takes advantage of my unwillingness to cut her off and seems to relish my embarrassment over hearing such personal details.

I do wonder why a matchmaker would be trolling for company in a bar, but then I figure, one, using her own website would be a conflict of interest, and two, bars provide a wide range of potential customers for someone like Cassie.

When I down the last swallow, I set the glass aside and stand. "Well, it's been nice meeting you, and I thank you for the drink. No strings, right?"

She nods. "No strings. But if you should change your mind, ask Peter where to find me. I'm usually around here most nights." Cassie nudges me with her elbow. "Including the rest of tonight."

Too late, I bite back a laugh that carries over the sound system and turns a few heads. She thinks I'll ditch Gen and throw myself at her? Wow, that's some serious overconfidence.

Instead of becoming offended, Cassie studies me coolly. "You might be surprised at the lasting effect I have on people." Then she just turns away, striking up a completely unrelated conversation with the businessman on the other side of her. I've been dismissed.

Right. Okay.

I head back to my table, still empty, though several empty glasses indicate it had a few takers over the course of the past forty minutes.

I make it halfway there when the room spins.

Intense concentration, placing one foot in front of the other, gets me to my seat. I ease into it, closing my eyes against the rocking, my hands gripping the armrests. I'm no lightweight. I can go drinking with the construction crew and hold my own just fine. That must have been some serious rum.

Could Cassie have slipped me something?

But Peter brought me the drink, and I had it in my control the entire time we chatted. It never left my sight. Maybe all the medication I've been on, even if I didn't take the heavy-duty pain drugs this evening.

Gen returns, telling me Allie and Steve left for Jelly Rolls, the dueling-piano bar next door. I like Jelly Rolls. It's a good place to kick back, drink beer, and sing along to some rocking tunes. But there's no dancing, and she came to dance.

"All rested?" she asks, sneaking a kiss on my cheek. It's dark. The table sits in a corner. And I'm apparently drunk. I don't mind the PDA.

"Few mr mints." And I'm slurring my words. Great.

Her narrowed eyes peer at me in the dim light. "How many drinks have you had?"

I hold up two fingers, which blur into four.

Oh, not good.

Dropping my head against the backrest, I close my eyes again.

Genesis crawls into my lap, her arms working their way around my neck. "If you were upset and had a few extra, you don't have to lie about it. I shouldn't have abandoned you. I can drive us home."

"Not lying," I say, trying to muster up some indignation, but I can't even lift my head. "Jus had a really strong one, thas all. Give me a bit lnger to let things wear off and we cn dance some more." Geez, I sound like I've suffered a brain injury. Dancing might help, actually, if the room stops swaying.

She sighs, and I doubt she believes me, but she snuggles in, resting against my shoulder, which doesn't hurt at all.

Things do settle after a couple more songs. I feel warm and comfortable, but not off-balance when I set Gen on her feet and walk her to the floor for a slow dance. Her curves meld with mine, a perfect fit, the top of her head tucked under my chin.

But it isn't enough. I want her closer. My skin tingles, and I ache to have her touch me without the layer of clothing between us. Heat builds, along with a deep, pooling arousal.

Since my doctor gave me the go-ahead, we've made love a few times, with varying success. At least once, Gen's dark magic addiction attempted to intrude on an intimate moment, and more and more often, the aches in my body make things difficult. I try to satisfy Gen first, but despite her efforts and enthusiasm, sometimes my needs go by the wayside. She so desperately wants to please me, but eventually I have to stop her, claiming exhaustion or, yeah, I know, faking satisfaction.

When the song ends, I tilt Gen's head back and kiss her deeply, my tongue snaking between her lips to deepen the sensations. By the time I pull away, we're halfway through another song, a fast number, and the other dancers sail their way around our two-person island. A few stop to applaud the kiss.

Gen stares at me, eyes wide with surprise, though she's smiling. "What's gotten into you?" she asks, poking me in the arm, teasing.

I blink at her, then shake my head. What *has* gotten into me? Dancing is one thing. Kissing the hell out of my girlfriend in the middle of a dance floor is quite another. I *do not* do this. What am I thinking?

I draw a slow breath and let it out.

I'm *not* thinking.

We dance to a few more songs, fast ones, and soon it isn't just Genesis lighting my fires. It's every attractive woman around me, and even some who aren't so attractive. My gaze lands on Cassie. All the while, she watches me, only me, sitting straight and tall on her barstool, her partially unbuttoned blouse revealing the rounded curves of her breasts and a hint of black lace, her eyes following my every move.

Once I notice her continued interest, I can't look away, to the point where Genesis glances over her shoulder several times to figure out what's caught my attention. I divert my gaze elsewhere each time, feigning a scan of the club, but it's hard. Too hard.

I find myself undressing Cassie with my eyes, peeling away her business jacket, unbuttoning her blouse one button at a time, slowly, smoothing the satin material across her skin. I hook my fingers in the waistband of her skirt and tug it down over her hips to drop on the floor by her high-heeled shoes.

Genesis spins into me, and I miss the catch, both of us stumbling before I right us. Gen laughs and smacks my shoulder, chastising me to pay attention. I *am* paying attention—to the wrong person.

Tugging Gen off the floor, I lean down to her ear. "We need to go."

Her smile fades, but she nods. "Whenever you want." She brushes my sweat-dampened bangs from my forehead. "You feeling okay?"

"I'm fine. Let me hit the restroom first. Can you settle our tab? Meet me by the entrance?"

She nods again and heads for the bar, where Peter grins and waves to her.

Cassie's barstool sits empty.

Relief and disappointment battle for dominance.

The walk to the bathroom provides its own set of challenges. Each step rubs the rough material of my black jeans between my legs, and the growing moisture there stuns me. My vest/ shirt combination restricts my breasts, hardening nipples straining beneath two layers of fabric, three counting my suddenly-too-tight bra.

I crave and enjoy sex as much as the next gal, but this is extreme in every way.

The dark blue carpeting leads to a narrow, mirrored hallway with entries to the men's and ladies' rooms on either side. Cassie leans against the small table between them.

I lock eyes with her as I approach. My body reacts to her nearer presence, throat going dry, knees weakening. I lick my lips and attempt to pass her by, but her fingers with their long, manicured nails close around my arm.

"You want me," she says, drawing me toward her, voice low and throaty, almost sultry. I can't look away.

"I—" My mind screams no, but my body says yes. My suede boots bump the toes of her high-heeled shoes. In the mirror behind her, I search frantically for any sign that Gen can see us, but no one's around. Not even other patrons headed for the bathrooms.

"Kiss me." A command, not a request.

An inner force pulls my lips to hers. When they connect, sparks flash behind my closed eyelids.

Cassie kisses like a pro, her mouth soft and pliant, her tongue dancing with mine. She tastes of rum and mint and—

What the fuck am I doing?

Instinct takes over, a force I've kept dormant rising up from within, power surging, pushing outward, while physically, I shove myself backward, away from her. Yes, I have magical talent of my own, a *push* skill that gives me an ability to drive external influences from me, as well as providing an affinity for the spirit world. It showed up when I was nine and I had a conversation with my dead grandmother, and reappeared during the Dead Woman's Pond fiasco. No, I don't want to pursue it or train it or acknowledge its presence at all, despite Gen's predictions that it will continue to manifest.

Guess Genesis was right. She usually is.

I stumble in my haste to put distance between us, colliding with the wall on my left, then using it for support.

"Who *are* you?"

Cassie smiles a wicked smile. "So, the rumors the Registry is hearing are true. You do have the *push*." She stalks toward me, studying me like an unusual specimen. "And strong too. Not an easy thing to resist my compulsion. Too bad for you, the rest of the spell is chemical. You're in for a long night, Flynn."

A flush of heat suffuses me as she speaks, the need for sexual release building and building. I want to grab her as she passes me, demand some answers, or maybe fuck her right there in the hallway, but all my effort goes toward remaining on my feet and not fondling my own breasts or reaching between my legs.

"Say hello to Genesis for me."

"Bitch," I mutter.

She vanishes around the corner, never having answered my question. Or maybe she has. The Registry. The goddamn National Psychic Registry.

Bathroom. She said the rest is chemical. I can make myself puke. But it's been over an hour since I accepted her drink. Too late for that.

Maybe I can *push* the... potion... out of me. I reach into myself, searching for my power, but find nothing but exhaustion. When it has appeared in the past, it's done so without bidding. Now that I want it, I can't find the damn talent. Or maybe I'm just too tired.

Too untrained, a little voice whispers in my head. I tell it to shut up.

The arousal persists. I can duck in the bathroom, hide in a stall and—

Shit, I'm in trouble.

Fierce determination enables me to turn from the ladies' room and walk stiffly to Gen's side. I must look like hell because she takes one glance at me and freezes in her conversation with Peter behind the bar. "What happened?"

"Let's go." I take her by the hand and pull her out the front entrance. The bouncer wishes us a good night, but I barely hear him. I'm too focused on making it all the way across the Boardwalk Resort property to the farthest self-parking lot—the one where it's free to park rather than costing fifteen dollars for valet. This is what I get for trying to save a few bucks.

We haven't gone twenty feet before Gen hauls me to a stop under one of the decorative lamps beside the Boardwalk's lake. The resort simulates Atlantic City's beachfront hotels, the lake serving as a substitute ocean. Hidden speakers pipe in sounds of seagulls and lapping waves.

Despite it being after midnight, it's brighter out here than in the club. Gen turns me to face her, searching for answers. She frowns and swipes a finger across my lips, her fingertip coming away with traces of dark red lipstick—not Gen's shade, and I don't wear makeup.

Shit.

"I… I don't believe it," she whispers, tears welling in her eyes.

"Oh, for fuck's sake." We've had issues with jealousy and insecurity in the past, on both sides of our relationship. But I'd hoped we were beyond this.

She backs away from me, then takes off along the boardwalk at a quick pace, leaving me standing beneath the lamppost feeling alone and stupid and frustrated. When she reaches the next circular pool of light cast by the lamps, she stops and yanks off the engagement ring I gave her. The light catches the miniscule diamond, sparkling in the darkness.

Since we received Leo's fortune, I've offered to replace that ring with something better, nicer, bigger, but Genesis refuses. This is the ring I proposed with, and she'd keep it. Forever. Her words.

I guess she meant it, because she returns to my side, staring from me to the ring and back to my face. "Okay," she says, sliding it on again. "Maybe I'm being an idiot. But you need to start talking. What happened in there?"

I tell her. It comes out in pieces, my thoughts and words distracted by whatever's going on inside me, but she gets the gist. Her expression moves from stunned to outraged to downright scary while I talk, all the while shifting my stance and crossing my arms over my chest to keep from touching myself. When I finish, she takes my face in her hands and looks through me, setting my teeth on edge. She's done this before, searching for spirit possession or any other magical influence within me, but it freaks me out every single time.

"You're bespelled," she confirms at last, releasing me and sighing. "What was her name?"

"Cassie." I bare my teeth in a feral snarl. "She said to tell you hello."

"Cassie went after *you*? That blond was Cassie? Fuck."*

I can't tell if she's more surprised by my attacker or the fact that Cassie attacked *me*, but regardless, my eyebrows jump toward the top of my forehead. Gen never curses. That's my territory.

"I should have recognized her," she says. "It's impressive you managed to avoid going home with her. Cassie's a powerful witch."

I shake my head. "She said she owned a dating service."

Gen laughs, but there's no humor in it. "She does. Orlando Match. Some of the strongest amongst us hide behind mundane occupations."

Like a witch who specializes in love and seduction spells running a matchmaking operation. Right. "But not you."

"No, not me. People accept tarot readers and psychics who talk to the dead. But I have many skills—granted, lesser ones—that I don't show."

Tendrils of cold work their way down my spine. Yeah, she has other skills, like tapping dark magic and using it to kill those who threaten her or the people she loves. It still scares me sometimes, and I have to remember this is Genesis. I don't want to fear her or hurt her with that fear.

"So," I say, fidgeting and tugging my vest down straight. Bad move. The additional friction against my breasts has me swallowing a moan. "What now?"

"Now," Gen says, taking my hand again, "we get you home as quickly as possible. If I know Cassie, this is going to get a lot worse very fast. Seduction potions don't count as dark magic. They take nothing from another person to create them. But unsatisfied, they can be nasty. The Registry forbids their use except between two consenting adults, kind of like Viagra on steroids. Doing this so obviously, so publicly, so traceably… to not get in trouble, she'd have to have special permission…." She trails off, frowning, considering.

"And how do we fix this?" I don't have time for consideration. I'm about to crawl out of my skin, though I try hard not to show it.

Gen shakes off whatever is on her mind. She licks her lips, a wicked glint coming to her eyes. "We satisfy it."

Chapter 4
Test Fail

ONCE FLYNN and Genesis exited the nightclub, Peter watched Cassie slip from the liquor storage room and return to the bar. She propped her elbows on the surface, leaning her chin in her hands and giving him a baleful look.

"Rum and Coke. Make it a double."

At this point, an hour before closing, he could turn the pair of conventioneers he'd been waiting on over to his assistant. He caught her attention, nodded to the other customers, and let her take it from there.

Peter poured Cassie's drink and set it before her. "Where's your victim? I mean, um, conquest? Sex slave? What are you calling them these days?"

"Powerful," she whispered, taking a heavy draught. "The board was right to pursue this. That Flynn woman has strength to spare."

"In more ways than one," Peter agreed, remembering the muscles in her biceps, the way she'd spun her partner on the dance floor. "So you're saying you failed."

Cassie clenched her hands around the glass. "I'm saying she defeated me, soundly, thoroughly. Pushed my influence out like flushing a damn toilet."

"No worries, love. It's what you wanted to find out, after all, right? And she'll still have the potion in her," he said, grabbing a cloth from beneath the bar and wiping up someone's spill. "That should give you some satisfaction. By the way, you owe me for that." He held out a hand to her, palm up.

She stared at it like a chef might eye a rat in his kitchen. "Lot of good it does me. She's with Genesis now. The 'nationally known psychic' will take care of her."

"You know her." It wasn't a question.

"We were into each other for a brief time. Long ago, years and years. I've lightened my hair color, changed my eye color, and a little sex glamour didn't hurt either. She didn't recognize me."

Peter didn't remove his hand. "Flynn will tell her who you are."

"Perhaps. Despite that itty-bitty diamond Genesis wears, I sensed some insecurity between them. Flynn may not admit what went on here."

"None of that matters. We had a bargain. If I'm going to deliver your 'liquid gifts' for you, I expect to be paid."

Cassie's gaze shifted with anger. The pupils of her eyes flashed with quick sparks before dying like embers. Peter swallowed hard.

"You know I cannot create more than a couple of potions in a night. You work for me, but I work for the Registry, and I have others who need my elixirs as much as you. You wouldn't want me seeking alternate sources of power…."

No, he wouldn't. Because he knew full well what, or rather *who* that alternate source could be.

"Perhaps you don't enjoy being my assistant, and the age-reversing tinctures you receive when your hairline recedes, your muscles flab, your sexual prowess falters." She pierced him with her stare. "Perhaps it's time to stop providing you with those things and more, let the early-onset Alzheimer's have its way with you and give all my energy to others in need." Her gaze went distant, her tone, melancholy. "I can't save them all."

Peter shook his head. No, he didn't want that.

But a small part of him wondered, more and more frequently, if he wouldn't be better off having the Alzheimer's erase all memory of the things he'd done for Cassandra Safoir at the Registry's bidding.

Chapter 5
Losing Battle

I'M NOT stupid enough to leave a McLaren in a Disney self-parking lot, even one no longer painted look-at-me neon orange, but rather a nice, unobtrusive blue. No, we'd brought Gen's black Charger. I'd driven over, but she sits behind the wheel now, casting worried glances in my direction every thirty seconds or so. Normally that would irritate the hell out of me, but I can't blame her. Not considering the pitiful whimpers escaping from my throat at uneven intervals.

When she said things would get a lot worse, she wasn't kidding. I huddle in the passenger seat, knees drawn up to my chest, soles of my boots on the leather cushion, seat belt recklessly off because I can't stand any more tension across my breasts. And the damn warning light keeps blinking red on the dash, the "fasten belt" chime ringing in counterpoint to my mewling.

I'd thought pressing my legs together would help, but every jolt of the Charger, every bump and turn, every vibration of the V8 engine sends spirals of sensation straight from the car, through my jeans, and into my core. I've gone from pleasurable, if annoying, arousal to a dull, throbbing ache, an emptiness demanding to be filled. I don't want to consider what might happen if I spread my thighs.

The result comes to me anyway. I'll freaking explode.

"Gen," I force past gritted teeth, "it hurts." Damn, I hadn't meant to admit that out loud. Hadn't intended to worry her. Then again, it's obvious.

As the crow flies, Disney's Boardwalk Resort lies approximately seven miles from Festivity. As the roads twist and curve, adding in the tourist traffic even at this late hour and the reduced speed limit to protect idiots from ending up in Dead Woman's Pond, the drive takes about thirty minutes. It's been less than ten.

"The more you resist, the worse it gets," she informs me, keeping her left hand on the wheel but resting the fingers of her right lightly on my knee. I hiss at the contact, the warmth of her skin through my jeans. She jerks away. "Shit. Sorry, Flynn."

"Profanity twice in one night. Edgy." My attempt to distract myself with sarcasm fails. I want nothing more than to slide my fingers beneath my waistband, into my undershorts, stoke the fires burning there. The ache reaches a more painful crescendo, the need rising and falling, teasing me rhythmically in time with my pounding heartbeat. My hand creeps toward the buckle of my belt.

"Go on," Gen whispers. "Just do it. It's dark. No one will see you but me, and I'm watching the road."

"I'm not masturbating in a car like some horny teenager." And I'm not letting magic control me. No more. This is my line in the sand.

"It's not like I've never seen you before."

I catch the note of humor in her voice, a bit forced under the circumstances, but she's trying to lighten the moment. And she's right. Early in our dating, when we were still getting to know each other's wants and needs, we'd had a few glasses of wine and shown each other exactly what we liked. I enjoyed the experience, the two of us on the carpet in the living room of Gen's old apartment, my inhibitions carried off by the alcohol, and Gen, well, no inhibitions there, ever. Her eyes closed, her head thrown back, her lips parted as her breathing hitched….

My hips twitch upward at the memory, the muscles in my thighs tightening. I picture different sizes of screws and washers, different brands of particle board, anything to erase the image in my head of my beautiful Genesis in the throes of orgasm.

"It's about control," I growl. "I'm not doing this on their terms." They, meaning the National Psychic Registry. I've let magic control my life enough these last couple of months. Both our lives. I'm not giving in without a fight.

A fight I'm losing fast.

"You can't win," she says, as if reading my mind. Sometimes I wonder if mild telepathy is another of her many talents she hasn't shared with me yet. "You can only delay the inevitable. Why torture yourself?"

"It's the—" I gasp as a surge of the spell makes invisible fingers dance over my nipples. Okay, that's just not fair. When I can breathe again, I finish, "—it's the principle of the thing."

We turn onto World Drive, the road that ends at the big Festivity concrete signage wall so terribly far away, behind which lies Dead Woman's Pond—not that the wall ever managed to stop the lake from sucking in its victims while it was still cursed.

But it's miles away, and a phantom hardness rubs me through my jeans, pushing the damp material inside, deeper, deeper….

"What—" I break off with a low moan, pressing my mouth into my arm to muffle the sound. Distraction. I need a distraction.

No, Flynn. You need to get fucked. Right. Now.

Trees, cars, streetlights. I count them as the Charger rumbles on. One, two, three—

"Uhnh." No chance to muffle the sound that time. The groan bursts free and echoes in the sports car. Cassie's potion lets me get so close, and then it pulls back, eases off, over and over. I'm going insane.

"Flynn…."

"No. I have to draw the line somewhere. I'm drawing it here." I set my jaw. I squeeze my eyes shut. Fifteen minutes and we're home, and I, or Gen and I, can take care of this on my terms. Maybe a small victory, maybe a ridiculous one, but a victory all the same.

Whatever's in me, it senses my renewed determination and ups the stakes.

My temperature rises. Sweat beads on my brow
despite the Charger's AC cranked to the max and all
the vents aimed in my direction. I'm hot as hell, and
yet I'm shivering.

"Flynn."

My mind and body come to alert at the shift in
Gen's tone, from concerned to a purring sultriness I
cannot ignore.

"Unfasten that leather belt, Flynn."

In my peripheral vision, she keeps her eyes dead
ahead, never taking them off the Saturday-night par-
tygoer traffic, which is thinning out the farther we
get from Disney, but she's a master of multitasking,
I know from experience.

"Gen, don't." Pleading. I'm freaking pleading.
If I ever catch up to Cassie, I'm going to beat the
crap out of her for this.

"Come on, baby. I know you want to. Undo
those jeans. Slide them down. I'll keep us in the right
lane. No one will see."

"Goddammit, Gen." But my hands move of
their own volition. A soft clink of metal and the two
ends of my belt fall to my sides. The button pops
free; the zipper sings soft and sweet as it slides, almost on its own.

If sex could talk, it would sound like Genesis.
"That's it. Good. Isn't that better? Slip your fingers
beneath the cotton."

I do it, finding ten times more heat than I experienced before. The potion nudges me on, a new

flood of wetness responding to my gradual surrender. I know what I'll find if I seek lower. My left hand clamps down on the armrest between us, short nails still managing to dig into the leather so tightly I puncture the expensive covering. Fuck it. This is Gen's fault. She can damn well pay for any damage I cause.

"Circles, Flynn."

Aw, hell. She's using what she knows about me, my body, my responses, and it's ripping away the last of my resistance. "N-no." My hand trembles, but I hold myself in check.

"Really?" She straightens in the driver's seat. "Fine. Let's try this, then. Do you have any idea how wet you've made me?"

I blink. "What? Um, no." Here I am fighting this violation for all I'm worth and she's aroused by it? What the fuck, Gen?

"I shouldn't be. I know. But I can't help how my body's responding. The moans, the squirming. I know what that potion does. I can imagine how you feel. It's driving me crazy."

"Driving *you* crazy?" That comes out as a squeak. I never squeak.

"You know what I want to do to you right now? I want to pull off on one of these exits, find an empty parking lot, and ease your seat back. Why don't you do that for me, Flynn? Ease your seat back. You'll be more comfortable."

I reach across my body and find the lever, not wanting to remove my other hand from my jeans, even if it's not doing anything. I like the pressure there. That's all. Just pressure. Not giving in. I'm not. I find the handle and release the seat, reclining it all the way until I'm lying almost horizontal. And yeah, it's better.

It's damn good.

"Perfect," Gen purrs. "Then I'd crawl in between your legs and lift them up, place those sexy boots of yours on the dashboard."

My mind registers what she's doing. My body can't help itself. She doesn't even have to ask this time. I brace the soles of my boots on the dash. This makes it much easier to slide my jeans down over my hips. My underwear follows. She hasn't suggested that; I just do it.

Tears burn behind my eyes, pressing to escape. If there's one thing I hate, it's being helpless, and that's what I am right now.

"Then I'd lean my head down, and I'd—"

"God, Gen, stop."

But she doesn't stop. She tells me everything her tongue and fingers would do to me, and my hands match her words. The pace, the intensity, everything she says, I do, her voice a direct line between my brain and my body. My hips rock upward, driving my fingers deeper, harder.

"You're so close," Gen whispers.

I moan in response. She keeps talking. Dammit, why won't she shut up?

Because I need this. I want this. She knows me better than I do.

And yet, a little part of me hates her for it.

Bright lights glare through my closed eyelids—the spotlights around the Festivity sign. We've made it to town, but our inherited mansion sits on the far side. Another seven minutes in the Charger. I'll never hang on that long.

"Let go," Gen says.

"Don't want to," I growl, hips picking up speed, that damn seat belt alarm setting my rhythm.

"I know. But let it go."

She reaches out with her right hand, finding and fondling my breast through my vest and shirt, then sliding it down, grazing my stomach, to my thigh, where she traces gentle, intricate patterns over my bare skin. She stretches farther, her fingertips searching, searching, then finding my center and dancing across it.

With a cry of defeat, I surrender.

Chapter 6
Aftermath

GENESIS FELT the eruption approaching, the fever-ish bucking of Flynn's hips, the loss of rhythm as primal instinct took control of her girlfriend's over-taxed body and resistance broke down. Flynn's thigh muscles clenched, then released, then clenched again as wave after wave washed over her.

Gen kept up the movement of her fingertips, maintaining the contact, easing Flynn through the downswing, the aftershocks, the inevitable collapse of muscular strength, all the while keeping the Char-ger from riding up on the curb or crashing into a median.

With Flynn panting, gasping, then—God, was she sobbing?—beside her, Gen withdrew her hand and made the final turn onto Royal Court Street, guiding the car around the curves toward their home. She turned into the driveway, parked, and shut down the engine, silencing the infernal seat belt alarm at last.

And yes, Flynn was crying.

Shit.

It sounded very loud in the sudden silence of the vehicle. And very embarrassing to someone like Flynn who rarely, if ever, cried.

Better to give her some privacy. Gen unlocked the doors and swung hers open, standing on trembling limbs. She hadn't lied when she said this affected her too. Her knees shook, and the dampness between her own legs made walking uncomfortable.

Actually, standing still was pretty uncomfortable, too, but she couldn't move from where she leaned against the warm hood of the car. Not without Flynn, who, so far as she could see at a quick glance through the windshield, hadn't moved at all.

Guilt gnawed at her. What she'd done to Flynn, she'd done for her lover's own good. The potion wouldn't rest until satisfied. The ache Flynn felt would have grown steadily worse. Without Gen's encouragement, Flynn would have been screaming in pain before they reached home. Gen couldn't sit by and watch that happen. She couldn't.

Better to take Flynn's anger, beg for forgiveness.

So long as Flynn forgave her.

Pushing the reserved and, really, rather shy Flynn to do what she'd done might just have been a last straw. Gen didn't believe that, or rather, she didn't want to believe it. But more than anything, Gen feared Flynn's hatred of magical influence would sooner or later extend to Genesis.

And Gen had just influenced the hell out of her.

The Charger shook with interior movement. Gen kept her eyes turned away. A minute later, the passenger door opened. Boots hitting asphalt. A choked-off sob. The car door thunked closed. Boots on grass, uneven steps. Quadruple thuds as knees, then palms, hit the dew-dampened ground.

"Flynn...." Gen was around the hood, crouching in the grass beside her, before Flynn could rise. In the moonlight and the mansion's security lighting, the tears ran in glistening streams down Flynn's cheeks.

"Don't," she said, almost too soft to hear.

"But—"

"Don't help me." The subtext came through loud and clear. *You've helped enough.*

Gen wanted to cry with her, but one of them needed to maintain her composure. "I'm sorry," she said instead, her voice cracking despite her best efforts. "I couldn't let it keep hurting you. I did what I thought was right."

A sigh. "I know." Less anger in her tone. "But leave me alone awhile." Flynn pushed herself upright on trembling arms, then stood on equally shaky legs. Her head hung down as she trudged toward the front door, her limp much more pronounced than usual.

Broken, Gen realized. She's broken.

No. Just damaged. She'd bounce back. She had to.

Flynn was her strength, the only thing standing between her and giving in to the dark magic that even now called and called. Worse than Cassie's merely temporary love potion, it whispered seductively in

Gen's ear, a constant murmur. With the dark magic, she could heal Flynn physically, emotionally.

At what cost?

The last two times she'd used it, people had died—one a stranger, one an enemy. Next time it could be her brother, Chris, or even Flynn herself. She didn't want to find out what healing Flynn might cost.

The front door opened and the hall light flicked on, casting a wide beam across the grass. Inside, Katy's joyful bark shifted to a whine as Flynn apparently passed the husky/shepherd mix by without a greeting.

Flynn loved the dog they'd rescued (for a second time) from an Orlando shelter. Now Katy was part of their family.

A family Flynn had just removed herself from, no matter how temporarily.

And it hurt. A lot.

Chapter 7
Pride and Guilt and Consequences

I LIE on the guest room bed, across the hall from the master bedroom where Gen will be sleeping alone for the few remaining hours of night.

No, not alone. The padding of four paws trails her soft footsteps down the hallway. Katy's not allowed on the bed with us. She has a cozy dog cushion thing next to it. But I'm betting Gen will make an exception.

The human steps stop outside my door, which I locked on my way in. The dog paws dance on the tile, eager and anxious. I didn't treat Katy so well when we got home.

Didn't treat Genesis well, either.

I didn't want to give in. Magic has fucked with my life as much as I intend to let it. I will not let it control me.

You didn't. You didn't go home with Cassie. You went home with Genesis. You stood up to it. You beat it. It's Cassie you should be pissed at, not Gen.

I know she wanted to help, make things easier, get me through it. But dammit, I asked, no, *told* her to leave me alone. And she ignored me. Always knows what's best. Always has to do things her way.

She'd say the same thing about you.

I tell my conscience to shut the hell up, but I know I'm hardheaded enough to choose the difficult path every time. Always have been.

Chris has tried to give me some pointers on being part of a true partnership. He's as bachelor as a man can get, but he and Gen had two solid, loving parents until their boating accident when Gen was sixteen. I got nothing. Dad left when I was little. Mom went nutso.

Chris says if I'm in it then I'm *in it.* There's no half commitment. Not if I'm serious.

And I damn well better be serious, considering what I went through to give her that ring and get her to accept it.

Gen's been outside the door, silent, waiting, while I let my anger run its course through my head. She tries the doorknob, and I can picture the sadness on her face when she finds it locked and turns away. A moment later, the other bedroom door closes. She doesn't click its lock.

So she's leaving me an open invitation to change my mind, and she's not mad. That's good. And bad. If she's not mad, she's upset. If she's upset, I'm still responsible. I'm pretty much always responsible.

Time to start being more *in it.*

I heave a sigh and throw my legs over the side of the bed, pausing to smooth the fresh-out-of-the-plastic-bag comforter in rich browns and reds. Strong colors to compete with the pastel flowery nightmare in the master. But Gen likes pastels, and I humor her. No one's ever slept in this particular extra room.

Shit, this place is large enough to be a small hotel. I will never get used to being rich.

Standing takes concentrated effort, and I frown at a renewal of arousal. So, it's not done yet, and it doesn't want me off the bed. Well, I guess that figures. I can't tell if that's a result of my own need or the spell's will. A spell with a will of its own. Now that's a terrifying thought.

I open the door, which doesn't creak, and cross the hall. Then, even though it's my room too, I knock.

Katy barks, just in case Gen doesn't hear me.

The door opens. I hold out my arms and find them full of Genesis. She cries a bit on my shoulder, then pulls back to study my face. "I'm glad you changed your mind."

I give a one-armed shrug. The other hurts too much to risk it. "My ego's taken a hell of a beating. What's a little more abuse?" My blush creeps from the collar of my shirt to the top of my forehead. "And, um, I think I need you."

"You *think*?"

I wince, but the twinkle in her eye tells me she's pulling my chain. "I *know*," I clarify. "I need you now and every day of my life."

"About time you figured that out." She bumps my good shoulder with hers, then frowns. "You're still feeling the effects?"

"Wasn't for a little while. Am now."

"And you're tired."

"Exhausted."

Gen pulls me to the end of the king-size bed and pushes me gently down on the soft mattress. The need eases off a bit, like it knows I'm going to give it what it wants. Creepy.

Take it easy, Flynn. Don't get weirded out.

I draw in a deep breath and exhale.

Genesis proceeds to undress me, starting with the vest, then the button-down, then my sports bra, tossing all three on the room's only chair. She's got my belt undone, again, when I catch her hands in mine. "What about your needs?" I have no doubt she told the truth earlier, about how I affected her.

She grins that wicked grin I both love and fear. "Oh, don't worry. You first. I'll take care of my own needs later." She winks. "Maybe I'll even let you watch."

From there she acts out everything she described in the car, in triplicate, finishing with a masturbation session on her part that would make a porn star blush, "Just to be fair." As much as I'm enjoying the show, I'm out before she reaches her third orgasm, but given where she was headed, she probably didn't notice.

"I THINK we have a problem." Gen's voice carries as if across a large distance, muffled by the pillow I pulled over my head at some point during the night.

"Come on, Flynn. It's after two. Get up. I need to show you something."

"You showed me something last night," I say, lifting a corner of the pillow away from my face so she can comprehend my words. I let my grin come through in my tone. "A lot of something." My stomach growls. If it's after two in the afternoon on Sunday, I haven't eaten in... hell, I'm too groggy for math.

Katy's wet nose pokes me in the thigh protruding from beneath the covers, and that's enough to make me sit up, then regret it as my head pounds. I cover my eyes with both palms, blocking out the too bright sunlight streaming through open curtains.

"God, you didn't tell me potions come with hangovers."

"Here." She pulls my hands away from my face and presses two orange tablets and a glass of water into them. I swallow the ibuprofen with a grateful smile. "Now come on. Downstairs."

"Um, clothing?"

"No one here but me and Katy."

"Don't care."

She rolls her eyes, but I'm not parading around the mansion naked. Too many windows. Big windows. Some with stained glass befitting the castle-themed architecture, but plenty with clear panes that the maid (good God, we have a maid) keeps very clean. Besides, Gen's dressed, her gorgeous red hair wet from a recent shower. Her white peasant blouse reveals both shoulders and a tanned midriff above her forest green tiered skirt, and I have a sudden urge to press my lips to her abdomen despite the headache. Not the potion. I can tell the difference. This is all me. Sadly, she dances away before I can grab her.

A pair of my jeans and a black tank top smack me in the head, thrown from the chair where I tossed them before dressing to go out last night. "Um, underwear?"

"Go kamikaze. Just hurry up."

"That's 'commando,'" I say, pulling the tank top over my head and fastening the jeans.

"Whatever."

I follow her down the stairs, Katy doing everything she can to trip me on the way, but we make it to the bottom unscathed. Gen passes through an arch into the kitchen. I follow to open the pantry and get the dog food, building the husky mix into a frenzy of yaps and leaps, but Gen stops me with a hand on my arm.

The other gestures toward the kitchen table.

Where a vaguely familiar envelope lies on the flowered placemat at my usual seat.

It takes a moment for memory to break through my hungover brain. When it does, I turn on Genesis, rage and irritation vying for control of my voice. "I thought I asked you to throw that thing away."

She flinches, and I tone it down a little, stalking to the table and seizing the Psychic Registry's invitation to their national conference in a crumpling grip.

"I did."

"You—?" I break off, uncurling my fist and taking a closer look at the envelope, noting coffee and chocolate stains, a smear of dried creamed spinach on the back flap. We haven't had spinach in weeks. This invitation has been in the garbage.

And it has returned.

Sentient spells and reappearing envelopes. Now, Flynn. Now you're allowed to get weirded out.

Chapter 8
Shopping Encounter

"YOU REALLY shouldn't have done that," Gen says, turning the Charger onto I-4 and picking up speed. We're going shopping. Gen's idea. And since last night didn't work out so well, I agreed to it. She wants to shop, and she thinks my wardrobe needs updating, hence the vest/shirt combo she gave me. I think we both need to get out, so here we are.

"It made me feel better."

The invitation, in all its grimy glory, lies in sixteen pieces in four different trash cans scattered around the house. I even dropped the final, seventeenth bit in a neighbor's recycling bin out on the curb.

Let's see those bastards get *that* back on my place mat.

"The letter was charmed. They'll find a way," Gen says, braking for a U-Haul that doesn't know the left lane is the fast lane.

She's followed my entire train of thought. "You do have telepathy, don't you?" I mutter.

That earns me a laugh—a wonderful sound. "Nope. I just know you that well."

Yes. Yes, she does. Sometimes it terrifies me.

"You know, I never really thought about it, but how did the Registry find out about me, anyway? I mean, you didn't tell them, and I'm sure Chris wouldn't."

Gen shakes her head in confirmation. "He wouldn't. He rarely has reason to interact with them at all. And as much as I think you should get some training, I wouldn't go against your wishes on this."

On this. On *this*. Masturbating in the car is a different story.

She catches my sudden stillness, a blush suffusing her cheeks, and fixes her gaze straight ahead, so I know she knows what I'm thinking now too.

Let it go, Flynn, I remind myself. I force my shoulders to untense.

Gen releases a soft sigh. "Leo, maybe?" she continues. "He said he'd get even when I—when he died. He could have had some fail-safe in place, if he didn't survive the lake. A message sent."

I consider it, staring out the windshield, watching the brake lights. Sunday traffic, the going-home-from-vacation traffic, can be a bitch around Orlando. "That would mean he planned or at least considered the idea to kill us all along, or kill me, anyway, assuming Max would take care of you and Chris. And if I took Leo out instead, then he'd have his revenge, turning me over to the Registry."

"Yep. Much more vicious than I would have given him credit for, but that sums it up. Don't know what I ever saw in him." She frowns. "And the dark magic changed him."

"It won't change you. I won't let it."

Gen reaches out and squeezes my knee. She changes lanes, heading for the mall exit.

"Of course, it could have been the old guy," I say, then stiffen in my seat. Wait. What? Where had that come from?

"What old guy? Who are you talking about?" Gen doesn't take her eyes off the road, but her hands tighten on the steering wheel.

My memory flashes back to the battle with Max, his backyard, and a homeless man who stepped from the shadows and saw me—*saw me*—even in spirit-walker form. And why the hell was I only remembering this now?

Could have been the snakebite poison. Could have been the fact that I was out of my body at the time.

Or maybe that creepy old man put a spell on me.

I fill Genesis in on the details I'd never told her before, never been *able* to tell her until now, breathing easier when she doesn't freak out.

"Dark practitioner," she says. "I'll have to check him over the next time we see him at Starbucks. As a mentally unstable homeless man," she amends. "His guard won't be up, then."

"Okay, wanna deal me a clue card? Because I'm totally out of the game here."

We pull into the expansive parking lots of Mall at Centuria. Not where I thought we were going. I buy my clothes at Walmart or Target, the outlet mall when a good paycheck comes in, Goodwill when I'm out of work awhile. Once a year, I might splurge on gifts for others at the Florida Mall. Only really rich people shop at Centuria. People like Genesis, who makes a boatload telling fortunes.

And with the inheritance, now me too. So fucking surreal.

At least Gen's not heading for valet. That would totally blow my mind.

"The Registry punishes users of dark magic," she says.

Shopping at Centuria. If I hadn't started this conversation myself, I'd think she's using it to distract me.

"I know that much." It's what she fears.

"But you don't know the how. An occasional practitioner gets a warning. A persistent one gets punished with madness."

I stare at her, knowing she can see me in her peripheral vision. She pulls into a parking place about halfway down a row.

"Don't look at me like that," she says, shutting off the engine. "It's not permanent. But it is effective. The offender gets a number of days each week which he spends in a semi-mad state. The worse the offense, the more days. The rest of the time, he's sane. Sounds like your homeless man/pawn shop employee got caught using the dark stuff."

And her wonderful Registry made him insane—how the hell did that work, anyway? "Is the punishment automatic? Did he get some kind of trial? Or did the Registry play judge and jury like they're doing with me?" They sicced Cassie on my tail. That's pretty much all the answer I need. "Nice bunch. You were on the board for a while. I've seen the plaque in your workspace. How could you have been part of—"

Her hands tighten on the steering wheel, her knuckles going white. "It's why I resigned the position, Flynn." Gen shifts to face me. "Look. We're not angels. That much should be obvious from the things I've done."

"I didn't mean—"

"Let me finish."

I shut up.

"I don't agree with everything the board votes to do. But you don't want dark practitioners roaming around unchecked. Just look at Leo."

Yeah, he was pretty bad.

"And what they did to you is unacceptable."

Unacceptable? Yeah, I'd fucking say it was unacceptable.

"But they have reasons. They want to know what you are. They want to know how strong a power and whether or not you have the moral sense to be trusted with that power. They want to know that you're trained well enough to not accidentally harm someone or draw on the dark without realizing. And if you continue to refuse to go to them for evaluation, they will continue to find alternative ways, like using Cassie, to test you."

I've heard all this before. It's nothing new. She's been trying to convince me for weeks, but I'm not having it. Gen can watch out for me just fine, and I'm not playing with my power. I'm not tapping it.

Not on purpose, a little voice nags from the back of my head. I shake it off.

"With you right here, around me all the time, keeping tabs…." I pause, frowning at the odd look on her face, putting pieces together, not liking the picture I form. "They don't trust you, do they? They know."

Gen lowers her head, red hair falling around her face, hiding her expression. "Not about killing Leo, no. But I got my warning when I saved Chris's life. When I went to them for help because I was horrified by what I'd done. Putting me on the board was one more way to keep an eye on me. When I quit…. No, they don't trust me. Not with you, and not with myself."

I DON'T care what other people think. I don't care what other people think. I don't care— Oh, who the fuck am I kidding?

I blend into the well-dressed shoppers at Centuria about as smoothly as a guppy in a piranha tank. What do these people need with more clothes, anyway? They're already wearing suits and dresses that cost more than a week's salary at the construction site. In tennis shoes with no socks, battered jeans, and my black tank, I'm catching some rather disapproving stares.

"You're worth more than any of them," Gen reminds me, her hand tucked in the crook of my elbow, alternately guiding and pulling me when my feet refuse to move out of sheer terror. Hell, I can walk a roof's crossbeam four stories up, but I can't comfortably navigate a ritzy shopping mall. I'm not sure if Gen's words refer to my financial status or my character—the loving look she gives me suggests the latter—but either way, it helps. A little. Up one corridor and down the next we go, with intermittent pauses for her to admire something in a shop display or duck into a store to try on a skirt or blouse. I come to a halt in front of a jewelry store, cocking my head at a shelf of engagement rings in the window.

I take Gen's hand in mine, turning it over to reveal the tiny diamond in its tiny setting—all I could afford when I'd proposed. "You're sure?" I ask. My other hand finds the wallet in my back pocket, the shiny new Platinum Visa tucked in its worn leather folds. No amount of money can buy what she deserves, but I can do better than this pitiful representation of what she truly means to me.

"Positive," Gen says, tugging her hand away. She holds the ring up to the light, letting the fluorescent tubes catch the minimal sparkle. "What you gave me is priceless."

I shrug and let her drag me into the next boutique.

This one's arranged by color: all the pink dresses on one rack, green on another, white hanging on one section of the wall, black on the opposite side, and so forth. I guess it's efficient, because Gen zeroes in on her best shades of green and blue, pulling several and disappearing into a dressing booth.

And leaving me to fend for myself against the assessing stare of the middle-aged saleswoman.

Okay, I'm officially sick of this shit.

I cross my arms over my chest and lean back against the nearest clear patch of wall between two hooks full of tan clothing. She approaches in her black pumps and tailored gray pencil skirt and jacket over a black silk blouse. Behind her stands a mannequin wearing the same shirt. When she stops in front of me, she removes round wire-rimmed glasses, takes out a white linen handkerchief with some fancy silver embroidering, and cleans the lenses, maybe hoping to improve the view.

The pursing of her lips when she puts them back on says the cleaning didn't work. I'm still here.

"May I help you with something?" she offers.

Like finding a way out? her tone suggests.

"No, thank you," I say through teeth gritted so hard in a smile that they hurt.

"I believe Florida Mall has a Hot Topic that might fit your tastes."

Okay, that pisses me off on two levels: one, that she has the nerve to say to my face that I don't belong in her expensive shop, and two, that Hot Topic is one of those stores I drool over and can't afford… *couldn't* afford. Past tense. Huh. I'll need to drop by there sometime in the near future. Great jeans, kick-ass leather accessories, and vintage retro T-shirts.

But at the moment, I don't like being sized up in a glance, and I hate even more that she's right.

Wait. No. I don't. I'm not ashamed of who I am. I paste on my friendliest smile.

"Yep, that's me. Grunge and garage bands all the way."

Her eyes widen in surprise that I'd admit to such taste. She hurries away, putting the check-out counter between us like a protective barrier.

Meeting my own eyes in one of the multiple mirrors on the dressing booths, I note my unwashed stringy brown ponytail and my ratty two-day-worn tank top and jeans. Maybe my image could use a little help, but not today, and not from her.

Chapter 9
Round Two

CHRIS WIPED down the Village Pub's outside bar and surveyed his domain with a contentment deep and satisfying. As owner and manager, he didn't get to work the bar often, but Shelly had called in sick. Since he knew the job and trusted his assistant manager to handle things inside, the duty fell to him.

No, not the duty. The joy.

He'd missed this, the simple pleasure of the outside afternoon air, the smell of an August storm on the way, the Yankees game blaring on the suspended wide-screen TVs. Buried under all the other responsibilities, sometimes Chris forgot he'd liked being a bartender for his late parents' restaurant.

And sometimes, if he concentrated hard enough, he could picture Dad, leaning against the bar, watching the waitstaff come and go, and Mom, presiding over the open kitchen. No, not their ghosts. Just memories with enough strength he could hear Dad's laugh and smell Mom's perfume.

Unlike Genesis, the only spirits he saw were the ones he poured. He had no gifts, no powers, other than a perfectly human yet uncanny way with numbers that kept the Pub in the black. But no matter how well he ran the place, he missed his parents' input… and everything else about them. Almost nine years gone and it hurt like yesterday.

"How about another round, snit?"

Snit? Who the heck called anyone snit?

Chris glanced down the bar at the older gentleman seated on the far end. Polo shirt, typical of Festivity's residents but out of place on him. Chris peered harder. Familiar. He recognized the man, but not from here, and not in those clothes. Maybe somewhere else in town?

Shaking his head, he poured a fourth gin and tonic and slid it to the man, who caught it in a wrinkled but steady hand. Not the well brand. If the guy wanted to spend that kind of money in Chris's pub, he could call Chris anything he liked.

The guy feigned interest in the baseball game, but Chris could tell he wasn't into the sport. While other patrons hooted at errors and cheered the runs, this man showed no reaction at all. In fact, he seemed so lost in his thoughts, Chris almost dropped the glass he was filling when the man spoke again.

"That sister of yours, Genesis, she coming around today?"

Ah, that explained a lot. A potential client for Gen's talents might have heavy thoughts on his mind.

"Sorry, no," Chris said with some sympathy. "Not today." He stopped. How did this guy know

Gen hung around the Pub most Sundays if Chris had never seen him here before? He shook it off. One of her other clients must have told him. Sometimes Gen brought her tarot with her and gave quick readings to the regulars. Or maybe it was the name. He had "Chris McTalish, Proprietor" emblazoned on a bronze plaque out front. The man could have seen it while walking by and stopped in looking for Genesis.

So why didn't any of those explanations feel right?

The not-quite-stranger took a long sip from his drink, a slight rocking in his posture the only indication the alcohol had any effect. "Damn meddlers," he mumbled. "What good is having the Sight four days a week? I'm wrong almost half the time." He fixed his gaze on Chris's face. "Best give her a message from me, snit. If the board has to, they'll go through her to get to Flynn."

Chapter 10
Indirect Approach

GENESIS MODELS each selection for me, searching for my approval, beaming when I nod that I like an outfit or the way a piece of jewelry sets off the emerald of her eyes. The hippy-esque peasant blouses and skirts suit her profession, but with her figure and poise she can carry off damn near anything, and I notice details I haven't before, like her professionally styled hair and manicured nails. Guess I'm more of a big-picture person.

When I need a trim, I grab the scissors, and for obvious reasons, construction workers don't get their nails done. Despite my earlier assertions to the contrary, I'm a little down on myself, looking at her.

It's exactly what Gen needs, though, and I'm not so insecure or vindictive enough to lie about what I like, hurting Gen's feelings and cheating the saleswoman out of her commission. I'm saving that pent-up revenge for Cassie when I catch up to her. I have no doubt we'll meet again.

Gen purchases two dresses in green and a skirt in white. The price tags make me hyperventilate, but I hide it well. Besides, my reaction to spending so much can't compare to the aches in my leg and shoulder, the ibuprofen long ago worn off. Sooner or later, she's bound to notice me struggling.

The saleswoman is so giddy about the final bill, she doesn't stop patting Gen's hand until I drag Gen away from the counter.

In the seventh store—or is it the eighth? I've lost count—she grabs a long blue sundress off a rack. Way too big for her. Unless she wears four-inch heels, it'll drag on the ground. I can't imagine—

"Oh no." I cross the index fingers of both hands in front of me, warding her off as she approaches.

"Aw, come on. It's a great color for you. Give it a try."

Backpedaling like it's a bomb rather than a piece of fabric, I bump another rack and scramble to steady it before it falls. The saleswoman—more middle-aged snobbishness—glares from behind the cash register, glasses sliding lower on her nose the better to look down on me. I'm starting to think the attitude is a Mall at Centuria job requirement.

"I'm not trying on a dress, Gen. Kamikaze, remember?" Places like these have cameras in the dressing rooms, or same-sex watchers behind the mirrors to discourage shoplifting. I'm sure of it. And I'm not trying on a dress, or anything else, while not wearing underwear.

"That's 'commando,' and who cares?" She waggles her eyebrows. "I'll come in and help you with the zipper, if you want."

Which translates loosely to sex in a dressing booth. Way beyond my comfort levels but well within hers.

"No dress," I state, planting my feet despite the renewed pain in my leg.

She reaches up to pull my ponytail from behind my back. "How about a wash and set, then? A curl would frame your face, gentle some of the hard lines—"

I catch her wrist in my hand and grip it hard. "Is that what you're trying to do? Gentle me?" Anger rises in my throat, all the out-of-place insecurities flooding to the surface. I'm aware of other shoppers stopping to stare, then glancing away. "What's gotten into you? I thought—" My voice cracks. Tired. Just tired. "I thought you liked me the way I am." In the year and a month we've been together, she's never tried to change me. Enhance, maybe, with better shirts, the vest, but nothing far from my own style, such as it is.

She's never made me regret being me.

Until now.

Teenage memories crack through a shell I'd built thick as steel over the intervening years.

"TRY TO be a little more feminine, Flynn. Brush your hair, put on some lipstick and rouge. You'll never catch a boy's interest in those jeans and T-shirts."

"What if the boys don't interest me?"

She had to have a clue. Okay, we hadn't seen as much of each other since her suicide attempt and institutionalization, but I'd dropped every hint in the book that I was gay. And the way I dressed and kept my hair short back then, I was practically the butch poster child. I hadn't wanted to add more stress to her, in her condition, but it was time to come right out—hah—and tell her.

"What if I prefer—?"

"Don't. Don't say it. And we'll forget we had this conversation. Wear whatever the hell you want. Go through your life alone. Bad enough I had to suffer the embarrassment of your father leaving. I won't have a… a…."

"Lesbian, Mom. The word is lesbian. And I have no intention of being alone."

"Don't use that language around me. The hospital staff might hear you."

I glanced toward the room's door and the well-lit corridor beyond and shrugged. Unless Mom set off an alarm by trying to leave without permission or opened a window, no one would check until it was time for her next dose of depression meds.

"Dad's gone. Grandmother's dead. Now you can't accept who I am. Seems to me the only one risking being alone is you." Two months. Two months of summer vacation, and then I'd be off to college in Florida. I got up to leave.

"Flynn."

Hope took root, ready to bloom, waiting for her apology, her embrace. I couldn't remember the last time she'd hugged me. I held my breath, not turning back, hand raised toward the doorknob.

"Maybe you should tell one of the doctors here. Maybe they can fix you."

I should have known better. "You mean the way they've fixed you?" I said.

She'd been in there six months with no discernible improvement. I'd visited her every day of most of my senior year, gave up friendships, the diving team, bowling leagues, a girl I liked. I'd managed the family finances, set up automatic payments from the substantial funds Dad had left us, hired someone to continue taking care of those things after I went to college.

I threw open the room door with more force than necessary. Rapid footsteps approached from the central nurses' station to make sure I was the one leaving and not my mother, though they could probably see me on the cameras mounted everywhere.

I never touched any of Dad's money for myself except what the two of us had needed to survive. I had a bowling scholarship to college, and financial aid would cover the rest.

I never visited Mom again after that day. Letters, cards at birthdays and Christmas, the occasional phone call, but I haven't seen my mother in almost ten years.

"OF COURSE I like you the way you are." Gen's voice pulls me from a red-tinged haze. "I love you. I just want you to try something new."

I gesture at myself. "Because the old me isn't working for you. Is that it?"

Gen's brow furrows. She blinks rapidly, then rubs at her eyes. "I… no, that's not it at all. I don't know why I'm—" From inside her satchel purse, her cell phone jingles with Chris's ringtone—"Tub-thumping" by Chumbawumba. Despite my glare, she digs for it. "This might be important."

"Because fuck knows *I'm* not."

"Flynn!"

I storm away to a corner of the store to give her and her phone some privacy and myself a chance to regain my composure. What the hell?

Movement in the corner of my eye has me turning toward the store's entrance, where a security guard stands and surveys the rows of clothing racks, gaze falling on me, of course. He's young, tall, well-built, and armed with nothing more than a rent-a-cop badge. If I need to, I can take him, and from his intense scrutiny, I'm betting he's figured that out, but another assault charge is not something I covet, even though the last one got dropped. The saleswoman nods toward Genesis, then me. Terrific.

In Walmart, an argument would be nothing out of the norm. In fact, it would provide some much-needed entertainment for the other shoppers. Heaven knows I've gawked at a few domestic squabbles in my time… and intervened when a couple of boyfriends got too rough with their girls.

Here, on the other hand, it's a get-kicked-out-of-the-mall sort of offense.

I force my arms to my sides, rotating the stiffness out of my shoulders, and smooth my scowl into a bored, bland expression. The guard looks from me to Genesis, who has fully engaged with her cell, then back to me and shrugs. After a few whispered words with the saleslady, he departs, but not before giving me a warning frown.

Pretending to study the clothes and avoiding the price tags, I place myself where I can hear Gen's end of the conversation. She's been yapping quite a while, even for her.

"But who was he?" A pause. "And he's gone now?" Another pause. "You're certain that's what he said?" A much longer pause. Gen thanks her brother, and a beep indicates the disconnect. More rustling as she returns the phone to her burlap satchel.

Okay. I mentally rub my hands together in preparation to continue our argument, and finish it if I have anything to say about it. No dress, no hairstyling, and if she can't accept me then I'll... I'll... I have no idea what I'll do, but it won't be pretty.

"Flynn?"

Love. Love means going from pissed to panicked in the span of a single word. I should write a fucking poem.

The thready tone of her voice has me spinning toward her. She's toppling even as I move, diving to my knees to catch her before she hits the tile floor of the shop. In my haste, I rattle the racks on either side, yanking down several outfits, which fall on us. I grab and toss them aside to land in a wrinkled heap and

stare down at Genesis. All the color flees her face.
She blinks at me, not focusing.

"Hey!" I shout, regaining everyone's attention,
shoppers and staff alike. "Hey, I need some help,
here! Somebody get her some water, and call first
aid." The mall has a first aid station, right? I think
malls do. It's been a long time since I've been in
one. When I'm certain the saleswoman has picked
up her phone, I focus on Gen. "What's happening?"
I ask her.

At first I worry she won't or can't answer, but
then the glaze fades from her eyes. "Another spell,"
she whispers, strain evident. "I'm sorry, Flynn, so
sorry. I love you as you are, everything about you,
but the spell…."

The spell made her ask me to change, made her
dissatisfied. Relief races through me, even as I struggle to make sense of it all. "Don't worry about that
now. What can I do?"

"Chris got a…." She searches for the right word,
one hand flailing until I capture it in my warm grip.
God, she's so cold. "He got an anonymous tip that
the board is trying to go through me to get to you.
Once I became aware of it, I could have negated it
myself, so a fail-safe kicked in."

"What does that—?"

"Miss?" The saleslady, much more polite now,
hands me down a bottle of water. Unopened. Good.
Because I'm pretty sure that first saleswoman was
the one who did this to Gen—all that hand patting,
very much like the way Cassie covered my hand last
night—and I'm not real trusting at the moment.

"Thanks," I tell the woman, uncapping the bottle and holding it to Gen's lips. She sips a few swallows, chokes a bit, then shakes her head. I set it aside.

"First aid's on the way," the woman assures me. She starts moving concerned customers away. "Let's give her some air. Probably just the summer heat. Unless someone's a doctor?"

Fortunately, no one is, which is a miracle considering the wealthy clientele. I'm worrying about first aid's imminent arrival. How am I supposed to explain "she's under a spell" to a bunch of normal humans?

And when did I stop thinking of myself as one of them?

Chapter 11
Bundle of Joy

"What do I do?" I ask, keeping my voice low.

"Nothing." A shudder passes through Genesis, visible tremors vibrating from her sandals to her head. She groans, pressing her face into my good shoulder.

"Bullshit," I say, holding her close, whispering into her ear. "If this is a test for me, there has to be something the board thinks I can do about it."

She takes a steadying breath and stares up at me, green gaze clouded with pain. "And if you do it, you're giving them some of the information they want."

From outside the shop, a small motor vehicle approaches, like a golf cart. Its puttering engine grows louder by the second, accompanied by the thin wail of a small portable siren. First aid.

"Then they win. For now," I amend. "Tell me." If I'm the one suffering, I'll fight. But I won't take chances with Gen's health and well-being.

Genesis studies my expression. I shoot for determined and unrelenting, and guess I accomplish it because she says, "You have to push the magic from me."

"Push," I echo her. "You mean *push* push?"

"Yes. You should—" Her next words break off in a sharp gasp.

Clutching her to me, I reach out with the power I keep trying to suppress. It pours forth, directionless, blanketing rather than focused. The first aid cart stops at the entrance. Two men climb off the vehicle, glancing at us through the open doorway, then hastening to the rear of the cart to gather their kits.

No time. No fucking time.

I close my eyes and concentrate, aware I have no idea what I'm doing. The *push* I've sent out expands like an extension of my self, my soul. It touches Genesis, it *infuses* her very spirit.

It encounters something alien.

I know the moment my power brushes it that it does not belong. Sometimes, when we are at our closest, I believe I touch that which is Genesis, and given what I now understand about my power, maybe I do. I know her in a way I don't even know myself. This is not part of her. The reverberations it returns sicken my stomach, set my head pounding, grease across my nerves like oily residue. More than anything, I'd kill right now for a hot shower.

Footsteps approach, the medical personnel closing in. I envelop the energy, grabbing every last ounce of it, and shove hard.

"Flynn...." My name escapes Gen's lips in a hiss, and I can't tell if it's pain or relief.

I snap my eyes open. Hers have gone wide, and she jerks upright, sitting straight on the floor.

"Miss, you should lie back down," one of the medics says, a man in his mid- to late thirties, the white jacket of his uniform stark against his dark skin. He places a hand on her shoulder while his partner, much younger—a trainee maybe—with a bad case of acne, attempts to catch Gen's wrist and take her pulse. Behind them, the saleswoman hovers, hands clasped together in front of her, eyes darting between us all.

A shoplifter could make off with half the store.

Gen's mouth gapes open. She stares at me, wild-eyed, panicked. "Pull back," she gasps.

The others give her a little breathing room, but I grasp her true meaning and reel in the power, the *push*. It surges into my body, an exhilarating rush. After a minute or two of panting, Gen slumps against me with a soft whimper.

God, what did I do to her?

"Are… are you better or worse?" I ask, afraid of the answer.

One of the medics soaks a cloth in water from the bottle and wipes at her sweat-covered brow.

"It's…." Mindful of the presence of null ears, she rephrases whatever she planned to say. "It's over. I'm better. Sort of."

Sort of? Shit.

I can't ask her what she means. Not with the first aid guys hanging on her every word. The younger one pulls a walkie-talkie off his belt. "I'm going to call this in, get an ambulance out here."

"No!" Gen and I both shout, loudly enough to send the saleswoman scurrying backward.

"Ma'am, your pulse is racing, you were hyper-ventilating, and—"

"And I'm going to throw up." Gen gives a sudden, violent lurch, pushing over to all fours.

I pull her hair behind her, holding it out of the way, just before she hurls all over the pristine white tile.

It's not a lot. We had brunch before hitting the road, but nothing for hours. She dry heaves for a few painful seconds, then rocks back on her heels. The saleslady's face scrunches in disgust. The younger medic uses the walkie-talkie to contact maintenance for a clean-up crew.

"Hey, at least she missed the clothes," I say, shooting for levity and missing by a mile.

"Now let me call that ambulance," the older guy says, taking the radio as the younger one signs off.

"No," Gen says again, "not necessary. You see, this is normal for me. I'm... I'm pregnant." Her hand reaches to clench around my knee, letting me know this is our cover story, but not before I manage to slosh the remainder of the water bottle I'm handing her.

"But... but you two are... are...." The younger one gets an elbow in the chest from the older one for his spluttering.

"Haven't you ever heard of artificial insemi-nation? Do they teach you anything in that nursing school you're going to? Shut up before you say something else stupid and insulting." The older medic offers an apologetic smile.

"No offense taken," I say while Gen pushes to her feet with some assistance from me. I leave her leaning on a clothes rack and grab her shopping bags from where she left them against the dressing booth. "Better get her home, though. Thank you for all your help." I wrap an arm around her waist, and we make our way toward the far-too-distant parking lot. Yeah, I'm wishing for that valet now.

Even though she's obviously still in a lot of discomfort, Gen's laughing under her breath.

"What?"

"You should have seen your face when I said I was pregnant. I'll never forget that look." It comes out amused but a little wistful, too, and I wonder if someday she wants….

God, I hope not. I have nothing against children, but kids and I do not mix, especially little ones with snotty noses and sticky fingers. I occasionally enjoy playing with other people's children, but I'd make a terrible parent. I can barely take care of myself.

No. That's a worry for another day. I've got more immediate problems to worry about.

Chapter 12
Guilt of Inaction

GENESIS VOMITS three more times on the route home.

I'm driving. She's facing me, curled in the passenger seat, an eerie reversal of last night.

"Do all spells have such negative aftereffects?"

Gen shakes her head, winces, presses her lips together, and waves at me to pull over. Again. I haul us off to the curb, not far from Dead Woman's Pond, mere minutes from the house, and watch helplessly while she throws open her door and dry heaves. So far we've managed to avoid her getting sick inside the Charger, but it's been a close thing every time.

"Sorry," I mutter when she closes the door. "Didn't mean to set you off."

She offers a half smile, closing her eyes and leaning back, but not speaking. From the way she clamps her jaw shut, I suspect she's worried opening her mouth might produce more than speech.

A million questions ramble like tumbleweeds through my head, but I hold them. I get her to the house, help her to the door, and hold Katy from pouncing on her until Gen can escape upstairs and into our room.

"Give her a break," I say, half to myself, half to the dog, and lead the husky/shepherd into the kitchen for her dinner. Once she's eaten, it's out for walkies (Gen's term, not mine), though I cut the stroll short in my hurry to return to Genesis. "Sorry, girl. You have to settle for being the second most important female in my life."

Katy gives a short bark and licks my hand.

It's a little weird for me, having a dog named directly after my deceased first serious girlfriend. She went by Kat, but the connection still freaks me out if I think too much about it.

I remember how happy Kat seemed once her ex-husband died. She faded into nothing, along with the ghost of Max's more recent wife, but I can't help wondering if they linger around here sometimes. One more thing to ask Genesis about when she's feeling better. And speaking of….

"You're gonna stay downstairs tonight," I tell Katy. "Got that? Downstairs?" An eighty-plus-pound dog jostling the bed is not what Gen needs right now.

Katy's tail droops between her hind legs, and she utters a little whine, but she heads into the spacious living room. My entire former hotel "suite" would have fit into that living room with space to spare. I lean through the arched entryway as the dog turns in a circle three times and curls herself on the rug in front of a massive, unlit stone fireplace.

Fireplaces in Florida. I'll never understand them, but I do enjoy cuddling with Genesis in front of one during the cooler months—cooler meaning the temperature drops to a mildly chilly fifty degrees and Gen claims she's freezing. It's all relative. I grew up in New Jersey. My blood's thicker than hers.

I fetch a dog biscuit from the box on the kitchen counter (yeah, I fetch, the dog lies on the rug) and toss it to her. She catches it in midair. "Good girl. Stay." Then I grab a spare blanket from the downstairs linen closet and head up to our room.

My soft rapping on the door earns the usual response of, "You live here too. You don't have to knock," so I step inside and stop.

My instinct served me well. Gen's in bed, the heavy comforter pulled up to her chin, skin pale, lips blue and trembling. I don't know how I knew. I just knew.

"Shit, Gen." First I spread the second blanket over her. Then I climb in beside her, slipping under both covers and pulling her against me for extra warmth. It's August. It's Florida. Despite the air-conditioning, the first beads of sweat form between my breasts and on the back of my neck, but I'll deal with it.

She presses herself as close as she can, sliding ice-cold hands beneath my shirt to rest on my heated stomach.

"Hey!" I say, arching away without success.

"You're too hot. I'm too cold. It averages out," she says, laughing a little. But it's weak, that laugh. I don't like it. I don't like any of this—how she looks, how she sounds.

"This feels wrong," I say. "I might not know a damn thing about your world, but whatever I did in the store, I fucked it up, didn't I?"

Almost a full minute passes before she replies, while I come up with all sorts of horrible consequences in my head. "Yeah, you did. Sort of."

That's what she said before. *Sort of.* "I need more than that."

Genesis sighs. "You did what I told you to. You pushed the spell out, stopped its influence. And again, I'm sorry. I could hear my words, see my actions, but I couldn't stop them. I can't imagine how I made you feel."

"It hurt," I admit, earning a look for the bold statement. Yeah, admitting pain. Big step. "I'll live. Will you?"

"Of course." She pulls one hand from beneath my shirt to cover one of mine. "Flynn, you need to understand, what you did…. You should be wiped out too. But you're not. You're fine. Better than fine, even after last night. I don't understand it."

Now that I think about it, she's right. Oh, my shoulder and leg ache as usual, but not as much, and unlike other times I've used the push, I don't feel tired.

I do feel a bit aroused, but I chalk that up to the last traces of Cassie's love potion in my system. And I don't mention it. It's not like Gen's up to doing anything about it. I'll manage.

"You're stronger than either of us suspected. Stronger than me." Gen holds her palm up to forestall the argument I'm about to make.

No way. No way am I stronger. I've seen her work, speak with the dead, channel spirits, drive one from me. Heal me.

Kill.

"Maybe not as diverse in your skills," Gen says, pausing to chew her bottom lip a moment. "Or maybe your other abilities haven't manifested yet."

Now there's a happy thought. Not.

"Regardless, you're strong as hell. Stronger than the Registry suspects, or they would have collected you by force."

"Okay, that's scary, and a topic for further discussion, but Gen, right now, tell me. What. Did. I. Do?"

She takes a deep breath, lets it out. "You didn't just push the spell from me. You pushed out all the magic, all my psychic energy down to the last iota. I'm null."

I'd swear my heart stops. I blink at her, letting the enormity of her words sink in. I think I'm going to be the next to vomit. "Gen, I—"

"No! No, not permanently. Crap, I'm sorry. I'm not thinking clearly. I'll be fine. Given time. I'm rebuilding my reserves, drawing from nature, letting my body regenerate its own innate power. But that's what's wrong, why I'm so drained. You... you removed all my strength. And that... that should be impossible," she finishes.

Chapter 13
In the Gutter

CHRIS AND I spend the next twenty-four hours rotating Genesis duty. I have to work the construction site Monday morning, so he takes the day off from the Pub and spends time with his sister and Katy. I swear he loves that dog as much as we do. Makes sense given the month or so he kept her for me while we got settled in the mansion.

When I get home, on time for once, from a frustrating day at work, he heads out to take the Pub's night shift. Chris owns and manages the place, but he leads by example, and he works as many hours on-site as the rest of his staff. I respect him for that and a lot of other things.

"You okay?" he asks, grabbing his keys off the peg rack by the front door.

I stop rubbing at my shoulder, face flushing. Need to be more careful about hiding pain, especially with Genesis incapacitated. She doesn't deserve extra stress. At least he hasn't seen how pronounced my limp gets after an eight-hour shift.

"I'm fine," I say with a little more growl than intended. He raises his eyebrows but lets it go. "How's Gen?"

"Better. Stronger."

"Add 'faster' and she'll be bionic." Yeah, maybe I watch too many *Six Million Dollar Man* reruns on the Syfy channel. "Really, though. She's okay?"

Chris rests a hand on my good shoulder. "She's okay. You didn't seriously harm her. You pushed the spell out and saved yourselves a major rift in your relationship. And she's regained enough strength to hold off the dark magic."

That's what we all feared, and why she'd insisted I call Chris in to help. With her own energies depleted, Genesis heard the call of the dark powers all the more strongly. I'd had to snap her out of tapping it several times during the night.

I slump against the nearest wall. "Okay. Good. And thanks."

His infectious grin has me returning it with one of my own. "No problem. Oh, two more things." Chris holds up two fingers in a peace sign. "One, she insists you go to your bowling league tonight."

Ah. Yeah. It's Monday. Used to be on Sundays, but when the laid-off construction crew's team had to drop out for financial reasons, our spot got taken by another group. We went back to work, money came in, but we had to switch to Monday nights when the lanes had an opening in their league schedule.

As much as I should be, I'm not thrilled at the prospect. I love bowling, went to college on a bowling scholarship. Seriously, they do exist. And

I haven't been out with the guys since my snakebite injuries, instead having the team plug in a number of substitutes in my position. Worse, I'm captain. I should be there to cheer them on, if nothing else. But I'm worn out, not from the use of my talent but regular work, and while it's my left shoulder that aches, not my right, hurling a sixteen-pound ball with speed and accuracy is not going to be pleasant.

I force a wider smile. "Sounds good." Fake it a few more hours, Flynn. Then use your favorite accessory, the mansion's hot tub, until you can crawl yourself into bed without whimpering. "What's the other thing?"

Chris blushes. Uh-oh. Not a good sign.

"Um, Gen's talking a lot about the, um, wedding."

Wedding? What wedding? We're not invited to a—Oh. Shit. Damn good thing I'm already leaning on the wall, because otherwise I'd fall against it. Even so, Chris grabs my arm.

"Hey! Steady there." He laughs. I don't join him. "It's just a little ceremony."

Not if Genesis has anything to say about it. I know her well enough to know she wants the whole shebang: the white dress, the huge guest list, the massive reception. Gown catalogs have been showing up in the mail for weeks, and she's looking at them every minute she can snag from her appointment schedule or spending time with me.

"Where, exactly, does she want to have this ceremony, and when?"

Chris straightens his Yankees cap over his short brown hair. Otherwise, he's dressed for work at the Village Pub—black pants, black shoes, white button-down shirt. "Atlantic City," he says, reaching past me for the doorknob and swinging the massive wooden castle-like door open. Katy hears the sound and races down the hallway for goodbye licks and pets. "She's got her eye on some place called One Atlantic. The building extends out over the ocean. I think she intends to fly the guests up there. Charter a flight or something." Chris reaches down to scratch the dog behind the ears. "For the reception, she's thinking one of the casino hotels."

Uh-huh. The National Psychic Registry's upcoming annual conference, the one they keep insisting I attend, is being held in Atlantic City. She won't force it on me, either the conference or the wedding, but I don't believe in coincidences. Not anymore. Not since my truck almost ended up in Dead Woman's Pond and my dead ex decided to appear for a little chat.

Then again, she can't possibly put together a wedding in just over two months, right? The conference is the last week in October, and today is August twenty-seventh.

"Just think about it," Chris says, oblivious to my other concerns. I doubt he has the details of the conference. He has no reason to. "You asked her. You must have known she'd expect follow-through. You did know that, right?" He's got an edge in his tone on that one. I don't blame him. He's looking out for his kid sister's happiness.

"I knew it," I confirm. His shoulders relax. "I just didn't think about doing it so fast. Figured we'd wait and watch the political climate for a while."

"You know you live in Florida, right? Biracial couples still catch some flack down here. They're going to waver back and forth on gay marriage." Shaking his head, Chris steps outside and shuts the door behind him.

Yeah. It's legal for me to marry Genesis now, but with the shifts in support from DC, there's no telling how long it will *stay* legal. Wouldn't be surprised if Gen's rushing it because she's afraid we'll miss our chance.

I use the wall for continued support and do some deep-breathing exercises. Katy wags her tail and licks my hand.

Come on, Flynn. You made a public proposal. You can handle a public wedding.

In Atlantic City.

Holy fuck.

"SHIT, FLYNN, you are way out of practice." Tom, my immediate boss at RPL Construction, strolls onto the lane and slings an arm across my shoulders. Together we watch my steel-gray/blue bowling ball bang and bump down the gutter.

"Lost my balance," I mutter.

Bowling has turned out to be everything I feared it would. My right arm works fine, but despite that being my release hand, the left gets thrown out to the side in a proper approach and delivery, compensating for the additional weight of the ball on the right. Except it hurts like hell to extend my left arm out, so I do it half-ass and end up staggering so as not to step in the oiled area of the lane and slip harder than I already have. End result? Bad release. The ball leaves my fingers a split second too early, flies about three feet in the air, lands with a thud, and hits the gutter.

I'm lucky it came down in my own lane.

I'm lucky I didn't launch the damn thing backward into my teammates.

"Don't sweat it. Happens to all of us." Tom wipes the sweat from his bald head on his bowling towel, then steers me around until I face the electronic scoring desk and seating area. The other three guys on my team—Alex, Diego, and Joe—also in matching RPL bowling shirts, hoot and applaud. It's all good-natured, and I love these guys like brothers, so I don't take it personally. The sneers and offers to give me bowling lessons coming from the other team, however, have me growling under my breath. "Come on. I'll buy you a beer," Tom says.

Allie's there, too, scribbling orders on her notepad to take back to Steve in Kissimmee Lanes' bar. She's wearing that cute plaid miniskirt I love, especially combined with her current white button-down and black patent heels. I'm careful not to admire too long or try to catch the reflection up her skirt in the polished shoe leather, though. I flirted with her once, under the influence of my ex's spirit.

Given she's dating Steve and the three of us have been solid friends for years, it didn't go over well.

She waves and offers me a sympathetic smile as Tom and I head over, then yelps and jumps forward, banging her thighs on the edge of the scoring computer desk. That'll leave a couple of solid bruises. Behind her, one of the guys from our opposing team, Delio Programming Systems, withdraws his fingers from beneath the pleats of her skirt. Allie whirls on him, her hand raised for a good slap across his face, but I get there first, sliding between them in shoes designed for just that purpose.

"You owe my friend an apology," I say, raising my voice over the crashing of pins in the background.

"Your *girl*friend?" the guy says, glancing between us. "Shoulda known." He and his teammates laugh and clink beer bottles together, the guy's lips wagging beneath a cartoonish handlebar mustache. Add in his cowboy hat and the boots by his bowling bag and he's a walking cliche. Except for the poser part. Given his slight build and utter lack of thigh muscles, he's never ridden a horse in his life.

His buddies present no more of a threat. Not compared to a team of construction workers, all of whom treat Allie like their kid sister or daughter.

"Flynn," Allie hisses in my ear, "it's okay. I can handle it."

"You hit him, in here or in the parking lot, and you'll get fired. Me, on the other hand…." I let my voice trail off. I've been in a fight here once before. The management might ban me for a week or two, but I'd survive another altercation.

"You, on the other hand," Tom finishes for me, "are the hero of Dead Man's Pond. Single-handedly saved a woman from drowning in her car." I don't correct his name for the pond. The nulls have no idea what went down there, literally. I'm just thankful that Tom has a gay sister, and he's very protective of her, and by extension, me.

"You, on the other hand," Diego says in his thick Mexican accent, "survived three consecutive water moccasin bites." He's the oldest member of the site crew, trained me, and I think of him as a replacement for the father who left when I was four. He moves to stand at my right shoulder, his bulk a reassuring presence. I'm confident I can take care of Mr. Happy Fingers, but I doubt I can take on his whole team.

"You, on the other hand," Alex puts in, "hold a brown belt in karate. Or is that a black belt?" I trained Alex. He's never forgotten all the tricks I showed him or the help I gave him when he came on board. He glances over at Joe as they both move to my left with Tom behind me.

Joe shrugs. "Does it matter?" He's the newest on the crew, a good worker with the right attitude of all of us being a family. He cracks his knuckles.

Actually, I hold no belts in karate, have never even attended a course, so I'm suppressing a grin. I've taken a few defense classes, and I'm a good scrapper in a fight, but no formal martial arts training. I don't correct my guys, though. Why spoil their fun?

Combined, we amount to a formidable mass of muscles, a veritable wall of brute strength. And Happy Fingers's buddies aren't jumping up to back *him*. They recline against the plastic seats, heads swiveling between us, watching the show.

Happy raises both palms in the air. "Aw, come on. You wear a skirt that short, you're asking to get your ass pinched."

My eyes narrow on him. "You wear a hat and a mustache like that, and behave the way you do, and you're just asking to get your ass *kicked*."

That earns a chorus of laughter from his teammates. Apparently, they think about as much of his cowboy style as I do. Mine aren't laughing. They're waiting for my next move, ready to back my play, whatever I do. It's a good feeling, knowing they care about me both on and off the site. For the past year or so, I've been the de-facto second-in-command at RPL. I've had their respect. When I was in the hospital, one of them called or snuck in after hours to visit me every day.

Nice to know I also have their love.

"Fine," Happy Fingers says. "You win. I apologize." He directs it over my shoulder to Allie, then focuses back on me. "We'll take our vengeance on the lanes. I'm not worried about *your* score."

Yeah, sadly, he's probably right not to worry.

We return to bowling. And our team does win, though it's close—two out of three—and my dismal night's average of 135 almost costs us the match. I used to hover around 190, 195 most games, and that's down from my college touring team average of 212.

I can barely walk when I leave, and my shoulder screams when I sling my bowling bag over it, so I end up carrying it down at my side in my right hand.

The click of high heels races up behind me, and halfway across the parking lot, someone snatches the bag from my grip.

"Hey!" I protest, spinning to find Allie and almost falling when my right knee buckles.

"Hey yourself," she says, steadying me with her free hand. "I've got your gear. Just lead the way to the McLaren."

My new sports car cracked up everyone in Kissimmee Lanes and at the construction site. Who drives a McLaren to a bowling alley or a half-finished apartment complex with dirt for parking? When I came in, the manager of the lanes said he was keeping one of the lot cameras trained on the "damn thing" so as to avoid potential lawsuits when someone tried to steal it.

No one has. The now blue car sits right where I left it, beneath one of the few uncracked lights. I pop the trunk with the button on the key fob, and Allie dumps my bag into the tiny space, then shuts it with a soft thunk.

"Thanks for tonight," she says, resting delicate fingers on my sleeve. Her nails have little Hello Kitties painted on them. Cute. "I told Steve what you did. He wishes he'd known so he could have come out of the bar and slugged the guy, but he says thank you too."

I shrug it off. "Anytime. Steve also needs to stay employed."

"Flynn...." She hesitates, and I'm worried she might bring up the pass I made at her a couple months ago. That has nothing to do with why I risked a fight for her. I did it because she's a friend, but I'd have done it for a stranger. No woman, regardless of attire, should have to put up with that kind of shit. But that's not where she's going. "Have you told Genesis how bad it is? Your leg and your shoulder? You're looking a lot worse than when you proposed a few weeks back. My brother's a physical therapist, and, well, that's not a good sign."

"I've just gotten back to work last week, and bowling strains a lot of unusual muscles. It's not always this bad." I limp around to the driver's side door and open it. Getting in is another story. McLarens, like most sports cars, sit low to the ground. I bite back a groan as I lever myself into the seat. Allie hovers outside, her face pinched with concern.

"Flynn...."

I sigh. "No, I haven't told Genesis. I'd appreciate it if you wouldn't either. Not until I know something more concrete than my leg and arm hurt."

"But you've seen your doctor."

I nod, and some of the tension leaves her.

Yeah, I've seen him to get stronger painkillers and have him tell me there's nothing else he can do and it will probably get worse, since he has no idea to the cause and I can't exactly tell him these were *magical* water moccasins.

Offering Allie a reassuring smile and wave, I shut the door, start the engine, which purrs like half a dozen cats, and drive home.

Chapter 14
Threat Assessment

NATHANIEL PACED in front of his computer screen, still dressed in khaki pants and a polo shirt despite the late hour, waiting for the Google chat invitation. He logged on three minutes ahead of schedule. Figured Miss Official Board President Linda Argyle couldn't show up early for once.

The chime sounded and he accessed the "room." When she didn't appear, he returned to his pacing. Four minutes, five….

"Will you stop that? You're making me nauseated."

Linda's voice halted him midstep. He dropped into the dining room chair and faced the laptop on the table. Lin stared back at him, blond hair sticking out in multiple directions, a faded Trump Marina T-shirt covering impressive breasts. She'd never show up this disheveled in front of anyone else, but they'd known each other since college. He forced his gaze up to her sleep-reddened eyes. His need for a chat had interrupted her sleep schedule. Good.

"What's so damn important? You could have waited until morning." She yawned, not bothering to cover her mouth so he got a great view of her tonsils.

Might as well cut to the chase. "You are a piece of work, you know? You had no right sending me after a succubus. No warning, no protection. I could have been drained!"

"What the hell are you talking about?" Lin rubbed her eyes, blinked, and tried again.

Could she truly not have known? She'd sent him and Tara to test that woman, Flynn, to ascertain the strength of her talent. If Lin hadn't known, Nathaniel could well understand her surprise. No one had seen a succubus in three, maybe four generations.

"I'm not referring to the mythological spirits, Ms. Argyle." He reached for the can of Coke just beyond the webcam's pickup and brought it into view, toasting her with it before taking a long drink.

"Don't call me that. We've been friends almost twenty years. And of course you're not referring to myths. They don't exist."

Not that the Registry knew of, anyway. Plenty of spirits enjoyed sex after death, came to their lovers in the night and seduced them. But they didn't drain them of their life energy. That's what defined the classical succubus, if it was a female spirit, or incubus, if male.

In terms of the National Psychic Registry, however, the words had different meanings. A psychic succubus/incubus could control the magic of others, pull it from another talented person and…

absorb it. Use it. If done to a member of the opposite sex, it could be a permanent loss. At least that's
what the archives said. No live ones, until now, had
blipped on the Registry's radar. Not in over a hundred years.

"If you didn't know, I might forgive you. Damn
good thing for her partner that Flynn's a lesbian."

"Flynn Dalton is not a succubus." Calm, firm,
decisive. Everything Linda, as board president,
needed.

And wrong.

He ran a hand through his shaggy brown hair,
frowning at the length. A trip to the barber was in order. "I saw it with my own eyes. After Tricia spelled
Genesis McTalish, I followed them from Tricia's
shop to the next bunch they visited. God, that woman
can spend money."

Linda glared. He hurried on.

"Anyway, someone tipped Genesis off, over the
phone, about the spell."

That raised Lin's interest. Her thinly plucked
eyebrows shot up, a shade or two darker than her
dyed hair. She needed a touch-up. "Who?"

"Don't know, but you might want somebody to
look into it." The tapping of keys over the microphone
indicated she was making a note to do just that. "Anyway, the fail-safes kicked in. Gen collapsed, and her
girlfriend used that *push* of hers…."

Linda waved an impatient hand at the camera.
"Which we already knew about."

Nathaniel nodded. "Yes, but when she stopped, instead of cutting it off, she pulled the power back in, right along with Genesis's."

"You saw this?"

That was his primary talent, seeing the talents of others, appearing to his other-sight in particle form beyond the normal visual spectrum. Occasionally he could see spirits in the same way, though that was a much weaker skill. Tricia's ability was encouraging a dissatisfaction in her targets' appearances, and in the appearances of whomever they shopped with, to get customers to buy more. A lucrative skill she applied in the perfect job for her, like most of the magically gifted, though after this, Tricia would have to transfer to another store branch.

"I saw it. Both the push and the pull. You know how strong Genesis is. Flynn drained her dry. Made her sick."

Linda's lips curved in a faintly pleased smile, making Nathaniel wonder if she had something personal against Genesis McTalish, or if Flynn's potential strength held some benefit for the Registry president.

Instead he said, "I don't think either of them realized what Flynn was doing. Gen had to know she'd been drained, but she may not understand that Flynn absorbed that power. And hey," he said, coming to a whole different realization, "wouldn't a succubus, by nature, be using dark magic? Taking another living being's energy for personal use?"

Linda shook her head. "Technically, no. The Registry's rules are very specific. We must make allowances for the gifts talented individuals are born with. A succubus taking magical energy, *psychic* energy, is doing what comes naturally. If she tapped into a person's *life force*, that would be dark, but that's not what Flynn allegedly did."

Nathaniel bristled at the "allegedly" but said nothing. In the room behind Linda, a flicker appeared. He stared at it as it coalesced into an almost manly shape, then dissipated. Hmm. Looked like Madame President had caught the interest of a ghost. Nathaniel should have mentioned it, but he was annoyed enough by her doubts to let it play itself out on its own. Linda had a mild affinity for the spirit world. If it continued to stick around, she'd eventually discover her visitor.

She continued her pronouncement. "The two of them will figure out exactly what transpired soon enough. Perhaps that will convince them both to attend the convention." Linda reached forward to cut the connection. "In the meantime, I'll arrange some further tests and do some research. If we have a succubus on our hands, we need to know everything our ancestors recorded about them. Including, if she should continue to avoid us, how to neutralize one. Natural skills or not, the Registry won't risk another threat to its members."

The two said goodbye, Nathaniel closing the window and shutting down his computer before Linda's words completely registered. "*Another* threat?" he muttered to himself. "Wasn't aware we had a first one."

Chapter 15
Building Things

ON TUESDAY, I leave the house for work in better spirits, knowing Genesis plans on taking four clients today. She says her skills are back to normal—a huge relief to me, considering I caused the problem. The passionate kiss she gives me as I climb in the McLaren doesn't hurt either.

Wedding. Yeah. We'll need to talk about that soon. With Gen by my side, I can handle anything.

I hope.

I park the ultra-expensive sports car in the least dusty section of our makeshift parking lot. The little bit of grass remaining might do less damage to the repainting I had done on the car. Of course, that means hiking even farther to the site since the grass lies at the edge near a planned conservation area. By the time I reach Tom's trailer, I'm already limping.

He meets me out front, iPad in hand. Tom's big on tech, using it to hone his somewhat blunted organizational skills into a sharpened blade of precision. To my surprise, he passes the device over to me.

"Jan's sick," he says. "I need you to run things this week."

"Jan? Your sister? What's up?" I like Jan. She's young, about nineteen, lives outside of Atlanta, and she "came out" two years ago, although her family had suspected for some time. Tom hooked us up in a sort of mentor/student way via the internet, and I'd talked her off a few sexual orientation terror ledges. Since she's now attending Georgia Tech, a fairly open-minded campus toward lesbians, she doesn't have nearly as many problems making friends and remaining unmolested as she had in her rural Georgia high school.

"Mono," he says with a twisted grin. "Her girlfriend has it, now she does. And the both of them are miserable, hacking up lungs and missing at least a week of classes. Thought I'd take some days off, go up and help them out."

"Girlfriend, huh? Good for her. Well, in every way except the mono." I glance at the iPad, scrolling through the pages one at a time. Standard stuff. Crew assignments, delivery schedules… uh-oh. My eyes snap to his. "Company inspection?"

He has the good grace to look sheepish. "Was kinda hoping you wouldn't notice that one. End of this week. And no, I didn't time it. Jan really is sick. Antibiotics and everything."

"Not OSHA?" I'd had a bad run-in with the Occupational Health and Safety Administration right before Dead Woman's Pond when I took a spill on the rafters of building three, now finished. We're working on buildings seven and nine these days.

Damn lake's sun-glare blinded me, and I lost my balance. I still wonder if that hadn't been another attempt on the lake's part to make me its victim, and how many other seemingly unrelated deaths might be attributed to the cursed medallion I'd retrieved. Anyway, when I fell, an inspector had apparently been lurking about. I never saw the guy, but the company got shut down for a while, putting the whole crew out of work while further investigations were conducted. Money was tight. It was an accident, but some of the guys blamed me—not my close friends, but still. It sucked.

I could blame Dead Woman's Pond, but mostly I blamed myself. I should have been more careful.

"Not OSHA. Company bigwigs. Flying in from the West Coast, checking out all the Florida crews." Tom bumps my good shoulder with his. "Make sure you watch your step if you go up top."

I bump him back. "No worries."

"I have none. Not with you in charge. Might even be a promotion in this for you. I've recommended you enough times."

"What, me? But I screwed up." I knew he'd been grooming me for a foreman job of my own. We'd discussed it. But I'd figured after the OSHA disaster, I'd blown my shot.

He fixes me with a stern look. "It was an accident. Everyone has them, and you've had a lot fewer than most. Not everyone can handle this site and these guys," he says, waving a hand toward the half-finished buildings, "along with the math, the record keeping, being civil with our suppliers, the way you can. You've got a college degree and a head for business. You're overqualified for what you do."

I have a degree in English Literature from the University of Florida. Not real pertinent to construction, but yeah, it's more education than anyone else on the crew has. Half the guys never finished high school.

Tom removes his hard hat and stores it in one of the lockers stacked along the outside of his trailer. "Everyone knows to bring all questions to you. I'll check in once or twice a day via cell." Tom tosses me a jaunty salute, and I remember he served three years in the Marine Corps before working for RPL. "They're all yours!"

With that, he heads for the parking lot and, presumably, Georgia.

Chapter 16
Doggie Abodes

I WOULDN'T call being foreman a cushy job, but it definitely exerts the body less than working on the construction itself. Plenty of walking from building to building, team to team, so my leg's a mess, but not much lifting, carrying, or swinging heavy tools around except when I volunteer to pitch in and lend a hand. We've got maybe twenty guys in total, not counting me (the only female) or Tom, so four teams, each assigned to different tasks. I double-check specifications, make sure they have the materials they need for the day's jobs, and troubleshoot/head off problems, hopefully before they can occur.

If I didn't know better, I'd think Tom's sister wasn't sick and he wasn't trying to avoid the company inspection, but he was attempting to give my injuries a break.

Not the case, of course. No matter how much he cares about me, he has a family to feed—a wife and two kids and a dog named Grasseater, of all things, Grassy for short. He's handed me the keys to the

trailer a few times before, and I get the impression
he would have been doing so even more frequently
if my injuries hadn't sidelined me.

And on Friday, the bigwigs are coming to evaluate the crew, but potentially to evaluate me.

I consider that while filling out the required
daily paperwork on Tom's desktop. I'd miss my
guys—Alex, Joe, Diego—but the extra money
would be....

Entirely unnecessary. Right. Me. Rich.

I like working up top, sweating from good, honest hard labor, building things from the ground up. I
like the banter, the camaraderie, the rapport I have
with the guys.

If my injuries heal, I might actually turn a promotion down. If they don't, well, I'm not sure foreman is the way I want to go.

FOR THE first time in over a week, I get home with
enough energy left to head around back and slip into
the pool for a few laps, followed by a quick shower
and a couple of hours in the room I converted to a
combo gym and woodworking shop. The strange car
out front tells me Gen's with a late client, so I don't
peek into the parlor/seance space she uses. Interrupt-
ing her mid spirit-channeling could send the session
in a bad direction.

Katy pads to stand beside me while I survey the
organized chaos of my work area. I own a custom
doghouse-building "business," really more like a
hobby that used to bring in a few extra dollars when

I was between construction jobs. I advertise on the internet, attend local craft festivals and shows, and have my work displayed in a number of Festivity backyards.

The half-finished Barbie Dream Doghouse model—pink with white trim and destined to become two stories with little dog-sized steps to the sleeping cushion in the upstairs—hasn't been touched since just after I got out of the hospital and discovered excessive hammering and sawing hurt too much. It's a display item, not a customer order, so I haven't failed to fulfill a contract, but staring at the unassembled pieces, I feel… inadequate.

Katy saunters to the first floor of the doghouse and its steps currently leading nowhere, and places her paw on one of them. It's way too small for her, designed for a miniature poodle or chihuahua-sized canine, and the incongruity has me chuckling. Katy glances back with her Husky side's blue eyes and woofs softly.

In other words, "Finish this, stupid human." Got it.

I pause long enough to grab and dry-swallow a couple of Advil from the bottle on my worktable. No sense inviting extra pain. That will take the edge off. Since they pack a serious punch, the heavy-duty prescription stuff waits for bedtime. Then I dive in.

Anywhere else I'd worry about the banging and electric drilling disturbing Genesis, but Leo's former home has great soundproofing. I wonder who his contractor was.

A couple of hours see the second story of the doghouse assembled and its interior painted and drying. Katy watches the entire process, lying in the corner, head on her paws, ears pricked forward at the high-pitched screeching of the drill. Tomorrow I can attach the two floors together and paint the exterior.

I'm cleaning up the tools and sweeping sawdust into a neat pile when two sounds interrupt me: Gen calling me for a late dinner over the house's built-in intercom (geez) and the chime of an incoming email on my new laptop.

I press the button on the wall speaker. "Be there in a few minutes," I tell her. "Just putting things away."

"I'm glad to see you in there," she says. "Been awhile. Don't let your shepherd's pie get cold."

Mmm. Gen's Irish heritage means a fantastic family recipe for shepherd's pie a person can't get anywhere but the Village Pub and her own kitchen. Ground lamb, green peas, and mashed potatoes, all simple ingredients, with a secret wine-based sauce and seasonings she hasn't revealed even to me. "I'll hurry," I assure her and release the button.

Logging on the computer takes a moment. I have to think about the password I chose. Haven't owned a laptop since I hocked the last one to make rent money a year back. Got it. Gen's birthday. And, shit, it's coming up. October twenty-eighth she'll turn twenty-four. I'll have to get her something special, but I have no idea what. And hey, another coincidence. Her birth date falls in the middle of the Psychic Registry's conference week. Great.

I bring up my email, sighing at three doghouse inquiries, all several weeks old. I'll shoot them a reply with my standard rates and designs, but by now they've probably found another builder. The fourth, however, just came in. I click it open.

Dear Ms. Dalton,

I am interested in purchasing a custom home for my English Mastiff. Cost is not a concern, but I am worried about the safety of my pet, the security of your electronic payment options, and I'll need you to keep this a secret since it's a surprise for my wife, Cassie, and I wouldn't want her to find out. If, perhaps, we could discuss this further in person, say a place where I can buy you a drink, I will come to a location of your choosing.

Sincerely,

Peter

I almost laugh, it's so poorly "coded." James Bond, he's not. But I'm too angry for humor. I'd wondered if, in addition to Cassie, the internet matchmaker, Peter, the all-too-friendly bartender had played a role in my "test" at Atlantic Dance.

My quick response asks him to meet me at Village Pub tomorrow—Wednesday—night. Guess I'll get the details then, and if it's another trap, I'm on my home turf.

Chapter 17
Secret Agent Stuff

I HADN'T planned on taking Genesis with me to my meeting with Peter. I hadn't intended to tell her anything about it. But when cornered naked in the shower by your girlfriend (equally naked) and told point-blank that you're overprotecting her too much, well, you cave.

Anyone would.

We park her Charger out back of the pub and enter through the kitchen, pushing open swinging doors into the main dining area and continuing outside to a comfortable covered bar with wide-screen TVs on the three walls. The Pub's a Yankees bar: autographed pictures, balls and gloves, team decorative items like the wall clock and some of the overhead lighting fixtures. Which explains why I wear some other team's jersey when I come here during baseball season.

An accident, really. I owned a faded Red Sox T-shirt I'd gotten at Goodwill during tough times and enjoyed raising Chris's hackles with it. Now I have quite the collection of shirts. Tonight my chest features the Tampa Bay Rays, and I wave at some of the sports fan regulars and grin at their good-natured jeers and teasing. Chris, hanging out by the cash register, glances at my boobs and winces.

"They aren't even playing the Rays tonight," he calls.

I shrug. "Who cares?"

Bigger wince and a clutch at his heart.

Sorry, I'm more of a football gal.

Genesis rushes over to give him a sisterly peck on the cheek, and then we're scanning the bar area, searching for… there. Seated at the farthest corner from the door in a spot where he can see both the Pub entrance and the two metal swinging gates in the little fence that surrounds the outdoor seating.

Peter.

I make a beeline for him, but Gen catches my arm. "Let me lead," she says. "He's a null. I'm sure of it. If Cassie's confided the Registry's secrets to him, that means he's either family, a boyfriend/husband, or she's breaking the rules."

I nod once, slowly. Peter's got his eyes on both of us. He knew the moment we arrived. "We can use that, if that's the case."

"Exactly."

Gen pastes on a friendly smile even I would believe, and I know her well. She crosses the open space, and we take barstools to his immediate right and left. Without looking at either of us now, he sighs. "What'll you have, loves? On me." His words slur, and an empty glass sits in front of him. I wonder how many he's already had.

"So long as you're not serving, I'll have a beer—Breckenridge Vanilla Porter." My favorite, shipped in from Colorado, and hard as hell to find anywhere but the Village Pub. Gen orders a white zinfandel.

When Peter signals the female bartender, his hand shakes. I wonder if that's nerves or something else. Now that we're closer to him, the paleness of his skin and the dark shadows beneath his eyes show more, along with the lines in his face. And—weird—his hair seems thinner and a touch grayer around the temples than last week. Instead of the late twenties I would have placed him in, he looks much more like late thirties tonight. Has to be my imagination. It was dark in Atlantic Dance.

He orders our drinks and another Grateful Dead for himself, which sends my eyebrows rising. Vodka, gin, rum, triple sec, tequila, and sour, topped with chambord—just one of those would send me staggering, and I get the vibe this won't be his second either.

"So," Gen says, picking up the wineglass set before her. "You wanted to talk to Flynn."

"Didn't expect both of you," he grumbles.

"Too bad for you."

More surprise. Gen's pissed. She might smile and look pretty, but her tone says if Peter tries any more crap with me, he'll have to go through her. A few months ago, that would have cracked me up and Gen would have smacked me for it.

Now I know what she's capable of.

"You work with Cassie," I say before the tension between the two of them rises higher. I'm off-balance, out of my element here. Usually I'm the one getting aggressive. In good cop/bad cop, I'm the don't-fuck-with-me cop.

"*For* Cassie would be more accurate," Peter says with another tired sigh, "though we once dated for a time, so don't get any ideas about blackmail."

Damn. So turning the tables on her with the Registry is right out. Peter attempts to take a sip of his drink, but sloshes more than makes it to his mouth.

"Are you all right?" Gen asks, some of the anger leaving her voice.

That's the Genesis I know, always concerned for others, even to her own detriment.

"I would be," he says, shooting her a pleading look, playing on her sympathy, "if your girlfriend would knuckle under and submit herself to the Registry for testing."

My mouth drops open. "Are you fucking kidding me? You drug me, and then you expect me to do you a favor?"

Peter manages to take a healthy (or not so healthy) swallow of his drink. "Not just me," he says, clattering the glass on the bar. "It would get them off your backs too. And for the record, I didn't drug you. Cassie made the potion. I just delivered it."

"And that makes things so much better?" I lean into his personal space. He draws backward so far, Gen has to grab him to keep him on his stool.

"Look, loves—"

"Stop calling us your loves. There's no love between us." Okay, this is more like it. Badass cop Flynn.

"Fine," Peter says. "Ladies. I'm a desperate man, here. Cassie gets orders from the board. I get orders from her. We fail, they give her a hard time, and she can't pay me. She doesn't pay me, and…." He holds out his trembling hand, shaking like a palsy victim.

Not fear. This man is sick. Very sick.

"What, exactly, does Cassie pay you with?" Gen asks, reaching out and covering his hand with her own, pressing it down until it's flush against the table.

He doesn't answer her. He speaks to me. "Life."

A weight forms in my stomach and chest, like rocks, tumbling into nausea, blocking my air flow. "You're not guilting me into going to the board," I say through my tightened throat. "I hate all this magic shit. Present company excluded," I hasten to add, shooting Gen an embarrassed smile. "I'm not testing, training, or joining anything related to your damn Registry."

"Flynn…." Gen whispers.

"No! No," I say more softly when some of the sports fans turn annoyed glares in my direction. I glance at the hanging screen. Score's tied, seven to seven, bottom of the ninth. Yankees versus Detroit Tigers. I wave an apologetic hand and focus on Gen and Peter. "*You* decided to work for that bitch, or date her, or whatever your relationship is. *You* made a choice. The more I see of the Registry's members and their manipulative little games, the more I'm determined to stay the hell away."

"Then I'm as good as dead." Peter finishes his drink and asks the bartender for another one, the irony of his order lost on none of us.

"Tough."

"Flynn!" Gen stares at me, horrified.

I take a long swig from my bottle, the vanilla porter no longer sweet, but souring in my mouth. I hate the callousness I hear in my own voice. But shit. I don't know this guy. I don't owe him anything. I don't want to be a hero. Not again. The one time I was, I paid for it in what will likely become a permanent physical impairment that may cost me my career. I want a life with Genesis and Chris and Katy and no magic. No magic whatsoever.

Looking from Gen's face to Peter's and back again, I know I'm not going to get it.

"Fuck."

"Look," Gen interrupts, "tell us what you need from Cassie. Maybe there's something—"

"I've got Alzheimer's," Peter says. "The early-onset kind. When she took me on, I was drifting off once, twice a week."

My heart sinks further. When I was a kid, a friend of our family's had Alzheimer's. He was much older, in his eighties, but we knew the end neared when his mind started wandering that often. A few months later, he died.

"I also have Parkinson's Disease."

Oh, holy mother of fuck.

"And she won't cure you unless you convince us tonight, right?" I say.

"Cassie doesn't know I'm—"

"Bullshit. You suck at coding. You wrote that email directly to me. If you're her employee…."

"Assistant," Peter corrects.

"Whatever," I say, "she set this up. She told you to write. She told you to play the 'dying' card. For all I know, you aren't even really sick."

"He is," Gen says softly. "I can feel it."

I look down to where her hand still covers his, resting on the bar.

"Cassie's best at love mixtures, but she's one of the top talents with life-extension spells and potions. She can't cure him, but she can buy him some years. If she chooses," Gen bites out. "No one else in the Registry would do as well for him."

"And you should know," Peter cuts in, "she's not the bitch you think she is. Someone she cares about is sick… sick like me. I don't know who, but she uses a great deal of her power on that person. And the Registry forces her to use the rest for their benefit or things go wrong for her and her business. And she needs the insurance money…. It's all a tremendous power circle."

And Gen once worked for these sadists.

Then she quit. I'm thinking she had more reasons for doing so than she's told me.

A sudden thought occurs. "Wait. Could I push the disease from him? Like I did with the snake venom?" Before Genesis used Leo's life force to heal me, I'd already pushed some of the poison from my body. It weakened me too fast for me to complete the job, but—

"No," Gen says, shaking her head. "Those snakes were controlled by the magic of the charm, their venom enhanced and altered. That's the only reason your power worked on them at all. His illnesses are naturally occurring. Only someone with a strong healing talent can help."

I finish my beer in one long gulp and thunk it down on the bar. The Pub's bartender raises a questioning eyebrow, but I shake my head. For a decision like this, I need to be sober. "So, basically, I can let a man die, or I can let the Registry blackmail me for the rest of my life." I stand, reaching around Peter to pull Genesis up with me. She hasn't emptied her glass of wine, but we're leaving. Now. "I need to think."

A sudden cheer erupts throughout the bar. Yankees must have scored. Goody for them.

"I beg you, don't take too long." Peter reaches into his pocket, pulls an expensive leather wallet, and drops his credit card beside his glass.

"I'll take as long as I need. Thanks for the drinks. Don't contact me again." Dragging Gen by the sleeve of her little white sweater, I head for the restaurant doors.

"WE CAN'T let him die," Gen whispers, both hands clutching the steering wheel of the Charger.

We're halfway back to the mansion, passing the K-8 school on the right, then the baseball field and the manicured lawns of the expensive Festivity homes. I'm stunned she's remained silent this long.

"There's no 'we' here." Just me. I shouldn't feel guilty. The Registry and Cassie are to blame, though I'm not so sure how much I should blame Cassie anymore. But the moment Peter told me his tale, he made it my responsibility too.

"I know about it. That makes me involved," Gen says, echoing my own thoughts.

"But you can't solve the problem."

"Actually, I could."

It takes me several blocks before I figure out what she means.

"Pull over."

"What?" She risks a glance at me, then turns back to the road.

"Pull the fuck over."

When she continues driving, I grab the wheel and pull to the right, jerking us and bumping the front right tire hard against the curb before we swerve back onto the street. It's not that big a deal. The town speed limit is twenty-five miles per hour, so we aren't going that fast, and Festivity doesn't get much traffic, so there aren't many other cars around, but it gets her attention.

She curses under her breath, letting me know I've really ticked her off, and lets the car roll onto the shoulder, then cuts the engine and turns on me. "Are you out of your mind?"

"No," I say. "*You* are, if you think I'm going to let you use dark magic to fix this."

"I could—"

"No. Just no. You save his life and someone else dies? And you're even more addicted than you already are? Is that what you want?"

Tears well up in her eyes. She blinks, fighting them back, but they fall in slow streams down her cheeks.

I take a shuddering breath, then reach out a hand and brush them away. "No matter what happens," I say with less rage, "you're not touching that power. Not for him. Not for me. He's not worth it, and I don't want it. You hear me?"

She nods, and I pull her across the armrest between us, holding her to my chest for several long moments.

"Just let me think, okay? I'll come up with something."

But now I have not only Peter, but Genesis to worry about. And I have absolutely no idea what that something will be.

Chapter 18
Family Line

"HEY! HEY, you!" Chris speed-walked across the street between the Village Pub and Starbucks, pursuing the man wearing a pair of jeans torn out at the knees and a ragged, sweat-stained Disney T-shirt.

Standing in the middle of Front Street, the old guy turned bleary eyes upon him. Four of the local teens skateboarded past, cutting their turns as close to his ankles as they dared, cursing at him to get out of the way.

Ignoring them and several cars that honked and weaved around them, the man studied Chris as Chris peered hard into his face. "Snit!" he announced, pleased as punch, craggy wrinkles deepening with his grin.

Nice, even teeth, Chris noted. In need of brushing, but much too intact for a homeless man. "It *is* you." The guy from the Pub's bar. The one who warned him about the Registry going after Genesis to get to Flynn. But what the hell had happened to him?

No, Chris corrected himself. What had *been* happening to him, on and off, for at least the past six months? Because he'd seen this man around here before, at the Starbucks, at the Panera at the edge of town, and panhandling by the stoplight at the entrance to Festivity. He'd looked nothing like this at the Pub in his polo shirt and shorts.

"Come on," Chris said, taking the man by the arm and leading him to the sidewalk by the coffee shop. "Let me buy you an espresso."

"Free coffee?" His eyes narrowed. "You aren't gay, are ya? I don't swing the same way as my daughter. Or maybe I do. She likes girls, I like girls…."

Chris froze with the man on the curb, blending the two images—the clean-shaven one and this one with three days of stubble threatening to become a beard, overlaying those with…. Light brown hair, high, sharp cheekbones, fierce brown eyes, broad shoulders.

Flynn.

Oh dear God.

He hadn't just known the man from around town and the Pub. He'd recognized him because, if one knew to look for it, his resemblance to Flynn was uncanny, especially clean-shaven as he'd been the last time they'd met. Chris's feet moved forward, walking him to Starbucks's patio on autopilot while his brain raced.

He knew of Flynn's broken childhood, both from the source and Genesis: raised by a single mom and grandmother until the older woman died when Flynn turned nine, father left when she was four, resulting in chronic depression for her mother including several suicide attempts, and a long-term stay in an institution where Chris believed Flynn's mom still resided.

"Here! Here!" The old man grabbed at two of the metal patio chairs, startling several birds into flight and causing the teenage girls at the next table to shriek and flee to other seats, though whether they were fleeing the crows or the scary homeless guy, Chris didn't know.

"Relax. I'll get your coffee. What would you like?"

New Jersey. She'd grown up in New Jersey. What had brought him down to Festivity, Florida?

Flynn, his internal analyzer told him. *Duh.*

The old man glanced up from the pages of the abandoned newspaper on the wooden table and frowned. "Tall, iced white mocha, nonfat, stirred, no whip."

A wealthy man's drink, ordered in the correct coffee shop terminology, the words pouring from the guy's mouth by rote rather than conscious memory. Blinking repeatedly, the old man seemed as surprised by the order as Chris.

"You got it."

"No. You still haven't told me why you're buying me coffee." He pressed his hands on the chair arms, preparing to rise.

Chris patted the air between them. "It's okay. It's fine. No, I'm not gay, not like—" He hesitated, then went for it. "—not like Flynn. Just paying you back for the information you gave me the other day about the Registry and Flynn and my sister."

"Oh. Oh, well, that's all right, then. Fine and dandy. Flynn. Chip off the old blockess, that one. Just like her mother. All wiles and wildfire, power and passion. Sucks to be her. Indeed, it sucks." He broke off in hysterics degrading into a coughing fit that had Chris slapping him on the back.

"Yes, yes it does," Chris said, no idea what the man found so funny. "Maybe you can tell me all about it. I'll grab the coffees." He pushed open the double doors, glancing backward to make certain the man had resettled into his seat, which he had. Chris got in line, breathing in the aromas of espressos and lattes, vanilla and caramel and chocolate. Not too many customers midmorning on a Thursday, so only a few minutes passed before he returned to their table with the drinks.

"They didn't stir it," the man complained, glaring into his cup where the white chocolate and coffee clearly separated.

"I asked them to."

"Ah well, beggars and choosers." He took a long drink of the sweet, icy concoction and sighed, leaning back in his chair.

"So," Chris said, feeling his way, "what do I call you? I'm Chris." He held out his hand.

"I know who you are," the man said, gripping for a shake with sticky fingers Chris didn't want to think too much about. "Ferguson. Or Fergie for short, though I quit going by that a few years back. Too many people mistaking me for female British royalty." Which resulted in another burst of laughter that went on long enough to attract a lot of stares from the other, more sophisticated customers.

"And you're Flynn's... father?"

Ferguson leaned across the table, blasting Chris with an exhalation of his fetid breath. "Our little secret," he whispered. "Too much. Told you too much."

No. No way. He couldn't keep this secret from his future sister-in-law. Though how he'd ever tell Flynn her father not only lived but was an on again, off again homeless man, he had no idea.

Flynn hated her father for leaving them and said so repeatedly. She wanted nothing to do with him whatsoever.

Maybe Chris could keep this secret, at least until Flynn's life settled down again.

They drank their coffees in silence, Chris sipping on a hot caramel latte despite the eighty-plus degree weather. Those cold, sweet drinks tasted too much like dessert. Over the course of an hour, Chris tried to direct the conversation back to Flynn, but Ferguson diverted it every time, though whether that was by choice or due to his odd sort of dementia, Chris couldn't tell. The topic wandered from soccer to gun control to gay marriage to pop music.

He got nothing else useful from the man and left with more moral dilemmas than he'd bargained for.

Chapter 19
One Step Forward,
Two Steps Back

"So, IF you gentlemen will follow me, I'll pull up the financial records and building timeline on the computer." I round the end of Tom's office trailer, leading three men sweating their collective asses off in expensive suits and hard hats.

The corporate executives arrived at 9:00 a.m. sharp Friday morning. I've spent the last two hours playing tour guide, showing them the finished apartment buildings, the half-finished ones, and the two that are no more than framework while trying not to be distracted by my ongoing disagreement with Genesis and my concerns about Peter and the Registry.

Two days of thinking haven't solved my problems there. Gen claims sympathy and understanding for my distaste of all things magical, the Registry's board in particular, but she wants me to help Peter.

And, I have to admit, so do I.

Once a hero, always a hero, I guess. Now if I can figure out a way to do it without subjecting myself to testing….

Meanwhile, the three executives talked among themselves, making me a little uncomfortable, and asked very few questions: "Are you on schedule?"

"No." Because the insurance company's investigation a couple of months ago set us back.

"Are you aware of the fines we'll have to pay if we don't complete the project on time?"

"Yes." The investors charge fees for every day we finish after the projected completion date.

"Are you going to get back on schedule?"

"That's the plan, and we've been closing the gap over the past two weeks." Duh. No, I thought we'd just drag our feet and hope for the best.

The insurance questions set my nerves on edge, but they don't seem aware that I was the cause of those problems. I've seen the official report—employee accident (unnamed and unspecified), investigation ordered, end result: no fines imposed, no corrective action taken.

Sites get closed down for investigations all the time. We've had fewer than our share. The big bosses shouldn't hold that against us.

But I'm still nervous.

I step inside the somewhat cooler interior of the trailer, though not as cool as it should be. "AC's on the fritz," I explain, opening windows on three sides of the long metal box. The air-conditioning unit works but stops lowering the temperature at seventy-nine. I also switch on a pair of stand-up fans

Tom bought with his own money and gesture at the two chairs in front of his battered metal desk. For the third man, I grab a folding chair and flip it open, placing it behind the other two; then I take Tom's regular seat behind the desk.

A few clicks bring up the requested information, and I rotate the screen toward them and shift the keyboard within their reach so they can peruse the files at their leisure. I'm not worried about them digging into anything else. Tom's got everything locked down pretty tight, and only he and I know the passwords.

While they drag their chairs in closer and one takes command of the mouse and keyboard, I get up and pace around the trailer. My leg complains. I've been on it all morning, but there's no help for it, and grabbing my industrial-sized bottle of Advil from the desk drawer will draw unwanted attention.

They're muttering among themselves again, so I wander to the farthest window, drawn by other voices outside. A glance out and down shows me Alex and Diego, taking a water break at the cooler right below the windowsill.

"You're not fooling anybody," I say just loud enough for them to hear me without the corporate men noticing. "I know you're eavesdropping."

Diego glances up with an unrepentant grin, then takes a long, slow sip from his cup of water. Alex has the good grace to blush at getting caught, but neither one of them moves from their positions.

I roll my eyes and sigh, turning my back to the window and leaning against the side of the trailer with my arms crossed across my chest. After another ten minutes or so, my guests mutter a few more unintelligible sentences to one another and click off the screen.

"Well, Ms. Dalton, we appreciate your time this morning. All the records seem to be in order, and it looks as if Tom's crew is, indeed, getting back on schedule."

As I said. I put on what I hope is a confident smile. "Assuming the weather holds, we'll bring in the project on time."

"Good. Good. However," the oldest gentleman, Mr. Carr, says, running a hand through his salt-and-pepper hair, "there is another matter we need to discuss with you."

Uh-oh.

I cross to the desk chair and retrieve the keyboard, turning the screen back to me. "What else would you like to see?"

"Oh, nothing on your computer," the second man says, straightening his suit jacket to better hide the wet stains beneath both sleeves of his white shirt. I can't remember his name. "We actually need to speak with you, specifically. You see, there's a certain matter of, well, company policy that's come to Mr. Ferbish's attention."

Mr. Ferbish, *Arnold* Ferbish, owns RPL. His elegant cursive signature appears on every electronic paycheck and corporate memo.

"Your foreman, Tom Bowers, has brought up your name in a number of emails, recommending you for a possible promotion to managing a crew of your own," the third man, Mr. Lipscomb, says. "Unfortunately, this has embedded your name in Mr. Ferbish's memory."

"Unfortunately?" How can an email of praise be unfortunate?

"You need to understand our position," the second man continues, a blush creeping from the collar of his shirt up to his receding hairline. "While we may not necessarily agree with everything in the corporate bylaws, we are required to enforce them if we want to keep our jobs."

"Mr. Ferbish is an extremely religious man," Mr. Carr says, "a prominent member of his Southern Baptist church."

He pauses while I digest that, a sick feeling forming in my stomach.

"And he's an avid watcher of the evening news," Mr. Lipscomb finishes for the trio, giving me a pointed look.

Considering the night he's referring to was one of the most memorable in my twenty-eight years of life, it doesn't take me long to piece this together. "And he lives in Florida," I say, not quite asking.

Carr nods. "Jacksonville."

I can't sit still any longer. My legs carry me, limp and all, back to the open window above the water cooler. The approaching afternoon storm's breeze does little to cool the heat in my face, but I take several deep breaths, trying to calm the racing of my heart.

When I rescued Arielle from her car sinking into Dead Woman's Pond, I caught the attention of all the local, and several statewide, news stations. The reporter at the scene had interviewed me and shared the story with a lot of channels. They broadcast my name as a hero. They showed me, standing at the lake's edge, wearing my dripping RPL Construction logo T-shirt.

And they captured it on camera when Arielle gave me a passionate thank-you kiss and I told her I already had a girlfriend.

According to Florida law, it's perfectly legal to fire someone for being gay. Generally, it's a "don't ask, don't tell, stay employed" sort of policy.

Except I'd told the entire news-viewing audience.

I know Carr's next words before he says them. "I'm sorry. I'm afraid we're going to have to let you go."

Chapter 20
And the Hits Keep Coming

APPARENTLY THE universe hasn't finished fucking with me.

The universe can go take a flying leap.

"So, let me get this straight," I say, wincing at the unintentional pun. I'm facing out the window. My elite group of visitors doesn't see it. Small favors. "You're firing me because I'm a lesbian."

Now I turn around, in time to catch Mr. Carr's grimace at my use of the dreaded "L" word and Mr. Lipscomb's averting of his eyes. Ashamed of their behavior or disgusted by mine? Don't know, don't care.

"Not so much that—" Carr begins, but the third guy cuts him off.

"Oh hell, Charles, we're firing the woman, by all accounts an outstanding employee, for no real reason at all. She deserves to be told like it is." Shifting to look me dead in the eyes, Mr. Sweaty-pits nods and says, "Yes. That's the reason."

He might not wear enough antiperspirant, but he's earned more of my respect than either of the others. Of course, that's not saying much.

A scuffling of boots on gravel comes from the open window, loud enough for me to hear, but not carrying over the background hammering and drilling and the fans whirring in the trailer.

Shit. Diego and Alex. I wonder how much they heard.

"It's effective immediately," Lipscomb adds, drawing some forms from inside his suit jacket.

No notice. I don't bother to ask if that's legal. If they can fire me, they can do it this way.

Sheltered. That's what I've been. An understanding foreman who surrounded me with accepting coworkers, a steady girlfriend whose only family has no problems with her, or my, sexual preferences, a town populated primarily by gay-friendly Disney personnel. I've forgotten what it can be like, what it's *still* like, living in a hetero-dominated world.

I want to kick myself. I want to beat my head against the wall for my carelessness at Dead Woman's Pond. Gen doesn't get my intense discomfort with public displays of affection, and lately I've been easing up a little, letting her lure me into hand-holding, hugging, kissing when we're out. I've thrown caution to the wind. I needed a reminder that I had good reasons for restraint. Now it's too late.

Lipscomb spreads the creased forms on the desk. Mr. Carr produces a fancy ballpoint pen from his shirt pocket. "If you'll just fill these out," he says.

Numb inside, I cross the three longest strides I've ever taken to the chair and sink into it as it creaks and groans beneath me. I scan the paperwork, not really seeing the words. "Terminated…." yada yada yada, "Immediate stoppage of payment…." No shit. "Surrender of all company equipment…." No surprise there. "Reason for dismissal—sexual deviancy/lewd public behavior."

What the fuck?

I stop initialing items. "Not signing this," I say, laying the pen down. Leaning back, I cross my arms over my chest and stare at my visitors.

"Please don't make this difficult." There's a note of pleading in Sweaty's voice. Please, just be a nice, compliant little lesbian, sign the papers, and we'll be on our way.

Except I'm not a nice little lesbian. "I'm not signing it, and I'm not taking this lying down." I have no idea what I will do, much like every other aspect of my current existence, but there must be some recourse. If that document gets around, I might never work in construction again.

Figures something like this has to happen to remind me just how much I really love this damn job.

Lipscomb sighs; Carr pulls out a cell phone and turns away in his seat. After dialing and speaking to someone on the other end, I catch "—need a security detail" in his conversation. He hangs up, and the three of them watch me, saying nothing, bracing themselves for my next move.

Shit.

A knock sounds on the door, and I jump a little. No way did they get some of their rent-a-cops down here that fast. Under other circumstances, I'd laugh. No one knocks before entering Tom's trailer. Hell, no one knocks before throwing open the doors to the Port-o-Potties out back.

Today, however, I sit up straight, put on my boss face, and yell, "Enter!"

The door swings open on creaking hinges. Tom should get that fixed. Alex and Diego stand framed in the entrance, not an easy position to maintain, considering each of them is broad enough to fill the limited space, but they aren't budging, and I grasp they're waiting for an invitation.

Rolling my eyes, I wave them inside. "Kinda busy right now," I tell them. Getting fired and all, it takes up a lot of my appointment schedule. "What do you guys need?"

They glance from me to the corporate guests. Alex swallows hard. Diego recovers first. He extends one hand, clutching what looks like my cell phone. I keep it in my locker when I'm working at the site, having smashed two screens in the past year trying to carry it around. Our lockers don't have actual locks unless we spring for them ourselves, so most of us just trust one another.

"It was ringing and ringing," Diego says. "We knew you had this important meeting, and we didn't want to interrupt, but we thought the call might be important, too, so we answered it."

Alex finds his voice. "The crew from Fox News called again. They want to know when you're going to give that second interview, you know, for that special segment on 'Local Heroes, What Happens Afterward?'"

A slow grin spreads across my face. The great irony is, they aren't pulling this out of their asses, at least not all of it. Fox *has* contacted me several times, wanting to do a follow-up, though I doubt they called in the last fifteen minutes. I keep turning them down. Fame isn't my thing, and cameras scare the shit out of me. I've mentioned it to the crew over beers at the Pub, and we laugh about it.

I'm not laughing now.

"Give me my phone." I hold out my hand. Diego drops the cell into my palm. With a wicked grin for my guests, I close my fingers around it. "So, gentlemen, what should I tell those reporters?"

Chapter 21
Ties That Bind

ONCE DIEGO and Alex leave, the corporate executives do confirm Fox News's interest. Then Mr. Carr makes some more phone calls. I get the impression he speaks with Mr. Ferbish himself because he straightens in his seat while speaking—an unconscious response to authority that the owner will never see.

When Carr cuts the connection, he turns to me with a tight smile. "Well played, Ms. Dalton. Well played. Mr. Ferbish would prefer to avoid any further media attention for RPL. You may keep your job." He reaches across the desk, takes the termination papers, and feeds them into the shredder Tom keeps off to the side. "However," he continues, "we'll be sending you some nondisclosure forms in the next few days. These state that you will not speak to the media about anything discussed in today's meeting, and in return, we will guarantee that you will not be fired for your sexual orientation at any point in the future."

"You can still be let go for other reasons," Sweaty interjects, holding up one finger for my attention. "But," he adds in a conspiratorial tone, "whatever that reason is will need to be thoroughly documented by your immediate supervisor, Mr. Tom Bowers. Otherwise, you could simply claim the company is creating false causes for your termination in order to let you go for your sexual preference."

"It's not your job to tell her that," Lipscomb says, pursing his lips.

Sweaty offers us both a shark-toothed grin. "I know." He extends a hand, and I shake it, ignoring the heat and slickness of his skin. "Keep up the good work, Ms. Dalton. Between you and me, I think you'll make a fine foreman, someday."

I escort them to the door of the trailer, but not out to the dirt lot. One, I don't want to try explaining the McLaren and who owns it, and two, I'm shaking too badly to go much farther.

IT'S FRIDAY, so after work, I buy Diego and Alex a couple of beers at the Village Pub. "Least I can do," I say, holding up a hand to forestall further arguments. "You saved my neck. And I owe you for backing me at the bowling alley too."

Diego wipes the foam from his salt-and-pepper mustache on the back of his sleeve. "Should've gotten a promotion. Instead they try to fire you. Utter shit."

"Who cares who you love?" Alex chimes in.

Yeah. My next sip of Vanilla Porter goes down hard, my insides tight with anger and stress.

While I'd chatted with the corporate visitors in Tom's trailer, I'd wondered if they had some sort of connection to the Psychic Registry, if it was another of the board's tests. That would have almost given me some relief. But I can't see any way magic would have played into that interaction.

Now it looks like I've got issues in every aspect of my life: work, health, social….

Personal.

The three of us sit at the outside bar, with me in my favorite spot on the far corner and the baseball game in the background. Genesis stands just inside the restaurant's doors, sequestered behind the hostess podium by her brother. Judging from their hand motions and facial expressions, they're engaged in a rather intense discussion—so intense, Gen hasn't noticed me yet. I hope it's not about me. I'm not sure how much more I can handle.

When one of the waitresses heads out to the patio with someone's food order, Gen follows her movement and spots me. Her eyes go wide, and she darts a few glances from me to Chris, then says something quick to him before pushing through the doors. He follows her, mouth grim and determined.

I sigh and rest my chin on one hand. So much for hoping.

The guys see them coming, assess the situation, and climb from their stools. "Thanks for the beers," Alex says. "Enjoy your weekend." He nudges Diego, and the two of them make their escape through one of the swinging gates in the low metal fence surrounding the outdoor area.

Chickens.

Gen and Chris take their abandoned seats, one on either side of me. I try to watch them in my peripheral vision, but I can't look both ways at once. After a long, uncomfortable silence, I stare straight ahead and say, "Okay, what's up? You've got me hemmed in like plywood in a vise, and I feel about that pressured. Spill it."

"How was your day?" Gen asks, too brightly, her smile too wide.

Oh, whatever's going on, it must be bad. And I'm in no mood to play.

I mimic her cheery tone, adding in a model-worthy smile for good measure. "We had our inspection. They tried to fire me for being gay. The guys came to my rescue. I'm still employed. I'm really pissed off. How was yours?"

Gen sucks in a sharp breath at my revelations, but Chris cuts right to the chase. "I had coffee with your father yesterday."

Damn good thing I'm already sitting down.

I turn my head slowly to stare at him, shaking off the hand Gen rests on my shoulder. "How... how would you know?" And what the fuck would he be doing in Festivity, Florida?

Unless... he's aware that I live here. And he's trying to find me.

"He told me. And he looks like you," Chris says.

A little curl of traitorous hope forms in my belly. I grab for my beer, almost knocking over the bottle, and take a long swig, but the alcohol doesn't drown it. I'm going to need a lot more Vanilla Porter.

I have no memory of my father, just a vague impression of a man with brown hair and eyes who could be half the guys I pass on the street in any given day.

He left me. He drove Mom into depression. Twenty-four years without a word, a card, a freaking text message. Nothing. I don't need him. I don't want him.

I hate him.

And yet, in a choked voice, I say, "Tell me everything." Now I can hate myself too.

While I start in on my third bottle, Chris relates his tale of coffee with my father. He doesn't get far into it before I put the pieces together.

The homeless guy/pawn shop dealer. The one who wielded magic well enough to erase evidence at Max Harris's murder/suicide scene, keeping me, Gen, and Chris out of the investigation.

The one who, according to Genesis, has likely been punished by the Registry for the use of dark magic. Punished with intermittent madness. I don't feel sorry for him, not in the least. I do wonder if that's why he left us.

I picture him in my head and give myself a mental kick. Knowing the family connection, the traits are obvious. But I hadn't possessed that information at the time.

I share my information, both Gen and Chris letting me get things out at my own pace, which is slow and stilted, interrupted by a lot of drinking and pauses to regain composure. Gen covers my hand with her own, gently prying my fingers from the edge of the bar. I hadn't even realized I'd dug them in, leaving scratches in the polished wood surface.

"Sorry," I mutter.

"Don't worry about it." Chris shrugs. "Adds character."

"Well, now we know where your power comes from," Gen says.

"What do you intend to do about him?" Chris asks.

I shake my head and rub my palm across my face, frowning at the oiliness of my skin. Exhaustion rushes over me in a wave. I want a hot shower, maybe some food, though I'm not sure my stomach can handle it, and bed. Anything else is beyond my capacity at the moment.

"Nothing," I say. I pull out my wallet and drop some bills on the bar. Been coming here long enough to know what everything costs. "I'm going home."

"You're not driving." Gen takes my arm when I haul myself upright with some effort. It's not the alcohol making me wobbly. At least I don't think so. My leg aches like a bitch, but I let her think otherwise.

"I'm sorry to drop this on you, Flynn," Chris says. "I know you've got a lot going on, but I didn't think you'd appreciate me keeping it."

"No," I say, finding a smile for him somewhere. "It's okay. I mean, it's not, but you did the right thing."

Gen drives us home in the Charger. The Pub's lot is very public and well-lit. I'm not too worried about leaving the McLaren.

Somehow I manage to wash up and change into sleeping shorts and a T-shirt. I have to eat something or nausea will wake me in the middle of the night, so I feed Katy and dig through the fridge for sandwich fixings. Gen's puttering around her workspace in the front parlor, setting up for tomorrow's clients, giving me some space. I hear cabinets opening and closing and throw pillows getting fluffed.

I turn to the table to set down my plate and freeze.

On my place mat lies an envelope, shiny with crisscrossing pieces of Scotch tape.

Chapter 22
Headlong Rush

I SLAM the plate atop the envelope so hard the plastic dish cracks—one of mine from my former weekly-rate hotel living, so Gen won't give me grief over it.

Too much. It's too fucking much.

My bare feet carry me into the hallway, past the parlor where Gen pauses in the middle of straightening her deck of tarot cards on an end table. "Hey! Where are you—?"

Her keys hang on a peg by the front door, and I take them without asking, then slam out of the house. The Charger sits in the driveway where habit had her park it earlier. The McLaren gets the garage, which holds two cars, but boxes of Leo's stuff fill one side—items we haven't managed to get rid of yet, or occult pieces we're afraid to unleash on the general public, locked in portable safes only I know the combinations to.

More magic shit to deal with another day.

With time spent on a shower and other getting-ready-for-bed routines, the alcohol has worn off, so I'm not concerned about driving intoxicated. I am worried about driving holy fucking furious, and I check my speed and slow down halfway through town. Damn good thing I didn't get pulled over. I don't have my wallet.

I don't know where I'm going.

It's not that late, a little after nine. I spend maybe a half hour traveling aimlessly up one street and down another, then end up without conscious thought in the parking lot of the pawn shop where I bought Gen's engagement ring.

My sleep shorts look like regular running shorts, and, okay, I haven't shaved my legs in a while, but no one will confuse me with a baboon yet. The navy T-shirt I grabbed after my shower hides the fact that I'm not wearing a bra. Biggest issue is no shoes, but I'm pretty sure Gen still stores a pair of flip-flops, along with a change of clothes, in the trunk. It's a holdover from our early dating days—never knew when the girlfriend might ask you to sleep at her place last minute. Except I never did. My place embarrassed me. She might have slept there twice.

My head spins with how much my life has shifted.

I step out onto hot but not scalding pavement, the sun having set a couple of hours ago, and hurry to the rear of the Charger. Sure enough, she's got her overnight bag back there. I swipe the shoes, too small for me so my heels hang an inch or so off the backs, but they'll do. Slamming the trunk releases a touch of my frustration, and I cross the lot to the store entrance.

They close in twenty-five minutes, so no one's in there except the sales clerk—a heavyset blond woman with a bad perm of tight curls and a horizontal-striped tank top that accentuates each roll of flab. She's spraying and wiping down the glass cases and doesn't want to spare time to chat, but I get that she's never heard of my father, either by his current name of Ferguson or the one I remember from my childhood—Robert. Which prompts the question, is either one his real name? And another question, just how strong of a magic user is he?

Did he spell the entire pawn shop two months ago? Of course, the "entire" shop might have been one employee then as it is now. Either way, it's a little scary.

From there I try Festivity's Starbucks, but they close in less than an hour, and it's cleared out too. At least their staff smiles and greets me when I enter. The baristas all know me and Gen, right down to our preferred drinks. I wave off the offer of a grande white mocha on the house and climb into the car.

Third time's a charm, right?

The Starbucks on Route 192 stays open twenty-four hours. I used to hit that one on my way back from bowling league night and pick up a coffee to make it home if I got really tired. My old hotel sat on the far side of Kissimmee, and after a long day of work and bowling, I often needed extra caffeine even to drive a few miles. The homeless tend to avoid the franchise in Festivity, but they love the one on 192 since they don't have to worry about closing time. It's also larger and has comfortable couches inside and out, unlike the downtown one with its hard wooden and metal chairs.

I keep my eyes peeled on my drive. Chris said he'd spotted Ferguson panhandling at the corner of Festivity Avenue and 192, but the beggars don't tend to do that in the dark.

Some of my former hotel neighbors did the street-corner panhandling thing, and while pedestrians sometimes feared them, shying away and crossing to the opposite side of the street, they, in turn, feared the nighttime drivers. I heard all sorts of horror stories, from bottles thrown from car windows to sideswiping by a bumper. But it paid better than minimum wage.

Open all night or not, the other Starbucks is almost as deserted as the one in town. These baristas know me, too, though not my specific drink, and I get a wave from one as I scan the few scattered customers.

Not inside. I step onto the patio where two teens who should be home hover around a computer screen watching anime. In the far corner, a man talks rapid-fire into his cell, an open briefcase on the too small table before him. No Ferguson.

I'm ready to give up and I'm crossing back through the inside of the coffee shop, when the men's room door swings open and he emerges, ragged clothes, scruffy beard, and all. Must be one of his madness days.

He spots me and spins toward the restroom entrance as if to escape, but I catch his shoulder. "Oh no, you don't. We're going to have a chat." A gentle but firm shove sends him in the direction of one of the pairs of armchairs by the front windows.

"Chat, skat, nothing to say, wouldn't make sense if I did," he says, then cackles like the crazy man he is.

The two baristas eye us but keep quiet as we pass. They're pretty cool about leaving the homeless alone, letting them take shelter in the air-conditioning so long as they aren't bothering the paying customers.

"Not safe, not like this, down the drain, drain me dry."

"You just did that," I say, pointing at the restroom where a male tourist in a Universal Harry Potter tee disappears through the door. "Come on."

I wait until Ferguson chooses a chair and take the one opposite him, resting my elbows on my knees and my face in my palms.

My father. Holy shit.

I want to deny it, call up Chris and tell him he's mistaken. Just some nutcase with no connection whatsoever to me. But now that I know to look, even with the beard and dirt masking his features, Ferguson matches up with my flashes of childhood memory.

He's my father, he's alive, and he's mostly insane.

Chapter 23
Research

DRESSED IN a pale blue business jacket and skirt, Linda Argyle click-clacked in her heels to the Registry's archives. She'd driven over an hour from her Jersey shore home, slipped through a rear entrance, taken an elevator down below street level, and descended a flight of stairs to reach the hidden storage rooms in a sub-basement of the Princeton University library, but she understood the necessity. The materials stored in the steel-walled, warehouse-sized space shouldn't be accessible to just anyone.

Linda passed through one more reinforced door to find herself before a mechanical archway resembling a metal detector. Only this device didn't register weapons. Designed by one of the other board members with an affinity for manipulating both electrical and magical energy, it detected psychic ability. Stepping beneath it triggered a series of red lights along its inner curve. The more lights, the greater a psychic's strength. A small smile of satisfaction curved her lips when all but the top eight lights lit with her presence. No one ever lit them all, and she was one of the strongest talents listed in the Registry.

Had she activated none of the lights, or if they had turned green, the machine would have sent a silent alarm to the welcome desk a few yards ahead and an armed guard would have been summoned. Not that they were out to shoot anyone—most wanderers turned out to be curious or simply lost—but a dark practitioner could gain invaluable information if he or she managed to access this facility. To date, no one had tried. As far as Linda was aware, no one but the board members knew of this place's location. But the possibility remained, and with Genesis Mc-Talish leaving the board.... Linda couldn't rely on the other psychic's oaths of secrecy.

"Madame President," an older gentleman greeted her as she approached the desk. He stood behind the polished mahogany antique, manning it the way a ship's captain might man the wheel. He reached out and shook her hand, his enveloping hers in a weathered yet firm grip. "Thank you for the advance notice of your visit. The computer alcove stands ready for your use, the relevant files already downloaded. Should you need hard copy, summon me with the intercom and I'll locate the volumes." Not a gray hair out of place, tan shirt ironed and starched, blue eyes piercing with a quickness she admired. Excellent.

"Thank you, Master Archivist." Linda wished she remembered his name. His diligence pleased her. "I may be most of the morning, and possibly into the afternoon."

He nodded. "There's coffee in my office. I'd be happy to bring you a cup if you'd like, and should you stay longer, I can have lunch sent down to you."

"Coffee would be wonderful." She waved a hand at the rows and rows of bound volumes shelved behind the desk, extending as far as she could see. "I haven't done this sort of research since my college days. Caffeine will come in handy."

The Archivist chuckled and turned to lead her off to the right where a small curtained area held a computer, desk, and chair. She settled in, waited until he returned with her coffee and left, and then began her task.

First things first—the anonymous tip Genesis had received that she'd been targeted by one of the Registry's people.

The Archivist had already compiled a list of registered psychics living in the Orlando, Florida, area. Linda scanned the names, finding mostly those loyal to the Registry, a few outliers, and one or two deviants. One in particular stood out as the most likely candidate—Ferguson Brigham (with a footnote stating this was likely not his real name). Seer, eraser, occasional dark practitioner, currently serving a sentence of madness three days a week for the rest of the year. Address unknown but suspected of living somewhere around Festivity. Linda made a note to set someone to find him.

The second file she opened contained basic information on succubi:

"Extremely powerful users of the *push* talent, succubi can drive out both spiritual and magical energy from any subject. However, succubi differ from other *pushers* in that they possess an equally powerful ability to *pull* the magical energy back into themselves *and* make use of those absorbed talents. Note: see *Walkers/Succubi*."

So essentially, psychic succubi were overly strong *pushers*. Many psychics had the *push* talent. Genesis McTalish had it to some extent, enabling her to *push* unwanted spirits from the bodies of those they possessed, though she couldn't affect another user's magical ability.

Flynn, on the other hand, was much, much stronger. The *push* comprised her primary talent, where Genesis's was communicating with the spirit realm.

Linda clicked open the file on *Walkers*, scrolling down until she reached the notations on the combination of *Walkers/Succubi*.

"While a *walker* is a particularly strong talent in the *push* skill like *succubi*, *walkers* differ in that they can literally *push* their own spirits beyond the living body to walk as a spirit would on the earthly plane. Should a *pusher* be strong enough to qualify as both *walker* and *succubus*, he or she may also have the ability to *walk* as a spirit through *time* as well as *space*, resulting in a tendency toward mental instability in later life. Last known psychics documented with this ability: Tempest Granfeld, (1879—). Banned from the Registry for dark practices. Punished with madness."

That was odd. The Master Archivist kept the records up-to-date. Linda never had reason to criticize him. So why was this one incomplete? With 1879 as a birth year, Tempest Granfeld had to be dead. Where was the date of death? Not to mention that the entry read "… last known *psychics*" with the ability. Psychics. Plural. Yet it only listed one.

Alarm bells rang softly in the back of her mind. *Erased*, a voice whispered. Someone had altered the documents, maybe gotten interrupted partway through. Worse, electronic tampering would have set off any number of security systems. No, this was magical in nature. And the Registry only had a handful of *erasers* on its rosters. An ability to erase evidence of all kinds from existence was rare and highly prized. The ones she trusted, she employed on a regular basis. And Ferguson Brigham happened to be one, and not one she trusted. Yes, they definitely needed to find that man. Linda didn't believe in coincidence.

And something else, an explanation for some of the odd occurrences the board had been experiencing of late. Members going missing. She'd looked into a few reports, hadn't liked what she'd found, or rather failed to find. Could it all have been connected somehow?

Linda stared at the rest of the seemingly innocuous description, her mind postulating all the potential risks someone with both skills might present. A walker through time. What damage might an untrained time walker (should Flynn Dalton turn out to be one) cause to the known universe?

And what might Tempest Granfeld have done with her own skills? No death date. It didn't make sense.

Linda had no reason to believe this Flynn woman possessed the same abilities, except she'd defeated Cassie's love spell and Tricia's dissatisfaction spell. Nathaniel swore Flynn to be a succubus of tremendous power.

Flynn Dalton had to attend the conference, had to come in and be assessed, had to swear to uphold the moral laws of the Registry. Linda couldn't take a chance with this one. And should Flynn turn to the dark powers or become mentally unstable.... Dear God.

But, on the other hand, should she be strong enough that Linda might make use of Flynn's powers....

Connections were forming in her mind, and while some were promising, she didn't like where others led.

Activating the intercom, Linda buzzed for the Archivist and requested every piece of information he possessed on succubus walkers and Tempest Granfeld.

It was then she noticed the ghostly flicker in the corner of the small room.

"Hello?"

The flicker brightened, then faded, a shadow of self, too indistinct to identify as any particular individual.

Linda contemplated her options. Spirit contact wasn't her strength. Her primary ability lay in dampening the powers of others. It gave her an edge over the more aggressive members of the Registry—those who would break the rules. A botched contact with her flickering visitor might result in damage to them both.

No, better to find a channeler, one she trusted with whatever information the ghost wished to impart. Because for a ghost to contact her, it was likely a matter of importance.

And secrecy.

Chapter 24
Bad Girlfriend

I'M NOT getting anything out of Ferguson, not while he's in crazy mode. Riddles and nonsense, incoherent babbling. My number one question is *Why?* Why did he leave us? Why is he here in Festivity? Why, specifically, did the board punish him? I get answers to Why is the sky blue? Why do fish swim? and Why is hell hot?

Sigh.

At midnight, I let him go and head for home, hoping to catch him on one of his non-insane days in the near future. I hope he survives that long. Crazy homeless guys have short life expectancies.

For half a moment, I consider taking him with me. The mansion has six bedrooms. We have plenty of space. But he's a dark magic user, and the last thing Genesis needs is that kind of bad influence taunting her addiction.

When I pull up to the castle house, I know I'm in trouble. All the downstairs lights blaze through the windows, casting streaks of yellow across the front lawn, and Chris's car sits in the driveway.

I pat my pocket for my cell before remembering I stormed out in my nightclothes. No pockets, no wallet, no phone. And no way for Genesis to reach me. She must have freaked.

Guilt sours the taste in my mouth. Or maybe it's the fact that I never did get any dinner. Resigned to my punishment, I flip-flop my way to the front door. It flies open before I touch the knob, and Gen's in my arms, sobbing against my chest. I wrap her in a tight hug, all the anger and stress pressing down until I can barely stand.

"S-sorry," I choke out, swallowing hard. "I'm sorry. I fucked up."

"Yeah, you did, Dalton."

I look over Gen's shoulder. Chris stands in the entry hall, arms crossed over his chest, still in his work clothes from the Pub. He's got that big-brother protective scowl on his face, but his eyes show relief and sympathy.

Gen's hiccupping, as she does whenever she cries, so I speak to him. "How long have you been here?"

"Since about fifteen minutes after you left."

So at least three hours. Shit.

He pulls his keys from his pocket and squeezes past us to the front door, but he's not finished with me. "You're not on your own anymore, Flynn. I know things have been screwed up lately, but it's not all about you. You're responsible for another person's happiness now, just as Gen's responsible for yours." He pokes me hard in the shoulder, my bad one, and I wince, but he doesn't notice. "Start acting like half a couple." Then he's gone.

I stand there holding Gen, waiting for her to calm down while Katy trots over and licks my hand.

Finally, she regains her composure enough to ask, "Where did you go? I saw the invitation in the kitchen. I knew you were already upset. You scared the hell out of me, Flynn."

I've already apologized. Doing it again won't change anything, but I say it anyway. "I'm sorry. There's no good excuse. I just saw the envelope and I had to get away from it. Fight or flight, you know? I guess I'm not up to fighting anymore." And suddenly I'm really not. I'm exhausted. My leg hurts, my arm hurts, my stomach growls.

Gen laughs at the long, rumbly sound emanating from my abdomen. "Come on. I'll make you something to eat."

I follow her to the kitchen, my limp pronounced and painful. Good thing she's ahead of me. The invitation has vanished from the round wooden table. Don't know if she threw it out for the third time, but I'm happy not to see it.

Over bologna and cheese sandwiches, I tell her about my failed encounter with my father and my near loss of employment. She listens to every word, shaking her head and making sympathetic noises, and she doesn't bring up my disappearing act until I'm finished.

"Next time, and I fear the way we're going there will be a next time, maybe you can talk to me instead of running?"

I stare at her, the realization that I *have* someone to talk to these days, that I'm not alone, hitting home with a force that staggers me. "God, I love you," I breathe.

"I love you too." She reaches out to touch my cheek. Then her expression hardens. "But don't do that again. Please."

Chapter 25
Beginning of the End

SATURDAY PASSES without disaster. Never thought I'd define a Saturday in those terms, but the way my life has been going, disaster versus non-disaster seems to be the right terminology. And I count a day of relative peace in the win column. I do worry about Peter and how I might help him without tying myself to the Registry, but nothing comes to mind, even when I brainstorm with Genesis. She wants me to go to the convention. She won't say it again out loud, but her eyes scream it when we discuss anything related to my talents.

On weekends, Gen often takes a lot of clients. I get the vibe she canceled some Saturday appointments to spend the time talking me down off the ledge, especially when a nonstop parade of customers starts showing up beginning at 10:00 a.m. on Sunday morning. While I appreciate her attention and concern for my mental state, I can't help the guilt over disrupting not just my life, but hers.

I spend the day throwing myself into building doghouses. One of the old email inquirers hadn't found another builder she liked and still wants to buy one of my custom creations. We exchange a few messages and settle on a Goth style complete with black paint and burnished metal accents for her Doberman. If it comes out the way I hope, I might even add a bat or a gargoyle on top (no extra charge).

Sawing and hammering takes my mind off my issues. I crank up some Alanis Morissette on the iPod and pound away in time to "You Oughta Know." When I construct a piece, I get lost in the work, and it's well after lunch before I glance at my phone for the time.

With the roof finished and the other major pieces measured, cut, and ready to assemble, I grab a towel and wipe good, honest sweat from my arms and forehead. The shoulder hurts, and my leg complains when I rise from the floor, but a couple of Advil should take care of the pain. Of course, I left the bottle in the front parlor when I sat chatting with Genesis last night.

Sighing, I check the kitchen for another pain medication, but there's only one pill left in the Excedrin container. Figures. Gen doesn't like to take full doses, so we always end up with one of this and one of that, and a single pill won't cut this ache.

I've got my heavy-duty stuff hidden in my nightstand upstairs, but I want to finish the construction of the doghouse today and maybe paint it after work tomorrow, and if I take one of my prescription meds, I'll sleep away the entire afternoon.

Nothing for it, then. I creep down the hall to the closed parlor door and listen outside to the voices coming from within.

"And do you think I should marry him?" That must be the client. I don't know the sultry female voice in a rich alto, and it's a typical question people ask of the spirit world.

Not sure I'd trust a decision like that to a dead person, but hey, who am I to judge?

"It's awfully fast. Only three months. There's no special reason you're rushing to marriage, is there?"

Okay, weird. Fucking creepy weird. A shiver crawls up my spine, and I let it pass through me, since no one's around to see. I will *never* get used to hearing someone else's words, speech patterns, and this time a Southern accent, coming out in Gen's voice. She's dropped her pitch by an octave, probably channeling a male. I shake my head hard, wishing I could empty the sound from my ears. No way am I entering while that's going on. I avoid seeing Gen possessed as much as possible.

"Oh, Dad, you always were too overprotective. No, there's no special reason. I'm not pregnant or anything. I just think he's the right guy. I love him."

"Then you don't need to be asking me. You do what your heart says is right."

A skeptical client would call that hedging on Gen's part. But I know those are the father's exact words. And judging from the pleased laughter, the woman knows it too.

The father and daughter exchange a few more pleasantries before Gen's voice shifts to her normal tones, tired, but hers. Channeling spirits wears her out. I hope she's planned in some downtime between sessions, but I've heard the front door opening and closing almost every hour all day.

The conversation shifts to payment and scheduling another appointment for next month, so I figure I'm safe to sneak in and grab the Advil. I crack open the door, spotting Gen first, then the woman, a tall brunette in dark green sweatpants and a lime tank top. She's muscular and athletic, around twenty-five, and I'm betting she's headed for the fitness center over at Festivity Health straight from here. Sunday clients fall into two categories: those coming from church and dressed to the nines, and the ones en route to other leisure activities.

Gen's head comes up at the creak of the hinges, and she waves me inside with a weary smile. I wave back, crossing quickly behind where they sit on throw pillows surrounded by six lit candles in a variety of ornate holders. The tarot cards lie between them in the usual cross and line down the side pattern with a few others placed atop the base reading for more detail. I worked for Gen for a short time, acting as her assistant, and I've observed a few sessions, so I know the basics, but I'm glad to be back at the construction site. No ghosts, no possessed girlfriends, no weirdness.

A quick look reassures me of no foreboding cards in the layout, at least not the ones I remember most: the Tower, the Devil, the Hermit. I'm sure others exist. It's a large deck with too many images for anyone other than a professional reader to memorize, and the intricate designs catch the eye—human figures with feline/alien faces in a variety of environmental settings. Beautiful artwork. Gen uses the cards to focus her energies, direct her questioning, and draw in the spirits she allows to temporarily possess her. I'm told other psychics don't work the same way, but it smooths the transition for Genesis, so she sticks with it.

I'm so distracted by the cards that I almost collide with the handsome gentleman leaning against the cabinet where Gen keeps her atmosphere-enhancing decorations and candles.

"Oh, I'm sorry. I didn't realize there were two clients this session. Or are you waiting for a reading?" I study him in his Bermuda shorts and polo shirt, with brown sandals on his feet and a healthy tan that sets off his just-beginning-to-gray brown hair.

He straightens slowly, coming to a full height of an inch or two past six feet. Intelligent eyes regard me with intense surprise and interest. "Are you saying, young lady, that you can also see me?"

"Also?" The room goes a little blurry as I process what's happening, and I make an unsteady grab for the side of the cabinet to stay on my feet.

"I wasn't aware Ms. McTalish worked with another psychic," the man continued in a slow Southern drawl.

"Aw hell," I mutter.

Gen's up and running for me, catching me when my knees buckle, while her female customer stares around the room asking, "Who's she talking to?"

"Fuck, fuck, fuck," I whisper, the shakes taking a firm hold.

Gen has me in her arms, and she guides me to the settee close to a curtained window. The oppressive heat of the afternoon sun carries through the heavy folds of blackout cloth, and it soothes me somewhat, driving away a few degrees of chill.

"Is she all right?" the woman asks.

"Claire, could you get her a glass of water? Kitchen, down the hall through the door at the end." Gen points in the general direction and the woman hurries away.

The ghost of her father remains.

"I'm guessin' this ain't typical for you," he comments.

"Not supposed to happen," I say over and over. I turn wide eyes to Gen. "You said I wasn't a full-blown psychic, just a sensitive." I shouldn't be able to see random spirits, only those of people who'd been close to me. Like my ex-girlfriend, Kat, and my grandmother when I was a kid.

Besides those two unpleasant moments, the single other time I'd seen apparitions was when I was out of my body, *walking*. Then, and only then, as a spirit myself, I can see any ghost who chooses to appear to me. Not an experience I wish to repeat.

But I'm not *walking*, and it is repeating.

"What the hell is going on?" I ask, squeezing my eyes shut and clinging to her like a child.

Get a grip, Flynn.

But I can't. I don't want this. Please, God, make it go away.

Gen strokes my hair, my back, soothing me as best she can. "I don't know," she says, then to the spirit, "It might help if you left for now."

"Not a problem, ma'am. Thanks for puttin' me in touch with my little girl. I figure she's the reason I'm still here. I might visit again sometime in the future…?"

"Yes, of course. Thank you for coming."

Polite ghosts. A small, semihysterical laugh escapes my throat. Gen's arms tighten around me, like she can hold me together with her physical strength. I'm thinking, no.

Claire returns with the water, pressing the glass into my hand since I'm not looking at her. I'm not looking at anyone until I'm sure the spirit is gone.

"Should I call someone?" she asks.

"No, it's… no," Gen says. "She'll be fine. Thank you."

"I'll just leave the money on the table."

"Right. Fine." She's distracted, trying to get Claire to leave as fast as possible without being rude.

I'm screwing up Gen's business. Shit. I draw a deep breath, which hitches through my lungs in short spurts, and pull away. No sign of the ghost. The next inhalation comes easier. "You two settle things. I'll…." The legs I attempt to stand on don't hold and I almost drop a second time, but I lock my left knee. The right won't support weight. Wonderful. "I'll wait here," I announce as if it were my intention all along. From the looks the two women give me, neither one's buying that.

They spare what's left of my ego, though, and move off to finish their business. Gen casts worried glances in my direction, and I know she's hurrying, but Claire doesn't seem to mind. Nice girl. Whoever her boyfriend is, he's a lucky man.

I'm stiff, straight-backed on the settee. When the door shuts behind the client, I slump into the cushions. Gen returns to sit beside me. "I'm assuming you don't know Mr. Hayworth?"

God, I wish. That would make sense. As if anything in the magical rule book makes any real sense. But it would be something.

"Nope," I say. "Never met him."

"I have a theory," she says.

"Go on." It comes out muffled, since I've buried my face in a throw pillow, but she gets the gist.

"You aren't going to like it."

I sit up and bark a sharp laugh, then another, until the hysterics that have hovered at the edge of my sanity burst through and boil over, and I'm laughing so hard tears pour down my cheeks and my stomach hurts from the effort. When have I ever liked any of this?

Gen's expression goes from surprise to deeper concern, and the arm around my shoulders trembles a little. Or maybe that's just me.

"You're scaring me," she says.

I'm scaring myself.

How much can a person take before she loses it? How much weirdness can the universe inflict on a former null, someone who blocked out her abilities from the age of nine and swore to herself that she possessed no magical talents whatsoever? Lots of kids wish for super powers. Any child who read or watched Harry Potter wants to go to Hogwarts.

I wasn't one of them.

I enjoyed stories about magic and monsters, but that's all I wanted them to be—stories. The closest I ever came to casting spells was role-playing games like Dungeons and Dragons in college.

Now my thoughts scatter like rolled dice.

Mix in the issues at work and trying to hold Gen's addiction in check and I'm heading for the asylum.

Like my mother.

Gen opens her mouth to say something else, probably to tell me what she thinks is going on, but I hold up a hand to stop her.

My mother. A woman who battled with depression for as much of my life as I can remember. I always thought it stemmed from my father leaving her when I turned four, but what if…? What if she'd had mental problems the whole time? What if they came as a result of my father's magical abilities and the effect they had on her? He used dark magic. God knows what kind of collateral damage that could have had on the people around him. Like her.

And me.

Mom lives in a mental facility in New Jersey. I don't want to join her.

"What are you thinking?" Gen asks.

"I'm thinking I'm in deep shit. Tell me your theory."

From her piercing look, I know she wants to press me for more, but she refrains. Gen takes a deep breath, steadying herself. Not a good sign. "Today was the first time since the Mall at Millennia that you came into the parlor during one of my sessions, right?"

I nod. It was the first in a couple of months. The last time I watched her work, we were living in her old apartment.

"I think I know why I collapsed in that store," she says.

Huh? "We already know why. I *pushed* your magic out of you."

Gen shakes her head and frowns, rubbing one ballet-slippered foot across the hardwood floor. "When it got to be too much, I told you to pull back. I think… I think you took me literally. Without any training, you did exactly what I said, acted on instinct." She looks me straight in the eyes. "I think you pulled my magic into yourself."

She lets me go, rising to pace the length of the room, circling around the throw pillows and tarot cards. "You can see ghosts of people unconnected to you. I'm betting if you knew how, you could call them too."

"No thanks," I say, wrapping my arms around myself. The parlor feels like a walk-in freezer.

"Well, let me test this idea, at least." Before I can stop her, she sinks onto the closest pillow and closes her eyes. "Mom, Dad, could I borrow you guys for a few minutes? Flynn needs your help."

Whoa. "Gen, are you telling me you can speak with your dead par—"

A man and woman shimmer into existence on either side of her. They wear shorts and loose-fitting matching shirts—white with blue trim—and deck shoes, and I remember Gen's folks died in a boating accident when she was sixteen.

Instead of blue-skinned, bloated corpses, though, they appear healthy, almost alive, with tanned skin and cheeks rosy from a sea-salt wind. They turn to me with warm, affectionate smiles, and my heart aches with longing. What I wouldn't give for parents like these, and God, what Gen has lost in their deaths.

That she communicates with them shouldn't surprise me, only she's never mentioned it, and she shares so much. I suppose she wanted to keep this special connection private.

No hard feelings here.

"What do you need us to do?" her father asks, tilting his head in my direction.

Gen ignores the question, asking me, "Can you see them?"

Oh yeah. I can see them.

I stand and cross the room, a little unsteady, but I make it. Can't shake hands, at least I don't think so, so I settle for a nod to each of them. "Mr. and Mrs. McTalish, it's a pleasure to meet you both. I...." What do I say? The first words that come to mind are, "I hope you're okay with my relationship with your daughter."

Stupid, I know. But when I proposed to Gen, I wished I could have done the traditional thing and asked for her hand. Not that it would have changed my actions, but I wanted their approval. I wanted another family, a real one. I'd spoken with Chris, of course, but while he filled a void I never knew I'd had, it wasn't the same.

Gen's mom laughs, a delightful, musical sound reminding me of Genesis in a million ways. "I wish I could hug you," she tells me.

"You might be able to," Genesis says. "You're able to hug me."

Gen possesses enough psychic strength to have physical contact with spirits. I know because she was able to touch me when I *walked* in spirit form.

"Maybe you should tell us what's going on, kiddo," her father suggests.

Before she can explain, however, her mother steps forward and embraces me.

I suck in a sharp breath at the spirit's touch, my pulse rate speeding up and every muscle tensing. Then a love so... well, there's no word to explain its overwhelming impact. It wraps around me, pierces me to my core, calms frayed nerves and eases racing thoughts. My sense of self returns when I hadn't quite realized it had fled—a scary awakening. In that moment, I'm loved and accepted in a way I've never been except by Genesis.

After a long moment, Gen's mom steps back, and her absence aches with a dull, throbbing pain in my chest and throat. I force down a swallow and wipe away the tears streaming over my cheeks. Not sure where those came from, but that needs to stop, now.

"Welcome to the family," her dad says, resting a brief hand on my shoulder. Not as life-changing as the hug, but it conveys a respect and admiration for me I never would have suspected, and I almost start bawling again. What the hell? He gestures toward the settee and I sit beside Genesis. "Now, let's talk."

Chapter 26
When *Push* Comes to Shove

So, I'm some kind of nymphomaniac dead thing.

Okay, okay, Genesis assures me the term "succubus" does not mean what I always thought it meant from my college course in Medieval mythology, but that doesn't make me embrace the term assigned to a "rare power like mine."

As a former member of the Registry's board, Gen had access to a lot of information other members don't, so she's somewhat familiar with what I am and what I can do, depending upon my strength, which has not yet been officially determined.

And if I have anything to say about it, never will be.

However, she hasn't served in an administrative capacity in several years, so her memories lack details, and she no longer possesses the passwords to enter the online archives. The Registry stores the real hard-copy documents in a secret storage facility in New Jersey (Gen won't tell me where), so we can't storm the castle, so to speak, either.

Which leaves me, as usual these days, in limbo.

That thought gets me laughing again, earning more concerned looks from my girlfriend across the dinner table, her parents having since departed.

Ack. Departed. I laugh harder and hate myself for it. Gen doesn't deserve that kind of insensitivity on my part, but I can't stop. Fuck, I'm in trouble.

"What's so funny?" From her tone, she's desperately hoping it's something tangible, because I'm not so stable right now.

I shake my head. "Nothing. Limbo. I was thinking I'm back in limbo, which, mythologically speaking, I think is the demon realm, which connects to succubi, who are demons, and—"

"You're not a demon. You're not in limbo. You're going to get through this. So stop it." She stabs at a forkful of Kraft mac and cheese. Yeah, we have a million dollars and we still eat Kraft dinners. The silverware hits hard enough to screech across the plate like a dentist's drill on a bad molar.

I close my mouth. The unwanted humor fades.

Just like the ghosts of her parents.

By the end of our lengthy conversation, their images had grown fuzzy and indistinct to my Sight, and they all figure whatever power I took from Genesis, it's only temporary and weakens with use. She tried calling a couple more benevolent spirits to the parlor, but I could neither see nor hear them, so my short-lived walk in Gen's shoes has ended.

The aftershocks have not.

Sadly, Mr. and Mrs. McTalish—who insist I call them Mom and Dad and have me blinking back tears whenever I think about them, dammit—know even less about succubi than Gen does. Her mother had some magical ability. She was a precognitive who used her foreseeing skills to read business trends and operate the Village Pub at a consistent profit, but that was the extent of it, so the Registry never took an interest in her or shared its secrets. Her father had no power at all.

Gen has some ancestors further back with greater strength, so that's likely where she got it from, but they're long dead and, according to Gen, crossed over, so any knowledge they had is lost to us.

One thing we do know, I'll need to be more careful. If I pull too much power from someone, I could drain them permanently.

I HIT the construction site on Monday morning suffering from little sleep and bad attitude. My fury burns from the Friday almost-firing incident, and the hearty hellos from my team don't lessen the anger.

Tom's back, so I turn over the iPad and the trailer keys and give him a rundown of Friday's inspection, leaving out the personal stuff. He'll hear the rumors soon enough. I'm not in the mood to rehash it.

"So, where do you want me?" My guys swarm like ants across the roof of apartment building nine, one of the last two to complete before we move to another site farther up the road and begin several rows of duplexes. I spot Diego and Alex working on shingles while Joe carries another batch up to them.

"Tired of the cushy air-conditioned life?" Tom waves at the trailer.

"I just want to get to work."

He frowns. "Something wrong?"

"It's nothing. Assignment?"

Tom scans me from head to toe, lingering on my leg and shoulder for a beat longer than necessary and focusing on my face. Even more I suspect his putting me in charge might have been a planned break for my recovering injuries, but I don't ask. "Join your team," he says.

Damn. I walk away toward the ladders leading up to the roof with a quick pause at the bank of lockers for my hard hat and tool belt. Should have asked about his trip. Should have checked on his sister's health. Time to get my head out of my ass.

I haul myself up the ladder, hand over hand, the pull setting a deep ache into the damaged arm. Great way to start my day. A week off made me soft, got me out of the exercise regimen, and even though I pitched in on occasion and worked out at home, I'm feeling it fast.

The steady monotony of shingle attachment dispels some of my anger, and I settle into a silent routine. Around me, the rhythms of the work blend into an intricate beat, Diego and Alex purposely timing their pounding to create a musical percussion. It makes me smile: the sun, the blue sky, the satisfaction of building, friends close by.

When the heat hits its midday peak, I pause for a break, leaning back against the sun-warmed roof where we've finished the shingling, sucking a long drink from my water bottle. Joe clambers down the closest ladder, calling that he needs to take a piss. No extra formalities because I'm a woman, and I appreciate that. Alex says he's gonna grab some more materials and heads down as well.

"Hot one. I'm worn out today." Diego drops beside me. "So, how go the wedding plans?"

So much for my improved mood. "They aren't going," I mutter. I eye him in my peripheral vision. He's red-faced and sweating. Good thing he's taking a rest.

"My Rosaline, she makes wedding dresses. Told me to let you know she'd give you a hefty discount." Rosaline's his wife, a beautiful Latina woman with shining black hair and dark, kind eyes. When I had financial issues last winter, they invited me several times to their home for Mexican meals that would put any restaurant to shame, and with their large family of four girls, they had less to spare than I did. But they insisted.

"You're family," she'd told me. "Diego calls you his *hija quinta* his fifth daughter."

Saved me from eating ramen noodles every night. They even thrust Tupperware filled with leftovers into my hands and made me take them back to my extended-stay hotel.

"Someday," Rosaline said, "I'll teach you to cook."

Not likely. I burn water. Genesis doesn't let me near the stove if she can help it, and I'm fine with that.

And a wedding dress? "Kinda saw me in a tux, actually," I say. Maybe with a more feminine cut to the jacket, but not a gown. "Dresses really aren't my thing."

Diego chuckles, scanning my well-worn jeans and short-sleeved white T-shirt. "No kidding. I mean for Genesis."

Gen's had her nose in a half dozen bridal mags since I proposed, but she might go for a custom-made dress. "I'll tell her."

We sit in companionable silence awhile; then he rises to get back to work… and gasps. I jerk toward him at the sound, shock and horror slowing my actions as he grabs at his chest. His right foot slips; his left knee buckles. The rooftop shudders with the impact of his body falling… and sliding.

"Diego!" I launch myself at him, landing flat on my belly, the new shingles scraping the skin of my stomach raw where my tee rides up. I dig in with the steel toes of my boots, the right leg screaming. Scrabbling, I grab two handfuls of his shirt before he can reach the roof's edge. Or I would have, if I could close the fingers of my left hand. "Fuck!"

Diego lets out a strangled groan while I will my hand to work, and fail. The whole arm from my shoulder to fingertips goes numb and lifeless. My right has him, but he's a large man, heavy with muscle and good home cooking, and we're both sliding fast toward the more-than-three-story drop to the ground.

Chapter 27
Breaking Point

DIEGO'S LEGS dangle over open air, his tool belt caught on the roof's edge. He's got his face turned up to me, eyes squeezed shut, muscles taut with pain. One hand scratches at the roof, scraping across the rough surface; the other is pressed beneath him.

His center of gravity and my single hand's grip are the only things preventing Diego from falling to his death, and I'm flashing back on my near fall a couple of months ago when Dead Woman's Pond caught the sun and blinded me and I lost my balance. Near miss then, much worse now.

I slide another couple of inches forward, the shingles pulling up under my boot toes. One shingle breaks off and skitters past me to drop into open space. The three-quarter-inch nails holding the roof pieces in place aren't designed to bear so much weight—aren't designed to bear any weight at all.

Below, the other workers, including Alex and Joe, mill about between the buildings, oblivious. "Help...." I call, but my belly flop knocked the wind out of me, and my voice carries no farther than my own ears.

And we're still sliding.

"Flynn, let go." Diego forces the words through clenched teeth.

"No way." I'll never get him back up the incline, but if I can hang on until help comes....

We slip another couple of inches toward the edge.

Diego flails, body jerking and twisting, and at first I think he's panicking. "Calm down! Don't move. You're making it worse." I can't do more than whisper, but I know he hears me.

Instead of grabbing at the rooftop, he's grabbing at me.

No. Not grabbing. Pushing. Pushing me away.

He shoves at my hand, my arm, his blunt nails still managing to do damage as he tries to dislodge my grip.

"God, Diego, stop!" I can't hold him as it is.

Alex happens to glance up at this point, staring for the longest second ever before breaking into a run toward the ladders. He's shouting, waving his arms, bringing every worker within range racing for building nine. A couple pause to snatch a tarp off a pile of lumber, stretching it out between them, but they're too far. Cloth tears, Diego's shirt ripping at the seams. I'm losing him, but I won't give up.

"Let me go, mija. Before I take you with me."

No. I think of Rosaline and his four daughters: Eleana, Isa, Alejandra, and Katrina—all beautiful girls who love their father more than anything in the world.

I love him too.

"Please," I beg him.

The ringing of boots against metal tells me the guys are coming, that they're climbing as fast as they can, but my leg aches and my hand sweats.

And my shoulder pops—a sucking, wet sound that fills my mouth with bile because my body comprehends the meaning before my mind wraps itself around it. My right hand, now as useless as my left, loses its hold.

"Hang—" Alex reaches the roof at the same moment Diego leaves it.

The dull thud tells me they never got the tarp in place. And there's shouting, so much shouting.

"No!" Two shingles detach beneath my boots and I'm falling, my head, neck, and shoulders over the edge, my eyes shut so I don't see Diego's shattered body or the death coming for me.

If I die, will Genesis call me back?

Strong arms wrap themselves around my lower legs, crawling their way up my thighs to my hips, and I'm moving backward, farther up the roof, to safety. "I've got you," Alex pants. "I've got you, Flynn."

I'm not sure I want him to. I dropped Diego. I let him die. I never should have been up here, working with my injuries, putting others at risk with my weakness. I should have let them fire me.

But if I fall, Gen will never recover.

"Don't worry." More hands, Joe's, at my waist. Then I'm hauled against a sweat-covered, muscular, heaving chest.

Shock and pain hit as one, and I'm sobbing, shaking. Someone screams "No!" over and over. I think it's me. I'm not sure I ever stopped. I think I've been screaming it since the moment Diego fell.

Joe rocks me in his arms. Alex strokes my hair. Guess I lost my hard hat somewhere in the struggle. I feel my friends' presence. I hear them. I can't respond.

"God, what's wrong with her arm?" Alex asks.

"Which one? The right's dislocated. The left one.... She caught it on the edge. It'll need stitches."

Warm wetness runs down my bicep over my elbow. It doesn't hurt. Some vague part of my brain knows that's wrong.

"Ambulance is coming. We have to get her down."

All my working muscles tighten. I've never been afraid of heights, but the idea of climbing over the edge, down a ladder, after what just happened… it's unthinkable. Thunder rumbles in the distance, dark clouds rolling in fast from the east. Of course. Tom would be bringing us all in now, regardless. Workers on rooftops tend to get struck.

"She can't do it without at least one good hand," Joe says.

And just like that, feeling returns to my left arm, blasting me with a wave of pain that sets my vision sparkling and blackening at the edges.

"I—" I break off whatever I intended to say, sucking in a sharp breath as more fire runs through my muscles. Breathing deep, I ride it out. When it ebbs, I try again. "I can manage," I tell them. Then with a sarcastic laugh, "Don't let me fall." Like I did to Diego.

"Never," Alex says, patting my thigh.

We shift to the ladder, moving slow, a few feet at a time. Alex goes first, then me, then Joe, who keeps casting worried glances over his shoulder. My legs are tucked in tight to Alex's chest, his head at the small of my back. We take it rung by rung, Alex calling the shots: he goes down a step, I wait, let him grip my waist, then I go down one so he can hold on to me when I release the ladder with my one good hand.

The wind picks up and the rain pours, soaking through my thin T-shirt, turning the white material transparent. When will I learn to stop wearing this color outdoors? Sirens wail in the distance, drowned out midscream by a close clap of thunder. My right arm hangs at an odd angle, even the raindrops enough to add to its pain.

It takes more than fifteen minutes to reach the ground, shouts of encouragement following us the final third of the way and ragged cheers erupting when our boots hit dirt now turned to mud. Flashing lights make me worry I'm close to fainting until I spot the ambulance parked between buildings seven and eight and the EMTs slogging through puddles and bent against the wind.

My first instinct is to head for where Diego fell, some stupid part of me clinging to a last thread of hope. Depending on how he hit, he might have survived, right? I turn in that direction, but Joe blocks my path and my view.

"You don't need to see that," he says, his mouth forming a grim line. Judging from his pallor, I'm guessing he's already risked a glance.

"Come on!" Tom approaches from the accident site, having to shout to be heard over the howling wind. He leads the way to his trailer, Alex and Joe on either side of me, neither willing to let me walk on my own. Good thing too. My right leg drags every third step, creating a trough through the mud.

The wind catches the trailer door when Tom opens it, slamming it outward against the exterior. Then we're inside, the door bolted shut and the worst of the noise blocked by the slightly swaying portable office walls.

Alex eases me into one of the metal and plastic chairs. I pull my knees to my chest, literally having to *pull* the right up under me with my no-longer-as-bad-as-the-other left arm. Ah, irony. My gaze focuses on the throw rug Tom tossed across the fake wood floor, a woven tiger stripe pattern in rich orange and black.

Tom crouches beside me, bringing him into my field of vision, not making me look up. "What happened up there, Flynn?" His tone is gentle, and it almost sets me sobbing again, which makes me realize at some point I stopped. Wonder when that happened.

I stare into his face for a long moment before answering. "My fault," I whisper. "Couldn't hold him."

"That's bullshit," Joe says from behind me. "She couldn't have held Diego even if she'd had two good arms. Not sure *I* could have. Quit beating yourself up, Flynn."

Something warm and heavy falls across my shoulders—Tom's leather jacket, draped carefully by Joe. The shaking eases off.

"What caused him to fall?" Tom asks.

"You gotta do this now?" Alex growls.

"There'll be another investigation." Tom rests a hand on my knee. "What happened?"

"H-heart attack, I think," I say.

"Well, that explains why he didn't pull himself back over the edge," Joe says.

"Shouldn't have been up there. I shouldn't have…." My gaze drifts from Tom's face, focusing on nothing.

The guys move off to the side, muttering among themselves. I can't make out any of the words, but I'm not trying real hard.

"…need to call her girlfriend," eventually drifts across the space between us.

"Already tried. Can't reach her. She's not picking up." Alex holds out my cell phone. He must have grabbed it from my locker. But when did he do that? I never heard him leave. Guess I zoned out for a while.

"Three rings, pause, three more rings, pause, three more…," I chant like a mantra.

"What's that, Flynn?" Tom asks, cutting me off. To Joe he says, "Get one of those paramedics in here. I don't like how she's acting. Shock maybe." The door opens. The wind howls. The door closes.

"Emergency code," I mutter. "Gen won't answer when she's working. Unless she hears the code ring...." I wonder who's going to call Rosaline. I wonder if someone already did, if she's on her way right now, or outside with her husband's broken body. How long has it been? A few minutes? An hour? It seems like we were just discussing wedding dresses.

"I'll try the code," Alex says and steps away. After a few seconds Gen must pick up. And of course, I'm fucking up her business with her clients again. "Hey, Genesis, it's Alex, from Flynn's work? Yeah. There's been an accident."

Accident. Right. Like it's a little thing. No big deal. Fixable.

"No, no," he goes on. "She's okay. Well, not okay. She's hurt, but it doesn't seem too serious. Look, she needs you here. Can you—? Right. Tom's trailer. If we're gone, we're on our way to the hospital and we'll meet you there." Alex stops talking. I'm assuming he's dropped the call.

The door bursts open and a bedraggled, sopping EMT steps in, shakes off the outer coating of wet, and sets a kit beside my chair. He starts to reach for my right arm, catches himself, and takes the other one for a pulse reading. He shines a penlight in each of my eyes, then pauses and studies my face. "I remember you," he says, his voice pitched low and soothing, perfect for his profession. "I treated you at the lake, for snakebite poisoning."

I blink at him. "Sorry, I—"

He smiles. "Oh, you wouldn't remember me. You were unconscious at the time. I'm Al."

Right. I passed out as that ambulance arrived, didn't wake up until we got to the hospital, and even then, I was in and out a lot. "Hey, Al," I manage.

He asks me some questions, basic ones to determine my mental state. Name, age, location, year. I answer them all, but from his frown, I don't think I get all of them right. "Okay, then. We're going to take you in with us, get that shoulder and your other arm fixed up. Looks like you've got some scrapes on your abdomen as well." He peels my bloodstained T-shirt up, exposing raw scratches across my stomach. These he treats with antiseptic and gauze, taping it in place. Then he waits until the silence draws my attention to him. "They told me you were up on the roof, tried to save him. They say you're blaming yourself," he says quietly.

The fresh tears push their way past my defenses, trickling down my cheeks.

"It was a massive coronary," Al says, pulling a packet of tissues from one of a multitude of vest pockets and offering me one. "You couldn't have saved him, no matter what you did, but you're a hero for trying so hard."

A hero. Again.

Fuck this shit.

Despite my aching leg, I push myself up, faster than Al or Tom or anyone else can stop me. I grab the chair with my good hand and hurl it across the room, where it slams into the metal wall and clatters to the floor.

Three sets of hands take hold of me. I kick and flail, my nerves shot, my temper gone, and my body determined to do as much damage to anything and anyone as I can. I'm not out to hurt my friends or Al, but the need to break things overrules common sense. A couple of grunts tell me my steel-toed boot connects with someone's shin before they force me into another chair and Al calls for a stretcher on his radio.

"That's enough of that," he pants, not unkindly, like he's dealt with crazed accident victims a lot.

Another pair of EMTs enters the trailer. They wrestle me onto a stretcher, though really I'm too weak to continue fighting, and strap me down. Holding Tom's jacket over my face, they carry me out to the ambulance. I'm not sure if the jacket is to protect me from the now drizzling rain or keep me from seeing the aftermath of the accident.

In the rear of the vehicle, Al hooks me up to an IV. "Sedative and painkiller," he explains when I raise my eyebrows. I don't argue.

I'm dimly aware of Tom next to me, riding along to the hospital. He alternates between watching me and staring out one of the narrow windows along the inside. We're in motion, and I feel when the ambulance leaves the bumps of the dirt roads and parking areas and hits the smoother asphalt of Festivity Boulevard.

The medication flows icy cold through my veins. Things go hazy, the sedatives kicking in, the pains receding to dull aches. Tom straightens beside me, pulling my cell phone from his pocket. From the conversation, I'm getting that Gen's Charger just passed going the opposite way, and he's directing her to follow us to the emergency room. When he clicks off, I fumble for his hand, and he takes it between his two large, warm ones.

"I quit," I mumble.

"No, you don't," he says.

"Yeah, I do. Should've done it a while ago. Too much ego. Too dmn stbborn." My words slur as my focus drifts.

"Sorry, Flynn. Company policy. I don't take any resignations from employees under the influence."

"Not fit to work…. Danger to everybody."

"You're no danger. I'll find something for you to do until you heal. I'll make them give you a foremanship of your own, even if I have to go to the main office myself. You just rest."

"Not gonna heal. Doctor said so."

That sharpens his attention. The soothing smile fades from his lips. "You talked to him?"

"Did. Not getting better. Getting worse." My eyelids grow heavy. I struggle to keep them open. Gotta make him understand and accept the inevitable, like I finally have.

Tom exchanges worried looks with the EMT. His grip on my hand tightens. "I don't care what he said. You're not quitting. We need you. You're too damn good at your job to let go. Take a few days, a few weeks if you have to. I know money isn't an is-sue. But I'm holding your position for you. Because you're coming back, Flynn. We aren't a family with-out you."

I close my eyes on a sigh. "Not a family without Diego either."

Funny. He has no answer to that.

I HATE hospitals. I hate emergency rooms even more. And I particularly hate Festivity Health. Not that they didn't do all they could for me on my pre-vious visit. But their religious affiliations prevented Genesis from seeing me the last time I was here, because, you know, homosexuality is a sin, and she didn't think fast enough to lie and claim to be a relative.

This time she can't get in because emergency room policy states only one visitor may be admitted and Tom's already with me. He offers to trade places with her. I can imagine how worried she is in the waiting room with Alex and Joe, but I don't plan on hanging around long, and I'm not sure I can take her fretting, so I decline.

Good thing too. Tom remains steady, no matter what the staff have to do to me. The worst moment involves popping my shoulder back into the socket. I think I do black out for a few seconds, and I hope my scream didn't carry all the way to the waiting area and Genesis.

The doctor wants to keep me overnight, but I refuse, so they patch me up, prescribe a lot of painkillers and some Valium, and send me on my way.

By the time I hit the exit, three hours later, the sedatives have worn off and the painkillers make walking bearable. I step through the doors, Tom close by my side. I think he's afraid I might drop at any second, and I'm not sure I won't.

Then I spot Genesis.

She's worn and pale and breathtakingly beautiful, still dressed in her psychic reader garb: flowing tiered earth-tone skirt, forest green off-the-shoulder blouse, and all the bangle bracelets that can fit between her wrists and her elbows. Alex and Tom flank her, but I barely notice them, my eyes only for the woman I love more than life.

Three steps, four, and she's embracing me gently, tentatively, as if she's afraid I might break. But I'm already broken, and the shudder that passes through me at her touch tells her that.

"It'll be okay, Flynn. It will," she whispers.

I don't want more lies. Lies won't bring Diego back. "Please," I tell her, "just take me home."

Chapter 28
Down and Down

THE MORE days that pass, the less okay I become.

Tuesday, Wednesday, Thursday—they blur. Restless sleep, painkillers, sedatives, and drug-induced oblivion. I eat when the hunger nausea gets too intense. I doze off on the couch in front of Game Show Network, at the breakfast table, wherever exhaustion takes me, Katy curled up at my side most times.

That dog. I swear she reads my moods better than I do. Always there with a lick or a nudge of her nose or a soft whine of sympathy. The fact that Max Harris and whoever her other former owner was mistreated her makes me boil with hatred for them. I play with her in our backyard, me sprawled in a lawn chair, her fetching the ball I throw on autopilot like one of those tennis launching machines.

In my few moments of industriousness, I finish the Goth doghouse I'd started before the realization that I'd co-opted some of Gen's powers for myself. Never let it be said that I didn't fulfill an agreement.

But I'm not taking any more orders. I have to stop every hour or so when my arm gives out and wait for enough feeling to return so that I can continue—an ongoing reminder of what I've lost.

And then there's Genesis.

I know she wants to help. I also know she's getting frustrated with my refusal to let her. For the duration of my convalescence, she's put her psychic reading business on hold, devoting her hours to me. Every day she comes up with some errand that needs running, some "fun" excursion for us to undertake: movies, picnics, a Renaissance festival one county over, which almost tempts me. I turn them all down.

What I'm doing, it's not healthy. I'm aware of that, but no amount of coaxing on her part pulls me from the lethargy weighing on my shoulders.

Tonight, Friday, the night before Diego's funeral in the morning, the offer is simple—iced tea on the upstairs balcony overlooking the Aurora Disneyalis.

"Please." She stands at the foot of the spiraling wood staircase, two sweating glasses in her hands, her eyes begging and shiny with unshed tears.

I'd rather go to bed. I'm half-drugged, and my sluggish thoughts wander unless I make a lot of effort to focus. Instead I give a curt nod and precede her up the stairs.

Off the master bedroom extends a wide balcony with ornate metal railings befitting the castle theme of the mansion. It never held chairs before, but we've got two of them now—comfy things with deep gray-stone-colored cushions that blend with the exterior—and I wonder during which of my drug-induced stupors Gen bought and placed them out there.

I accept a glass and sink into one of the chairs, raising my bad leg to the matching footrest, leaving the other planted firmly on the floor. She takes the other, and her hand reaches out to cover mine as the light show begins.

As the crow flies, Festivity lies about five miles from Disney World, and if a house in town faces the right direction and nothing obstructs the view, residents can catch the Disney fireworks every night from the upper floors of their homes. Gen's apartment had no balconies, and all the windows looked out the wrong way, but this place....

Blues and greens, reds and yellows, the glows color the night sky. At this distance, the actual sparkles and flashes aren't visible, but the rainbow of hues makes for pretty entertainment, especially with a glass of wine or a cold beer. Since alcohol doesn't mix well with my meds, I'll have to make do with iced tea. Gen nicknamed the phenomenon the Aurora Disneyalis, and between the two of us, it stuck. In fact, we've shared the title with other residents who've adopted it as well.

I let the psychedelic display lull me into a semi-hypnotic state, the drugs turning the event into an LSD-like trip. Well, at least I think it would be like that. I've never tried any illegal drugs. Getting rather fond of the prescription ones, though.

Getting rather fond of losing myself.

"Flynn?" Gen's voice cuts through my dazed drifting.

"Yeah?"

"You know it wasn't your fault, right?"

I guess I take too long to answer because her fingers squeeze mine hard. She doesn't say anything else, just lets me be.

I DIDN'T plan on attending the funeral, but we skipped the viewing, and Gen says I need closure, whatever that means. She stands in front of me, hands on hips, already wearing a short-sleeved black dress she must keep in the back of our closet because I've never seen it before. It's a little tight in the bust line, and I can't help wondering if she wore it to her parents' funeral.

She pulls the dark slacks I used to wear to work at the Village Pub, along with a black button-down and my dress boots, and lays them out on the bed for me.

We arrive a few minutes late, mostly because I'm dragging my feet, and end up at the rear of the crowd, far from Diego's family, to my relief. It's a sunny Saturday, all blue skies and bright sunshine, much too nice for such a somber occasion, and everyone's sweating in their dark clothing.

A few of the guys notice me, and Alex gestures for me to move up beside him, but I shake my head, the muscles in my chest clenching. I don't deserve to be up there. That's for Diego's friends. I'm the one who, quite literally, let him down.

We listen to the pastor's solemn words, his voice carrying over the gathered assembly, though I cannot see him from where we stand. "…soul at rest…" yadda yadda, "…better place…" bullshit, bullshit.

Sorry, but no one would prefer to be dead.

Throughout it all, Gen's a steady presence at my side, her arm hooked around my waist, her head leaning against my good shoulder.

The sermon ends, and folks shuffle forward to pay their last respects. I catch Gen's arm and turn her toward the line of parked cars filling the narrow lanes between the segmented grassy expanses of gravestones. The Charger blends in well with the other black and gray vehicles.

"Don't you want to—" she begins, but another voice cuts her off.

"Flynn!"

I'm knocked back a step by the impact of a young body embracing mine, soon followed by three more girls—Diego's daughters.

"…so glad to see you…."

"…calling and calling…."

"Mama! She's over here!"

Aw fuck.

Rosaline approaches, teary-eyed like her daughters but smiling through them. Dear God, the woman has the strength and endurance of a Mack truck. I'm a wreck, though I'm not crying for a change, and here she is hugging me, thanking me. *Thanking me* for trying to save him at the risk of my own life. And she encourages the girls to thank me, too, which they do with little prompting. Bile rises

in my throat, but damn, if they can bear it, so can I.
I swallow it down.

She rattles on in a mixture of Spanish and English I only half follow until I catch the words "…
tried to tell him. Chest pains, on and off for months.
Little things, he said. Heartburn. No insurance. No
doctors." She shakes her head.

I pat her shoulder, unsure what else I should do,
while Gen gives me a sympathetic look.

No insurance, I understand. When business was
booming a few years back, the construction crew had
a great group plan. These days we were all expected to fend for ourselves. Until the inheritance thing,
I wouldn't go near a doctor unless I was dying. In
fact, that's exactly what it took to get me through a
hospital's doors. Now I have private coverage, like
Genesis, and we're paying an arm and a leg (no pun
intended) for it, but it beats taking risks like Diego
did. Like we all did and most of us still do.

I should talk to Tom about petitioning the company to reinstate the company coverage now that the
economy has improved.

That train of thought derails with a screech of
brakes and a crashing of engines in a head-on colli-
sion. Right. I don't work for them anymore.

I manage to disentangle myself from Diego's
family once they elicit a vague promise to come
to dinner sometime in the future, with no firm date
chosen. I can't imagine what they'll do now. He was
their main source of income, with Rosaline's dress-
making service a nice supplement.

Gen leads me away as family members swarm in, and we go several yards before I notice we're heading in the wrong direction. Instead of going to the car, we're crossing the graveyard, picking our way between headstones, toward a small copse of trees separating two of the plotted areas.

"Um, Gen?"

"We need to talk."

Uh-oh.

She pulls me deep enough into the wooded patch to not be seen by the funeral attendees. I plant myself against one of the oaks, leaning back and crossing my ankles, bracing myself for yet another lecture on beating myself up, taking the blame, quitting my job, abusing the painkillers, whichever topic she's seizing upon today. And I'll take it without argument, because she's right, at least on most counts. I'm just not in the mood to change.

"I want you to draw power from me."

Okay, I didn't expect that.

Chapter 29
Insight

IT TAKES a moment for her full meaning to hit. When it does, a shiver runs from my neck down my spine. "No."

Gen crosses her arms over her chest, and I know I'm in for it. That's her "I'm not budging on this one" pose, and when she strikes it, I lose every time.

"I'm fucking sick of you feeling sorry for yourself."

My eyebrows hit the top of my forehead. Gen never curses. On the rare occasions she does, it's usually at or about me.

"Your friend's death isn't the start of it. It's just the latest in a string of excuses to avoid who you are. You mope around the house. You take too many pills…. Don't you think one addict is enough for one household?" Her voice cracks. I hadn't realized how much my actions affect her.

I haven't paid attention to anyone but myself.

"Everyone's told you you're not to blame for this. You're to be commended, not condemned. If you won't listen to the living, maybe you'll listen to the dead. Now, take the damn pull." She grabs my hands and places them on her shoulders, then grips my forearms. I flinch back, but she's got a tight hold. Her tone softens, though her grasp doesn't. "I need you, Flynn. I need you strong. Maybe I'm being selfish, but I don't care. You're not the same person I fell in love with, and I'm scared I'm losing you."

I'm not the—? "Are you falling out of love with me?" I'm terrified to ask. I have to know.

She shakes her head, strands of red hair falling across her face, but she makes no move to push it back. She'd have to let go of me to do that. "I'll always love you," Gen says. "But you're making it harder than it should be."

Well, shit.

I close my eyes. I search inside for that part of me I avoid like splinters under my nails—that sense of myself that inevitably reaches for my perception of *her*. Not love, not friendship, not affection. A primal connection I've felt on the periphery since the first time her magic collided with mine.

It's duller than I remember, and I wonder if the drugs I'm taking interfere with the power's flow. If I take more, will it—?

No. Stop it, Flynn. You're not hiding behind narcotics.

Isn't that what you've already been doing for a week?

I tell my conscience to shut the fuck up and let my energy touch Gen's. She sucks in a sharp gasp, and my eyes snap open while sparks literally fly between us, though I suspect they're visible to no one but us.

"Careful," she cautions. "Just pull a little. I don't want to end up bedridden again, and vomit will look awful on this dress. I'll tell you when to stop."

I nod. The power drives itself, instinctively seeking what it needs for completion—the magical energy of others. Now that I've done it once, now that I know what I am, it's easier, almost too easy, and my attempts to go slowly, to draw in a gradual stream, quickly give way to a greater rush. The stream becomes a river, the river, an ocean, and I'm filled with it, euphoric with it, unable to stem the tide even if I wanted to.

"Stop. God, Flynn, stop."

I've never been trained. I don't know how.

Gen's voice carries across a great expanse, but I'm caught in the flow, hurtling over cresting waves and crashing on the other sides, each great swell lifting me higher and higher, each drop less frightening, less painful. This second time touching her power, it's so much better than at Centuria Mall. It feels so good….

My muscles tense. My body trembles.

With one great shove, Gen pushes me away, and I slam into the tree, the back of my head cracking sharply on the solid bark.

We stand there, in the late-afternoon heat (and when the hell did it get to be late afternoon?), panting for breath. Gen's bent over, her hands on her knees, her back rising and falling as she draws air into her lungs. I want to touch her, to make sure she's all right, but I'm afraid of hurting her further.

"Say something," I wheeze. My lungs ache like I took a soccer ball to the chest.

At last she raises her head, revealing shadows around her eyes that weren't there before. "That… didn't go… quite like I planned."

A semihysterical laugh escapes me. She moves to my side, letting her hand rest on my arm, letting me know she still trusts me. The power rises a bit at the connection, then flutters and falls, spent.

"That was… intense," I say, for want of a better description. "Orgasmic" might define it best, and the dampness between my legs confirms that, but she pushed me away before the final climax. I'm more than a little frightened of what might have happened if I'd reached it.

Maybe I'm not a succubus in the classic sense, but some similarities definitely exist.

God, that felt good. I'm more vibrant, more alive than I've been in days, maybe weeks. It feels like….

It feels like that little taste of dark magic Gen gave me once, when she accidentally tapped it while making love to me.

"Gen," I say, waiting until I'm sure she's concentrating more on me than her still ragged breathing, "am I evil?"

Her eyes widen, and she wraps her arms around me, pulling me close. "God, no!" Her hand slaps my upper arm, kinda hard. "Don't think that. You're just doing what comes naturally to your skill. But I'll say it again, Flynn. You need training. And I want to attempt it as soon as possible. In the meantime, though—" She tips her chin up, aiming it over my shoulder. "—do you see him?" Gen's last words come out soft and a little sad.

I follow her line of sight to a familiar figure standing between two nearby trees, and a sob breaks through my determination not to cry anymore. Of course it's Diego. Of course that's who wants to speak to me. And I knew that when Gen asked me to pull from her power. But it's still a shock.

He looks as he did before the heart attack: same work clothes, same paternal expression, though I sense a touch of disapproval in his gaze, and I lower my head. "I'm sorry. I—"

"Oh no. None of that," Diego interrupts my apology. "In the years I've known you, in all the time we've worked together, I've never once been disappointed in you, until today."

The words send me staggering backward, once more cracking my head on the tree. I'm going to have a serious lump there tomorrow. I figured he might feel that way, but I never thought he'd say it out loud. Maybe ghosts have less discretion. I mean, why not? They really have nothing to lose.

The spirit strides to stand in front of me, so real, so solid, I could reach out and touch him, but the flash of anger in his eyes prevents me from throwing my arms around him. I'm tall, but Diego's taller by several inches, and he glares down at me.

"I've never let my daughters, how do you say it? Willow in self-pity. And that includes you."

Oh.

"Wallow," I correct him. It's not sarcasm or attitude. Diego always encouraged me to fix any mistakes he made. He wanted to improve.

Encouraged. Wanted. I hate thinking of him in the past tense.

"Wallow. Thank you." A touch of a smile curls his lips. "Come here," he says and opens his arms.

I step into them, feeling his embrace for what will likely be the last time.

"This is a neat trick you have, seeing and touching the dead," he says into my hair. "I'm glad to get to speak to you."

Me, not so much. Diego and Gen's parents aside, I would be quite happy without it.

"So, no more of this, yes? You quit your job, and I understand why. But you will go get another one, for at least until things change with your arm, your leg. You will take your medication only when necessary. You will let your lover help you with this power. You will visit my sweet Rosaline." His voice breaks on that one, and I pat his back in an awkward movement. "And you will stop beating yourself up with a two-by-four."

I bark a laugh, muffled against his chest, and pull away. "That's a lot of orders."

"I trained you," he says. "I'm allowed to give you orders."

And he's the father I wish I'd had.

"I'll do my best."

"That's all I've ever asked of you."

Chapter 30
Career Move

I'M LEARNING to tend bar.

The Pub's outdoor bartender had to go part-time. Sheila's taking care of an elderly mother, and she can't work the afternoon shifts, so over the next couple of weeks, I pull out and iron my black slacks and white button-down and haul my sorry ass to the Village Pub for bartending lessons from Chris. The staff knows me. I worked there briefly a few months back. And the transition flows smoothly.

Gen's ecstatic. Tending bar sure as hell beats construction work for safety. And I have to admit, the job's kinda fun.

I don't have to walk farther than the length and breadth of the bar, so my leg holds up well. I've learned to spot the signs when my arm's about to go dead (around once a week), so I don't drop a lot of bottles, and I think the gig helps with my shyness. Through Gen and Chris and general hanging out there, I already know a lot of the regulars, and I'm good with names and faces. Making small talk is an art, and I'm a novice, but I'll get better. Everyone comes to the Pub, from the lawn service guys to the golf pros and movie stars who own mansions scattered around town.

And when there's a Yankees game on the widescreen, you can't tell the difference between them.

I'm learning a lot about baseball, and I might even grow to like it. Someday. But probably not the Yankees.

The cooler air of late September dries the touch of sweat on my brow. Busy day, lots of customers, and I've been in nonstop motion from noon on. In the corner of my eye, a newcomer steps into the bar's courtyard, and I turn to take his order. And freeze.

The phrase "dead man walking" takes on a whole new meaning.

Peter shambles to the bar, hauling his emaciated body onto one of the stools with more than a little effort, and in the end, I reach across the polished wood surface to steady him before he slides off the seat. His hair has thinned so much, scalp shows through in a number of places. Craters darken the skin beneath his eyes. His hands tremble so badly he can't hold the one-hundred beers list and has to set it on the bar to read it.

"What... happened to you?" Not the most polite question, and I already know the answer, but my shock outweighs sense.

"You happened," he says without bitterness in that rich British accent, only it's not so rich anymore. It's wavery and a little hard to understand.

My eyebrows rise. In his place, I'd hate me.

I take his order, a hearty stout, and set it in front of him. "On the house."

"No," he says, eyes crinkling and a touch of the old humor in his voice. "On the bar."

I smile at the joke and leave to tend to a few more customers. Mostly Buds and Bud Lites on draft. There's something about a baseball game and cheap American beers, but I don't really get it. We have over one-hundred varieties, including my favorite vanilla porter, and these wealthy men and women prefer to drink what amounts to fizzy, mildly alcoholic, brownish water.

The Yankees score. A cheer goes up. A glass hits the patio.

Damn.

"Sorry about that," the red-faced man in an old Jeter jersey calls to me. "Too much team spirit, I guess."

Too many spirits in general, judging from his unsteady stance.

One more frequent casualty of baseball—a lot of glassware.

Not spotting any of the busboys outside at the moment, I grab the dustpan and broom and sweep up the mess, all the while casting glances at Peter on the bar's end. He's barely moved, barely touched his glass, just staring at the milling patrons with an occasional scowl at the game. Once I've dumped the shards in a waste bin, the bits clattering in the metal interior, I ask if he needs anything else.

"You know what I need, Flynn. Have you at least done me the courtesy of thinking about it?"

I hate to admit it to anyone besides myself, but I nod once, slowly. "I have." And it's the truth. The Registry sets off all my alarm bells. They're nasty, vindictive, controlling assholes. But Gen knows little about succubi, and the bits of training we've tried haven't done me much good. I need knowledge. I need help. And I'm not getting either anyplace else. I made promises to Diego. I need a way to keep them. "Haven't made a final decision yet. Haven't told anyone but you. So keep it to yourself for now."

The sudden lift of his head, the flare of hope in his eyes, break my heart. "Won't tell a soul," he says, placing a shaky finger over his lips. "And perhaps I can offer a little more incentive." He reaches into a pocket of his knee-length beige cargo shorts, which looked much better on him when he had some meat and muscle on his now spindly legs. Peter pulls out a folded piece of paper and passes it to me.

Unfolding it reveals elegant calligraphied handwriting in black ink curling and swirling across the page:

Ms. Dalton,

I'm certain you find my actions to date distasteful in the extreme, but I hope you'll at least acknowledge the sort of pressure the Registry board can bring to bear on the organization's members.

Since the old saying states more flies may be caught with honey than vinegar, let me try a different approach—come to the October conference, let the board evaluate you, sign the moral and ethical restrictions paperwork... and I'll heal your arm and leg.

Sincerely,

Cassandra Safoir, owner Orlando Match.com

By the time I finish reading the note, I'm shaking more than Peter. And that's saying a lot. Half excitement, half anger. The idea that Cassie could heal me at any time, could have healed me before Diego's accident, makes me want to run the McLaren through her Winter Park office's front window.

But the bottom line is, she can do it.

Unless she's lying to get what she wants.

I lift my head from the note to stare at Peter, superimposing the former image of him from my memory—vibrant, energetic, handsome, quick with a joke or a gallant gesture—over what he's become. If Cassie could give him that quality of life....

She can heal me.

If I'd still been on the fence about the convention at all, I'm certain now. I'm going.

THE REST of the day passes in a blur. I throw myself into the job to keep my mind off the possibility of recovery, but it doesn't work. Drifting thoughts and traitorous hope have me making mistakes: serving the wrong drinks to the wrong customers, staring into space instead of taking orders, even knocking over a beer bottle, the contents barely missing a well-dressed woman's white skirt.

The regulars forgive me and even offer sympathy for whatever's troubling me. The tourists, not so much.

After I present a man with a root beer instead of a rum and Coke, I spot him talking with Chris just inside the Pub's swinging doors. Chris nods and smiles and guides him to the interior bar, where I'm sure the customer receives a free drink—mixed by a different bartender.

The last straw comes when I drop a full bottle of expensive champagne on the very solid patio tile. It shatters, of course, spilling its pricy contents in a wide, bubbling pool. I stand there staring at it, guilty over the waste. Not Dom or Moët et Chandon, but one of the upper echelon of champagnes.

A gentle hand falls on my shoulder. I know it's Chris without pivoting.

"You okay? You've been distracted all day."

No, just since Peter, who left a couple of hours ago, gave me that note.

"I'm sorry. I'll pay for it." I reach for the mop I've left leaning within the square of the bar since I've been using it so frequently, but he catches my arm and pushes it gently down to my side.

"That's not what I asked you. Are you okay?"

I face the concern in his deep brown eyes and wonder, not for the first time, why he hasn't found a life partner for himself. He's the perfect catch: good-looking, considerate, a great listener, hard-working, and well off. Any straight woman should fall all over herself to catch him. And yet he remains single, saying his job takes too much time for relationships.

When he realizes I'm not talking, he signals to one of the waitresses to man the bar and hooks his arm in mine, then leads me inside and into the kitchen. He finds a quiet corner, not easy with all the cooks and waitstaff bustling about, and leans me into it. "Speak, Flynn."

"Woof?"

"No treat until I know what's up." His hand reaches out and grabs one of their signature yeast rolls off a plate on the closest counter. He dangles it in front of my nose.

I want to be offended, but they are fantastic, and I snatch it from his hand and take a large bite. "I've decided to attend the conference," I say around the mouthful.

Twirling a half circle, Chris lets himself flop against the wall beside me. "Oh, thank God."

"What?" I cast him a sidelong glance. "Didn't know you had so much invested in it."

He has the good grace to look sheepish. "We all have," he admits. "Did you think only the bad guys were catching flack from the Registry?"

My mind takes a minute to process. When I put it together, I frown. "They've been pressuring you too?"

"Pretty much daily, but don't tell Genesis I told you. We've held up all right. I'm a null, so there's not much they can do to me, though we've had an inordinate number of roaches and ants, deliveries inexplicably delayed, and a purchasing check that bounced despite plenty of money in the Pub's business account."

God, I hate those people. "You're making me rethink my decision."

He moves to stand in front of me again and rests a palm on each of my shoulders. "You do what *you* want. We'll continue to weather the coercion. It's your choice."

God, I love this man. The rest of what he's said hits home.

"Gen too? I mean, the mall thing was bad, but has there been more?"

"Yeah, but you didn't hear it from me."

I fix him with my best glare. "You know I'm not keeping anything from Genesis." At least nothing I don't want kept for my own reasons.

That actually earns me a smile. "Good. That's how it should be. I'll take the heat. Talk to her about it. She's gotten some additional pressure."

Which might partially explain her outburst with me at the funeral a couple of weeks ago. Not that I didn't deserve it. Not that it didn't help in the long run. I'm happier now. Far from whole, but happier. Still, she usually puts up with my shit, and yelling at me stepped outside her nature. If the Registry applied pressure, I can understand it more.

"What made you change your mind?" he asks.

I swallow hard. "Cassie sent a note. Says she'll heal me if I go to the conference and get her off the hook with them."

"Hmm. Make sure you know the details of that agreement. A permanent healing would be worth it to you, I'm guessing."

It's not a question, but I nod anyway.

"Just be certain permanent is what she's offering, and know exactly what the Registry expects from you. When Gen got elected to the board, they demanded some pretty intense shit, which is why she ended up resigning."

Which they didn't like at all. Yeah, I know the story. Not the details, but the generals.

"I'll be careful." I head for the door to the dining area, but Chris catches my arm for the second time today.

"You do that," he says. "I mean it. You don't have the best track record, Flynn."

Like I didn't know that already.

I COME home to an unfamiliar car in the driveway. Nothing unusual about that. Gen's clients drive all sorts of expensive vehicles, ranging from DeLoreans (my favorite, and I'm half tempted to trade the McLaren in for one of those) to environmentally I-don't-give-a-shit Hummers. Except this one doesn't fit the wealthy customer parameters.

I climb out of the McLaren and circle the beat-up, rusting, nineteen-ninety-something Ford Escort, fond memories of my long-gone Chevy pickup truck curling my lips into a wistful smile. Owning a vehicle like this one and keeping it running earns a certain class of folks an unsung badge of honor. The older the car, the longer it's on the road, the bigger the badge. Your friends might not say a word about it, but inside they're nodding their heads and praising your frugality—and your mechanical hoodoo.

This one looks not long for this world, though. Duct tape and zip ties secure the rear bumper and muffler to the chassis. Crouching down, I spot wire coat hangers holding some of the other parts to the underside. The pronounced rust, if equally prevalent on the undercarriage, will likely eat through the flooring any day now. I could eke a few more months out of her, if she were mine. Keeping the Chevy going taught me some tricks. Maybe I'll tip off the owner if I run into him or her.

I tear myself away and head into the house. Muffled voices carry from the front parlor where Gen does her readings, so I wander to the kitchen. Huh. No dinner. It's seven at night, and Genesis loves to cook, so she usually has leftovers waiting on the table or warming in the oven for me. No, I shouldn't expect it. She holds a job just like I do, and even if she chooses her own hours, I'm not counting on her to take care of me. Fixing myself a sandwich isn't beyond my meager cooking skills.

Roast beef, aged cheddar, mayo, and a dash of salt on rye make for a fine meal, and with my conference decision made, I eat more ravenously than I've done in weeks. Gen's noticed me losing weight. I think it's just muscle. My workout routine has suffered from my weakened arm and leg.

The backyard, in-ground pool beckons, and I figure I'll ask Genesis to join me for a swim and maybe something more, but the voices continue flowing from the front room. A glance at my cell phone tells me they've been in there longer than the average session. I know what Gen charges—fifty dollars for fifteen minutes. No one who drives the Ford Escort outside can afford that kind of money.

When a sudden yelp from my girlfriend reaches my ears, I burst through the door... and skid to a screechy halt on the hardwood floor. Two sets of startled eyes meet mine, one pair belonging to Rosaline, who kneels on a couple of throw pillows, the other Genesis's, who's standing on top of the coffee table.

Wearing a wedding gown.

Chapter 31
Negotiations

"OUTOUTOUTOUTOUT!" ROSALINE shrieks, laughing and shouting at the same time. She pushes to her feet, crosses to where I stand openmouthed in the doorway, and smacks me on the bicep. "Don't you know the rules?"

Rules? What rules?

I duck under Rosaline's arm—no easy feat considering she stands about four inches shorter than me—and stare at Genesis.

Radiant. That's the only word for her. Well, maybe "angelic." Or "mesmerizing." Or—

"Flynn!" she says, blushing a deep pink that contrasts sharply with the white of the gown. White with sparkles, no, rhinestones, sewn into every seam, shimmering like stars each time she shifts her position. God, she's heavenly.

The dress has short sleeves resting off-the-shoulders like that shirt of hers she knows is my favorite, and I wonder if she's having it designed that way just for me. The bodice curves low to reveal the very tops of her breasts, form-fitting to the waist, where it flares into a skirt that's knee-length in front, ankle-length in back. She's barefoot now, but I can imagine heels that will accentuate her already shapely legs, her muscled calves, her tanned skin….

"Earth to Flynn, dammit!" She's giggling, but her tone holds a note of exasperation.

"What?" I ask as Rosaline tackles me from behind, grabbing me around the waist and hauling me toward the hallway. She's short but stout, with muscles built from hard work. I could break her hold if I chose, but she's stronger than I expected.

"You aren't supposed to see the bride in her dress before the wedding," Gen says.

"It ruins the surprise, the mystique," Rosaline adds.

"Nothing will ever ruin that mystique," I tell them both, nodding toward my girlfriend. If anything, she blushes more deeply.

Rosaline wrangles me into the hall and pulls the door shut behind us, but not before Gen calls, "I love you, now stay out!" sending a warm rush throughout my entire body.

Then I'm standing in the dim corridor, alone with Diego's widow.

"Why did you barge in like that?" she asks, hands on her hips.

"I heard Genesis cry out. I thought she'd been hurt."

Rosaline's face softens. "Always the hero," she mutters. "A pin. I accidentally pricked her with one of my hemming pins. Do not worry. No blood was shed. So you like the dress, yes?"

"You do amazing work." It's honest praise. I don't know how to give any other kind.

Her face flushes with pleasure. "Your Genesis, she is indecisive. Had her design narrowed down to three, but could not choose. She showed me pictures. I combined them into what you were not supposed to see. But I am glad you approve."

I nod, a thought occurring to me. "It's almost finished. You've been sneaking over here for weeks, haven't you?"

"Sí," Rosaline says. "And I might add, *you* have not come to see *us*." She pokes me in the breastbone with one red-painted fingernail, the polish chipping a bit.

By "us" she means herself and Diego's daughters. Whom I promised I'd visit. Nothing like breaking an oath to a dead man and his wife to give myself a massive guilt trip. "I'm sorry," I whisper.

"Do not be. I am just teasing. Genesis and I, we talk. I know some of what you are going through—your arm, your leg. But soon you come, yes? I make those enchiladas you love so much."

My mouth waters at the thought of them, the sandwich I made nothing by comparison. Cheddar cheese, ranchero sauce, sour cream, and homemade guacamole on the side with rice and beans. "Soon," I tell her. My stomach rumbles in confirmation.

She laughs. "Let's make it official. No more—" She waves a hand in the air in a random pattern. "—vagueness. That is the word, right?"

"Right."

"Today is Tuesday, September twenty-seventh. Saturday you will come to my house, you and Genesis, and we will have the enchiladas." She pokes me in the chest again. "Bring salad. I am assuming you can make something as simple as salad?"

I've never tried, but it's just chopping stuff up, right? How hard can it be? "Sure," I tell her.

"And while you are there, we will discuss what *you* intend to wear to your wedding. Because if I know you at all, I'm betting you have not yet even considered it."

"Um," I say, shuffling my boots on the tile. "When, exactly, *is* this wedding?"

Rosaline's hands fly to cover her mouth just as the parlor door swings open and Genesis emerges. She's changed into a denim miniskirt and a black T-shirt with metallic blue stars all over it. Cute.

"October thirtieth," she informs me, bringing the conversation back to the big event.

"And Flynn didn't know?"

Gen shrugs. "She told me to plan it."

And Genesis took me at my word and ran with it. My own fault, and I'm not angry, just flustered. Chris suggested the wedding might take place in October. I hadn't thought she could pull it all together so fast, but money talks, and we have plenty of that.

"In Atlantic City," she finishes.

I run the dates in my head. "Two days after your birthday, and in the middle of the Registry's conference. How did you know I'd agree to go?"

"The cards told me."

"Of course they did," I mutter, frowning.

Rosaline looks from one of us to the other, realizes this conversation doesn't involve her, and disappears through the open door into the parlor. She's gathering her things: pin cushion, sewing kit, a huge bundle in a zippered ivory plastic bag I'm assuming to be the gown. When she has it all, she pushes between us and heads at a brisk pace for the front door. "Saturday," she calls.

Gen hurries after her, I suspect as much to escape my displeasure as to help Rosaline with her exit.

"Hey," I say, "if you don't mind, I'll bring some tools and patch up a few things on that Escort."

"That would be wonderful," Rosaline agrees, and she's gone.

Pivoting slowly, Genesis turns back to me.

"I think," I begin, leaning against the wall and getting comfortable, "you'd better give me some details on this wedding you've planned. Because," I add when she opens her mouth, "it's definitely sooner, and probably a lot bigger and fancier than I really expected."

Chapter 32
Fate

"SO, SHE'S decided to attend after all. Whom do we have to thank for that?" Nathaniel asked, speaking into the microphone pickup and facing the computer's camera lens.

On the screen, President Linda Argyle straightened in her office chair. She'd called from their main building in Atlantic City rather than her oceanfront home. Behind her, a bay window showed glittery casino signs and high-rises. "Me, of course," she said, preening. "It was my idea to place the bad luck spells on Chris McTalish's business and send Genesis a string of clients who wanted contact with those deceased through violent means."

Nathaniel shivered despite himself. He couldn't see spirits clearly or speak with them, but his contact with those so inclined told him all he needed to know about violent demises and seances. The medium, in this case, Genesis, tended to experience whatever caused the ghosts' deaths. It might be only briefly, while the spirit settled into its host body, but it was never pleasant.

"Oh, I suppose we'll have to toss Cassandra some bit of compensation as well. I'll stop the computer virus spell caster from messing with her online dating business. Was rather amusing having all those heteros matched with homosexuals, complete with the incorrect photo cross-references, though."

"Yes, I'm sure it was hilarious," Nathaniel said dryly. Sometimes Linda's flair for punishment pushed the radius of his moral compass.

"All worth it." She tapped her nails against something solid off camera, probably the desktop, the repetitive noise grating on his nerves. "In less than a month, we'll have Flynn Dalton under our control. In the meantime, however, I have a couple of tasks for you."

Uh-oh. Tasks meant trouble. He'd had enough of that. He'd lost his job as a high-end restaurant host due to the hours he'd already taken working for Linda. Yes, her assignments paid well, but they couldn't compensate for steady income. "I hope they're brief," he ventured. "I'm job hunting."

She leaned in to the lens, resting her chin on her crossed arms. "Are you suggesting the Registry doesn't come first?"

Nathaniel practically threw himself backward in his own chair. Anything to escape those demanding eyes. "No," he said. "But I have to have money to maintain my position here. Rent, food, gas, they all cost."

"You'll be paid well for these jobs," she assured him and began ticking off the duties on her fingers. "One, I want you to continue to keep an eye on Flynn Dalton. Let me know of any other usage of her skills or if any new talents emerge."

Nathaniel smiled with satisfaction. If Linda had this many concerns about Flynn, that meant she believed the woman to be a succubus, just as he'd said. Nice to be right once in a while. In fact, she seemed to almost have too much concern. He wondered exactly what the board president had discovered in her trip to the archives.

"I haven't finished tracing her heritage," Linda continued. "I've got two of my best local people on it. What little I've found indicates a strong magical lineage. Secondly, find a man named Ferguson Brigham. He's likely the father and formerly one of us, and I think he's been up to something in the archives."

Nathaniel's eyebrows rose at that. The archives were known as one of the Registry's most secure locations.

"Nothing definitive," Linda said, reading his expression. "Just a feeling. No luck with finding the mother yet. Might be a null. Might not. Lots of Daltons in the world. We'll keep searching. She's bound to turn up sooner or later. Also, it seems I've picked up a ghost."

Ah yes, the pixelated poltergeist Nathaniel noticed during their previous online chat.

"I've brought in a channeler. According to her, Leopold VanDean, of all people, wants something from me. So far, his spirit hasn't regained enough psychic strength to communicate, but I'm assured that's who this ghost is."

Nathaniel tapped his chin. "Odd. VanDean died of a heart attack. He shouldn't be having power issues in spirit form."

"Exactly. Unless that's not the true cause of his demise. Look into it."

He nodded. To Nathaniel's knowledge, the only sort of death that could cause such a significant drain in psychic energy would be a magical one. Which left one very important question: Who was responsible for that death?

Chapter 33
Out of Element

TWO DAYS later, I'm still reeling over Gen's wedding plans. "I can't believe I'm getting married in a casino," I mutter as I settle onto the throw pillows in the parlor. It's harder and harder for me to maneuver my injured leg into an Indian-style position, but it's Gen's preferred seating arrangement for our practice sessions. And sitting prevents falling over if things go wrong.

"You aren't," she says with an exasperated sigh. "The wedding is at One Atlantic in Atlantic City. Beautiful views. The *reception* is at the casino."

Like that makes a whole lot of difference. Either way, it still means a big, flashy party with me as half the center of attention. I grumble something noncommittal and stretch my arms behind my back, cracking the tightness out of it.

Gen thinks she's compromising, and I suppose in a way, she is. The actual ceremony will be rather low-key, especially for her, with a few close friends and family members at One Atlantic. We then travel by limo to Harrah's Atlantic City Casino Resort, where we meet up with the rest of our friends, coworkers, and apparently a fourth of the guest list of the Psychic Registry Convention (the ones Gen likes), which happens to be taking place in the same resort.

She's rented out both the pool reception area—an indoor balcony overlooking the glass-dome-covered pool and holding about a hundred people—and a second ballroom of a more traditional nature with vaulted ceilings and gilded mirrors and other kitsch that can accommodate a hundred more. Where she thinks we're finding all these guests, I have no idea. But between my bowling alley friends, my construction site friends, our friends from the Village Pub (both local residents and coworkers), her Registry friends, her regular client list, and a few scattered others, Gen assures me we'll fill both spaces.

She's chartered a private plane to fly the Floridians up and back, along with booking (and paying for) a block of rooms for them in the casino hotel, so our less-than-wealthy acquaintances (mostly mine) don't need to worry about funding the trip.

I roll my eyes at the thought of it all while Genesis fetches the tarot cards from the wooden cabinet and passes them into my hands. The tiniest of electric shocks transfers from the cards to me, but otherwise, I detect no affinity for them. These are Gen's focus, not mine. But when she's trying to help me work on controlling my power, she says they help her concentrate.

Shuffling them, I consider the other wedding details—she's picked flowers, colors (pink and ivory, gah), and a strawberry cake with cream cheese icing, which happens to be my favorite and also fits the color scheme. I think it's a consolation prize for putting up with the glamour and glitz. She's hired a photographer and a videographer. She's bought me a ring, which I'm not allowed to see until the big day. She's even taken care of the nondenominational reverend, though that's supposed to be my job, and since we're going to be in Atlantic City anyway, it's kind of a given that we'll honeymoon there, so I don't have to plan that either.

My duties? Dress myself appropriately and pick someone to give me away at the ceremony. I already have the ring. The engagement ring I gave Gen came as part of a wedding set. Rosaline's handling my clothes. We're doing what she calls a strategic planning session before dinner at her place this Saturday, though the idea that she feels the need to call it that does give me some pause.

No, the biggest issue here is someone to stand in for my dad in the wedding, because there's no way we're going with the real thing, and Mom, even if she did approve of my orientation, doesn't possess the mental stability. I'm starting to sense a theme in my parentage.

My first choice of replacements would be Chris, but he's obviously giving Genesis away, and doing so for both of us would look a little strange to the officiator.

Diego would have come second, but, well, he's gone, and even with my new skills and Genesis's talent, I don't think a ghost guest would go over well.

Which pretty much leaves me shit out of luck. I mean, I could ask my former boss, Tom, and that's probably who I'll go with, but hell. It's more than a little depressing to really have no one closer to me to fill that role.

"Flynn, whatever's wrong, it's not the tarot's fault."

"Huh?" I glance up from shuffling, shoving the two stacks into a semi-neat pile with more force than necessary. "Oh, sorry."

"Something on your mind?" She reaches and takes them from me, laying them out in the familiar pattern.

"No." The catch in my voice surprises me. The burning in my eyes makes it worse. I order myself to get a fucking grip. Weddings are supposed to be happy occasions.

Gen peers into my face, and I know she sees right through me, but she shakes her head, letting it go. "Try to relax," she says, flipping over one card at a time. "You know this won't work otherwise."

"I know." I take a slow breath and let it out, then close my eyes. The cards don't matter to my skills, and I don't like seeing what my future holds, anyway. They're only there to help Genesis keep her own concentration.

"Okay, let's try this again," she says without impatience. "The more you practice, the more control you'll have. And the Registry's expert teachers can help you refine things even more."

"Right." We've been working on me tapping just the slightest touch of her power, pulling a… taste, so to speak, and then cutting the connection before I give in to the desire for more. I've only made her sick once since we began training. Since then, I've managed, with varying levels of success, to break away. More often than not, I still take too much, enough to weaken her and leave her exhausted for hours. I hate this, but she swears it's necessary.

"Let's try something different. We've only narrowed in on the power itself. Maybe if we broaden things, you won't overpull. Focus on me, my voice, my being," she whispers. "Not just the power. Picture me in your mind, everything you know of me, mentally, physically."

The last comes with a little giggle, and I smile. Yeah, I can do that.

In my mind, I undress her, pulling the short-sleeved gray summer sweater she's wearing over her head and running my callused hands back down her rib cage. I unfasten her leather belt and ease her white capris over her hips, leaving her in just her lacy white bra and panties.

"Are you picturing me, Flynn?" she asks.

"Oh yeah." It's more of a growl than an intelligible response.

She laughs again. "Good. Keep forming the image in your mind, but don't try to tap my energy yet."

I nod, knowing her eyes are open even though mine aren't, and in my head, finish removing her undergarments, leaving her naked and beautiful and—

A sudden surge of pure, raw need courses through my veins, sending waves of the most intense desire I've ever known flowing outward from my core. I snap my eyes open. The sensation has manifested as a visible wall of fiery electrical power, and it's moving toward Genesis.

"Shit!" I mentally grab for it as she reels backward. I pull the energy into myself as fast as I can, but it's too much. It overflows my senses, deafening me to the words Gen's trying to form. Her mouth moves, but I hear nothing. My limbs tremble. My body heats, then breaks into a cold sweat. If I don't find someplace to dump the excess, I have no idea what will happen to us, but I'm certain it won't be good.

My mind scrambles for a solution, skimming through everything Genesis has taught me in the past few weeks, and screeches to a halt on a tiny bit of information.

Nature. She says a psychic's power comes from within, but also from nature. If I can get power from there, maybe I can dump it there too.

As my vision clouds, then darkens to black at the edges, I use every bit of control I have to *push* the energy from me, aiming it into the backyard, the trees, the grass, the weeds, whatever. I'm aware of my body rocking, slipping, sliding to the side. I impact the pillows on my bad shoulder. My head misses the cushions and smacks the wood floor. Wincing at the pain, I fade into nothing.

Chapter 34
Formative Years

NEXT THING I know, I'm standing outside in the dark, the solid concrete of the sidewalk coming up to meet my knees as they buckle. The impact hurts. A lot. But it grounds me too (no pun intended).

I can't say I'm used to my spirit *walking* without the rest of me, but at least I now know how to recognize it when it happens—disorientation, mild dizziness, a distinct sense of fish-out-of-water syndrome.

The weirdest part is being able to touch, to feel the world around me even when my physical body lies unconscious on Genesis's parlor floor. According to her research, most walkers can't make that contact, but I'm powerful. Lucky me. And oh, Genesis must be panicking right about now.

My first thought is, in my efforts to push the excess power into the natural, outside world, I somehow pushed my spirit out as well. I recognize the street I stand on. It's Festivity Avenue, though not quite the one I remember. I'm in front of the school, the one right across from the downtown area, but it's different, and it takes me a moment to figure out why.

Festivity K-12 School.

I read the sign out front of the multiple two-story buildings over and over again before it hits me. Festivity School isn't a K-12. It's a K-8. The sign has changed.

Not something I'd normally notice, but Gen's told me about her high school days, attending the school when the town first got built. She'd gone there from grades seven through twelve, was part of their last graduating class before a separate high school was constructed—the one out on the edge of town where my guys are finishing up those apartment buildings.

Across from the K-12, the newer town homes stand half-complete, though they've been inhabited for at least five years; the trees form less of a canopy across the road because they're shorter.

What is happening?

I focus on the school. Ah, high school. I remember my high school days none too fondly. An image of my younger self forms in my mind.

A chilling wind catches the branches, rustling them in the darkness. It's one of those freakish late-fall Florida nights when the temperature actually drops into the fifties, and I pull my red-and-black letterman jacket closer around my—

What the fuck?

I stare down at the almost forgotten jacket, a high school treasure I lost when I first moved from

New Jersey to attend the University of Florida. My palms rove over the leather sleeves and down the wool front with the big P.H.S. for Pennington High School on the breast. Girls didn't normally get them, but I'd asked for it when in my junior year I led the swim team to a state championship, and my coach arranged it for me. Valued it even more when I had to quit the team to take care of Mom.

Moving more slowly, I zip it and examine the rest of myself: white sneakers, blue jeans, black T-shirt hanging just below the jacket. I raise my hands to my hair, feeling around the nape of my neck—the *bare* nape of my neck. I haven't had short hair since I was a teenager, still trying to decide between butch and femme and eventually settling on something in the middle when I got to college.

This is too weird.

Maybe I'm not out of my body after all. Maybe I passed out, or I'm dreaming. Nothing else explains all this. But why would I dream about Festivity's past? In my teenage body? And the better question: How do I wake myself the fuck up? My teenage years kinda sucked. I really don't want to relive them.

One thing I've learned about dreams, they take you where they want to. Might as well start walking.

As if drawn, I head toward the school gym— separate from the classroom buildings and almost a block away. The original builders had considered aesthetics over practicality, leaving a wide expanse of forest "conservation" in between and forcing students to get even more exercise hiking back and forth from one site to the other.

I wonder what time it is. No foot traffic and very few cars. I haven't encountered anyone else since my "arrival." Then a low moan reaches my ears.

I follow the sound to an open window in the side of the gym, one of those storm windows that opens outward using a crank handle, and then only a few inches. But there's no mistaking the soft, repeated moans or the likely cause of the sensual noises. They're feminine, and there's more than one.

Ooookay.

Figuring I'm supposed to, I locate the nearest entry—a set of double doors with the right one standing ajar. Upon further inspection, I discover the interior push bar has a bit of twisted metal in its lock, preventing it from closing fully. I step into the even darker darkness of a short corridor leading to another set of doors at the end and flanked on either side by entries to the men's and women's locker rooms.

Well, I heard girls, so I enter the left one and stand, listening for further guidance.

Nothing. Silence. Rows and rows of lockers block my view beyond the row I'm standing in. Pale streetlight shines through frosted glass windows set at intervals along the walls, including the window that I found half-open.

Maybe they left. Or maybe dreams don't follow logic.

Nothing else in my life does.

"God, that feels good," a hushed female voice sighs. "Do that again." Some rustling follows the request, along with another moan.

My hormonally charged teenage body responds to the sounds and implications, dampness forming between my legs. It figures this succubus stuff would trigger wet dreams. If I interrupt the girls, maybe they'll stop and I can wake up.

And find Genesis, fast.

I sneak forward to the end of the row, careful not to squeak my tennis shoes on the tile, and lean my head around the corner.

As I figured, two girls lean against a small expanse of wall between banks of lockers. The one facing out has long blond hair curling down and hiding what I'm certain would be a beatific expression. The other has darker hair—red, maybe—and faces away from me, toward the subject of her attentions. They both wear school uniforms—short, dark pleated skirts in a color indistinguishable with all the shadows, and button-down long-sleeved white shirts. A couple of jackets lie discarded on a bench running the length of the aisle.

The redhead has her lips pressed to the blond's, one hand inside her untucked blouse, obviously fondling a breast, though I can't see that with her body between us, and the other hand resting on the blond's hip. They continue making out for several minutes, me feeling like a total voyeur but unable to tear myself from the sight. My own nipples harden beneath my jacket and T-shirt, and I resist the urge to touch them.

At last they break for air, both panting, the sound very loud in the echoing locker room. I wish the redhead would turn around. She's petite and curvy and soft in all the right places, and I'd love to get a look at her face.

"Let's try a different experiment," she says, and I can practically hear the wicked grin in her voice… and something else too. Something familiar.

My brain works on piecing it together while my body does all it can to distract me. The redhead's hand leaves the blond's waist and slides up from her thigh to vanish beneath her miniskirt. She lowers her head, using her other hand to open the blouse farther. Soft kisses and then gentle suckling sounds carry throughout the room.

I know the second the redhead's searching fingers reach their lower goal, because the blond suddenly stiffens, jerking backward and flinging an arm to the side to clang against one of the lockers. She clamps her hands on her partner's shoulders, then, to my surprise, pushes her away.

"Genesis, um, hey, maybe we should stop."

Chapter 35
Time Walker

GENESIS....

I grab for the nearest wall, glad they're too focused on each other to hear the thud I make when I lean into it. I can still see them, barely, around the corner, from where I stand.

Dream. Dream. It must be a dream. Gen told me about her first girl-girl affair, a "fumbling, awkward teenage thing" resulting in her partner leaving her at the end. In fact, she said her second attempt had ended much the same way.

But why in hell am I dreaming about this?

"Stop?" Gen says, tone a mixture of hurt, confusion, and anger. "Why? This was your idea, remember?"

"I know. And it was a bad one." The blond straightens, tossing her long hair over her shoulders, and I receive my second shock of the night.

Cassie. It's Cassie. Younger, less painted, less polished, hair a little darker, but there's no mistaking that face. At Atlantic Dance, Cassandra indicated she knew Genesis, and Gen had confirmed it. Now I knew exactly how.

"There's something wrong with us," Cassie goes on, fingers working to button her shirt. "We're not normal." She pauses, hands stilling. "No, scratch that. *You're* not. *I'm* not giving up my life, my reputation, my family."

"You weren't worried about that a minute ago!" Gen puts her hands on her hips, but the posture doesn't fool me. Her voice broke on those words.

"It didn't hit home until a minute ago."

It didn't hit home until Gen touched her sex and Cassie realized how much she liked it, I'm thinking. Yeah, that can be a real eye-opener. One not everybody can handle, especially as a teen.

"Your brother can't afford to push you away, not with your parents dead," Cassie continues, ignoring Gen's gasp at the mention of her folks.

God, what a bitch. Genesis looks about eighteen, meaning she lost her parents only two years back.

"I'm not losing mine." Cassandra snatches her jacket off the bench and tugs it on with one vicious pull. Fully dressed, she faces Genesis with an angry scowl. "Don't talk to me at school. Don't sit with me at lunch. I've already heard the whispers. You're not influencing me anymore."

"Influencing *you*?" Gen's voice is incredulous. "What the *fuck*!" she shouts, stunning everyone in the room. Cassie flinches back, but not in time to avoid the hard shove Gen gives her, sending her careening into the bank of lockers with a resounding metallic slam. "*You* flirted with *me*."

Given what I understand of Cassie's love magic, I don't doubt it. I wonder if Cassie even knows yet about the power she holds. I wonder if Gen knows.

"You knew about the broken door," Gen goes on. "You planned this whole night, down to the last detail. Now you're blaming me because you're too chickenshit to accept who you are. Well, fuck you. Someday you'll figure it out, that you can't change." A flash of green lights her furious eyes.

The dark magic.

Shit. Two years after her parents' deaths, maybe mere months since she used the dark powers to save her brother's life. She'd still be fighting off that addiction, struggling to overcome the need.

But it's a dream, I remind myself.

No, it's not, a little voice screams in my head. Too real. It's all too real. And if it's real, how the hell am I going to get back? I have to have contact with my physical body to rejoin it. At least that's how it worked the last time. But my physical body at this point would be... I do the calculations in my head. Gen's a senior in high school. I'm five years older. Just graduated college, settled in Kissimmee.

Physically, I'm halfway across Osceola County.

Fuck. Really hope this is a dream.

"What... what's wrong with your eyes?" Cassie whispers. Faced with Gen's rage, she's lost control of the situation—a circumstance I suspect, even at that age, she's unfamiliar with.

Cassie's question has an immediate effect on Genesis. Gen blinks, rubbing at her eyes with both fists before sagging onto the center bench.

"Nothing," she says, defeated, the tears falling at last. "Just go."

Which presents me with a whole new problem. I stand between Cassie and the door.

If it's a dream, it won't matter. If it's not... I have no idea.

Cassie takes her chance at escape, whirling toward the exit, rushing toward... and through... me. A shock passes through us both at the contact. I feel her body tremble literally within mine while my stomach turns over uncomfortably. Then she's past. She pauses only a second, staring into the space I occupy without focusing on me at all. With a sharp intake of breath, she breaks for the locker room door and disappears into the dark hallway beyond.

I exhale, which, given I'm a dream or a spirit, seems pretty bizarre. I still don't know either way. If I'm out of body and somehow really here in Gen's past, Cassie would neither be able to see nor touch me. At least in my admittedly limited prior experience with this shit, nothing with a spirit of its own, with the exception of a psychic with an affinity for spirits, like Genesis, can have contact with my out-of-body form. Of course, if I'm a mere dream.... God, my brain hurts, trying to sort it all out.

I stop trying and listen to Gen's sobs. I hate feeling helpless, but what can I do in this state, whatever this state is?

After several minutes of convulsive crying, mixed with the hiccups she always gets when she cries, she reaches beneath the bench, dragging out an overnight bag I hadn't noticed before, then cries some more. Figures. If she'd been planning to spend the night with Cassie, either here—though I can't imagine how that would have been comfortable—or at Cassie's house, then a reminder that she needed to go home likely dug the knife of rejection in deeper.

Gen unzips the bag and digs through its contents, coming up with something thin and plastic with a flash of metal I can't quite make out. She stands on shaky limbs and stumbles toward the women's showers, vanishing from my line of sight. A light snaps on, temporarily blinding me. Guess she doesn't care anymore if someone catches her here. The squeal of heated water rushing through metal pipes carries back to me.

She's taking a shower? Now? Washing off Cassie's scent, maybe. Or the taint of the evening. But it doesn't feel right. And what had she pulled from her bag?

When my sight clears, I follow the sound around the corner, where steam flows in a vision-blurring cloud from one of the stalls.

Yeah, high school gym class. Showering surrounded by naked teenage girls, no curtains, open to ridicule, or in my case, the embarrassment of getting turned on by all the tits and ass and praying like hell no one noticed.

Still fully dressed, Gen has her face turned to the spray pouring from a nozzle on the right-hand wall of the stall. She's rolled her sleeves up and holds her hands out before her, one clutching the thin object, the other letting the water fall through her spread fingers. The bare bulb overhead glints off the object's flat metal end.

And suddenly I know exactly what she's holding, and what she intends to do with the blade of that razor.

Chapter 36
Once More a Hero

I HAVE seconds to act, and I do the only thing I can think of. I feel around the corner of the wall and flip off the lights.

Three things happen at once: we're plunged into darkness, Gen shrieks, and the razor clatters on the tiles. Thank God.

"I didn't figure you for a coward and a hypocrite," I say, my voice threatening to crack. Damn, that was too close. What would have happened if I hadn't been here? I'm more and more convinced I've traveled through time as well as out of body. Gen's alive in the future, so she must not have gone through with the suicide attempt, but it sure looked like she planned to.

And shit, I still don't know how I'm getting home.

"Who... who's there?"

Heart pounding, I answer her. "A friend... I hope."

The water shuts off. Squishy footsteps approach. She steps around the corner, back to where the lockers are. Her face comes into the dim light from the windows. She peers at me through the shadows. When her hand reaches for the switches on this side of the wall, I catch her wrist to stop her.

"Don't. You're just asking to get caught. Personally, I don't need a rap sheet." I also don't need her seeing me clearly. In five years, I'll meet her at the Pampered Pup festival, and she'll ask me out for the first time. No way do I want to mess that up, and I've watched enough science fiction to know how badly I could screw with the time lines. I let her go and take a seat on the central bench, waiting to see what she'll do.

Her head tilts to one side. Droplets of water patter on the floor at her feet. "What's your name?"

"F-Fran," I stammer, almost giving myself away. Not too many girls named Flynn. If I tell her the truth, she might still put it together in the future.

"Where did you come from? You don't go to school here."

Right. Fran's not a popular name either. She'd recognize it if we were in the same grade. "I'm visiting friends in town. Thought I'd check out the school. Heard noises and investigated."

"Spied, you mean." Her tone's accusatory. "What are you, a peeping Tom?"

I don't blame her. I *was* spying. "Nope, a peeping Fran."

Genesis laughs despite herself, but she hasn't come any closer. It's dark. She's rattled. I want to hold her, tell her it's okay, but I'm a stranger to her. Doesn't stop me from speaking, though.

"She's wrong, you know," I say, feeling my way.

"Huh?"

"That girl. The idiot who ran off. She's wrong about you. There's nothing the matter with you. You're perf—" I catch myself. "You're beautiful." *Not much better, Flynn.* But I can't help it. Gen tried to kill herself. I can't fathom what went through her head, but I'm determined to erase it. "Anyone who can't see that is a moron who doesn't deserve you."

Genesis lets that sit a minute. I can almost see the wheels turning. She shuffles over and drops onto the end of the bench, keeping distance between us, but still, it's a step. "Are… are you gay?"

It's a bold question to ask a stranger, but given what I've been saying, I'm not too surprised. "If I say yes, will that make things better or worse?" One thing to have a person come upon you while you're making out with another girl. Quite another for that person to likely have been affected by what you were doing.

"I'm not sure," she admits. Well, she's always been honest. Wish I could say the same.

"Fair enough. Yeah, I'm a lesbian. Hate me, now?"

"You saved my life. I can't hate you."

Right. Flynn the hero.

She goes on, "That wasn't really me, you know. The whole suicide thing. I wasn't thinking clearly. There were… other influences involved."

Gen must mean the dark magic. Maybe it exacted a punishment for her touching it. But I can't admit understanding that without giving a whole lot more about myself away. So I shrug and do my best teenager impression. "Whatever. Just glad I was here."

"How old are you?" she asks.

"Eighteen." And the lies just keep on coming. Then again, I'm *physically* eighteen. Just not mentally. So, not a total lie. "You too, right?" God, if I just watched a minor making out....

"Just turned."

Whew. Dodged a bullet there.

"And you're comfortable with who you are," she adds. It's not a question, but I answer it anyway.

"Completely. I don't march in parades and wave rainbow banners, but I'm out, and I'm pretty obvious." Not at eighteen. At eighteen, I kept things on the down low. Friends knew. Mom knew but stayed in denial. I didn't get blatant about it until a few years later. I don't shout it from rooftops, but anyone with half a brain would figure it out. At least working for Chris, it's not necessary to hide in order to stay employed.

"No one else is gay or bi in my school. No one except Cassie, and she—Well, you saw what she did."

"They're there. They just aren't admitting it yet. Most people come out in college."

"But not you. You were brave."

Not as brave as you think, Gen. I've got my hands clamped between my knees so she won't see the way they're still trembling from a few minutes ago.

She turns her face toward me, the moonlight catching the green of her eyes (normal now), her wet hair and skin glistening, her white blouse soaked and semi-transparent. So fucking sexy. "You think… you think you could tell me about it?"

I shake myself, blinking to refocus. "If you promise you won't try that stunt with the razor again, yeah. I'd be glad to."

Chapter 37
Any Port in a Storm

THE RAIN gave Genesis McTalish's castle-like mansion an even more foreboding ambiance, making Cassie shiver in the cool night air. She held her black umbrella over her head and tromped along the stepping stones to the front door, her high heels slipping on the wet walkway.

"Fucking psychics and their theatrics," she muttered. "Couldn't have a simple sidewalk like everyone else." Under the awning, she shook off the rain and closed the umbrella, then pressed the doorbell, which chimed a deep, resonant gong far within the house.

She'd come out here to double-check Flynn's intentions of attending the conference. The Registry received the woman's RSVP—tattered, torn, taped together, and stained with garbage, according to Cassie's New Jersey friends—but she had to make certain it wasn't some ruse to buy more time. Trust but verify. Her livelihood depended upon it.

And the life of her daughter.

One failed marriage, one wonderful result—a beautiful little girl, now four years old and stricken with leukemia. Between the best medical treatment money could buy and Cassie's own potions, she'd kept little Tracy alive and could continue doing so indefinitely.

So long as the Registry left her and her business mostly intact.

Even now, Tracy waited at the hospital for her return. She'd taken a turn for the worse, and though the doctors had stabilized her, they wanted to keep her overnight.

And then the damn Registry had called with this task.

Cassandra squared her shoulders. The sooner she got this over with, the sooner she could return to her daughter's bedside.

Cassie didn't know what she expected from whomever opened the door. Both Flynn and Genesis had plenty of reasons to hate her. She didn't fear the former. Flynn's full recovery hinged on Cassie's ability to heal her. And Genesis wouldn't harm her until that had been completed either. But she braced herself for some sort of animosity.

She certainly didn't expect what she got.

Genesis threw the right-hand wooden door open, letting it slam against the interior wall. Her wild eyes scanned the porch, peering at her visitor in obvious shock. She flipped a switch just inside and bathed the step in yellow light from a flickering fake candle encased in a glass lantern overhead.

"Cassie!"

Cassandra raised an eyebrow. "Yes?"

"You're a healer."

She raised the other eyebrow. "Yes…?"

Gen reached out of the doorway, wrapped both hands around Cassie's forearms, and yanked her into the house. The umbrella clattered onto the stone step, and Cassandra bent toward it, but Gen kept tugging and she had to leave it behind. Ah well, at least she wouldn't drip water all over the entry hall.

"Genesis, what the hell?" Her former schoolmate pulled her along, not stopping for pleasantries or explanations. She made the first left through a door, halting in a cheery parlor decorated with candles, a window settee, and bright-colored throw pillows, along with a cabinet containing more candles, several decks of tarot, and some other occult knickknacks.

But none of that drew Cassie's attention like the familiar woman sprawled across the floor, half on and half off a set of red-and-gold cushions.

Flynn Dalton.

A large dog, some mix of husky and shepherd, pranced in nervous circles around her, whining and darting a tongue out to lick her hands and face.

"Crap." Tossing her purse on the settee, Cassie crossed to Flynn's body and knelt. The dog growled, but Genesis caught its collar and hauled the dog through a door on the far side of the parlor. Cassie caught a quick glimpse of a half bathroom before Gen shut the animal inside and returned to her.

Cassandra took quick stock of Flynn's condition. Pale complexion, shallow, too slow breaths, sporadic tremors in the limbs. Someone had tucked a pillow under her head, presumably Genesis, but judging from the reddened lump on Flynn's temple, she'd initially struck the hardwood floor.

"What happened?" Cassie asked, not turning from the prone figure. Dammit, the woman couldn't die. Not now that the Registry was getting what it wanted from her.

"I don't know." Genesis sounded near collapse herself. "We've been training, trying different things. There was some kind of surge. At first I thought she'd fainted, but I can't wake her. I've tried *everything*…."

Something in that word made Cassie shift her focus to Genesis, whose eyes flickered once, then twice with sparks beyond the normal green. "Jesus, Gen, don't touch the dark." She'd seen that happen once before, all those years ago, in that gym locker room. But that had been before Cassie had known of her own power, or Genesis's, or anyone's. A year later, when the Registry identified Cassie, they'd clued her in on the local talent, even set her to keep an eye on Genesis, who was on probation, but other than that night, Gen had never faltered.

Or had she?

Chapter 38
Alternate Beginnings

"HOW DID you first know you were gay?" Gen asks. She gives a violent shiver on the hard wooden bench, and I remember she's soaked and it's maybe fifty degrees in the gym locker room.

"First things first," I say, grabbing the jacket she'd left on my end of the long seat. "Change. You'll get pneumonia."

"In front of you? You'll see everything."

I give her my most disarming smile. "It's a locker room. And I can already see pretty much everything." The high-set windows might prevent any actual peepers, but they're placed at just the right height to let the streetlights and moonlight shine through. Plenty of shadows, sure, but Gen's wet white shirt leaves little to my imagination. Besides, I've seen it all before, but I won't tell her that. "I'll turn around if you want."

Before I can shift my body in the opposite direction, she catches my arm and stops me. "No, it's okay."

Huh.

"I mean, we're both girls, right?" The tiny smile tells me she knows what she's saying.

Now, that's more like the Genesis I fell in love with—complete sexual confidence and a tendency toward the wild side. "Right. Both girls." I swallow hard, the room warming by a few degrees as she removes her shirt, button by button. She hesitates over the bra, a brief flash of modesty turning her away from me while she reaches back and unhooks it, then drops it to join her shirt on the bench. Without facing me, she takes the jacket from my suddenly nerveless fingers and slips it over her shoulders. Gen pulls it around herself but doesn't bother zipping it, so when she turns back to me, I get tantalizing, teasing glimpses of soft, pale skin.

Her smile has broadened to that familiar wicked grin. I have no doubt she knows exactly what she's doing to me.

"To answer your question," I begin, my eyes glued to the space between the two sides of the zipper. I have to stop, clear my throat, and force my gaze to meet hers. She giggles. I ignore it. "I just knew. Are you asking because you aren't sure of yourself? Is that what this thing with the blond was all about? Some kind of test?"

Gen looks away, a blush turning the skin of her cheeks a shade darker in the moonlight. Her right sneaker traces patterns on the concrete floor, scuffling softly. "I guess," she admits. "I mean, I like guys. But girls… they do something special to me, you know?" She stops herself, blushing deeper. "Duh. Of course you know."

Yeah, I know. Like right now. Teenage Genesis is so damn cute. I wish I'd known her then. I think it would have helped both of us through some difficult times.

"I just want to be sure," she goes on. "I don't want to start something with someone, lead them on, and then…." Gen trails off, and I'm sure she's thinking of what Cassie just did to her.

"Well," I say, straightening on the bench and summoning my best counseling voice. Why is this so difficult? I've done this before, with my boss, Tom's, sister. Except that was over the phone and by email. It's a helluva lot harder in person.

It's a helluva lot harder when it's Genesis and I'm in love with her.

"Tell me what you like about girls," I say, my words coming out huskier than I intend.

Her features soften, changing her expression from nervous to almost dreamy. "It's hard to put my finger on it. I like the curves, and the way they smell, and their softness…." Gen glances at me from the corner of her eye. "Although I'm finding I like the slightly harder variety too."

Oh, dear God.

Before I can say another word, she leans in closer, so close her lips fill half my vision. "I really like the effect I'm having on you."

My breath catches, and she blinks up at me, studying my face.

"I *am* what's making you breathe like that, right?" she asks.

"Um, yeah."

"And it's not just the letterman jacket heating you up?" Gen touches my cheek with her fingertips, ice to my fire, tracing the cheekbone, then curling around behind my neck. It's one of my erogenous zones. With my shorter haircut, it's even more sensitive, and I shiver beneath her touch.

"No, not just the jacket," I admit in a hoarse whisper.

"I'm not the only one who's wet, am I?"

Oh, wow. Just… wow. I guess innocent and vulnerable time is over.

Chapter 39
Back and Forth

I'M ACTUALLY about to answer her question, in the affirmative, when she giggles.

I've been played.

I have to chuckle with her. It's either that or kiss her, and I'm not making first moves, here. Mentally, I'm twenty-eight. She's eighteen, inexperienced, and virtually untouched. If anything happens tonight, it's got to be her call.

Except she's fast wearing down my resolve.

"Sorry," Gen says, regaining the ability to speak. "Your face. You should have seen your expression when I said that." She erupts into another fit of the giggles.

I grind my teeth a little. Eighteen, I remind myself. She doesn't know better.

When her hand drops from my neck to trace patterns on my jean-clad thigh, I catch her fingers in mine. "Not okay. Teasing isn't cool with girls any more than it is with guys."

Her demeanor sobers at the seriousness in my tone. I hate being harsh with her, but she's got me so hot, I can barely stand it. This needs to stop. Or go somewhere. But it can't continue as it is.

"Got it?" I ask, softening.

"Yeah." A whisper. At least a full minute passes while she looks at me, studies me, tracing my outline in the shadows with her eyes. She lingers on my muscular legs, my solid arms, my shoulders, finally settling on my face. At last she says, "Fran, I'd like… I'd like to keep touching you. For real. Would that be okay?"

I swallow and nod once, slowly. If this is what she needs to convince herself she's bi, then I'll be her test subject.

Reaching out again, Genesis unzips my jacket down the front, revealing my too tight black T-shirt and the hardened nipples straining through the sports bra beneath it. She eases the jacket off my shoulders and folds it, then lays it neatly across the bench behind her. Her hands return to me, running over my shoulders, hesitating at the muscles in my biceps. At that stage of my life, I swam and bowled daily. My arms were in great shape even at eighteen, and I never lost that. Well, not until the snakebite thing.

At that thought, my body stiffens. I don't hurt. My leg. My arm. No pain. Because this version of me hasn't been bitten yet. Which starts me down a different road. What if—? What if I could *walk* out of body to a time before Leo sicced the snakes on me? What if I could prevent that from ever happening?

Except then I wouldn't have gone out of body in the first place, wouldn't have saved Genesis and Chris from Max Harris. They'd be dead. Leo would likely still be alive, and I'd be much, much more of a basket case than I already am.

No. I need to go with the cards I've been dealt. Cassie will heal me. Or not. But I'll live with it, either way.

"Hey, you okay?" Gen asks. "You zoned out for a second there."

"I'm… fine," I say, breath catching as her hands leave my shoulders and find my breasts.

She runs her fingers across the tops of them, sending tingles of intense pleasure through the thin shirt. I shiver, goose bumps flaring up and down both my arms. She's so focused on me, she hasn't noticed her jacket gaping open, revealing the inner curves of her own breasts. I can't resist slipping my hands to her waist, then up the sides of her rib cage. Her skin's so smooth and soft, still cold, though warming beneath my palms. I stop just short of my goal.

I wait until her eyes meet mine, then send a silent question.

Gen bites her lower lip and nods.

I cup the soft mounds, kneading them gently and running my thumbs across the nipples, which immediately harden.

"Oh." Her single word conveys a million emotions and revelations. Then, "Yes…." Gen's eyes close on a sigh.

And she's mine.

One huge advantage to my out-of-body walk through time—I already know what she likes, even if she doesn't yet know herself. Another huge advantage—I get to show her.

Her hands fall away from me as I lower my head to one breast and apply my mouth, placing kisses on the pale skin. She's losing herself to sensation, and though she's no longer touching me, I don't mind. This was all about her and her self-discovery. And I love watching her like this.

Everywhere I kiss or lick, I pause to blow cool air across the moistened skin. Her body trembles, her hands find the back of my head, pressing me harder against her, and she moans, long and low.

Oh, it's going to be one of *those* nights.

From experience, I know that sometimes, if I play things just right, I can bring Gen to orgasm just by teasing her breasts. It's a talent I'm proud of, and I'm thrilled I can make this happen for her tonight for her first time with another girl.

I refocus my attention, never letting either breast be neglected. While I explore one with my lips and tongue, I fondle the other, neither nipple allowed to soften. Gen's nails scrape down my back, something I love, but I don't let it distract me for long. Her breath hitches in her chest. She's got one leg on either side of the bench, and her hips shift erratically back and forth on the wood surface as she loses control.

"You're making me… I need… I think I'm…."

You're incoherent, Gen. Exactly how I want you.

My amused laughter against the nipple I'm suckling sends her into paroxysms of twitches and jerks, and I almost lose contact with her. Time to readjust.

"Come here." Pausing for a moment and earning a moan for the delay, I set my hands on her hips and lift her easily onto my knee, straddling and facing me. "Right here."

Before I can return to her breasts, her mouth finds mine, and the intensity of her kiss steals my breath. Here's something she already knows, and she demonstrates the full range of her expertise, teasing my lower lip, slipping her tongue inside to play with mine. I taste cherry ChapStick and peppermint, and my mind hazes over.

Cherry ChapStick. Huh. I can't remember exactly what year that Katy Perry song "I Kissed a Girl" came out, but I wonder if the choice was conscious on Gen's part, chosen for Cassie, not me. I'm appreciative nonetheless.

Mentally giving myself a quick shake, I retake control. If this is the way she wants it, I can handle that.

Both hands recapture her nipples, and I flick and pinch them in time with my tongue darting in and out of her mouth. Gen squeaks in response, the sound resonating through both of us. Then she groans and presses down harder on my knee. I swear I can feel her heat through my jeans.

"Please," she gasps, breaking from my lips with an effort.

No problem.

Clasping her breasts together, I alternate my tongue fast between them, teasing, tasting, occasionally biting, while she goes wild. My hands massage her. I pull back so I can watch her expression shift from pleasure to astonishment. My thumbs work her nipples harder and faster.

"Oh God, I'm going to… just from you…."

I lean in close to her ear. "Yeah," I whisper, feeling her thigh muscles clench around me, "you are."

With a strangled scream, Gen throws her head back, nearly slamming into my chin on the upswing, but I've guided her through orgasm before, and I know when to get the hell out of the way. Her spine arches, her body goes rigid, waves of pleasure sending tremors coursing through her. She jerks and twists, helpless against the intensity, and all the while I continue to tease and massage and stimulate her now hypersensitive breasts.

As her limbs slacken the tiniest bit, as she starts to come down off the high, I slip one hand beneath her skirt, pull the cotton panties aside, and press two fingers to the wetness I find there. Her eyes fly wide, her body spasming. Her grinding tries to force them inside her, but I don't let them enter. I have no idea how far she's gone with guys or by herself, but I won't risk stealing her potential sexual innocence. Besides, the mere contact is more than enough.

"Again…," she cries in utter amazement, right before she loses it a second time.

This one's bigger than the first, leaving her panting and whimpering, leaning against my shoulder as she recovers from the aftershocks. Gradually, I slow the motions of my fingers and ease my hands away.

I wrap my arms around her and hold her close, my own heart pounding and my pulse racing in sympathy. Watching her, it almost took me over the edge myself. "So," I say, shooting for nonchalant but failing when my voice cracks, "made up your mind yet?"

"That was… I've never felt…."

And you're still incoherent. Heh.

I can't resist a smug smile as I murmur calming words into her hair.

Then I feel the pull.

I don't know how to describe it, the visceral yank from within, a tugging on my very soul. But instinctively I know what it is, and its timing sucks.

"I've got to go."

"Hmm?" Gen's in a postorgasmic haze. It takes her a minute to process. When she does, she sits up and stares at me. "You aren't serious."

I make a show of glancing at the clock hanging on the wall, lit by the nighttime security lighting. "'Fraid so. The, um, people I'm staying with get freaked if I come in too late. And didn't I overhear you have a brother? He'll be worried about you."

"He will, but…." She moves off my lap, allowing me to stand. "I'll see you again, right? Where are you staying?"

"I'm *not* staying. I leave in the morning." Actually, with the pull growing stronger, I'm worried I'll "leave" at any second, poofing out of existence before her very eyes and leaving her more traumatized than if I'd never been here. I've gotta get out of this locker room, but she's got a hold of my hand and she's not letting go.

"How about a phone number, then? An email address? We could keep in touch, talk about… stuff."

Lesbian stuff, I'm guessing. And if we really were both eighteen, and this hadn't all already happened, I'd have loved having someone to talk to. But not now. I disentangle my hand from hers. "I can't."

Genesis bites her trembling lower lip while I straighten my clothing and retrieve my jacket. Who knows what would happen to it if I left it in the past? I hand her her still damp bra and shirt.

"You have someone. Back home. Wherever home is. Don't you?"

"No, no one." Not counting her, anyway. "I just don't believe in the long-distance thing. It never works out, and one of us will get hurt." I head for the glowing red exit sign.

"One of us is already getting hurt," she says softly, stopping me in my tracks. "I'm so alone here."

Shit.

I close my eyes and take a deep breath, then turn back to her. I cross the small distance between us, take her chin in my hand, and kiss her gently on the lips. "I'm sorry," I say with as much feeling as I can put behind the words. "I wish I could stay. I wish it were possible. But it's not. All I can promise you is that someday I'll come back to Festivity and we'll run into each other again. Trust me. There are others in your school who feel the way you do. Be who you are. Own it. Don't be ashamed of it. They'll make themselves known to you, and they'll respect you for it." I'm not making shit up. I already know I'm right. Gen's told me how she came out during her senior year, started the first Gay & Straight Alliance club in her high school. It helped make her into the confident adult I know and love.

With that thought, I'm struck by a dizzying sense of chicken-or-the-egg syndrome. Does the advice I just gave her end up guiding her? Or did her stories about her high school days guide *me* into giving her that advice?

My brain hurts.

I make my escape as fast as I can, pushing into the dark hallway, down the corridor, and out through the broken double doors.

I stand, panting for a moment in the cold darkness, her stricken expression emblazoned in my inner sight, but I'm afraid she might try to follow me, so I run. No direction, no goal. I just run.

The trees on Festivity Avenue flash by, then the apartment buildings and downtown shops. I pause in front of the coffee shop, no longer a Starbucks but a Barnie's. Guess one bought out the other somewhere along the line. With my hands on my knees, I bend over, taking panting breaths.

"Are you all right?" asks a familiar voice.

I straighten, meeting my father's eyes. He stands beside the shop's patio, leaning against the brick wall, a steaming cup in his hand. Clean clothes and clean-shaven—either the Registry hasn't punished him yet, or this is one of his "sane" days.

Ferguson, or Robert, or whatever he's going by blinks when he recognizes me. "No," he says. "I don't think you are all right. Rather far from home, aren't you? And I don't mean New Jersey."

So he knows I'm *walking*. Makes sense. He's a user of magic himself. I'm surprised Genesis didn't recognize me as some sort of walking spirit, but then at this age, she hasn't fully come into her own abilities. As for dear old Dad, I have no idea what to say, so I say nothing.

"Always wondered which gifts you got. Rather wished you'd gotten none of them."

"You and me both," I mutter.

That sparks a laugh from him, a sharp bark that echoes along the nearly empty street. I wonder what time it is. No one's out, and the coffee shop looks like it's closing up for the night, which would put it around eleven if Barnie's keeps the same hours as the more modern Starbucks in town. Good thing it's deserted, actually, because people wouldn't see me. They'd only see him talking to himself like the crazy man he'll later become.

"I get the feeling you've lost your way back. Dangerous. Stay too long in the wrong place and you'll disconnect for good."

Okay, that's scary. I search inside myself for the pull I felt earlier, but it's faded. "How long is too long?"

"Depends. How far away are you?"

"In distance or time?"

Ferguson's eyebrows shoot up. He fumbles the cup of coffee, then grips it so tightly the lid pops off and the hot liquid spatters his white shirt front. He doesn't even seem to notice. "How old are you?" he demands.

"Ten years older than I look," I say, clamping down on the nerves and adrenaline building within me.

"Oh…." He takes three strides forward, closing the distance between us, and places his free hand on my cheek. His eyes slide closed, intense concentration forming wrinkles across his forehead. "You're in trouble, girl. Listen," he whispers. "Listen hard. Listen good. She's calling you, and you need to answer."

Um, what the fuck? I don't hear any—

And then I do.

Flynn? Come back to me, Flynn. We can't find you. Please….

It's Gen's voice, and not. An echo of herself, a sense of her more than actual sound. And it pulls me like a milkshake through a straw—thick and slow, but steady. And sweet.

"Someday," Ferguson says, "we need to sit down for a long chat. Get to where your physical form lies in the future. You should reconnect if you stand in the same space. Safe journeys." Then he turns and walks to the closest side street and disappears between two buildings.

JOGGING ACROSS town when I'm exhausted and sexually aroused ranks pretty close to the top on my list of least-favorite activities. The longer it takes, the more tired I become and the less I feel the sidewalk beneath my sneakers. By the time I reach Leopold VanDean's castle/mansion, I worry I won't have the strength to get myself inside.

The place looks much as it does in the future, with its manicured lawns and security spotlights highlighting the gray stone blocks of the exterior. The McLaren is nowhere to be seen, but I'm guessing it's in the garage. Then again, Leo is only a few years older than Genesis. He might not even live here yet.

I stalk up to the front door, but of course it's locked. Casting about, I come up with one of the large rocks lining the front hedges and bend to pick it up.

It takes three tries and a lot of concentration. The first two attempts, the stone passes right through my hand, and my panic threatens to overwhelm me when I finally get it. Hurrying now, I hurl it through one of the parlor windows, smashing out the glass with an impressive crash.

Alarms sound within the mansion—the shatter sensors registering the break-in. Footsteps retreat down the hall outside the parlor. Figures Leo or whoever lives here now wouldn't investigate on their own. The residents are probably heading for a phone to hurry the police who've already been called.

I scramble over the windowsill, careful of the glass. Don't know if cuts from the past will carry to my body in the future, but they'll hurt regardless. My feet hit the floor with a soft squeak of rubber on wood. Different furniture from Leo's, much more tasteful décor, so, yeah, some other owner, or he remodeled over the years.

I only have to take four steps into the room when the fish-on-a-hook sensation hits.

Darkness and swirling and a horrible sense of motion sickness wrap me in a nausea-inducing grip. My spirit flails, helpless against the drag. My head pounds with a dull, persistent ache, and I recognize the physical pains of the body I left behind in my hurting arm and leg.

The warm glow of candles still blinds me when I open eyes I hadn't realized I'd closed. I stand just inside the now intact window, Genesis kneeling beside my fallen figure, along with Cassandra, of all people. Katy barks from behind the closed bathroom door. A large bruise swells on my forehead, red and angry. And have I mentioned that I will never get used to looking down at myself?

Well, the bruise explains the headache. And the sudden blurred vision. And the dizziness.

Shit.

I hit the wood on all fours, drawing the attention of Genesis and by association, Cassie following Gen's gaze. "Flynn," Gen breathes, diving for me, wrapping her arms around my shoulders. Her warmth dissipates some of the disorientation, but not enough for me to stand.

It must look pretty weird to Cassandra.

"Flynn's… there?" she asks, staring through me, then back to my body.

Gen hesitates, probably not wanting to give too much information to this woman. And I still want to know what the hell she's doing here, but my mouth doesn't work well enough to ask. "Yes," she admits.

"My God. She's a walker. That's impressive."

And a time traveler. And that makes me really powerful, if what Gen and my father have told me is true.

Cassandra approaches the space I occupy, waving her hands around and through me. My stomach roils at the contact with my spirit.

"Tell her to stop," I say through gritted teeth. "It's making things worse."

Gen relays the message, but Cassie's staring at the ceiling, not listening. "I know that feeling. I've felt it once before."

Fucking hell. The locker room, when she walked through me and hesitated.

Her eyes go wide, and I know she remembers exactly where and when she encountered the sensation. And what it means I can do.

Chapter 40
Strange Alliances

"SHE CAN walk through *time*?" Cassandra squeaks, reeling back on her heels just as footsteps pound down the hallway toward the parlor.

I'm waiting for Genesis to lose her shit right along with Cassie, but at that moment, Chris bursts into the room, shirt untucked, car keys clutched in one hand. His eyes scan until they find first me on the floor, and then Gen and Cassie crouched beside the other me—the me that's conscious, though he can't see that me.

Okay, I'm officially confusing myself.

"What… are you doing?" he asks. To him, Gen appears to be hugging empty air.

She huffs an impatient sigh. "It's Flynn. She's out of body again. And since none of you can help me with this, can you all clear out of the way? She needs to go back."

"Your lives just get weirder and weirder," he says, flopping onto the settee.

Yeah, no kidding.

Gen half drags me across the floor, and I reach a trembling hand to touch my own forehead. My skin burns beneath my fingers, and I open my mouth to tell Genesis, but my spirit is grabbed and hauled forward, and a second later, I'm blinking physical eyes at three concerned expressions.

Even Cassandra, which surprises me. Though she might be more worried about my skill set than my well-being.

"What the fuck are you doing here?" I growl at her, pushing up to all fours. It would have been a lot more menacing if I hadn't immediately thrown up right after.

"Ugh," she says, stepping her expensive leather shoes out of the splash zone.

I manage to keep it all on one of the area rugs, which can be rolled up and washed, rather than across the polished wood. Gen holds my ponytail out of the way. Chris returns to my side and pats my back.

"And what brought you here?" I ask him once I can breathe again.

"Gen called. Said you'd collapsed. I got here as fast as I could." The last sounds apologetic.

Genesis reaches out and touches his shoulder, and inside, I smile. What I wouldn't have given for a brother like that, growing up.

"Are you all right?" She presses her palm to the side of my forehead that isn't bruised and frowns. "I think you're running a fever."

"Yeah," I say, wiping sweat from my face. "Feel like shit. Dizzy and achy, like I'm fighting the flu and losing."

Genesis grabs one of the water bottles she keeps in the parlor to refresh herself after a client reading. After uncapping it, she passes it to me, and I take a long drink. Then I press the still cold plastic to my forehead and groan.

"Did your temperature go up the last time?" Chris asks. He and Genesis each take one of my arms and pull me up, then guide me to the settee. I sink into the cushions and lean my head sideways against the pillows.

"No idea. Probably. But it would have been hard to tell considering everything else that was wrong with me." Like three water moccasin bites.

"She's done this *before*?" Cassandra. Still squeaking. The pitch of her voice could rival a kid sucking helium. I get the vibe she doesn't squeak often, so this must really be rocking her world.

"Yes," Gen admits. "She's a walker. She does it when she's distressed. I guess our training session got out of hand." She turns to me, taking my hands in hers. "I'm sorry, Flynn. Focusing on all of me instead of just my power wasn't such a great idea."

I offer a lopsided grin. "I like focusing on all of you. Just maybe not when we're having a lesson."

"All right. Seriously. You two need to stop the lovey-dovey crap for a minute." Cassandra paces the parlor floor, her heels click-clacking and setting off my headache again. "She's a walker," Cassie continues, oblivious to my pain. "But I don't think you've quite grasped the implications... the potential for disaster here." She turns wide, wild eyes toward us.

"God, what if she's already changed something? What if the whole world has shifted? What if—?"

"Who are you, if I might ask?" Chris looks her up and down, an appreciative, if wary, glint in his eyes.

Uh-oh.

I open my mouth to warn him, but Gen beats me to it.

"Cassie. This is Cassie. From high school. She's changed a lot, but we had her over to the apartment enough times." Her jaw sets. "I'm sure you remember."

Chris's eyes narrow. "Yes, I remember." His tone isn't pleasant. I'm guessing Genesis brought a lot of the pain of that break-up night to him for comfort. But he shakes his head, dispelling the flash of animosity from his features. "That was a long time ago." The appreciative look returns.

Double uh-oh.

"Will you all focus, please?" Cassandra says. "We might not even be the same people we think we are. Or were. God, the possible ramifications...."

Moving to her side, Chris slips an arm around her shoulders. It has the same effect on her that it always has on Genesis, or me, for that matter. Cassie visibly calms.

Next to me, Gen glares daggers at them both.

"Why don't you have a seat and explain exactly what you're talking about?" Chris suggests.

"Time," Cassie whispers, dropping from beneath his arm onto the floor pillows, legs askew and showing lots of skin in her short skirt, as if her puppet strings were cut. "I'm talking about time."

Chapter 41
Paradox

THREE TYLENOL and another bottle of water later, I'm tucked into the downstairs guest bed, mostly because I don't think I can manage the stairs. Cassie's gone, ushered out the front door by Chris, who's also left for the night. Katy curls at my feet on top of the comforter I've got pulled up to my chest, because no matter how hot September is in Florida, and no matter how high a fever I'm running, I'm freezing.

Gen slips in the door, quiet as one of the spirits she contacts, until she sees I'm awake. Then she crawls into the queen-size bed and snuggles with me under the covers. "It took another ten minutes of babbling in the driveway," she says, stroking my arm with her fingertips, "but Chris finally got her on the road."

I let out a long sigh.

"You want to tell me what that was all about?"

Not really, no.

I had Gen get rid of Cassandra because I didn't want to share details about my abilities in front of her. But the woman's already made up her mind. She knows. And I'm certain within the next hour, the entire Registry will know.

Which leaves me with one even more immediate problem. Genesis, and how to tell her what happened to me tonight. Like I even understand it myself.

Suddenly I'm really, really tired.

I close my eyes, working through how I want to explain.

Gen's lips find my cheek. She kisses me softly and waits.

"Tell me about your first sexual experience with a girl," I begin.

The mattress shifts abruptly and the comforter jerks. I guess that wasn't what she expected to come out of my mouth. "Um, why?"

"Just indulge me, okay?" I walked. It wasn't a dream. But I need confirmation that what I think happened is what actually did happen.

"All right...." She proceeds to relate the events of the locker room, pausing when she can't remember specific details so fresh in my mind, but years ago for her. Gen reaches the part where Cassandra freaked out. "And then she—"

"Cassie, you mean," I interrupt. Gen's been referring to Cassandra as "she" or "my first girlfriend" throughout the narrative.

Gen's fingers tighten on my arm. "How did you figure it out? It was a long time ago," she adds in a rush.

I tilt my head toward her and open my eyes. Hers search my face, but I'm calm. "I'm not jealous or upset," I tell her. "You said you'd known her."

"I should have told you everything. But I was angry. She dumped me because she couldn't handle the baggage, but then she's there in Atlantic Dance kissing you. I know she had ulterior motives, but it still hurt."

And if I hadn't been caught up in a love potion and my multitude of other issues, I might have noticed that.

No. No excuses. I love her. I *should have* noticed that. "She's older now. And she was acting under the Registry's orders. I doubt she had any real attraction to me. And what *was* she doing here tonight?"

"Confirming your attendance at the conference. But you'd collapsed, and I thought maybe with her healing skills she could help you, so I dragged her into this. I'm sorry. I wasn't thinking."

I tug my arm from beneath the blanket to reach over and stroke her hair. "Forget it. We'll deal with her later. Go on."

"Well… then this other girl showed up. Out of nowhere. She'd overheard us and she decided to comfort me and, well, take matters into her own hands, so to speak."

I chuckle softly. No "so to speak" about it. I took everything into my own hands. I also notice Gen skips the part about her suicide attempt. Did she suppress that memory? Or does she not want me to know about it? Maybe it's just something she'd rather not discuss.

"What do you remember about the other girl?" I rub Gen's back through her pajama top, wondering when she had a chance to change clothes. I'm still in my T-shirt and underwear, my jeans having ended up on the floor somewhere with my boots.

"Her name was Fran. She was from out of town, leaving the next morning. She was my age, but she seemed older, wiser. She was taller than me, and strong, with short hair and an amazingly sexy voice." Gen pauses. "You don't really want to hear this."

It's all I can do to keep from laughing. Gen's worried I'll be jealous. Of me.

"I do," I say. "I really do."

"Well, okay. But I don't see what this has to do with—"

"Just tell me, please."

Gen studies my face a moment, then shrugs and continues. "She showed me things," she admits, biting her lower lip. "About my body. About what a woman could do for another woman. As strong as she was, she was so very gentle. She taught me a lot that night, and she made me feel…." Her voice trails off in a sigh.

"How?"

"She made me feel the way you do. Safe and valued and loved. You remind me a lot of her. I couldn't see her clearly in the shadows, but I've always imagined she looked like you."

More than you know.

"And then she left." Gen's tone turns bitter. "Just up and left, exactly the way Cassie did."

Uh-oh. "Really?"

Genesis sighs, her breath warm against my skin. "No, not really. Not like that. She said some nice things, gave good advice. And looking back, she did the right thing. A long-distance romance would never have worked at that age. But still. I spent weeks searching for her, Flynn. She had on one of those high school sports jackets. You know the kind I mean?"

I nod, swallowing hard.

"It had initials on it. P.H.S. I used the internet. Hundreds of schools have those initials. Maybe thousands. I went through yearbook after yearbook online. Stared at so many girls' pictures, each and every Fran. There were more than you might think. None of them fit what I knew of her."

Because, for one thing, besides the wrong name, she was looking at the wrong year. Since I'm five years older than Genesis, I would have graduated five years earlier. God, this isn't what I wanted—her hopelessly pining after me and searching for a girl she'd never find.

"You got over her eventually, right?"

She nods, and relief floods me. "I did. I started the Gay & Straight Alliance in my school, met another girl, dated her and a few guys too. But every month or so, I'd do another search. And I always kept my eyes open whenever I walked around town. She said she'd come back to Festivity someday, and I believed her, but she never did."

Pressing my lips to the top of Gen's forehead, I whisper, "You're wrong. I did come back."

Time stops.

For a second, I wonder if I've stepped out of body again, things are so surreal. The wall clock ticks—a pale wood mechanism that shows the cycles of the moon in addition to the time of day. Katy makes soft slurping noises as she licks her paw. Gen's breath picks up hard and fast against my neck.

"Oh my God," she says. "Flynn, what did you do?"

Chapter 42
Chicken or the Egg

"I... DIDN'T *do* anything. I was focused on you. The power sent me there... or then... or whatever. I didn't have a say in it."

Gen's up and out of the bed, waving her hands in the air, picking up knickknacks off the dresser and end tables and putting them back down as if she doesn't know what to do with herself. She probably doesn't. I've had a few hours to come to grips with all this. She hasn't.

"It's not possible," she says.

"Oh yeah, it definitely is." I still feel her lips on mine, her soft skin. I picture the stricken expression on her face when she grabbed the razor from her bag.

"But I'd told you about it, the experience, before you went back, or whatever it is you did."

"You told me it had been awkward, that both your first and second girlfriend had left you...." And it hits me then. I'm the second girlfriend who left. "Oh...."

"Yeah. Oh." Returning to the bed, she sits next to me and takes my hands in hers. "How could I have told you about something that happened when it hadn't actually happened until tonight?"

I shake my head, regretting it when my migraine threatens to split my skull. My wince catches her attention. She presses me back down on the pillow since I'd been leaning up and strokes the hair from my face. "Maybe time is one big, continuous loop," I say. "Or one of those… what do you call them…. Mobius strips. You know, the twisting paper chains that never end if you try to draw a line down the middle of one. Who the fuck knows? All I know is I was there. It was real. And I love you more than ever."

"I love you too." So much behind those words. Knowing your first love is your true love, like fate or destiny or something. It's awesome and terrifying, and I don't blame her for being freaked out.

She curls up again, and we lie in silence for a while, laughing softly when Katy pushes between us and rests her massive, furry head on Gen's arm. One big happy family.

I'm almost asleep when Gen whispers, "Cassie knows. The Registry knows. This is going to make things difficult for you."

"When hasn't it been?" I ask around a yawn. Then I'm out.

AS PROMISED, I take my tool kit out to Rosaline's house to work on her car on Saturday. Gen goes inside right away, carrying a large blue plastic bowl containing the salad I made. Well, helped make, anyway. I chopped stuff.

Rosaline needs her for a final dress fitting, and since I'm not supposed to see the gown—okay, not supposed to see it any *more*—I jack up the Escort and slide underneath to see what's what.

Damn, it's a mess under there. The patient has suffered fatal injuries, but I might be able to prolong her life and improve the quality of it for a little longer.

I do an oil change, replace the filters, tape a lot of dangling pieces back into place, and make a list of things, in order of priority, for Rosaline to get done at a real mechanic. She needs the brake pads changed out. I can handle that in my next visit, and the pads themselves won't cost her much. But the transmission gasket also needs replacing. Transmission fluid is leaking, and it could catch fire if she's unlucky. Sadly, it's a job I can't do, and a costly one. But it's a wonder Diego's girls haven't lost a second parent to this car.

Oil covers my hands and the old clothes I wore on purpose to do the job, and I don't want to go in the nice clean house like this, so I press the doorbell with my one dirt-free knuckle and wait.

It swings open and Diego's youngest throws herself into my chest. "Flynn!"

Katrina's a preteen, about twelve, but already showing the Latina beauty of her sisters and her mother. Shining dark hair hangs almost to her waist, and her tan skin is flawless. Well, not so flawless when she pulls back from her hug. Laughing, I point at the oil smudge down one of her cheeks. "Great. Now we both need showers."

She sobers when she meets my eyes. "I'll lead you to the back bathroom. Don't touch anything. Mama will kill you."

I nod. Rosaline keeps an immaculate home.

We parade through the house, picking up Isa and Eleana along the way. The oldest girl, around eighteen, has my bag from Gen's Charger. It contains my change of clothes. The other, sixteen—I remember because I went to her quinceañera last year—carries a fresh towel that she won't let me touch until I'm clean. "Where's Alejandra?"

"Helping Mama with dinner," Isa tells me.

"And Genesis?"

Katrina laughs. "Learning how to make enchiladas the *right* way."

Awesome. Gen's a great cook, and Rosaline's Mexican food is to die for. I'd love it if Gen made some of those dishes at home.

We move down a long hallway, passing the open doors to the two girls' rooms, two girls per bedroom, both nightmares of pinks, purples, and yellows, lots of frilly things and flowers. I suppress a shudder. The hall's walls display family photos, framed in carved wood or intricate metal. The pictures progress in age from one end of the hall to the other, beginning with a wedding portrait of Diego and Rosaline, then baby pictures and images of the girls as they grew, and ending with several of the whole family together. I'm choked up and teary-eyed by the time the hall dumps us into a laundry room and bathroom.

"It's okay," Isa says, touching my shoulder. "We're all sad. But the memories make us happy."

"Right," I croak, then swallow hard. "Right." It comes out stronger the second time, and I force a smile for them.

"Now strip, and I'll wash your clothes while you shower and we eat." Eleana holds out a hand.

I backpedal, heat flooding my cheeks. "Um, how about you guys go away and I'll strip, shower, and wash my own clothes?"

All three burst into laughter, and I realize they planned this just to see my reaction.

Sisters.

I always wanted one. These girls are as close as I'll ever come.

Extending my greasy, oily hands toward them, I pretend I'm going to smear them all with dirt and grime. Much squealing and chasing around the laundry room ensues, earning us a humor-infused warning shout from Rosaline to keep the noise down. But it gets everyone else out of the room so I finally have privacy to clean up.

Scoured, scrubbed, and red-skinned from the harsh soap I brought, I emerge from the shower and dress in the spare jeans and T-shirt. Pulling it over my head results in a shock of pain through my bad arm and shoulder, but I grit my teeth and breathe deep until it passes. I overdid it working on Rosaline's car. Damn, I'll have to watch myself tonight so I don't pick up any delicate glassware with that hand. Wouldn't want it giving out on me while holding something breakable.

Delicious smells set my stomach growling and my mouth watering. Dinner must be ready.

I follow the aromas of tortillas, yellow rice, and beans into the dining room, where everyone already sits at the large oval wooden table. Gen's saved me a place on one side between her and Isa, and I take my seat while Eleana heaps generous portions of everything onto my plate.

We talk about inconsequential things: politics and weather, my new bartending gig, Gen's tarot readings, the girls' school classes. No one mentions Diego except during the pre-meal prayer, a quick blessing for him in heaven.

I cast a questioning glance at Genesis during the prayer, wondering if his spirit is around and knowing she'll understand what I'm asking her without words. She nods, and some of the tension leaves my shoulders. He's watching over them, as he should be. Someday I'm guessing he'll move on, but for now, his family needs him.

"So," Rosaline says to me once we're all stuffed and the girls are clearing the table, "now we see to your fitting, yes? I'm assuming you will wish to wear a tuxedo rather than a dress. How do you feel about pink and white?"

I grin, looking to all the other faces in the room, figuring this is another attempt to get a rise out of me. My smile fades. Everyone else looks completely serious.

Chapter 43
Drawing the Line

"No," I say while Rosaline shows me picture after picture. "Just no."

She's got a catalog of tuxedo designs, and she's flipping the pages, pointing out all the "benefits" a white or ivory-colored tux has over a black one: less hot, makes the wearer stand out, will match Genesis's dress and flowers and the wedding colors, will go better with my light brown hair.

"I'll look like I'm working in a 1950s ice cream parlor."

She stops and stares at the current image before us, the catalog lying in her lap and me beside her on the living room couch. Everyone else has conveniently vanished, including Genesis. Because she's smart. Laughter carries down the hall from the girls' rooms. I think they're playing Twister.

Wish I was. I'm twisting in a whole different way.

Rosaline studies the photo of a skinny male model with hair the same color as mine. He sports an ivory tuxedo, pale pink cummerbund, and matching pale pink bow tie. I want to order a strawberry shake from him. With whipped cream and a cherry. And maybe some sprinkles.

Leave it to Genesis to accidentally choose wedding colors that will leave a fairly butch lesbian woman looking like a flamboyant gay man.

After turning the picture one way and then the other and looking from it to me, she sighs. "You have a point."

Crossing my arms over my chest, I sink back into the couch cushions. The worn furniture, patched here and there and scuffed and scratched in the wood places, feels like home. I scrunch my sock-covered toes in the thick-pile beige carpet. "So how do we compromise?"

"Hmm. Good question. Gray? No, that will wash out your skin tone. We could do black…."

I perk up at that.

"…but keep the tie and cummerbund in pale pink."

So much for perking.

"I'm really not a 'pink' kind of gal." Like, to the point of nausea.

She fixes me with a hard glare. "Look. This is Genesis's day. Technically two brides, but still her day since you choose the more masculine role in your partnership. It is a day most women dream of their whole lives. And she wants it to be perfect. And that means—"

I hold up a hand to stop the femininity lesson. "I'll wear it."

Rosaline's jaw snaps shut and her eyes widen. "Really? Diego always told me how stubborn you are. I thought I'd have to argue much longer."

Stubborn? Me? Go figure. With a shrug, I pull the catalog from her lap to mine. "I love her. What can I do?" I continue turning pages, searching for a cut of tux I can live with and a shade of pink that doesn't scream Barbie. When the silence lasts too long, I finally glance at Rosaline and find her still watching me, her brow furrowed in contemplation. "What?"

"You do love her." It's not a question, but she sounds surprised.

"Well, yeah, of course." Why else would I go through all this? I don't say that part out loud, but it's true, and I'm not just thinking of the wedding. I've been to hell and back with Genesis these past six months. And I suspect I've got several more levels of hell to visit before I'm done with the Registry, or Gen's addiction, or all the other crap. But Gen loves me and accepts me and makes me a better person. I'd suffer anything for her.

I'll even wear the white tux if she insists on it, but I won't tell Rosaline that.

"I was speaking with her in the kitchen, at length. She loves you too."

"Um, good to know?" Okay, where's this going? And what, exactly, were they discussing about me? I'm insecure enough without this sort of bullshit.

Rosaline must sense my discomfort because she reaches out a hand to pat my knee. "Oh, we didn't say anything bad, just spoke of how you've supported one another through difficult times. It's only… I never understood how two women could love each other." Her eyes flick to my face. "I hope that doesn't offend you. I have much respect for both you and Genesis, and I've always thought of you as another daughter. But the woman/woman thing, it never seemed real to me, more like a very strong friendship that some mistake for love. Then I see the two of you, and there's no mistaking it. It's as strong and real as anything I've seen between a man and a woman. Perhaps stronger."

That last carries a note of personal pain, and I wonder. I take her hands in mine. "You know Diego loved you very much, right? He talked about you all the time, always bragging on your cooking and your sewing, but he also adored you as a person. He could never believe you chose him over all your teenage suitors."

"He told you about that?" she asks with a little sniffle.

Aw hell. The last thing I want to do is start her crying, but there's no avoiding the subject now. "The senior prom and the four guys who asked you to it? Yeah, he told me. He said when you agreed to go with him, he danced around his house for two weeks trying to 'perfect his moves.' He broke two vases. His mother wanted to kill him. And by the time the dance came around, he had blisters on both feet from the dress shoes he'd been practicing in, and he could barely walk."

"Sí, sí." She's laughing now, and crying, and I pass her a tissue from a gold metal box on the coffee table. Never understood those things. Companies decorate tissue boxes in pretty flowers and such. Why do people cover them up in gaudy metal or ceramics?

Rosaline accepts the Kleenex and dabs at her cheeks and eyes. "Thank you, mija. One more happy memory I'd nearly forgotten." She smiles at me.

I glance around the otherwise empty living room, wondering if Diego is there and if he's smiling too. I hope so.

We return to the catalog, the daunting task still before us. It takes another hour of "negotiating" to settle on a style, and even then, nothing feels quite right to me. I study the image. No tails, a simple design, though the shorter jacket has a military dress uniform look to it. In the end, she convinces me that she can alter it so it isn't quite so manly. She'll curve the lines of the jacket to match my more feminine form, accentuating my average-sized chest. Not sure about that, but she swears I'll look great and Genesis will love it.

After seeing what Rosaline's done with Gen's gown, I have to bow to her skills.

"So, we're decided, then? After I take your measurements, I'll order it and get to work right away."

"Um, there's one more thing," I say, reaching into the pile of pattern magazines on the table. I pull one featuring cocktail and party dresses and set it in my lap.

This is huge. A step I've never taken. A step much, much worse than the whole tux thing. But I snuck onto the Registry's website and scanned the conference events, and I read the descriptions of some of the gatherings I'll be expected to attend and escort Genesis to.

Our wedding is personal. We should be ourselves. The conference is public. And I don't want to embarrass Gen or feel out of place more than I know I already will.

I can't help remembering the whole Mall at Centuria fiasco, and what Genesis asked me to try on. Maybe she was under the influence of a spell, but I suspect some truth underlay the request.

I also have this sudden, obscene desire to blow my girlfriend's mind.

"Rosaline," I say, opening the catalog, "I want you to make me a dress."

Chapter 44
Wild Blue Yonder

CONFESSION TIME—I'VE never been on an airplane before.

Growing up, Mom, Grandma, and I had enough money to live on. We ate well. We bought clothing from real stores, not secondhand shops and Goodwill. We went to movies and amusement parks. We took summer vacations. But we traveled by car or once or twice by train when we went into the city. Of course, all that ended when Mom got depressed and ended up in the institution. But the bottom line is, we did not fly.

Second confession—the idea of flying terrifies me.

I promise myself I won't let my terror interfere with our trip. Our jaunt to Atlantic City is stressful enough: the conference, dealing with the Registry, the wedding, and the reception, not to mention Gen's birthday, for which I still haven't made plans. It's a mishmash of positives and negatives, pleasant experiences and unpleasant ones, at least for me.

Gen, on the other hand, practically skips through the Orlando terminal to our designated departure gate. She's got the garment bag containing her wedding dress in one hand and her carry-on luggage in the other. I have no idea where she's getting the energy, but I guess she's excited.

It's oh-God o'clock in the morning on a Sunday. The weeklong conference starts today, and she doesn't want to miss any of it, but Saturdays are busy at the Pub and I couldn't leave Chris without a bartender, so I worked yesterday. The only flight available after that was a red-eye leaving at 7:00 a.m. That meant getting up at four thirty, arriving at the airport by five thirty, and sleepwalking through baggage check-in and security.

"Here it is, A17," Gen announces, draping her dress over one of the plastic chairs in the passenger waiting area. She drops into the second chair in the row, setting her carry-on at her feet.

"It's way too early for you to be that perky," I mutter, stifling a yawn. I drop my own duffel and fold my garment bag over another seat. My shoulder aches, and the limp I no longer try to hide becomes more pronounced as the walkways seem to get longer. Cassandra better keep her word to heal me. The bag holds my tux, but that isn't the only thing inside, and the thought of the dress Rosaline made for me does bring a smile.

True to her amazing skills, Rosaline created something I could not only live with, but that makes me look… well, pretty isn't the right word, but it shows off my best features, and I can't wait to hear what Genesis says when she sees me in it.

"We're boarding in thirty minutes. You want a snack from the convenience store?"

I peer along the corridor where other weary travelers shuffle between the gates and the bathrooms. A baby screams in his mother's arms. A couple of toddlers chase each other around a dad who stands with his eyes closed. I'm not sure he's awake. "Is anything open?" I ask.

"There's always something," she says in a tone that implies I should know that. And I would, if I'd ever been in an airport before. Genesis fishes in her bag for her wallet, pulls a twenty, and shoves it into the pocket of her jean miniskirt.

I consider her offer. We left too early for breakfast, but the idea of eating anything, considering I'm about to be thousands of feet up in the air, doesn't sit well. "No thanks," I say.

She peers at me. "You don't want food? Are you feeling okay?"

"Nice."

"No, really. You look a little pale."

I scrub my palms over my cheeks, waking myself up and hoping to get some color in them. "I'm fine. Go get whatever you're getting. I'll watch our stuff."

Gen pauses a moment longer. I'm not fooling her. She knows something's up. But when I don't offer further details, she shrugs and heads off.

I spend the time people-watching. A dark-haired guy in a polo and khakis strolls up to the gate, checks the arrival times, and finds himself a seat by the windows. Facing me. When we make brief eye contact, he looks away, but I can't help feeling I'm still the focus of his attention.

By the time Gen returns with juice and a banana, we've been joined by a number of businessmen, a few older ladies with colorful purses featuring different casinos, and the family with the rambunctious shrieking toddlers. I eye them with a frown, a headache starting at the bridge of my nose.

"Don't worry," Gen says, patting my jean-clad knee. "I doubt they're with us in first class."

I tilt my chin toward the neatly dressed man by the windows. "Know him?"

She follows my gaze. "Ah. Nathaniel. He's a reader."

"Like of tarot cards?" Wouldn't she just call that a psychic? My confusion must show on my face because she laughs.

"He reads the powers of others. That's his talent. Don't worry about him. He lives in Orlando, and he's probably just heading for the conference, same as we are."

Right. Makes sense.

As with most things, wealth has privileges, and we're called to board ahead of everyone in coach. Two men in suits follow us, but Gen and I are actually the first ones on the airplane. Lucky us.

An attractive blond flight attendant shows us where to hang the tux and gown, then leads us to our row near the front of the cabin. Though she offers to do it for us, I wave her off and lift first my bag, then

Gen's into our overhead compartment. The flight's only a couple of hours or so, so I don't bother grabbing the paperback I'm reading. I've got my phone in airplane mode and a set of headphones for music, so I should be good to go.

If my palms would stop sweating. And my stomach would cease churning.

Unlike the seats farther in, first class has only two chairs on each side, both wide and comfortable, with plenty of leg room. "You want the window?" I ask.

"You sure?"

A view of clouds, open air, and nothing below us? Oh yeah, I'm sure. If we crash, I don't want to see it coming. A gallant sweep of my arm ushers her into the row while she giggles. Her skirt rides up to midthigh when she crosses one leg over the other, and she waves her hand in front of my face. Her eyes twinkle when I meet them. "You want coffee?"

"Huh?"

"Coffee." Gen points over my shoulder where the attendant hovers, a pushcart in front of her and a white coffee mug in hand. Geez, I wonder how long she's been there. Judging from her grin and the look she gives each of us, I'm guessing it's been a while.

"Um, no thanks."

Genesis frowns.

Shit, I should have taken a cup, just for appearances. Behind the stewardess, Nathaniel passes, carrying his small bag. He doesn't give us a second glance and heads on back to the coach section, so I return my attention to Genesis. I always have coffee in the morning, or grab a Starbucks on my way in to work at the Pub. Her narrowed eyes tell me she's not letting this one go as she accepts a steaming mug and pops open her tray table to set it down.

Once the cart rolls through a curtain into the business-class section, Gen shifts to face me. "Okay, spill. And I don't mean my coffee. What's up?"

"Nothing." I fish my phone from my pocket and plug in the headphones. "I don't want to have to use the bathroom, that's all."

It's a good excuse. From all I've heard, maneuvering in an airplane restroom is a study in acrobatics, and though I have the athletic background, it's not a feat I want to attempt.

That seems to satisfy her. She makes a little noise of acceptance and settles into her seat. I shove my ear buds into my ears and tune out the disturbing sounds of a whining engine as we taxi down the runway.

When the safety announcements begin, I turn off the music and pay close attention. I memorize where the exit doors are, and the procedures for loss of cabin pressure and how to inflate a life vest. Beside me, Genesis flips through the in-flight magazine. She's found a pencil somewhere, and she scribbles a word into the crossword puzzle on the last page. How can she be so nonchalant? This information could save her life!

I don't get it, but I let her be, figuring if I have to, I can help her with her oxygen mask and vest.

I suspect she's watching me in her peripheral vision, but I ignore her and tighten my seat belt as much as possible before forcing my muscles to relax. The engines rev; the plane increases speed. We're hurtling down the runway, bouncing on cracks in the tarmac.

And then we're airborne.

"Flynn."

"What?" I say through clenched teeth. I don't look at her. I stare straight ahead, focusing on the seat backs, the narrow walkway between the chairs, anything except the window on the opposite side of her.

"Flynn, look at me."

My breaths come short and fast. I grip the armrests hard, digging in my blunt nails, but I don't turn toward her. Gotta calm down. People fly all the time. Safer than driving, according to the internet.

"You're scared of flying."

Crap.

Very careful not to glance out the window, I meet her eyes. She's half smiling, half grimacing. I can't quite read the emotions there, but I think part of her is laughing at me.

"How'd you guess?" The change in pressure fucks with my hearing, and I swallow hard to clear my ears before she replies.

"Well," she says, taking a sip of her coffee, "for one thing, you listened really intently to the safety speech. Anyone who flies a lot has heard it a million times and knows that none of that will save us if the plane actually crashes."

Oh, thanks, Gen. That's a big help. My hands clench even more tightly on the armrests.

Her grimace deepens. "For another, you're clawing my arm."

"What?" I look down to where my nails dig into the sleeve of her white lace sweater and the soft skin beneath. "Oh shit." It takes effort to disengage. I roll her sleeve up to examine the damage. Little half-moon indentations, angry and red, mark her arm between wrist and elbow. "God, I'm sorry," I moan, rubbing at them.

"Shh," she says, stopping me by pulling away and wrapping the arm around my shoulders. She tugs me down for a kiss, and I allow it since no one's watching us. "It's okay. But I don't get it. You deal with heights all the time."

"Heights I can control are different from putting my life in the hands of someone else, and a plastic and metal thing that rattles like it's about to fall apart."

She cocks her head, listening, like she hasn't noticed before, but I'm right. The plane makes disturbing noises, creaking and growling around us. No one else seems to care, and I guess it's normal, but if a car sounded like this, I'd junk it.

"It'll be fine," she says.

The plane drops at least three feet, then rebounds upward. "Fuck," I hiss.

A chime sounds through the cabin. "Ladies and gentlemen, we're currently experiencing some mild turbulence—"

"Mild?" My voice squeaks. The businessman across the aisle from me offers a sympathetic smile.

"—so please remain in your seats with your seat belts fastened. We'll get through this as soon as we can. Thank you."

Wonderful.

The plane jolts and shudders, jostling the bags in the overhead compartments and sending something crashing in the small kitchenette between sections. Outside, the sky grows dark and ominous. Lightning flashes. I force my gaze away from the damn window.

It goes on and on.

The attendants come through with more drinks and breakfast offerings, but the scents of scrambled eggs and sausage turn my stomach. Gen takes a full platter onto her tray. I decline everything, but Genesis waves her back.

"She'll have a rum and Coke," Gen says, nodding at me.

"It's eight fifteen in the morning," I remind her.

"First time flying?" the woman asks.

And now everyone knows.

"The sick bag is in the pouch in front of you, if you need it."

Oh great, like I wanted that thought implanted in my head.

She pours the drink, including a generous percentage of rum, like more than half, and passes me the glass of amber liquid.

Genesis toasts me with her coffee mug. "Down the hatch," she says.

I examine the drink with a skeptical eye. "This will help?"

"Absolutely," Gen and the attendant say together.

I chug the whole thing.

"Keep 'em coming," Gen says.

I accept a second rum and Coke.

I don't usually drink the hard stuff, and I'm doing it on an empty stomach. By the time I swallow the last of this round, I'm more than a little buzzed. The rocking and jolting continue, but it's like getting stuck on an endless roller coaster rather than being in a contraption about to go down in flames. No one occupies the chair behind me, so I fumble with the seat controls, and Gen helps me recline until I reach a comfortable position.

"Sleep, Flynn. We'll be there in about an hour." She presses a kiss to my cheek. I must be pretty far gone. I hardly notice the PDA.

I close my eyes. The vibration of the engines lulls me until I doze.

"Ladies and gentlemen, we're hitting some fairly rough weather. Please continue to remain in your seats with the seat belts securely fastened."

In the next half hour, I learn the difference between mild and fairly rough.

Thunder cracks and lightning flashes constantly outside the plane. The toddlers in the rear howl so loudly the sound carries all the way to first class, and they aren't the only ones. Several women scream, and the men give the occasional grunt or growl of discomfort as the plane bucks like a bronco. Someone vomits into a rustling paper bag, the pungent odor carrying in the recycled air. I risk a quick glance at Genesis. She's gone pale.

And me? I'm a freaking disaster.

I want to be strong, especially with Gen beside me, but I'm bordering on hyperventilation. I double-check the positioning of Gen's arm and grab the armrests so tight I think I puncture the faux leather. When the plane takes another six-foot drop, I scrunch my eyes shut and vow to just hang the fuck on.

Positive thoughts, Flynn. Think positively.

All my focus goes toward arriving safely.

I imagine myself in the Atlantic City arrivals terminal. We're strolling down the gangway, moving with the crowds of travelers toward baggage claim. In my head, I create an image of the place so real I can almost touch the luggage on the carousels. I've seen pictures. When I did my internet research to try to fool Gen into thinking I've flown before, I studied the Atlantic City airport.

And then, quite suddenly, I'm there.

Sort of.

Chapter 45
Arrivals

I STARE around the airport terminal, wavering slightly on my feet while travelers pass me on both sides. Plastic seats, gift shops, food kiosks—I could be anywhere. Except the shops feature T-shirts from the various Atlantic City casinos: Harrah's, Trump, Caesar's, and the lit signs lining the walls advertise the same.

I've arrived at my destination. Without my luggage or Genesis or an airplane.

Or my body.

"Goddammit!" I scream, because I know no one can hear me. And no one does. One guy even swings his hand across the space I occupy, causing a pins-and-needles sensation to flutter through me where it passes. I shake off the feeling and turn in a slow circle.

Bad idea. The mild vertigo increases to major, and I grab for the nearest seat back to steady myself. Then I wait for it to fade.

Except it doesn't.

It takes me several minutes to figure out what's wrong. When I do, I want to do more than curse.

"I'm out of body, *and* I'm half-drunk. Can this day get any worse?"

"They won't be here yet. We're almost an hour early," a familiar voice behind me says.

When am I going to learn not to ask that last question?

I turn, more slowly this time to cut down on the room spinnies, and face Cassandra—the speaker, along with Peter and a woman I don't recognize. Peter looks a helluva lot better than the last time I saw him. His hair has thickened and his waistline has filled out. Guess Cassie rewarded him for his service in getting me to attend this damn conference. They stand in a clustered triangle, eyeing gate B14 for United Airlines, the one my plane will arrive at in about forty-five minutes.

And oh shit, Gen's got to be having a fit right about now. She'd know the minute I "stepped out," so to speak. I tend to flop over when I abandon the physical. She'll need to come up with some kind of plausible reason to give the flight crew—I've passed out from the drinks, or I've gone to sleep, or something. But when they land….

I can just see it: paramedics, security, and God knows who else rushing to my unconscious aid after the plane touches down. I've got to reunite with my body before that happens.

I've also left poor Genesis alone on that shaking, bouncing, dipping deathtrap in the middle of a freaking thunderstorm, which just now arrives outside the airport's windows with a distant roll of thunder and a flash of lightning. The pelting raindrops sound like a thousand cockroaches dancing on the concrete roof and metal awnings.

"We needed to be here early in order to intercept them," the unfamiliar woman says. "Nathaniel assured me they'd gotten on the plane."

Uh-oh.

"Are you sure you have enough power for that, Madame President?" Cassie asks.

So this is the Registry's board president. Huh.

I check her out from her austerely styled blond hair, down the lines of her pale blue business suit, to the pair of nicely shaped legs extending beneath the knee-length skirt. The outfit screams power and fits her every curve, some nice ones at that. She's probably in her mid- to late forties, judging from the handful of stress lines and the way she carries herself, but she has the body of a twentysomething.

"That is my talent, blocking others' skills," she says, pursing her lips together in an unpleasant frown afterward. I doubt many people question her abilities. "Would you care for me to demonstrate?"

Some of the blood drains from Cassandra's rouged cheeks. "No, ma'am."

Much as I dislike Cassie, I almost have to feel sorry for her. Almost.

Peter steps between them in one smooth motion, and I have to admit, it's good to see him able to move that way again. "What she means, I'm sure, is that she's simply concerned for you, President Argyle. The Flynn woman has proven to be extremely strong, what with her ability to not only *push* but to *pull* magic from others, not to mention her *walking*."

"And to do it through *time*," Cassie says, finding her voice.

Fuck. It was naive, I know, but I still had clung to the hope that maybe Cassandra hadn't figured out exactly what I could do, and if she had, that she'd keep it to herself. Chris had later said that he'd turned on the charm for her, and that he'd thought she'd expressed a bit of interest in him. Not that I wanted those two getting chummy, but if it kept her quiet....

Clearly it hadn't.

"I didn't become board president by being a psychic weakling. Besides, I'm not making any overt moves right now. Just a 'testing of the waters,' so to speak. We're here for me to introduce myself to our new prospective member, present her with her obligations while Genesis attends the conference, and during the course of our conversation, I'll extend a temporary block."

"Just to make sure you can," Cassie mutters.

If President Argyle hears it, she doesn't let on, but her eyes flash at the suggested insult.

The whole thing pisses me off. Here I am, doing what they want, and they're still plotting against me. I consider *pulling* some of Madame President's power out of her, just to teach her a lesson, but I don't do it. If she's that strong, she might sense the attack and figure out that I'm listening to their conversation. And I'm not sure I can *pull* in this form, anyway.

I cross my ephemeral arms over my chest, glaring at the three of them in impotent fury.

"Let's get breakfast," Peter suggests. "It'll kill time and top off everyone's strength."

Argyle gives one curt nod before leading the way down the corridor toward the food kiosks.

Leaving me standing around in a terminal filled with people who can't see or hear me.

I entertain myself for maybe twenty minutes screwing with people's minds by playing the poltergeist. Nothing too obvious: sliding a coffee cup across a slick table, billowing curtains beside a closed window—things that could be explained away. I'm not so out of it that I want to announce magical ability to the world of nulls. Gen's instilled in me the need to keep the extent of psychics' powers a secret.

The amusement wears off fast, and I end up staring at the sealed gangway door to gate B14.

God, Gen, I'm sorry. I didn't mean to do this to you.

The cabal of evil returns with their steaming coffees and little breakfast sandwiches and takes up a position in the seating area of the gate across the walkway. Guess they hope we won't see them until they're upon us.

The overhead speakers give a pleasant chime; then a practiced male voice announces, "Attention, passengers for United Airlines flight 701 bound for Orlando, Florida. The gate has been changed to D17. Please proceed to the new departure gate. Repeat—"

I don't wait for the recap. I'm already racing to the closest terminal map, lit and hanging on a nearby support pillar—along with several dozen other people. At least I am able to race now. My drunken buzz has worn off.

One good thing about being out of body. I don't have to worry about crowds. Much.

It takes a bit of steeling myself to push through the first person at the rear of the cluster. The older gentleman shudders with my passing, and my stomach turns over, but I make it. The second one, a middle-aged woman with a toddler in her arms, goes a little worse. Goose bumps flare over my invisible flesh while she sneezes violently and the kid shrieks.

I glance down at the small boy, and he looks up at me. He reaches out a tiny hand, waving it through my forearm, then screams again and buries his face against his mother's chest.

Interesting and disturbing. Kids, at least this one, can see me. Either it's an age thing or he has some magical ability of his own. I'm glad he's too young to speak coherently. Otherwise I'd be responsible for who knows how many child psychologist appointments in his future. Considering how loudly he's wailing, I still might.

I have to get through three more bodies to reach the display, and by the time I can see it, I'm sucking great lungfuls of air into my nonexistent chest. The map increases my distress. D17 lies two terminals over. I have to take a monorail, and even with that assistance, it's at the farthest end. And Gen's plane is minutes from arrival.

Fuck.

Heaving a deep breath, I plow back the way I came, through five or six people... and face-plant onto the industrial grade, too thin carpeting.

God, I hate this.

Swirls and patterns float dizzyingly in my vision until I figure out it's the spirals on the carpet itself. I lever myself upright, weak and shaky. So I do have limits. Good to know.

The race to the new gate becomes more of a zombie-esque stagger and shamble. Down one long-ass corridor, wait for the tram, be sure to board when the others do. I can walk through living creatures. I can't walk through nonliving material, except, apparently, when it's attached to a living being, like clothing. I give a quick eye roll at that thought that never occurred to me before. Who makes these rules, anyway?

I hit the gate out of breath, barely keeping my feet under me, and brace myself against the wall beside the gangway door. When it opens, I'm the first one stumbling down the tunneled ramp. The plane's entry hatch stands open, the familiar flight attendant assisting a woman into a wheelchair while her male traveling companion waits to roll her into the terminal.

There's no way I can manage another pass through a living human spirit, so I wait, tapping my ethereal foot, until they clear the passage. Then I'm in the plane... and faced with an aisle crowded by passengers gathering their personal belongings from the overhead bins.

Thank goodness we're in first class and close to the front in the third row. I can just make out Genesis, leaning over my "asleep" figure, and I wave frantically to get her attention.

Her face shows obvious relief at my arrival, and she beckons me forward, but I point at the four people between us and shake my head.

"You have to," she mouths, then glances backward pointedly. I follow her gaze to a second flight attendant, male this time and model-quality good-looking, engaged in rapid-fire conversation with a man in a dark gray suit, carrying a black medical-type bag. The attendant gestures toward my body, slumped in my seat, not waking despite all the noise and disruption. Nathaniel hovers behind them, frowning.

Okay, then.

Instead of going down the aisle, I climb, over the seats, over the seat backs, stepping on cushions, cracking my knee against an unfolded tray table. All the rows are vacant, since everyone except me and Genesis is already up. I misjudge the final drop and fall, quite literally, into my prone form.

Chapter 46
Delayed Anger

"I'M READY to kill you right now," Gen whispers into my ear as I come back to my physical senses.

Not the affectionate concern I'd hoped for, but I can't blame her. "How bad was it?" I mumble through a mouth not quite working yet.

She takes a breath before answering. Not a good sign. "I convinced them you'd taken a sleeping pill on top of the rum and Cokes. And that you were a really, really sound sleeper in general. That didn't stop the doctor five rows back from checking your pulse and kinda freaking at how slow it was. I think they've called an ambulance."

"Fuck." I push myself upright in the seat, then go to stand, only to be restrained by my still fastened seat belt. One flick of the buckle and I'm free. But my drained body doesn't want to get up. "You wouldn't believe what I've been through."

"It's been no picnic here either," Gen says.

"Right, sorry. I didn't mean to abandon you." It comes out more pitiful than I intended, but I really feel like hell. The vomit bag in the seat pouch looks better every second, and I swallow a mouthful of bile. The heat in my face isn't just embarrassment. I'm running another fever.

Gen's face softens, and she presses her cool palm to my forehead. "Can you walk?"

"Not sure yet."

Glancing past my shoulder to the center aisle, she mutters, "Better *be* sure."

"Ma'am."

I shift toward the new voice, a deep baritone emanating from the guy with the medical bag. Behind him, the male flight attendant has stopped passenger traffic from disembarking, holding everyone up while the doctor checks me out and generally pissing off a plane full of people. I can't spot Nathaniel anymore, but I'm certain he's in the crowd somewhere, watching.

If his talent is reading others' powers, could he tell I was out of body? Is a spirit the same thing as magical energy? Questions for later.

The doctor reaches for my wrist, but I wave him off. And hey, my hand doesn't even shake. Much. "I'm fine," I tell him.

He shakes his head. "You weren't fine an hour ago."

The little chuckle I make sounds false even to me. "Yeah, well, booze and sleeping pills don't mix. Guess I should have paid better attention to the warning label."

He's peering at my face, where a trickle of sweat runs down my temple, so I add, "Toss in a touch of the flu and you've got this."

That last came out a bit too loud. Behind him, the passengers grow more agitated. Right. Flu on an airplane. Close quarters. Recycled air. They'll think I've exposed everyone on board. Hope they've had their shots or they'll worry themselves for the next several days.

"I was fine this morning," I say even more loudly. Last thing I need is an angry mob.

"We've called transportation for you to the nearest hospital," the attendant puts in, giving me a serious stare that erases some of his handsome qualities.

"It will be here in a few minutes." That voice comes from my opposite side, where the female attendant from when we first boarded wrings her hands with worry. She's still pretty damn attractive.

In fact, she's fucking hot. The rough flight tousled her some, and her uniform's a bit askew, the shirt half-untucked. An extra button has come undone, revealing a good amount of cleavage and—

Shit. With an almost audible groan, I clamp down on the sexual arousal building between my legs. Succubus. Right. And the powers attached to the title carry erotic side effects.

Have I mentioned I hate this?

"I'm not going to the hospital. I'm going to my hotel. And to bed." With a force of will, I press both palms on the armrests and stand. Gen rises behind me, I suspect as much to catch me if I fall as to present a united front. "You can't make me see doctors. And I'm fine now."

"You're declining medical treatment?" the male attendant asks.

I cock my head at him. Very precise phrasing, and I get it. He's covering his legal ass. No problem. "Yes," I say. "I'm officially declining medical assistance and treatment. United has taken great care of us. Thank you for your concern."

The poster-boy smile returns, flashing bright white teeth. He nods. "You're welcome. I hope you're feeling better soon. Have a safe trip to your hotel."

The doctor blusters and fusses a few seconds more, but they've released the tide and he can't do much with people pushing and shoving past him. Still no sign of Nathaniel. Maybe he ducked in the bathroom. The male attendant grabs our carry-ons for us while the woman fetches the dress and tux. I hate that Genesis takes them all herself, slinging my duffel over her shoulder, draping two garment carriers over her left arm, and holding her own bag in her right, but I'm doing well to walk at all. For once, the narrow airplane aisle works to someone's advantage. It means I can grab the seat backs to get myself off the damn plane.

The connecting tunnel isn't as manageable. I have to stop and lean against the side for a minute before I can keep going. While the remaining passengers pass us, I bring Gen up to speed on our welcoming committee. I also mention Nathaniel's sudden disappearance and the fact that he might yet be behind us, so we keep our voices low.

She looks like she wants to cross her arms or stamp her foot, but she can do neither while carrying all our stuff. And there's still more to collect at baggage claim. Weeklong conference plus wedding plus reception means a lot of luggage.

"You'll have to let President Argyle block you," she says. "You don't have the strength to fight right now. If you attempt to push her power out, you'll collapse."

"Yeah, kinda figured that out. What should I expect?"

Gen purses her lips. "I've never been blocked. But I've heard it's like being wrapped in psychic cotton. You lose a sense of a piece of yourself, sometimes a piece you weren't really aware of before. Imagine not being able to see or hear or taste or smell for a while. It doesn't hurt, but it's not comfortable."

"Dandy."

"Don't sweat it, Flynn. It should only affect you while you're in close proximity to her. Once we reach the hotel, it will fade. And besides," Gen adds with a sly grin, "it might not be a bad idea to give her a false sense of security when it comes to you. She doesn't know you're weakened. She'll think this is all the power you have."

"*Is* it false? She's supposed to be this badass president, right?"

Gen fixes me with her no-nonsense look and lowers her voice further, even though we're alone in the tunnel. "I've watched you for months. I've seen what you can do. Untrained, you're one of the strongest powers I've ever encountered. And trained…." She breaks off, letting the implications sink in, the words coming through loud and clear though she doesn't say them.

Trained, I may be stronger than the president of the National Psychic Registry.

Gen seems proud, but I've seen Madame President. That's a woman who will not welcome any challenge to her skills or authority, not that I want to challenge her at all. I just want enough instruction to get a grip on my skills so I don't go haring off every time I'm under stress. Then I want to be left alone.

Somehow I don't think what I want will matter.

Chapter 47
First Impressions

"GENESIS, WELCOME," President Argyle says, opening her arms and expecting Gen to step into them. Gen does it. Reluctantly. The hug is neither warm nor sincere—merely an acknowledgment of another psychic who's been absent from the area for a long time. I've seen it before, among corporate types at the Pub, and I've never understood it. On the rare occasions I embrace someone, it means something. "I understand you had a rough flight. You're looking rather pale."

Gen nods, and I examine her. She is pale. Another worm of guilt wriggles through my belly. Gen's a seasoned flier, and that trip terrified her. And I left her alone. I've got to get a grip on all this.

Behind Argyle, Peter offers me a smile, which I find myself returning. Despite the manipulation, I like the man. And what choice did he have?

Cassie's another story. She's shifting her weight from high heel to high heel, staring anywhere but at me while casting impatient glances at her cell phone.

We were the last out of the tunnel and we made them wait. Good. They weren't supposed to be here.

Then Nathaniel strolls from the tunnel doorway, jaunty as you please and bag in hand. He gives President Argyle a nod and a wave and heads for baggage claim, just another conference goer. Not spying on me and Genesis. Nope, nothing like that.

Asshole.

By now, the area's pretty much deserted. Must not be another flight due in for a while, and public address announcements inform us that passengers intending to take our plane back to Orlando have been rerouted with another gate and now an aircraft change. I know security cameras must be everywhere, but I wish more people were around.

At last President Argyle turns her attention to me, and I resist the impulse to shudder under her gaze. "So, you must be Ms. Dalton."

"Madame President," I return, and inwardly kick myself. I shouldn't know that method of address.

Instead of surprise, she smiles. "Ah, I see Genesis has instructed you on the formalities. Good. But please, call me Linda. If I may call you Flynn? And what a lovely and unusual name." *For a girl*, goes unsaid, but I hear it in her tone.

"Call me whatever you want," I say, shrugging. "I'm not particular." *Or impaired by a stick up my ass*, goes unsaid on my end. Genesis suppresses a snicker, covering it with a cough.

Cassandra looks ready to spit. Guess "Linda" doesn't let just anyone call her by her first name, and certainly not Cassie.

"Excellent," Linda says.

And then I feel it. Damp and heavy like fog. Soft like mounds of cotton balls. It settles over me, pressing into my skin and beneath, seeking out my magical center. It doesn't find much. I've got precious little energy left. But what it does locate, it cuts off from my access with an internal snap that sends me reeling into the closest blue plastic chair. For a few seconds, my vision blurs and a roaring echoes in my ears. Then both fade, leaving me trembling.

"That wasn't necessary," Genesis snaps, dropping her bag to grab my arm. Peter takes our other things from her so she can wrap both arms around my waist.

"My apologies," President Argyle offers. "But Flynn is an unknown. It's a standard precaution, until she joins us and we can trust and train her."

The need to *push, pull,* or *walk* becomes so intense I can barely stand the pressure. I can't, so I *have* to. Like when people blink repeatedly in a dark room until their eyes adjust, or when I had to clear my ears on the plane. The loss of my normal hearing felt too unnatural. I *had* to do something about it. It drove me crazy until they popped.

Only there's nothing I can do here. I'm too damn tired.

I hate this. I hate this a lot.

"If you focus on other things, you won't notice the loss as much," Argyle says, then spins on one heel and waves a hand over her shoulder. "Come on, let's get the rest of your baggage. We have a limousine waiting." Cassie and Peter, still carrying everything, fall into step behind her, the perfect little toadies. And that's that. End of discussion.

"You all right?" Gen says.

"No, but I'll manage. Let's get this over with so we can lock ourselves in our hotel room. I want food, sleep, and a shower, in any order." *I want access to my fucking power.*

The irony registers when we've gone halfway through the terminal, and I wave off Gen's incredulous look at my sudden laughter. First I want the magic gone. Now I want it back. I really need to make up my goddamn mind.

IN THE limo, Cassandra goes over my schedule for the week. It's long and detailed, filled with meetings with the board members, something she calls a power assessment, introduction to my instructors, and training sessions. In and around those, I'm permitted to accompany Genesis to a variety of conference events and social functions.

Wednesday is Gen's birthday. I still have no gift and nothing planned. The wedding and reception come on Friday, with one more conference day after that.

I hope Gen's keeping track of everything, or they've got it written down somewhere, because I'm zoning out and dozing after about five minutes of dates, places, and times. Really, I wish I could enjoy the limo ride. I've never traveled in one, and the buttons and little doors pique my curiosity. I want to sip a drink from the built-in bar, stick my head out

the sunroof like Richard Gere in *Pretty Woman*, but I
can't keep my eyes open.

At some point Gen presses a couple of aspirin
into my palm, and I swallow them with a few sips
of cold Sprite from a can she holds to my lips. Then
I'm out again.

Our arrival at the hotel wakes me. The chauf-
feur opens the door, letting in a stream of bright sunlight and cold October-in-New-Jersey air. Harrah's
Casino Resort sits right near the water, so a steady
breeze blows, carrying a pleasant briny scent I asso-
ciate with oceans and beaches. But the temperature
reminds me I'm not in Florida anymore.

Or Kansas, Dorothy.

I'm in Oz.

Twinkling lights, bustling valets, squeaking luggage carts. We're ushered into a lobby of polished
pale woods, gold fixtures, and not-so-tastefully embedded neon lighting. One of several casinos bor-
ders the lobby, and bells and chimes and happy "You
won!" music carry through an open archway.

Gen parks me on the closest empty sofa—a soft
red velvet monstrosity that attempts to swallow me,
ass first. But it's heaven. When she returns, she's got
room key cards in hand and a bellhop in tow dragging a cart stacked with our bags, the garment carriers hanging off either end. And Cassie, Peter, and
Madame President have vanished.

I poke at my power. Nope, still blocked, so the
bitch prez must be in the lobby somewhere.

We board a glass-walled elevator. The bellhop
takes one of the keys and inserts it into the slot by the

buttons. "Top floor," he muses. "Honeymoon suite?" He sounds a little confused.

"Yep," Gen says, wrapping her hands around my bicep.

"Ah, I see. Congratulations." He's blushing, but he recovers quickly, so I don't give him my patented scowl.

The doors slide shut with a soft thunk, and my power returns in a staggering surge—a wave of pure ecstasy flowing from my boot soles to my brain, sending little tremors cascading through my entire body. Gen must feel the twitching because she shoots me a concerned glance, but I shake my head.

I'm fine. I'm more than fine. The temporary block has sharpened my acuity to the magic, or intensified it somehow. Having it gone and then having that one sense return, I can focus in on it specifically, isolate it from my other five senses that often interfere. I have a clearer estimation and understanding of my abilities and limits... and those limits stun me.

Even tired from my airplane excursion, I've got energy to spare, because I know how to draw upon it, know where to find it.

I tap into it several times on our way to the suite, just to solidify my relationship with it. Damn, I wish Linda Argyle and Cassandra were around now. I might teach them a lesson in manners.

The elevator glides to a halt and we disembark, following the bellhop down a short corridor to a set of double doors. I turn in a slow circle. There are no other doors. We have the only room on the floor.

An engraved gold plaque identifies the room as the Honeymoon Suite. A doorbell sits below the key card slot.

Doorbell? Why would a hotel room need a doorbell? How big is this freaking suite, anyway?

I get my answer when our guide swings open both doors with a flourish that would make a magician proud.

Gen strolls straight into the room, though "room" would be a tremendous understatement. Me? I stand in the doorway, gawking at our residence for the next seven nights.

One would think living in a mansion would make me accustomed to opulence and grandeur.

One would be wrong.

Our bellman parks his luggage rack in the marble-tiled entry hall with small doors on either side and an archway leading into a living area bigger than the entire hotel room I occupied before I moved in with Genesis. I sneak a quick peak into the two doors: coat closet on the left, half bathroom on the right.

"For guests," the bellman explains. Even without a shower or tub it's bigger than my old hotel room's bathroom.

Guests, right. A suite with a doorbell and a guest bathroom. Sure. Why not?

I push on through into the living room. Soft blues and golds create a color scheme soothing to the eye and spirit. A large couch and two easy chairs face a flat-screen TV. A wet bar, fully stocked, takes up the front area. But it's the ten-person jacuzzi in the far-left corner that draws my attention. I walk to its edge and stare into it, empty now, imagining it filled with water and people doing God knows what.

Or me and Gen doing exactly what I'd like to do to her right now.

I have more in common with the traditional succubus myth than I want to admit, and using my power always results in an increase in my sex drive. So, yeah. I like the jacuzzi-in-the-living-room idea. And from the smirk Gen gives me from her perch on the couch's arm, she's reading my mind, and she likes it too.

The zing of a cord draws my attention to the thick gold curtains extending across the entire rear wall of the room. They part at the center, letting in blinding sunlight, and I raise a hand to shield my eyes from the glare. When I can see again, I'm met with an incredible view of the Atlantic Ocean and the boardwalk far, far below us. White-capped gray waves crash against the stone breakers while people in coats and hats admire the beauty of it all.

Two more doors to investigate. Before doing so, I step behind the bar, pull open the three-quarter size fridge, and grab a Coke Zero. Something tells me I'll need the caffeine for the rest of my tour.

Fortified, I follow the bellman through the single door on the left into a bedroom containing two double beds. Comforters displaying seascapes in pastels decorate the mattresses. There's another flat-screen, and the attached bathroom contains a shower bigger than a walk-in closet with dual showerheads. A basket of high-end toiletries waits on the double-sink counter.

I'm a little confused by the separate beds. If they're going for traditional, which I honestly can't imagine a casino hotel doing, then why would we be sharing a room at all? But I have limited (okay, nonexistent) experience with these things.

"If this is the bedroom, where does the other set of doors on the far side of the living room lead?" I ask, hoping I'm not showing too much ignorance.

Apparently I am, because the bellhop raises an eyebrow which he quickly lowers, and Genesis giggles from the doorway to the living room.

"The master bedroom, ma'am," the bellman explains.

"Um, are we expected to sleep apart?" I direct it to Genesis, who looks ready to choke on her laughter. My face heats.

"I wouldn't presume to judge, ma'am," the poor bellman mutters.

That does it. Gen loses it, bursting into hysterics and flopping on one of the made double beds. She rolls around a bit, holding her middle as if she's afraid the laughter might dump her insides out.

I want to crawl in a hole somewhere. I'm not mad, just humiliated, and when she finally regains some control, Gen looks at my face and sobers. "Sorry, Flynn," she says. "It's just… the expression on your face… of course I wouldn't dream of sleeping without you. This room is for Chris when he arrives on Wednesday morning."

Of course. He's not attending the conference, so he's coming in later, for her birthday and then the wedding. And since he's going to help her get ready and such, it makes sense he'd stay in the suite.

I have nothing to say, so I step from the room, cross the living area, and throw open the double doors leading into the master. And freeze again.

It's... impressive. And gaudy. And a lot erotic.

I kinda like it.

Huge four-poster bed. A chest at the foot of it, but no drawers, and I can't find a way to open the top. There's a button on its side, so I press it, hoping I'm not summoning security or something. A humming ensues, a panel in the top slides open, and yet another flat-screen TV rises from the chest's depths and locks into place atop it. Huh.

But the most unusual feature (or maybe not, since this is Atlantic City) is the ceiling of mirrors directly above the bed.

"Oh wow," Gen breathes behind me, peering around my shoulder.

"Yeah."

"That could be fun."

"Yeah." I'm short on words, imagining the possibilities. Gen runs her fingertips down my arm, raising goose bumps. I slide that arm around her, snuggling her in close. It's a bold move for me, with the bellhop in the suite somewhere where he could see us, and she laps up the affection like a cat with cream.

At that moment, the bellhop in question clears his throat loudly, making us both jump a little. "I'll just hang the garment bags in your closet and place the rest of the luggage in your bedroom, all right?"

"Right," I say, still staring at the bed and the mirrors.

"Um, if you'll step aside?"

Oh. Duh. We get out of his way. He places bag after bag on the plush gray carpeting with threads of pale blue and gold running through it, then disappears into a huge walk-in closet in the corner.

"If this is the bedroom, I can't wait to see...." Gen says, taking my arm and pulling me toward the bath.

Mind-blowing. An even bigger shower, this one with maybe twelve nozzles up and down the three tiled walls, the fourth frosted glass door etched with a seascape of sand dunes and gulls.

"Oh yeah." Gen's breathing comes a little faster than normal. I swallow hard.

"So, ladies!" the bellhop announces, stepping into the bathroom with us. I get the distinct impression he's laughing inside, and I can't really blame him, the way we're ogling the chrome fixtures. "Will there be anything else?"

"No," I say, shoving my hand into my pocket and passing him a bill. I meant to grab a ten. I think I gave him a twenty. At the moment, I don't really care.

"More towels, blankets, pillows?"

"No," Gen says, placing a gentle hand between his shoulder blades and giving a small shove.

"Perhaps I can fetch some ice for—"

"No!" Gen and I say together.

He's grinning from ear to ear, his shyness and embarrassment forgotten. Turning to face us, he offers a sweeping bow. "Then I'll take my leave, ladies, and once again, congratulations on your upcoming wedding. I foresee a long, happy life together for the two of you."

The bellman disappears from the bathroom. A moment later we hear the door to the hallway shut.

"So," Gen says, that I'm-going-to-eat-you-alive look in her eye, "shower, bed, or the swimming pool in the living room?"

"Hell," I say, setting my Coke Zero on the counter, "why not all three?" I pull my black T-shirt over my head and toss it aside, ignoring the jolt of pain the movement gives me from my shoulder.

Okay, body, you want this. You'd better not give out on me today.

She steps into the shower fully clothed and turns the nozzles all the way on. The sprays shoot from a dozen directions, soaking through her white shirt and making her shriek before the water warms up. The chilled blast has her nipples already peaking, clear and obvious through the thin material. "Love the way you think, Flynn," Genesis says, and pulls me in with her.

Chapter 48
Party Time

Genesis forced a smile on her face to hide her anger as she stepped through the ballroom doors. The reserved space glittered with tiny gold bulbs hanging from the ceiling and silver-and-white tablecloths adorning the scattered high tables where conference goers stood chatting and drinking. The opening-night cocktail reception.

And Flynn was upstairs, asleep.

Genesis wasn't mad at her lover. Gen's legs carried a pleasant ache, her entire body suffused with a comfortable lethargy from their intense lovemaking. They'd made it through round one in the shower and round two in the mirrored bed, before Flynn's energy gave out and she fell into a heavy sleep.

A sleep that might not have been necessary if not for all the stress of the trip, the out-of-body accidental shift, and then the temporary block on her power that President Argyle had imposed.

Unreasonable and uncalled-for. Flynn had never shown any aggressiveness with her magic, had never harmed anyone with it except in self-defense.

Okay, yes, she'd unintentionally harmed me, but that had been at my own request.

And she'd killed Max Harris, but with a gun, not with her power, at least not directly.

The dark magic writhed inside her core, the desire to make Argyle and all the others pay for what they'd done to her and Flynn barely containable. She had the strength. She had the skills. Genesis curled her nails into her palms, the perfectly manicured red surfaces digging into her skin. Somehow she had to hold on. She searched the room.

No sign of Madame President.

Thank God.

With Linda Argyle's absence, the need for vengeance faded. But it served as a reminder of just how much she depended upon Flynn's steadying presence and how much she missed it now.

Genesis stepped farther into the room. Heads turned at her entry, and there were a lot of them to turn. The Registry had several thousand members, and there looked to be about five hundred in this gathering alone. Hotel staff had opened the accordion doors between two ballrooms to accommodate them all.

Friends she hadn't seen in two years smiled and waved, several different clusters of people beckoning her to their tables from multiple directions. Unfamiliar faces, both male and female, showed appreciation of her attire—the same spaghetti-strapped, black tiered, thigh-length dress she'd worn the night Flynn proposed to her.

Her frown returned. She brought the dress with her to please Flynn, and now Flynn was upstairs sleeping the sleep of the truly exhausted.

Nathaniel approached out of a talkative group to her right, a big grin on his face and his hands extended to take hers. She'd always considered him a friend, a fellow talent in the Orlando area she could trust. She'd invited him to the wedding. But he'd also gone to college with Linda Argyle.

After what Flynn had told her in bed between rounds, she wasn't sure of him anymore.

And all the while, the darkness whispered suggestions in her ears.

"Good to see you again," he said. "Glad to know you had a valid reason for skipping out on us last year. Getting married, huh? And that woman I saw you with at the airport is the lucky one, right? She's impressive."

Genesis allowed him to take her hands, but she squeezed them back a little harder than necessary before dropping them. His eyebrows drew together in brief confusion, but he said nothing.

"You would know. You can see how much power she has," she said, keeping her voice low. And cold, so cold. She hardly recognized it. "Besides, you were spying on us at the airport. That wasn't coincidence. Just how long has Linda had you watching Flynn?"

He had the good grace to look sheepish. "A couple of months, since she sent the invitation. You know how it is, Gen. What the president wants, the

president gets… or you suffer some inexplicable
bad luck. I've been in and out of work. Every time
I even think of saying no to her, I get laid off or my
next interview goes poorly. It's like she knows, and
she probably does. I'm betting she has a clairvoyant
keeping an eye on me."

"Which seems fair, considering." She would
have harangued him further and possibly done much
worse, but another figure arrived in the entryway,
drawing her attention.

Soft brown suede boots ran to midcalf. No
heels, but the woman was plenty tall enough. A
long-sleeved deep blue velvet dress wrapped her in a
crisscross pattern that pulled in at the waist but flared
at the hips to flatter her curves and ended just above
the boots. The neckline plunged into a sharp *V*. The
matching brown suede belt tied it together, along
with a silver necklace and bracelet.

Gen reached the woman's face, wearing taste-
fully applied, minimal makeup, the long light brown
hair twisted over her shoulder in an intricate braid.
Genesis's mouth went dry. The woman smiled at her.
Because she knew her.

Because it was Flynn.

Chapter 49
Lessons and Teachers

OKAY, YEAH, I lied about being tired, and I faked going to sleep. But how else was I going to get Genesis out of the suite so I could shower—again—and change into Rosaline's creation?

I'd kept an eye on the clock throughout the mind-blowing sex, well, most of the time with a few minutes or… um… hours lost here and there. When I saw it nearing five with the reception at seven and dinner set for eight, I closed my eyes, slowed my breathing, and fought not to really doze off.

I think I zoned in and out while Gen showered and changed, with me sneaking peeks at her when she emerged from the bathroom, naked, and stepped into a black thong and fastened a strapless bra. She kept darting glances at me, so I had to be careful, and when she crept into the closet and returned in that amazing spaghetti-strap dress, I knew why. She'd set out to surprise me as much as I intended to surprise her.

The last time I saw her in it, my jaw dropped and my feet nailed themselves to the floor of the Pub. She'd had to come fetch me and walk me to the bar.

Well, two could play that game.

The second I heard the door to the suite shut, I sprang into action. Quick shower, into my clothes—I'd shaved last night, another reason I'd gotten little sleep—then makeup and hair.

Diego's daughters had spent hours teaching me how to do both. I proved a slow learner. But I practiced whenever Gen was with a client, so I had it down now.

The boots slid onto my feet with ease, and I finished the ensemble with the jewelry I'd so carefully hidden in my tool kit where Gen would never find it, stowing it in my carry-on at the last minute.

Great big pain in the ass. I don't know how other women do it day after day. But it was all worth it to see the current look on Genesis's face.

She approaches slowly from where she stands with Nathaniel—and what the hell is that about?—but I don't have time to worry over it because she's scanning me from boots to hair and back down again.

"Why?" she whispers.

My smile fades. Not quite the first thing I expected to hear out of her mouth. And why does this scenario feel familiar? Oh, I know. Because the last time I tried to surprise her, she left me standing with an engagement ring in the middle of a dance floor.

Like I said, I'm a slow learner.

Genesis must pick up on my distress because she grabs both my hands, then lets go and wraps her arms around me. "No, Flynn. You look fantastic. I mean, more than fantastic. I love the dress, and the hair, and everything else. But I need to know. Why? Does this have anything to do with what happened at the mall?"

I guess I hesitate a little too long, because she squeezes me tighter.

"There is nothing, absolutely nothing about you that I want changed," she says. "For tonight, I'll enjoy the exception to the rule. I'll savor the moment, emblazon the image in my memory—" Gen glances up at me with a quick grin. "—and use it for blackmail material next time we're out for beers with the construction crew." Before I can stop her, she pulls her phone from the tiny purse she's slung over one shoulder and takes a picture of me, dress and all.

"I'll just say it was a costume party," I grumble.

She laughs, then sobers. "Seriously, though. Don't do this for me. If you want to femme up, femme up. But for you. Not for me. Got it?"

"Got it." And that, folks, is just one more reason why I'm marrying this girl.

Chapter 50
Face to Face

WE MAKE it through the reception and dinner without me spilling anything on my dress. Living in Florida, I'm not used to long sleeves. Combining them with a fabulous meal of roast pork in burgundy sauce, sweet potatoes topped with marshmallows, green beans cooked with lime so even I'll eat them, and pumpkin pie for dessert, writes a recipe for potential disaster. And yet not a single stain mars my clothing when we push ourselves away from the table.

Gen and I ate with a couple of talents she knows who hail from Virginia—Luke, a tall, strikingly handsome blond man who works in some capacity for the US government (and can't tell me exactly what he does), and his wife, Sara, who is as plain as he is good-looking yet whose smile invites one into conversation. She's a psychokinetic, also working for the government, manipulating metals and other materials in dangerous places such as nuclear facilities to perform maintenance and effect repairs.

They invite us to hit the casino's dance club afterward, but we decline. The sex and the food and the plane ride have caught up with us, and faking sleep doesn't count for real sleep. Besides, I doubt my leg can handle dancing anymore. I want bed.

Unfortunately, the Registry has other ideas.

"Ms. Dalton!" a male voice calls as we wait for the elevators. Harrah's has notoriously slow lifts and way too many guests for those lifts. It's working against me now.

I turn toward Nathaniel, the voice's owner, already predisposed to dislike him.

"What?" I growl, backing him up a step.

"Your schedule. You're supposed to be in a meeting with the board. Right now."

I shoot a glance at Genesis, who raises both palms in the air. "Don't look at me. I wasn't much more awake in the limo than you. If they want you to follow a time line, they need to email it to us or something."

"We did." Nathaniel sets his hands on his hips and waits, the very picture of the perfect flunky.

With a long-suffering sigh, I nod. No need to give them any reason to invalidate Cassie's promise to heal me. "I'll meet you back at the room," I tell Gen. "Lead on, Nate."

"It's Nathaniel."

"Right, sure." Good, I know what annoys him, and I intend to every chance I get.

Gen steps on the elevator as Nate leads me off down the hall between conference rooms, "The Inlet Room," "The Promenade Room," "The Bayfront

Room," and stops beside the entry to "The Coney Island Room," which somehow seems fitting for this three-ring shitshow. Pushing open one of the swinging doors, he gestures for me to precede him. "After you."

I step inside, Nate so close behind he's practically stepping on the heels of my boots. I'm about to tell him to back off when I realize the purpose—to prevent me from turning and making a break for it.

Before me, at a long table, sit ten people I assume to be the board members, and a more imposing bunch I doubt I've ever encountered. They all face me, the table between us, with Madame President Argyle at the center of the row and an empty seat on either side of her. I'm wondering if she likes her personal space or if two of the members are absent.

"Glad you could join us, Flynn," she says, the word "finally" understood in her tone. "You look… nice."

Don't sound so surprised, bitch. I didn't dress up for you. "Thanks," I say instead. Gen would be so proud, though I can't quite muster up a smile. Argyle seems nervous, her fingers plucking at the white tablecloth while she shifts in her seat. I expect the block to fall on my power again, but it doesn't come.

"Well," she says, a little too fast and high-pitched, "now that everyone is present, let the testing begin."

Chapter 51
Battle of Wills

AH, THAT explains it. They can't block me if they want to test my abilities. And that puts them in a dangerous position. Two male board members at the end of the table whisper to one another while never letting their eyes leave me. One woman has her hands braced on the table's surface, like she's ready to use it as a barrier.

Holy shit, they're afraid of me.

And I'm an opportunist. A fucking tired opportunist. "I'm not great at tests when I haven't had any sleep," I say.

"Or when you've been traveling out of body within the last twenty-four hours?" Nate suggests. "You took a trip today, and I don't just mean the airplane ride. I saw the power surge. Where did you go?"

"None of your business." Magical asshole spy. Just what I need.

A side door opens and Cassie steps in, carrying a glass of red liquid that sparkles in the light cast from the candles placed on the table at each board member's seat. The dimmed chandeliers add a shimmering effect to the drink. I've served some sparkling red wines at the Pub, but this has an intensity beyond the norm. She offers me the glass—a crystal affair she must have borrowed from one of the casino bars, judging from the "Harrah's" etched into its base. "Drink," she says.

"What is it?" I hold it, the ridged surface digging into my palms with my tense grip. The red depths mesmerize me.

"My end of our bargain."

My eyes shoot to hers. The cure? This is the cure? Now that I'm paying attention, I note the strain in her features, the shadows around her eyes, the slight slump of her normally perfect posture. She's worn, like she's poured all her energy into something else.

The glass I hold.

I raise it a few inches toward my lips, then stop. "What should I expect?"

Cassie's lips curve upward, like she approves of my caution. "Pain," she says simply. "The potion, along with my added power, will drive the remnants of dark magic from your wounds. It should also restore you to full strength so that you may be properly assessed tonight. The experience won't be pleasant, but it shouldn't last long, and when it passes, you'll be healed."

"Permanently," I confirm.

"Yes." The single word comes out on a sigh. Oh yeah, she's exhausted. I hope her talent returns quickly, for Peter's sake.

I bring the glass up, noting a fruity, spicy aroma, and take a tentative sip. My eyebrows rise. Not nasty at all. For some reason, I assumed any magical beverage would taste like crap. Instead, it's more like a mixture of a sweet wine and a touch of cayenne pepper, the effervescence leaving my tongue tingling and the spice clearing my sinuses, but not overly burning my palate. I down the contents in several large swallows. A warmth fills the pit of my stomach, radiating outward in pleasant, soothing waves.

Cassandra retrieves the glass, and I wonder at her hurry to take it from me.

Then the pain hits.

Fire erupts in my nervous system. I trace the path of each searing flame along every single nerve. My eyes roll up; my legs buckle. With an echoing thud, I hit the parquet wood floor. The sound of tearing fabric reaches my ears, but I barely notice.

My mouth opens in a soundless scream, the muscles of my throat distended and taut.

My body flops onto its side and I writhe, trying to escape an inescapable internal agony.

Ash. I'm turning to ash. Organs, muscles, bone, they melt.

Tears stream from my eyes, and I blink to clear them. Defenseless, helpless.

Cassandra kneels beside me, her hands extended toward my twisting form. I can't wrench away. One hand falls on my leg, the other on my shoulder, and what I thought couldn't possibly get any worse manages to double in torture.

Now I do scream—a hoarse, shrieking wail that rises and falls with each pain wave. It blocks the room, the world, my senses shattered, my existence one tremendous agony.

When it recedes, I hardly dare to believe it. I lie on the cool wood, panting, gasping, while Cassie strokes the side of my face and murmurs quieting noises to me. "I'm sorry," she whispers. "But it's done."

Heartfelt sympathy. From Cassandra. If she's not the monster I've believed her to be, I wonder exactly what the Registry holds over her. Peter once mentioned she has someone very ill in her life, someone she has to take care of that the Registry's meddling threatens. As for her past with Genesis, well, she was young and scared and confused. Gen might never forgive her for that night in the locker room, but I can.

I blink up at her, then roll onto all fours and push upward with arms and knees. Stiff, yes. Sore, a little. But nothing of any consequence. I rotate my shoulders, completing the full circular motion for the first time in months. My limbs tremble, not with weakness, but with an internal energy that sparks and pulses. I'm alive with power. It radiates from my core and settles into a tight, firm resolve deep in my heart.

Rising, I face the Registry board, cold determination tightening the muscles in my face. I'm dimly aware of the potion glass, kicked to the side and cracked across its base, and the long, ragged tear in the skirt of Rosaline's beautiful dress design running from hem to hip and leaving most of my right leg exposed. I'll mourn that later. For now….

"You're going to test me," I say, voice hoarse from the screaming. I like the effect. It suits this moment. "So get on with it. Test me. Train me. Do what you need to do to reassure yourselves I'm no threat. Then leave me and Genesis the fuck alone."

Cassie struggles to stand, but her knees won't hold her weight. Without letting my eyes leave the table of board members, I reach down a hand to her and feel her ice-cold fingers wrap around it. One strong pull of my formerly damaged left arm brings her to her feet. "Thank you," I murmur, still looking straight ahead.

"You've earned it," she returns, equally low. "You're about to earn it further. Be careful."

Great.

Nathaniel approaches in my peripheral vision, carrying something mechanical in his hands. Red and green lights blink on the end of the small metal box. The outline of a recessed handprint covers its otherwise flat top surface. I never saw him leave to fetch it, but I was otherwise occupied.

"Here." He lays the box on my open left palm. "Press your right hand onto the impression."

Huh.

Before I do, I examine the thing further. Lights not just on the top edge of the rectangular box, but up the two sides as well. Nothing on the back or the underside of it. "What's it do?"

"It's a power measuring device," President Argyle calls from her seat at the long table. "A miniaturized version of a larger machine, designed by Charles, there." She points a long-nailed finger at the hawk-nosed blond male on the far-right end. He nods once, eyes darting between my face and the box.

"The more lights that run a steady red, the stronger your talent," he says with a Southern drawl that surprises me. It's smooth and cultured, not twangy—an educated accent for an obviously intelligent man if he invented this machine. "I can understand your concern, given what you just experienced. If you'll allow me to demonstrate?" Charles holds out his hand for the box.

I take a few steps toward him, then stop, a plot forming. "I think I'd rather your president show me that it's safe."

His eyebrows fly up. Behind me come a couple of coughs and a clearing of a male throat, both Nate and Cassie struggling to hide their surprise. Or is it amusement?

Glad I'm so entertaining.

Linda Argyle's nostrils flare with her deep, thoughtful intake of breath while she mulls over my request. Clearly, this isn't something she wants to do, and I'm wondering if it hurts or shocks or causes some other discomfort. I'm not in any mood for further pain. On the flip side, she can't very well refuse either. Doing so would imply weakness or a fear to show her own power levels to the assembled audience, though surely everyone here must know her strength. Genesis said she was incredibly powerful.

And that I might be stronger.

Ah. So that's it.

She appraises me with her eyes, likely remembering the ease with which she blocked me earlier this morning. When I was tired. When the release of that same block hadn't yet shown me how to channel my abilities. *Yeah, lady, that's it. I'm a real wuss. You're superior. Come on, bitch.*

Bring it.

Argyle settles her shoulders back, coming to her decision, and holds out her hand for the machine. Nate takes it from me and passes it to her, shooting me a wink on his way back. He's seen my power. I'm betting he suspects what the outcome will be.

Placing the device on the table before her, Linda Argyle rests her hand in the indentation, takes a deep breath, and closes her eyes.

The lights along the sides flicker, first slowly, then faster, alternating between red and green. One by one they settle on flashing red, climbing up the sides of the box toward the top edge where the tiny LEDs meet. Almost... almost... they don't quite come together, the four across the very top remaining green before all the lights stop blinking and hold steady—most red, the last four green. The president of the National Psychic Registry opens her eyes, sighs with satisfaction at the results, and leans back in her seat.

"There. Nothing to be afraid of," she says, as if speaking to a small child. She holds out the box toward me. Maybe no one else notices that it shakes in her hand, but I do.

Nathaniel transfers the device from her to me. "One thing I'll say for you, Flynn Dalton, you have balls of steel," he murmurs while still close enough not to be overheard.

"Agreed," Cassie whispers just behind me, raising the hairs on the back of my neck.

I snort. Either that or balls of stupidity. I'm about to find out which.

"What am I supposed to do?" I ask, holding my hand just above the machine.

"Just rest your palm on it and focus your power." President Argyle pauses, smirking. "As well as you know how."

Oh, I know how. She taught me a lot by blocking me off. I'm sure there's still much to learn, but I've made tremendous progress today.

I fit my palm onto the indentation and close my eyes.

It takes a few moments to center myself, to tap my core of energy and narrow the surge into one tight beam, which I direct from my chest, down my arm, into my hand, and then into the device. In the intervening seconds, the board members mutter to one another, a chair shifts, squeaking on the wood floor, a woman clears her throat. Someone whispers, "Wasting our time."

Then utter silence.

I open my eyes.

Every light on the box is a strong, steady red. Every. Single. One.

"Told her so," Nate says beside me while Cassie and a number of others catch a startled breath.

Argyle half rises from her seat, staring in disbelief, before she remembers herself and settles once more. But the wonder, the *fear* in her expression is undeniable.

Why do I get the feeling I've made a potentially fatal mistake?

It might not be a bad idea to give her a false sense of security when it comes to you. Gen's words from this morning float back to me. Too late.

And I'm not finished yet.

Without meaning to, without my doing anything, the top four red bulbs grow brighter and brighter and then burst, scattering tiny bits of plastic across the floor. The board members rear back as if burned by unseen fire.

I get the impression that's never happened before.

Great.

"Impossible," Charles mutters. He rises and approaches, wary and hesitant, but he makes it to my side. After taking the device from me, he turns it over and over in his hands, running his fingers across the casing. "It's hot to the touch," he tells me.

I hadn't noticed.

I shrug, trying for innocent and nonchalant. "Um, sorry?"

"What are you?" he says, peering at me.

So much for innocent and nonchalant. Though I didn't plan it, it's probably a good thing I'm wearing a dress. If I had on my usual attire of jeans, T-shirt, and steel-toed boots, they'd really be wary of me. "One of you," I say, putting as much reassurance into my tone as I can. "So stop staring and start teaching. The sooner I learn to fully control this power, the sooner you'll be able to trust me."

Though, judging from the incredulous expressions, I'm thinking that's a never.

"It's late," an older woman two seats down from Argyle pipes up. Her voice wavers, though whether from fear or her age, I can't tell. "Why don't we table this until tomorrow? There are things we should discuss before proceeding further."

Several board members nod or indicate their agreement, but Madame President has other ideas.

"We'll adjourn soon enough. But first, I need a demonstration of her skills. It's one thing to possess power and quite another to use it. Niki, come in here, please!"

That same door on the side opens, and an elderly woman, hunched and hobbling, makes her way to the end of the table. Even dressed in a semiformal black dress with some glittery accents at the shoulders, she's the picture-perfect witch, complete with a wart at the end of her nose and wrinkles so deep you could lose something in them. Age may have slowed her down, but the spark and fire in her gaze knocks me back a step. There's power there. No doubt about it. And with my new-found senses, I can feel it crackling beneath her surface.

"Flynn, meet Niki Meyer."

Niki nods to me in formal greeting.

Argyle goes on, "Nathaniel claims you to be a psychic succubus, capable of tapping the power of others and using it for yourself. He's made other claims as well, but we'll address those in due time. For now, I'd like you to tap Niki, here. Draw from her energy and show us what you can do with it." Argyle sweeps a hand in the old woman's direction.

Niki watches me steadily, unflinching.

"I don't want to hurt her," I say, eyeing the frail figure. Strong magically or not, I've seen what damage I can cause to Genesis when things get away from me. My magic is more controlled than it was, but I don't fully trust it yet. Last thing I want is to give some poor old woman a heart attack.

Her chin snaps up, its angled tip pointing at me. "You can't hurt me, child. I'm stronger than your lover. Have no worries and do as the president asks."

Her voice isn't unkind, just informative, without a hint of doubt or fear, so I nod and concentrate.

Slowly, carefully, I send a tendril of energy toward her. It flares when it encounters her own power, a flash of red on orange to my sight, then blends, drawing the combination back into me.

As I absorb the magic, a glowing shape forms to President Argyle's right, standing behind her shoulder. It coalesces into a figure, a male figure.

A male figure I think I recognize just as it occurs to me to question what kind of talent I've co-opted for my use.

My widened eyes must give away my shock, because Linda Argyle nods and smiles like the predator she is.

"You see, Flynn, it occurs to me that someone with as much power as you do apparently possess would be of great value to the Registry. We have any number of tasks you could perform for us that no one else can, especially if the other rumors about you prove true."

"I'm not working for you. I'm a bartender, not a magician." I might even be a construction worker again, given the return of my physical prowess. But my words fall flat as the ghostly figure sharpens into clarity.

"I think you're about to change your mind," Leo VanDean says, strolling around the table to stand before me, hands on his hips. "Payback's a bitch, isn't it, Flynn?"

Oh, hey, I'm totally fucked. Again.

What a fucking surprise.

Chapter 52
Contractual Obligations

"I WANT to talk to you and VanDean," I say to President Argyle. "In private."

From the tracking of their gazes, I can tell some of the board members can see VanDean standing beside me, smirking. And at least one or two heads cock in his direction, indicating they hear him but maybe can't make him out. Others stare blankly around the room or watch me for my next move. Regardless, this conversation needs to happen elsewhere.

"Not completely private," Linda says. "Seeing ghosts isn't my specialty. I'll need Niki to translate and act as witness to whatever we agree upon."

"Then I want one too."

"And whom, precisely, would you trust with such a task?"

She has a point. I consider Genesis but quickly discard the idea. This is blackmail, and I'm betting Gen's the lynchpin. She killed VanDean using dark magic, an offense punishable by madness or even death, depending upon the severity. And it wasn't her first time to dip into that seductive well of evil power. My stomach tightens with worry for her.

I'll do anything to keep Genesis safe, but I'd rather not have to agree to carte blanche if I can help it. Which means I'll need someone on my side who knows the ins and outs of this shit.

Without looking away from Argyle, I say, "I'll take Cassandra."

"What?" she squeaks, moving into my line of sight and blocking my view of the table of board members. Pieces of hair have come loose from her braided blond bun, and she's smeared her makeup, a dark streak of mascara marking her temple where she likely rubbed at tired eyes. "Are you out of your mind? You hate me." The last comes in a rapid whisper, but Leo hears it and snickers.

"Not as much as you think I do," I say, shooting a glare at VanDean. I keep my voice low. "I'm betting they've got a hold over you, too, forcing you to do things you don't want to in order to protect someone you love."

Something in her eyes flickers, just once, but it tells me all I need to know.

"Help me work this. Maybe someday I can return the favor. Unless you weren't just young and inexperienced and you really do want to see Genesis get hurt."

Cassie's eyes fall from my face. "I never meant to hurt her. I loved her. But I wasn't ready for that."

"You were a kid. I get it. But you're an adult now. What do you say?"

"Do you accept the appointment to be her witness and advocate?" President Argyle calls from behind her. I can't see her through Cassie, but her tone mocks us both.

"Yes," Cassandra says, and the room falls silent once more.

One heartbeat. Two. Three.

"Very well. Everyone with the exception of myself, Ms. Dalton, Cassandra, and Niki, and Mr. VanDean of course, is excused." When some of the board members grumble at that, she adds, "Whatever we agree upon will come to the board for a vote tomorrow morning at our meeting." That quiets them.

Chairs creak and the table groans as the other Registry executives push themselves up and shuffle from the room. Nathaniel places a brief, comforting hand on both my shoulder and Cassie's and then departs with the others.

The five of us stare at one another.

I stifle a yawn.

It's been a helluva day. I'm nowhere close to tapped out magically, but the stress is catching up to the rest of me. And I'm aroused, like I always am after messing with the psychic energy of the succubus skill set. I want Genesis. I want to wake her with soft kisses and caresses, tease and taste her until she cries out my name. And then I want to sleep for a week.

"Let's get on with this," I say. "What, exactly, do you want from me?"

Argyle sits down. She'd risen when the others left, out of respect, I guess, though I think it's more of a practiced formality than actual admiration. She shows deference because she needs them, not because she believes it. Until I came along, she was the biggest, baddest bitch around.

Well, honey, you've got a new contender for your title.

"I want you to be yourself. I want you to be the hero you are," she says softly.

"Huh?" Okay, not the snappy comeback I wanted. Then again, Madame President didn't say what I expected her to.

"Hero," she repeats. "That's what you are. I've been researching you, having you followed, studied. You saved a woman from a sinking car, you tried to save your construction teammate from falling, both despite great risk to yourself. You'd do anything right now to save Genesis from the Registry's standard punishment for the usage of dark magic, correct?"

"Don't agree to that," Cassie whispers urgently, but I'm already nodding.

"Yes, I would. I'd give my life for hers."

"Idiot," Cassie mutters, though there's no heat in it, only pity. Beside her, Leo laughs.

"Then help me," President Argyle says, and it's almost a plea. "Help me save us all."

I have no idea what she's talking about, and this looks like it's going to take a while, so I walk to the end of the table, drag the last chair around to the front facing where Linda sits, and plop myself in it. Cassandra and Niki fetch chairs for themselves.

Leo remains hovering behind me, an unwelcome and unnerving presence.

"Be specific," I say, starting to pull one knee up, then remembering the skirt. I plant both boots firmly on the floor.

Linda heaves a deep sigh, and for the first time tonight, I notice the weariness. Up close, makeup fails to hide the dark shadows beneath her eyes, the deepened lines in her face, the paleness beneath the rouge. Between me, Cassie, and the registry president, we're one big bundle of exhaustion. She gestures with both hands to the empty seats on the right and left of her, the ones that have been vacant since my arrival in the conference room.

"Missing," she says, simply. "Two strong psychics, one with an aggressive telekinetic gift, therefore perfectly capable of defending himself, the other a powerful precognitive who should have foreseen any danger to herself. Gone. Erased. Vanished like they never existed."

"I don't understand," Cassie puts in. "What do you mean, 'vanished'?"

Linda reaches beneath the table, and for a second I tense, wondering if she'll come up with a weapon of some kind, but instead she brings forth a leather-bound journal, thick with jagged-edged pages, like a diary only bigger. Linda flips open the book, turning pages until she finds the one she's searching for. She points at numerous blanks appearing seemingly at random in the otherwise continual black script.

"Vanished," she repeats. "And getting worse with each passing day. All references to these two psychics—" She pauses, shakes her head. "No. These two *friends*, fellow board members, comrades. All mentions of them are fading from existence. I noticed the odd spacing and incomplete sentences a few months ago. This is my journal. I don't write this way, don't leave things out." Linda's hand shakes. She clamps it onto the side of the diary. "So I started searching, found a few referrals to Tom and… and…. Dammit!" Her other hand clenches into a fist, which she slams onto the table's surface.

"Anger won't help," Niki cautions in her wavering voice.

"I know." The registry president sits up straighter, grasping for her fleeting composure. "But I'm forgetting them. The more time that passes, the less I remember and the more information that disappears. I *know* we had twelve board members. We have twelve of everything: goblets, place settings, chairs, robes for formal gatherings. But now there are ten of us, and I'm afraid—" She catches herself. "More of us will follow."

I shake my head, trying to make sense of what she's saying. "What, exactly, do you think has happened to them?"

"I think," she says, focusing her gaze on mine, "they're being removed from time."

"Oookay."

"No, really. It's the only explanation. If they'd been murdered or kidnapped, that wouldn't cause their apartments to empty, their belongings to disappear. It wouldn't explain this journal. I found an address, before it erased itself. An apartment in Princeton. Tom's address. I spoke to the couple living there. They said they'd been there for years."

"And how do you know it's not just you? Maybe being the president of this organization is driving you crazy." I know contact with these people is driving *me* crazy.

Mom, save me a spare bed. You may be getting a roommate soon.

"I've talked with a few carefully selected members of the board. They have fleeting memories of the missing people. And now that we've realized the danger, we've found evidence of others, not board members, but other psychics who've suddenly ceased to exist, reports from terrified members who can picture friends, relatives, husbands, but there's no longer a record of them. And then the memories fade and the reports stop coming, but I have documented them. Blank reports filed by those left behind."

God, what would I do if Genesis simply disappeared from my life? I'm a succubus. I walk through time, backward and forward. Does that mean I'd remember her when no one else would?

Cassandra stood from her seat and paced behind me, her heels drumming up an annoying clicking on the wood. "What would be capable of such a thing?"

And then I know. I know exactly what could do it. And from the look Argyle's giving me, so does she. I brace my hands on the arms of the chair, ready to make a break for it or defend myself. "You don't think I—"

"No," she hurries to reassure me, though I'm not very reassured. "No, I'm certain it wasn't you. I've had you watched, remember? You haven't gone out of body enough times or for long enough periods to do what's apparently been done. This would be someone completely detached from her physical form, someone who spends all her time *walking*."

"Just how many people do you think have disappeared?" Cassie asks. She's moved to stand beside me, and her eyes dart to the corners of the room, as if searching for an invisible threat.

Linda stares down at the open pages of her journal. "At least twenty, maybe more."

"Twenty!" Niki's startled blurt bounces off the high ceilings. "Oh dear God." She presses an age-spot-covered hand over her heart.

"You said *her* physical form. You have some idea who's doing this?" Stop panicking. Get to the heart of the problem. Solve it. Because if psychics are in danger, that now includes me. That includes Genesis. And I have a very good idea of what President Argyle wants from me.

She's nodding now, confirming my suspicions. "Tempest Granfeld," she says. "A walker from the 1800s. Another psychic succubus. Like you. We have records of her date of birth, but no death date.

I think…." She pauses to take a sip from her water glass. The liquid shimmers from her shaking hand. "I know how insane this sounds, but I think she never 'died' in the strictest sense. I think she separated from her body, and she's been *walking* through time ever since. Eventually, she would have been buried, but if her spirit wasn't in the body…."

A cold chill settles in my core, raising goose bumps along my arms despite the full-length sleeves of the dress. *You're in trouble, girl*, Ferguson told me when I'd been out of my body too long. I remember the pain, the sense of fading, pulling apart, the disorientation and vagueness of the world around me. Detached, cut off. Unable to touch anything, unable to communicate with anyone other than those with the psychic ability to see and talk to spirits.

I'd go insane.

The longer I remained apart from my physical form, the less ability I had to interact with the world around me. But if I'd been a little stronger, or trained….

What if I were a succubus who could continue to affect the physical world while outside of my body indefinitely?

I'd be the most dangerous creature on earth.

"What has she got against the Registry? If she's from the 1800s, attacking your people seems like a weird choice."

Argyle shrugs elegantly. "The bits and pieces we've managed to find in the records state that the former Registry policy was to hunt succubi and punish them if they used their skills. We've since modified that policy. What you do is your nature. So long as you don't tap the dark and don't permanently harm anyone, so long as you abide by our moral code, we won't intervene."

Considering how Gen and I have been treated lately, I have a few thoughts about their "moral code," and I don't hide my smirk.

She ignores it. "Back then... let's say psychics were less enlightened. They punished Granfeld, the Registry of that time. They drove her even more mad than the constant use of her skills would have."

I don't like the sound of that. Is she suggesting succubi go nuts over time? But I don't interrupt her.

"Regardless, she seems to have declared war on our generation. She may be targeting other eras as well. It wouldn't surprise me. She has all of time to play with. Though she might be avoiding her own lifetime and anything before it to protect her own existence. Alter something in her past and she might not be born."

A good thing for me to keep in mind as well. "You want me to stop her." It's not a question. I don't have to ask. I know.

But President Argyle shakes her head. "Not until you're trained. I'm not throwing away my greatest asset. Because I think I've done that before. Or my predecessors have. The records suggest there have been other succubi between Granfeld and you, but again, there are no names. The information is gone. I suspect others have tried to stop her and failed."

The information is gone. Because the other succubi were killed by Granfeld and therefore removed
from existence? Or because the data *itself* was
erased. I know one person who could do that. My
father, Ferguson/Robert Dalton. But why?

Maybe to protect himself. My skill set is descended from him. If he's got some of the same talents I do, in addition to his ability to erase information, he wouldn't want the Registry calling him in
for an assist with Granfeld. Given what they've done
to him, he has no reason to trust them.

And given that he was punished for the use of
dark magic, I remind myself, bringing him in might
be replacing one problem with the greater of two
evils.

Still, I'm really wishing we'd had that talk he'd
mentioned before I got on that airplane to Atlantic
City.

"Who knows how long this has been going on?
The Registry may have been dealing with this since
the 1800s," Cassie says.

"Certainly it dates back several Registry presi-
dents," Niki puts in. "I can't remember details. That
could be my age, or it could be tampering with time.
But I have a notion of a wave of psychics experiencing memories of lost companions back when I was a
young girl. Our leader at the time explained it away
as a quirk of the psychically gifted mind, but it left
folks uneasy."

"So what's in it for Flynn? Other than survival,
of course. Any one of us could be Granfeld's next

victim, but we're asking her to take a tremendous additional risk."

Good, Cassie. Keep us on track. And way to look out for me. I'm glad I wasn't mistaken about her.

"We don't know that it *is* Granfeld. Not for certain," Niki reminds us.

"We have to work with some sort of hypothesis. For now, we'll go with that one," Linda says. "As for Flynn, she's motivated beyond survival." She waves at Leo, who's been silently smirking at me this whole time. "Succeed in stopping Granfeld and I will not punish Genesis for her actions against Leo VanDean."

"What?" Leo shouts, making me and Niki both wince. No one else hears him. "McTalish killed me. With dark magic. And she gets no punishment?"

I get up, right in his face, forcing him to take a step backward, because with the power I've taken from Niki, I can hurt him, even while he's in this form. "*I'm* serving her punishment."

"And," Linda says to him after Niki translates, "I've had Nathaniel looking into the incidents surrounding Festivity's Dead Man's Pond. Given your track record, you're likely responsible for a lot more dark magic use, a lot more *deaths* than Genesis McTalish will ever be. I suspect she's done us a favor eliminating you. And I suspect it was self-defense. That doesn't change our rules," she adds, holding up a hand to forestall any arguments from me, "but as president, I can choose to overrule them. Or defer punishment."

"Not good enough," Leo says through Niki.

"It will have to be. We need Flynn to do this. It involves great risk. I want her to have great incentive. And if you attempt to cause problems for her or me, I'll have Niki dispel you for good."

That shuts him up, but he crosses his arms over his chest and moves to pout in the corner. I doubt I've heard the last from him.

"Flynn," the registry president says to me, drawing a folded paper from the back of her leather journal and opening it on the table before her, "I offer you this deal. Stop Tempest Granfeld from tampering with time and the lives of our members, and in return, I will never punish Genesis McTalish for her use of dark magic. Ever." The last word is stressed, and I raise my eyes from the written contract to meet her intense gaze. She wants me to understand something. Something important.

And I get it.

Now that Gen has used dark power twice, it's even more of a temptation for her. She may use it again. She's already come close on several occasions.

This is my only way to protect her, for now and forever.

It also tells me just how desperate President Argyle has become.

"Refuse," she says, "and Genesis receives a year of madness, three days out of every week. And you doom the rest of us, including yourself, to life in constant fear of oblivion."

I scan the contract, saying pretty much exactly what Linda just stated, while Cassandra reads it over my shoulder. She and I exchange a look, and she nods.

Okay then.

I hold out my hand. "Got a pen?"

THE SUITE is dark and silent when I finally return, a little after two in the morning. I've got my copy of the contract in hand, and I creep into the master bedroom, then the walk-in closet, and tuck the paperwork into a zippered compartment of my suitcase. The board still has to agree to it in the morning. Otherwise we have to negotiate all over again, but President Argyle seemed certain that it wouldn't be a problem. Don't know when, if ever, I'm going to discuss it with Genesis. She'll blame herself, even though her reasons for using the dark magic were valid. With her addiction, that's a stress she doesn't need.

Not wanting to wake Gen, I cross back through the living area and use the secondary full bath to strip, shower, and remove the makeup. I tie my hair into its usual simple ponytail and I'm back to being me. Carrying my ruined dress and undergarments, I return in bare feet and a towel to the master bedroom, dump the clothes in the corner, and fumble around for sleeping shorts and a T-shirt. It takes a while to find my stuff. Gen unpacked while I was gone, and of course, my things are in the last drawer at the bottom of the dresser.

She's left the curtains open, and the casino hotel's exterior lighting, plus the moonlight off the

Atlantic, give me enough light to see by. It casts a soft glow over her peaceful sleeping features, her hair falling in soft waves across one side of her face. She's kicked about a bit in her sleep, and the blankets only come to her waist. She's wearing some sort of white lacy negligee I've never seen before, something she must have bought just for this trip.

Just for me.

The satiny fabric with its spaghetti straps reveals her delicate shoulders and the tops of her breasts, dipping to a low V between them.

I have to pause to catch my breath.

For her, I'd do anything.

For her, I'll be a hero.

As if she feels my eyes upon her, she stirs and wakes, blinking at me in the semidarkness. "What time is it?" she mumbles, half out of it.

"Late," I whisper, sliding in beside her. "Go back to sleep."

But with my body so close to hers, the arousal I've held in check for the last several hours flares to life. My skin heats. A tremor works its way through me, transferring to her wherever we touch.

"I don't think so." She cups my cheek with her hand and brings my lips to hers to kiss me long and slow. The darting of her tongue sends pleasant tingles skittering throughout me like tiny electric shocks.

Her hand trails down my chest, pausing a moment to tease a nipple into erectness, then continuing onward to slip inside my shorts. She presses a finger to my center and sucks in a breath at the moisture she finds there.

"They had you using your power," she guesses.

I murmur an affirmative, unable to concentrate enough to form actual words. She's got a gentle in-and-out motion going, and my hips rock against hers, trapping her hand between us.

"At least there's an upside." She chuckles, low and throaty and sexy as hell.

Upside. Right. The Registry uses me. I get to put my life on the line. But hey, the power gets me horny, so it's an even trade. Not.

I want to laugh at the unfairness of it all, but all I manage is a strained groan as Gen applies pressure to my most sensitive spot, then massages it firmly. I flop helplessly onto my back, giving her better access, and find myself staring at the two of us in the overhead mirror.

My hands go to her negligee, easing it off her shoulders and slipping her arms out of the straps one at a time. She has to pause to pull it over her head, but the delay in my pleasure is worth it for the full revealing of her body in the moonlight: her flawless skin, the curve of her perfect bottom moving above me, uncovered by the blankets.

Instead of returning her hand between my legs, she slips one of her thighs between mine and presses down firmly. Her body takes up a sensuous motion, creating intermittent contact and alternating speeds, fast then slow.

I watch it all in the mirror, the sight of her from above a definite turn-on.

This position is good for her too. Her eyes close, and her breathing picks up its pace. Her lips part with her continuous soft cries and moans. I grasp her beautiful ass, pulling her into me to increase the friction while I buck my hips up against her.

In the throes of our release, we both lose the rhythm, and we're wildly rocking and thrashing in orgasm, the mirror reflecting it all for me to watch and carry me into a second wave.

Afterward, we lie panting, Gen's body collapsed atop mine, her cheek resting upon my breast.

"That was… amazing," she breathes.

"You should try it from this angle." And I use my left arm to flip her onto her back.

"Flynn!" She studies my face, searching for I don't know what. "Your arm," Gen explains. "Didn't that hurt?"

I grin down at her. "Cassie healed me."

"She kept her word. I wasn't certain she would."

"Well," I say, "I'm determined to give both the arm and the leg a thorough workout, just to test things." But instead of copying our earlier lovemaking in the reverse, I lower my head between her thighs.

And do my damnedest to make her scream.

Tomorrow, or really later today, I begin my training for the weirdest, craziest task I've ever tried to accomplish. Not long after, I'll put my life on the line to hunt a dead woman through time to protect people I've never met.

Somewhere in there, I have to celebrate Gen's birthday and, oh yeah, get married.

But tonight I'm just a woman in love with the most amazing girl in the world. Tonight I don't have to be everyone's hero.

I only have to be hers.

The End
(to be continued in DEAD WOMAN'S SECRET)

Keep Reading for an Exclusive Excerpt from

Dead Woman's Secret

By Elle E. Ire

Nearly Departed: Book Three

Coming Soon to
www.dsppublications.com

Chapter 1
Making Mistakes

"OOOF." MY impact with the conference room wall behind me knocks the wind from my lungs and rattles the lighting fixture hanging above my head. I slide down the smooth surface to thump ass-first on the parquet wood floor.

"Let's go, Dalton! It's not nap time. Heroes aren't born. They're made."

I favor Nathaniel with my best glare, a little blurry from the disorientation of the hit, but still formidable judging from the way he clamps his jaw shut. He's not part of this fight. He's not even breaking a sweat. He's the coordinator, the spectator, the assessor, standing off to the side in his neat tan trousers and white Polo shirt, leaning against the wall with his loafer-clad feet crossed at the ankles like he's waiting for a golf match.

"Look, asshole," I wheeze, and that's as far as I get before another blast of psychic energy wraps around my torso and drags me upright until my steel-toed boots leave the floor. I'm reminded of a scene from *Poltergeist*, helpless and flailing, Harrah's

Casino t-shirt riding up to reveal my white sports bra beneath, before I'm tossed aside to land on my left shoulder.

Two days ago, that would have hurt like a bitch. Okay, it *still* hurts like a bitch. But Cassandra, the National Psychic Registry's best healer and love potion maker took care of the water moccasin bite damage there. So it *only* hurts like a bitch rather than like a sonofabitch.

I roll sideways with the landing, the first move I've done right this whole match, and come up on my feet, panting and sweating. Turning, I face my attacker, and even though I've been fighting her for the last half hour, I blink.

Emily is, at most, 5'3", and that's counting the white tennis shoes she wears. Slight of build with delicate hands and feet, and spindly limbs. Pixie-style, blonde hair, bright blue eyes, a narrow face with high cheekbones and a slightly pointed chin. Add in her brown corduroys and green sweater, and she'd blend in with storybook forest nymphs.

At 5'8" I tower over her. My strength, built from years working in construction and a youth of competitive bowling, gymnastics, and swimming, could snap her tiny body in two.

And she's got me completely, utterly whipped.

She gives me a sympathetic little smile as if to say, *Sorry, it's not personal*, and extends her hands toward me again.

I bring my own up out of instinct, palms toward her, in a pointless attempt to ward her off. It does me no good whatsoever.

The megablast knocks me ass over tea kettle, so hard I do a perfect backwards roll, and again plant my soles firmly on the floor to stand. Muscles I haven't used since high school scream their protest, but memories of my gymnast days reawaken in the rattled corners of my brain.

I'm supposed to be fighting back. Using my succubus power, I took a *pull* from Emily's telekinetic energy a half-hour ago, and if I could concentrate for one goddamn minute, I could figure out how to manipulate that power to return fire. Except she hasn't given me the chance. She hasn't given me a single break.

Just like a real enemy, dumbass.

I tell my internal critic to shut the hell up and cartwheel right as another orange-yellow—at least to my sight—beam streaks my way. She misses my moving target. Her first miss since we started.

Might just be on to something here.

If I can't fight back, at least I can keep myself from being turned into one, massive, purple bruise. Though judging from the welts already visible on both my arms and the soreness in my back and legs, it might be too late for that.

And I'm supposed to take Genesis out for her birthday tonight.

I do a dive-roll that brings me up beside Nathaniel, studying the sparring session with his magic-sight; he sees power usage and can identify it, analyze its type. I can only see what I'm immediately using and interacting with.

"You're not fighting back. You're not using her energy at all. You're never going to survive a confrontation with that rogue succubus, Tempest Granfeld, if you don't start taking the offensive."

"Only thing I find offensive around here, is you, you little toad," I mutter, scrambling sideways like a crab to avoid another jolt. The telekinetic power zings close enough to raise the hairs on my arm and lift the long, brown ponytail off the back of my neck like extreme static.

Emily pauses to gather her strength. I'm wearing down her reserves, but that's not a technique I can use in a real fight where someone's actually trying to kill me. I would have been long dead by now if I faced Tempest instead of Emily.

In the brief interim, I grab a hold of the telekinetic power I absorbed, turning it over inside myself, trying to narrow its intensity to a beam like my opponent's.

And failing.

Her next blast hurls me into the double entry doors, slamming the pushbar inward and tossing me across the outer hallway running the length of the convention center of the hotel. I hit the carpet hard enough to shove my t-shirt upward and give me rug burns down my spine. The startled elderly couple standing over me stares, mouths agape, no words coming out.

I use the gray-haired woman's walker to haul myself upright, then pat her wrinkled hand. "Thanks. And sorry. Stunt man convention."

Her husband, I presume, glances toward the still-swinging doors to the conference room, eyes wide as if he expects god knows what to come out after me. He's not too far off the mark.

Emily steps into the doorway, holding the right-hand door open with her palm and shooting me a disapproving look. "You're breaking the boundary rules," she scolds. "You never know who might—" She spots the couple and freezes, face blossoming into a friendly smile. The slight gold spark, easily explained away by the gaudy overhead chandeliers, fades from her eyes. "Oh, hi! Martial arts class," she says.

"I thought you were attending a stunt man convention." The old woman narrows her gaze on me, like she's caught an unruly student cheating on a test. I'm betting she's a retired teacher.

"Yep, martial arts demonstrations are part of the convention activities. Gotta go!" I hobble away from them, sliding past Emily into the conference room. The doors bang shut. Her power catches me between the shoulder blades and flattens me.

"Aw, come on. That was a time out," I groan.

"Granfeld won't give you time outs," Emily says. Then, "Sorry, Flynn. I'm under orders to work you hard."

And I know just whose orders she means. Linda Argyle's. Madame President. The woman who blackmailed me into the Registry's service by threatening to punish Genesis for her second use of dark magic.

What Argyle doesn't realize is I would have agreed to help, anyway. Granfeld's tampering with time has put all the Registry members at risk. Including Gen. Including me. Any one of us could vanish from existence, and we have no idea who her next target will be. Which means they needed a hero. And I'm just a sucker that way.

Being the only other succubus alive with the ability to walk through time doesn't hurt, either.

I lever myself upright once more, frustration and failure warring for dominance. Can't get out of the way. Can't use Emily's power.

But I can still use mine.

I turn and face Emily just as she hurls another blast, and catch the beam mid-arc, *pulling* it into myself. It surges in my core, mixing with the rest of the energy I obtained from her. Her eyes widen, and a grin curls her lips.

Between my legs, arousal builds, a heated, aching need that always comes as a direct result of the usage of my skills. I swallow a moan and picture innocuous images in my mind: Mother Theresa, Ghandi, the Pope. Not enough. Casino mogul Donald Trump. The lust vanishes, replaced by faint nausea.

Emily tries again, and I do the same thing, storing more and more of her telekinetic power and draining her of her ability to use it herself. She's already tired, her levels, low. It doesn't take long before she has nothing left.

Then, suffused with her energy, things click into place. I'm still too clumsy to create a nice, narrow beam, but I can throw a wall of it in her direction, and I do it, with all the grace and finesse of a sumo wrestler in a ballet recital. She flies backward, slamming into Nathaniel who happens to be right behind her, which he mistakenly assumed to be the safest place in the room.

"Take that, spy."

President Argyle had Nathaniel watching me and Genesis for months, spying on my abilities, testing and tormenting us both. It felt good to toss Emily into him.

Then I notice neither of them is moving.

Aw, hell.

"I REALLY am sorry," I say, placing two ice-cold beers on the table in front of Emily and Nathaniel. I take the black leather-covered bar seat opposite them, hauling myself onto its cushion. Much of the Irish-pub themed establishment is empty, the hotel guests preferring to get their drinks for free at the gambling tables and slots, and at six dollars for domestic, I don't blame them. But a few customers occupy tables scattered throughout the small lobby bar, so I keep my voice low.

Emily gives me a wry smile while Nathaniel presses the chilled bottle of Bud to the swelling lump on his temple. He got cold-cocked when Emily flew into him, the back of her skull connecting with the front of his.

"Are you sure you don't want a doctor?" she asks, studying him. I'd only stunned her, but he'd been out for a few seconds before we revived him.

"No, thank you." He glances at his cell phone. "I'll have Cassandra take a look during the session break in an hour."

"Well, at least I managed to *do* something," I say, folding my arms on the table's surface. I'll need to wear long sleeves tonight to hide the welts. Genesis doesn't know anything about my upcoming mission. She knows I'm being trained, but not the aggressive nature of that training, or its purpose. And I'm not telling her. She'll worry. And she'll blame herself.

"Too little, too late," Emily says, watching my face for the inevitable scowl.

I don't disappoint her.

"Sorry Flynn, but you know it's true," she continues. "It took you too long to figure out how to defend yourself and how to defeat me. We need to get you to the point where you can channel any psychic's talent and make use of it immediately. Tempest Granfeld was a succubus, but many have multiple skills, like Cassie with her love and healing magic."

And Genesis who communicates with the dead. And uses dark power to kill people who threaten those she loves.

I shake that image away with a jerk of my head, then regret it when the bar rocks around me. Emily grabs my arm, holding me on the chair. Damn, I hate these high bar seats.

"You need some rest," Emily says, frowning. "You look flushed. Go upstairs. Take a nap. Get a meal."

"I always get a low grade fever when I use my—" I can't quite bring myself to say *magic*. "—abilities.

I'll just grab some aspirin. There's no time for anything else." I glance at my own phone and slide off the chair, on purpose. "It's Gen's birthday. I've got an hour to shower and change before I take her out to dinner." The limo would pick us up in front of the casino to drive us to a romantic restaurant the concierge had recommended. I'd made reservations, but apparently the place was small, well-reviewed, and always booked solid, so we didn't want to be late. It was also about forty-five minutes away.

"Well, that's rest of a sort," Nathaniel puts in. "I'll let Linda know we made some progress today. I'm sure she'll have something else to throw at you tomorrow."

"Try to make it something soft. I'm getting married in two days. Don't need to break bones before the ceremony." That earns me a chuckle.

"And if I don't see you again," Emily says, "good luck, with both the training, and the wedding."

"Thanks." Damn. I could get to like the little pixie. But she's right. New day, new challenges. I never face off against the same person for more than an hour or two, tops.

I make my way from the bar, across the lobby, past the casino entrance to the tower elevators. My arms and legs ache while I wait for the car to arrive. How I'm gonna keep this hidden from Genesis, I have no idea. She's occupied by panels and meetings in the daytime while I'm training, but at night, she wants to show me affection, and normally I'd be all for that. Not so much when every inch of my body hurts. Maybe the hot shower will help.

A well-dressed, middle-aged couple reeking of cigarette smoke shares the elevator with me to the twelfth floor. They've had a few drinks, and the woman wobbles a bit on her high heels. The man busies himself with his phone, scrolling through what looks like his appointment book on the screen, but the bleach blonde examines me out of the corner of her eye. When the doors open and they step out, she turns back and holds the car open. "Don't let him beat you up like that, honey. Get some help. There's a good shelter on Bayfront Drive."

I laugh and hold out my hand at about shoulder height. "Would you believe it was actually a girl, about this tall?"

She stares from my fingers to my face and back again, then cracks a wide smile. "Kinky," she says, and steps into the hallway, letting the doors close.

I ride the rest of the way to the penthouse honeymoon suite alone.

Two bedrooms, two and a half baths, a living room with a ten-person jacuzzi and a wet bar, all done in blues, silvers, and golds, and all irrelevant compared to the bed. It takes a force of will not to drop onto the king-sized mattress in the master bedroom. Maid service has made it and fluffed the pillows, and I can't think of anything more inviting.

Have to shower. Have to change.

God, I'm tired.

I indulge in a quick lean against the wall, closing my eyes, feeling the weights of the lids holding them down, blocking out the sunset outside the huge windows. I drift, forgetting what I came upstairs for.

"Flynn?"

Male voice. Close by. Threat.

I throw out my hand toward the sound, a perfect, narrow beam of telekinetic energy shooting from my palm across to the master bedroom door, wrapping itself like a lasso around the speaker and yanking him off his feet. He yelps, his head bumping the ceiling, looking down at me with wide, innocent eyes.

"Chris?" The shock of seeing Gen's brother in my room breaks my concentration, and the beam cuts off, dropping him eight feet to the carpeted floor. He lands with a dull thud and a muffled groan. "Shit."

I crouch by his side, legs aching in protest, and help him sit up.

"That was… impressive," he manages, his usual cocky grin returning. "You're definitely getting better at picking up guys."

I bark a quick laugh. "Funny. You're okay?" Should have known he'd be here. He flew in this afternoon to help us get ready for the wedding, and he's occupying the other bedroom in the massive suite, the one across the living room from ours.

"I'm fine," he says, rubbing at his backside. "You been tapping into telekinetics?"

I spread my hands. "Training," I say, avoiding details. Chris knows enough about the magical world from his sister and his parents, though he has no obvious talents himself, save an uncanny way with finances that keeps his business, the Village Pub, going strong back in Festivity.

"I'd say you're getting the hang of it."

Yeah, interesting that. Panic and adrenaline help me focus. Good. I'm sure I'll have plenty of both when I find myself in a real fight.

We give each other a hand up, and he studies my face while I grimace. I know what's coming next.

"Flynn, you look like hell."

Yep, that was it.

A hint of perfume wafts off him, a scent I can't quite place, though it's very familiar. Not Gen's, and while I like it on her, I don't wear flowery stuff, or any stuff, for that matter. Hmm.

Before I can sort through it, or he can corner me on how worn I look, I catch sight of the bedside table alarm clock's glowing red numbers. "Gotta hurry. I'm taking Gen out tonight, and I'm running late." Avoidance—always a great strategy. Except when I make my quick turn toward the master bath, my back locks up and sharp pain shoots across it. My breath hisses between my teeth.

Chris grabs my arm, right atop several bruises, and a humiliating whimper escapes my throat.

"What the—?" Without another word, he drags me over to the bed, pushes me face-down onto it, and shoves my shirt up. He's close enough to me now that the mysterious perfume on him smells much stronger.

My brain finally adds up two and two and comes up with…. *Cassie.*

Oh boy. Gen is gonna shit.

"Holy fuck," he breathes, stealing one of my favorite epithets and cutting off whatever I might have said about his secret relationship with Gen's biggest enemy.

"That bad, huh?" My voice is muffled by the comforter, but he gets the gist.

"You've got a band of bruising all the way across the center of your back, and it's swelling up, too."

"Yeah, that would be from when I got thrown into a door's pushbar."

Chris grunts and starts rolling up my sleeves, then my pant legs as far as he can. When he's done, he plops down beside me on the mattress which sinks under his added weight. "Why do you look like you just went twenty rounds with Mike Tyson? And your skin feels like it's on fire. You wanna tell me what the hell is going on?"

"Not really. You wanna tell me when you started dating Cassandra Safoir?"

Dead silence in the master bedroom.

"I'm not the only one who needs a shower," I add. "You'd better wash off that perfume before you run into Genesis."

"You aren't going to tell her?" His voice is soft… and hopeful.

Dammit.

I let out a long sigh. "Not really my business to tell, is it? Cassie and I are cool, but Gen… she's not gonna let that breakup go."

"She's going to have to. Cass and I are pretty serious."

Yeah, I kinda figured. "Good luck with that." I use the interruption to try to squirm away, off the opposite side of the bed, but he catches my arm and tugs me back toward him.

"Flynn...."

I know that tone. It's the same one Gen uses when there's no way I'm getting out of something she wants me to do. Must run in the family.

I heave a defeated sigh. "If you can listen while I shower, I'll tell you what's going on."

"Deal."

ELLE E. IRE resides in Celebration, Florida, where she writes science fiction and urban fantasy novels featuring kickass women who fall in love with each other. She has won local and national writing competitions, including the Royal Palm Literary Award, the Pyr and Dragons essay contest judged by the editors at Pyr Publishing, the Do It Write competition judged by a senior editor at Tor publishing, and she is a winner of the Backspace scholarship awarded by multiple literary agents. She and her spouse belong to several writing groups and attend and present at many local, state, and national writing conferences.

When she isn't teaching writing to middle school students, Elle enjoys getting into her characters' minds by taking shooting lessons, participating in interactive theatrical experiences, paying to be kidnapped "just for the fun and feel of it," and attempting numerous escape rooms. She is the author of *Vicious Circle* (original release 2015, rerelease 2020), the Storm Fronts series (2019-2020), the Nearly Departed series (2021-2022), and *Reel to Real Love* (2021). To learn what her tagline "Deadly Women, Dangerous Romance" is really all about, visit her website: http://www.elleire.com. She can also be found on Twitter at @ElleEIre and Facebook at www.facebook.com/ElleE.IreAuthor.

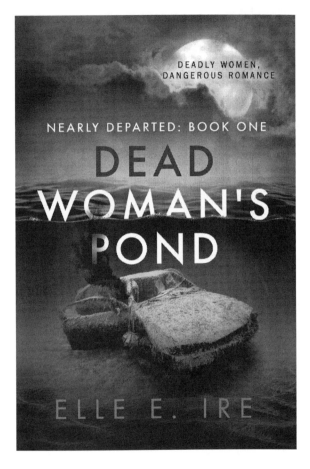

DEADLY WOMEN,
DANGEROUS ROMANCE

NEARLY DEPARTED: BOOK ONE

DEAD
WOMAN'S
POND

ELLE E. IRE

Nearly Departed: Book One

No matter how Flynn Dalton tries to avoid it, the supernatural finds her.

At first it's not so bad. Flynn's girlfriend, Genesis, is a nationally known psychic, which makes Flynn uncomfortable for both paranormal and financial reasons, but she can handle it. As long as no one makes her talk about it.

Then, on her way home from her construction job, Flynn almost ends up the latest casualty of Festivity's infamous Dead Man's Pond. And when her ex-lover's ghost appears to warn her away, things get a whole lot weirder.

Flynn might not like it, but the pond has fixated on her to be its next victim. If she wants to survive, she'll have to swallow her pride, accept Gen's help, and get much closer to the psychic realm—and her own latent psychic abilities—than she ever wanted.

www.dsppublications.com

DEADLY WOMEN,
DANGEROUS ROMANCE

REEL
TO REAL
LOVE

ELLE E. IRE

Finding the right romantic partner is always a challenge—especially when your first spouse turns out to be a greedy, business-obsessed hardass who winds up on her CEO office floor with a bullet through her brain.

After the murder of her first wife, Elaine is ready for a vacation and a solid relationship with a woman who only has time for her. Thanks to some found alien technology, Elaine can get what she wants… sort of. Okay, so a computer-generated tangible holographic image of a twentieth-century film star is about as far from "solid" as it gets. But as her themed pleasure cruise on a passenger starliner progresses and an additional plot to murder Elaine reveals itself, she finds herself inexplicably drawn to her fantasy companion.

Ricky might be the result of exceptional programming, but she proves to be more than the sum of her particles. She shows Elaine more affection, and eventually more protection, than any so-called "real" woman in her life ever has, leaving Elaine to wonder—are Ricky's feelings for her truly artificial? Or is this *REEL TO REAL LOVE*?

www.dsppublications.com

ELLE
E. IRE

Deadly Women,
Dangerous Romance.

VICIOUS
CIRCLE

Assassin meets innocent.

Kicked out of the Assassins Guild for breach of contract, hunted by its members for killing the Guild Leader, and half hooked on illegal narcotics, Cor Sandros could use a break. Down to her last few credits, Cor is offered a freelance job to eliminate a perverse political powerhouse. Always a sucker for helping the helpless, she accepts.

The plan doesn't include Cor falling in love with her employer, sweet and attractive Kila, but as the pair struggles to reach the target's home world, pursued by assassins from the Guild, Cor finds the inexplicable attraction growing stronger. There's a job to do, and intimate involvement is an unwelcome distraction. Then again, so is sexual frustration.

www.dsppublications.com

ELLE E.
IRE

THREADBARE
STORM FRONTS: BOOK ONE

DEADLY WOMEN,
DANGEROUS ROMANCE

Storm Fronts: Book One

All cybernetic soldier Vick Corren wanted was to be human again. Now all she wants is Kelly. But machines can't love. Can they?

With the computerized implants that replaced most of her brain, Vick views herself as more machine than human. She's lost her memory, but worse, can no longer control her emotions, though with the help of empath Kelly LaSalle, she's holding the threads of her fraying sanity together.

Vick is smarter, faster, impervious to pain... the best mercenary in the Fighting Storm, until odd flashbacks show Vick a life she can't remember and a romantic relationship with Kelly that Vick never knew existed. But investigating that must wait until Vick and her team rescue the Storm's kidnapped leader.

Someone from within the organization is working against them, threatening Kelly's freedom. To save her, Vick will have to sacrifice what she values most: the last of her humanity. Before the mission is over, either Vick or Kelly will forfeit the life she once knew.

www.dsppublications.com

FOR **MORE** OF THE **BEST GAY** ROMANCE